# THE
# RECKONING
# STONES

# THE
# RECKONING
# STONES

Laura DiSilverio

MIDNIGHT INK
WOODBURY, MINNESOTA

FIRST EDITION
First Printing, 2015

Book format by Teresa Pojar
Cover design by Lisa Novak
Cover images by iStockphoto.com/4940449/©EasyBuy4u
iStockphoto.com/346477©Lobsterclaws
iStockphoto.com/2584456/©swaite
iStockphoto.com/7738545/©bartvdd
Editing by Rosemary Wallner

Midnight Ink, an imprint of Llewellyn Worldwide Ltd.

This is a work of fiction. Names, characters, places, and incidents are either the product of the author's imagination or are used fictitiously, and any resemblance to actual persons, living or dead, business establishments, events, or locales is entirely coincidental.

**Library of Congress Cataloging-in-Publication Data**

DiSilverio, Laura A. H.
  The Reckoning Stones : a novel of suspense / Laura DiSilverio. — First edition.
    pages ; cm
  ISBN 978-0-7387-4511-4 (softcover)
1.  Child sexual abuse — Fiction. 2.  Life change events — Fiction. 3.
Self-actualization (Psychology) in women — Fiction. 4.  Domestic fiction.
I. Title.
  PS3604.I85R43 2015
  813'.6—dc23

                              2015009934


Midnight Ink
Llewellyn Worldwide Ltd.
2143 Wooddale Drive
Woodbury, MN 55125-2989
www.midnightinkbooks.com
Printed in the United States of America

*For my Thomas, the love of my life.*

# PROLOGUE

## MERCY

*Thirty Years Ago*

THE FEATHERS, TEENY DOWNY ones, clung to the rough wood of the coop and swirled across the yard like gray and tan snowflakes. Too many. Eight-year-old Mercy Asher hesitated, wind slapping her skirt against her bare calves hard enough to sting. The hens were quiet, not clucking and mumbling like usual. Egg-collecting basket slung in the crook of her elbow, Mercy poked the door with a tentative finger. It sighed inward. An explosion of flapping and wings pushed her back. A solitary white hen burst, squawking, from the coop. Its flurry stirred the slithery odors of chicken poo and blood. After a single glance at the shed's interior, Mercy fled, crying for her parents, Noah, anyone.

———

Hunched under the kitchen table late that afternoon, Mercy ran a cloth over the baseboards, a task she usually resented. Today, for the first time, she was glad she was a girl so she hadn't had to clean out the coop with her older brother and their father. The smell would have made her throw up. Just the thought made her reach for the pendant around her neck, the piece of obsidian her Uncle Fred, a missionary, had sent from Indonesia, on the other side of the world from Colorado. Sometimes when she clutched the stone she thought she could feel the volcanic heat, the shock of cold ocean water turning the lava to black glass. Today, the stone lay inert against her palm. "Why do the foxes kill all the chickens when they can't eat them?" she asked her mother.

"It's their nature," her mother said with the *tch* of annoyance that said she thought Mercy was being too curious or too nosy. Too. "Don't forget to dust—"

Her father came through the door, bringing the musty odor of wet wool into the kitchen. He had been at the church, and an elders' meeting, for more than an hour. His expression was grim, almost as dark as the time they got word Grandma Asher had died. Her mother looked up from scouring a pan, used her wrist to push hair off her forehead, and said, "Neil? What did the Community decide?"

Mercy's father gave his wife a look and she bowed her head, as if it was suddenly too heavy for her neck to support. "May God forgive him and have mercy on him," she whispered.

"What happened?" Mercy asked from under the table. Her long, mink-dark braids flopped over her shoulders and she flung them back impatiently. What she wouldn't give to chop them off, but Jesus didn't like women to cut their hair. Realizing her parents hadn't heard her, she asked, "Did someone die?"

"Mercy?" Her father bent and peered under the table at her. His head's funny angle made the pouches under his eyes sag sideways, showing reddened rims at the inner corners. His smile was more than usually sad. "I didn't know you were here, punkin."

Before Mercy could respond, her mother ordered her out from under the table. "That's good enough for today, Mercy. You may be excused from the rest of your chores. Find your brother and the two of you spend the afternoon in your rooms, memorizing your Bible verses for this week."

"But I want to know what happened. Why are you upset, Daddy?"

"It's not a fit subject—" her father began.

"Young lady, did I tell you to do something?"

Reading imminent punishment in her mother's eyes, Mercy curled her toes under inside her shoes and forced herself to say, "Yes, ma'am. I'm going." She left the kitchen, torn between frustration at not hearing more about whatever was making her father sad, pleasure at not having to finish her chores, and resentment at being confined to her room.

An hour later, having spent three minutes reciting her Bible verses for Noah and the rest of the time trying to perfect a drawing of a horse, Mercy ditched her sketch pad and grabbed for her Bible at the sound of her parents' voices in the hall.

"—of course Roger needs to be punished," her mother said, passing Mercy's barely open door.

Roger? Mercy didn't know a Roger.

Her father mumbled something, but the only words she caught were "harsh" and "reckoning stones." Holding her breath, she tiptoed to the door. Not daring to open it wider for fear her mother would catch her, she listened. "You stay home with the children, Marian," her father said, "and I'll go tonight."

"Whatever you think best, Neil, but it feels like something we should do together." Her words made it sound as if she was waiting for her husband's approval, the way a wife should, but Mercy could tell she'd made up her mind to go. "Noah can keep an eye on Mercy for the short time we'll be gone."

The two-tone creak of the bedroom door told Mercy they'd gone into their room. Wanting to know more, she waited a beat and then eased her door open the slightest amount possible and slipped through it. Her bare feet made no noise as she crept down the carpeted hallway toward her parents' room. She ghosted past Noah's door, willing him not to look up from his studying and notice her, and let her breath out when she was safely by. When she had drawn within two feet, her father's voice, much louder than she expected, startled her.

"Roger, an adulterer. He's the last man I'd have thought—"

Mercy's eyes widened; she knew about adultery from the Ten Commandments. She inched closer. Wood smacked against wood, and Mercy jumped. Two steps down the hall toward her room, she realized her mother must have closed one of the dresser drawers. She let her breath out slowly, silently, fighting an urge to giggle. It wouldn't be one bit funny if her parents caught her eavesdropping. Clapping a hand over her mouth, she moved toward their room, drawn by the lure of knowing. Her father was saying, "Thank God the children aren't called to witness the ritual."

Something in the timbre of his voice as he pronounced the words made the hairs prickle on Mercy's arms. *What ritual?* Her mother said something Mercy didn't catch and she leaned in so her ear was almost pressed against the door. A soft thud jerked her head up and it took her a second to realize the noise came from behind her. She started to turn, but over-balanced and fell heavily against the door. Noah stared down at her, his brown hair sticking out on one side, a "gotcha" expression on his face. Before she could scramble to her feet, he yelled, "Mercy's spying again! Mercy's spying."

Someone yanked the door inward and Mercy sprawled across the threshold on her back, looking up into her parents' surprised and angry faces. She was in for it now.

———

Dark had fallen by the time Mercy could escape her brother's surveillance and sneak out of the house. Her parents had left a full hour earlier; if she didn't hurry she'd miss the whole thing, whatever it was. She'd had to wait until Noah went to take his bath, and she'd spent the time copying the first three chapters of John into her notebook, her punishment for eavesdropping. She flexed her fingers now inside her mittens; they were stiff from the cold and the writing exercise.

Snow sifted softly onto her uncovered head as she hurried toward the church, less than a half mile away. She steered clear of the houses by skirting the perimeter of the small town, sticking close to the forest that cupped the Community in a large horseshoe. Mercy looked around nervously as something rustled in the underbrush. Probably a mouse. It was a little spooky to be outside at night, by herself. The trees that edged the Community seemed taller, the spaces between them darker. Two inches of powdery snow muffled her footsteps. A break in the clouds let the moon shine through and it stenciled tree lace onto the snow. Mercy kept her eyes trained on the church where a yellow glow flickered through the windows.

Nearing the church, she felt exposed as she crossed the open expanse of lawn. She'd be grounded until Christmas if her parents came out now, but determination kept her moving. Her reason for coming had somehow changed from wanting to know about Roger and the reckoning stones to proving that her parents couldn't stop her from knowing whatever she wanted to know. Mercy scurried the last few yards until she was pressed up against the church's rough stone foundation. It snagged her scarf. She tried to peer in the nearest window, but it was set too high. Her mittened fingers barely reached the sill and she couldn't get a good enough grip to pull herself up. Faint chanting filtered through the window. The cadence didn't feel like a prayer she knew. The congregation intoned the unintelligible words slowly, with less familiarity and unison than they did the Lord's prayer during worship services.

Without warning, the double doors opened wide and the congregation poured out, forty or fifty people. Their quiet was like the hens' and Mercy's stomach went all hollow. Candles cast long shadows that shuddered on the snow. Mercy froze. If anyone looked her way, they'd see her. No one did. They were all focused on the brown-robed man in the middle. He didn't carry a candle, but a woman near him lifted hers so it illuminated the man's face briefly and Mercy gasped. It was Mr. Carpenter, Seth and Luke's dad. His face was scrunched up like he'd been crying, and Mercy looked down at her boots, somehow embarrassed.

When she raised her eyes, the congregation was straggling toward the woods, forming itself into a ragged column. No one spoke, not even Pastor Matt who led the way with a fat candle lifted high. Mercy let them get almost all the way into the trees before she moved to follow. She had taken three steps out of the church's shadow and was as visible as a dot of ink on a white page when the last person in the line looked over her shoulder, as if wanting a final glimpse of the church. Mercy could tell the exact moment the woman spotted her because she lurched and had to look forward to regain her balance.

Not waiting to see if the woman raised an outcry, Mercy turned and ran as hard as she could for the woods. Her braids slapped her back. Thin branchlets whipped her face as she stumbled pell-mell through the snow and over roots. She didn't hear any yelling, or sounds of pursuit, but that might have been because her labored breaths and the muffled thuds of her feet deafened her. She paused only once, risking a glance behind her. Faint pinpricks of light danced deep in the trees beyond the church, winter fireflies. A cry carried to her, deadened by the falling snow.

Putting her hands over her ears, she hurried on. By the time she reached the house and stood shivering in the mud room, stripping off her snow-sodden boots and tights, Mercy had convinced herself that what she'd heard was an animal, a rabbit maybe, falling prey to a fox or owl.

# ONE

**IRIS**

NEWS OF PASTOR MATT'S resurrection ambushed Iris Tuesday night.

Sitting on the butt-smoothed wood of the barstool, her ankles hooked under the brass rail so she could tilt the stool back on two legs, Iris paid no attention to the talking heads mouthing headlines from the TV above the bar in Lassie's Pub. One of the mounting brackets had loosened months ago and the TV listed to the right. Appropriate, Iris had teased more than once, since Lassie's news show of choice slanted to the right, as well.

The Portland bar held only a sprinkling of customers before nine o'clock, most of them in jeans, like Iris. George Strait sang from the jukebox, and a girl, barely legal, laughed too loudly at something the heavy-lidded man beside her said. He dropped a beefy arm over her shoulders and she inched away with a nervous titter. Two women in their mid-forties wearing high-end costume jewelry talked in low voices at a table littered with empty glasses. Remnants of a girls' night out, she decided, reluctant to return home to husbands or surly teens or empty beds. A man hunched at the end of the bar, nursing a Jack and Coke, sliding her sideways looks.

Iris ignored him; his posture said old, defeated, definitely not fun. Her eyes followed the movements of two twenty-somethings playing pool at the table nearest the bar. The blond one, she thought, watching a tattooed bicep flex as he leaned across the table to make a shot. He was young but not sub-twenty, attractive but not movie-star, although a slightly snub nose made him look a bit like Matt Damon. If she could get him to buy her a drink within the next five minutes, maybe she'd take him home. She checked the time on her watch. When he glanced her way, she caught his gaze for a carefully calculated moment, then looked away, taking a long swallow from her Rolling Rock, knowing his eyes were locked on the way her mouth fit around the bottle opening, the long line of her throat as she swallowed, the fall of dark hair draping her shoulders. She'd promised herself she'd quit playing this game, knowing it had a dark side, but somehow, every few weeks, she found herself drawn to it again. Pool balls clicked. A minute ticked away. The barely legal girl made as if to get up, but her date pushed her down with a hand on her thigh.

"I need another beer," the blond man told his buddy.

*Oh, yeah.* Iris smiled to herself. His friend convinced him to play his next shot and she silently urged him to hurry up. Two and a half minutes and counting. Clearly, he needed motivation. Draining the last swallow of her beer, she snapped the bottle onto the bar. If he didn't take that hint, he was going to miss the deadline and miss out. Four minutes. Her foot jiggled. He said something to his friend and headed her way; she watched his approach in the mirror behind the bar, mentally running through the next moves. He'd ask if he could buy her a drink, while giving her a once-over. He'd turn to face her, crowding her a little, his hip bumping her thigh. She'd smile, look up from under her lashes, let her arm brush his as she reached for her beer. He'd forget all about the pool game. A flush prickled her chest. Ten, nine …

"Don't."

Startled, Iris met Lassie's disapproving stare. Coming up on fifty, he looked like what he was, a former lumberjack turned bar owner. He'd swapped plaid flannel shirts for a tan polo with "Lassie's Pub" embroidered over the pocket, but his weathered face and forearms still spoke of days spent outdoors rather than nights spent pulling beers. His usually pleasant face was set in a way that emphasized the grooves beside his mouth, the line between his bushy brows.

"Lighten up, Lassie," Iris said.

"Don't give me any of your shit. That's Karen's baby brother Greg and he's off-limits. What if I told you he's only twenty-four?"

"I'd say 'yippee.' Lots of stamina. What's fourteen years between consenting adults?" Her flippant tone wasn't making a dent in Lassie's disapproval.

"I'd never get laid again if I let him go home with you."

"Like I care about your sex life. He looks like a big boy. Maybe you should let him make his own decisions." Iris arched her brows a hair and half-turned on the stool to smile at the young man.

"Rolling Rock, Lassie," Greg said, sidling between the barstools just as Iris had predicted. He looked at her almost empty bottle. "Two."

Damn. He was four seconds too late. Iris gave an inward shrug. Lassie could relax.

"I'm Greg."

"So I hear. Karen's brother, right?" They shook hands. "I'm Iris."

"Karen told me about you."

"Warned you?"

"Yeah, maybe." He smiled, self-assured for a twenty-four-year old, young and strong and taller than he'd seemed by the pool table. He smelled faintly of the outdoors and spice-based cologne.

Iris felt a lick of real attraction. "And do you always listen to big sister's warnings?"

Greg grinned. "If you buy me a beer in the next five minutes, maybe you'll find out."

Whoa. Iris's eyes opened wide. Lassie—or Karen—had apparently briefed baby brother Greg pretty thoroughly. She slid him a speculative look, unused to having the game turned around on her.

Lassie thunked two bottles onto the bar. "Six fifty." Iris met his gaze briefly as Greg pulled the money from his wallet, and was surprised to encounter a level look that said their friendship was in trouble if she left with Greg. Shit. She'd finished a major piece that afternoon, was in the mood to celebrate. Greg was the only prospect in sight with potential.

"On me," she said, sliding a twenty across the bar. "Use the change to get her a taxi." She nodded toward the young girl who had managed to escape her date and was scurrying toward the restrooms, her lips folded in, blinking damply. Lassie took the bill without comment and went to the cash register, upping the volume on the television on his way, probably to make it harder for them to talk, Iris thought, half-admiring his tactics. Greg started to say something, but the newscaster drowned him out.

"... and in Colorado today, a man who spent the last twenty-three years in a coma has awakened. Doctors say Matthew Brozek regained full consciousness today for the first time since being viciously attacked and left for dead almost a quarter century ago. It's a real life Rip Van Winkle story ... "

The news, the name, hit Iris like an ice spear through the chest. Cold radiated down her spine and to her extremities. Her fingers went numb. The Rolling Rock bottle slipped from her hand and banged onto the bar, spattering the three of them before Lassie righted it.

"Jesus, Iris," Lassie said, swabbing the spill.

"Sorry," she managed. Her barstool wobbled, and she leaned forward to keep from going over backward. The stool's legs clunked down, jolting her.

Greg motioned for Lassie to bring her another beer, but she shook her head.

"No, I just remembered, I've got to—"

Lassie gave her a grateful look as she tried to think of a reason to bolt from the bar. "Excuse me." Sliding off the stool, she headed for the ladies' room. Locked. She ducked into the men's room and shut herself into the one-holer. Bracing herself against the sink, she stared into the mirror, not seeing the wild-eyed, too-pale woman looking back. Pastor Matt. Awake. Conscious. Remembering. Iris splashed cold water on her face and shut her mind down hard, knowing she'd lose it if she couldn't block out the memories. A Faith Hill song trickled through the thin walls and she focused on the lyrics, mouthing them to distract her thoughts as she opened the door. Greg was leaning against the bar, looking hopeful, and he stepped forward to greet her.

"I got you another beer."

"I've gotta go." She felt for her keys in her jeans pocket, already moving toward the door.

"I could take you home—"

"No." The walls of the bar were closing in. It was too hot, airless. Iris strode away from the bewildered Greg, trying not to run. The pub felt twice as long as normal, but finally she burst through the door into the parking lot and sucked in a breath that was almost a sob. She caught a whiff of dead cigarettes from the butt can near the entrance and coughed. The chill of an April night bit into her and she realized she'd left her jacket draped over the barstool. Fuck it. She couldn't go back. Tucking her hands into her armpits, she headed for her car, slammed the door, and pulled out of the parking lot.

He'd been as good as dead for twenty-three years. There were times when she almost forgot. And now—Memories threatened to overwhelm her and she pushed in a CD, trying to lose herself in Rascal Flatts' harmonies. Without warning, an image of her last time with Pastor Matt swam into her head and she knew she was going to throw up. Jerking the car toward the verge, she flung open the door while the wheels were still rolling, leaned out, and retched. Her stomach heaved again and again, and bile burned her throat. She finally sat up, wiped her mouth with a fast-food napkin she found in the passenger seat, and leaned back. She hated it that he still had this power over her. *Hated* it. After a few deep breaths, she put the car in drive and continued toward home.

The notion of going back to Colorado poked into her head. She could confront Pastor Matt, her family, the whole damn Community. No way, no how, she thought fiercely, turning into the driveway of her two-bedroom rental house in Portland's Montavilla neighborhood. Her life was here for the moment, anywhere other than Colorado. The girl she'd been, the Mercy Asher who'd lived in Lone Pine, was as dead and gone as she'd thought Matthew Brozek was. Deader. Goner. Turning the ignition off so sharply that she bruised her finger on the key, Iris left the car at the curb and climbed the two shallow steps to her bungalow. As far as she was concerned, Pastor Matt was still as good as dead. Nothing would ever get her back to Colorado.

# TWO

Portland's gray skies seemed to be trying to compress the space between themselves and the city streets the next morning. Iris cast the lowering clouds a look as she locked her bicycle to a lamppost outside Eclectica, wondering if their proximity was what was making her feel constricted, squashed, edgy. She pushed through the gallery's door, not open to the public until ten o'clock, but unlocked nonetheless, and headed past the displays without examining them. Jane had some new pieces that she'd want to study later, but not now. Appreciating art meant opening herself up, letting in the shapes and colors and feeling of the piece, whether it was a painting, a sculpture, or a piece of jewelry. She'd rarely felt more closed off.

"Jane?"

"Back here."

Iris followed the aroma of coffee to the small kitchen behind the gallery space, poured a cup, and opened the sliding glass door to the courtyard. Ferns and other greenery made the walled space feel like a rain forest. Climbing roses had budded and Iris could see hints

14

of the yellows and pinks to come. No matter how annoyed she got with Portland's drippiness, she had to admit it made for lush gardens. Burning her mouth with a sip of too hot coffee, she stepped down into the garden, hoping to feel the peace that sometimes settled on her there. Nothing.

Jane Ogden sat on a wooden bench, eyes closed and face tilted up to where the sun ought to be, still in a blue bathrobe, stroking the marmalade-colored cat draped over her lap. Her glasses lay on the bench beside her and without them she looked older, Iris thought, the crepeyness of her fragile skin more evident, the sparseness of her brows giving her face a disconcerting lack of expression. Jane shifted, her robe gapping near her ankles, and Iris spotted a large square bandage on her shin

"What'd you do to your leg?"

Jane opened her eyes and looked at Iris. "Banged it against the damn dishwasher. Doc says it's turned into cellulitis. I'm choking down antibiotics the size of the Hope diamond and soaking it in Epsom salts four times a day. Pain in the patootie."

"I wish you'd get one of those Life Alert gizmos."

"So you've told me. I may be seventy-eight, but I haven't lost all my marbles. I don't need an electronic babysitter."

Iris knew enough not to pursue the subject when Jane used that tone. "If it looks worse, or you start running a fever, call me." Crossing to the birdfeeder, she filled it as a blue jay urged her to hurry up from his perch in a crabapple tree. The tree cast a tracery of shadows that overlapped the lines of the paving stones and caught Iris's attention. She studied the patterns, wondering if she could recreate them in silver.

"I heard about Matthew Brozek on the news last night," Jane said. "Quite the miracle."

Iris turned to see the woman and the cat regarding her, blue eyes faintly questioning, golden eyes annoyed that the patting had ceased. In years past, the cat would have striven to keep the garden bird-free, but now he merely shifted on Jane's lap. Had he grown wiser with age, Iris wondered, wise enough to recognize that birds were a fact of life he couldn't obliterate, or had he become lazy or tired? Perhaps he'd become kinder, more willing to share the garden's bounty. Not likely. Iris had never noticed a correlation between increasing age and increasing kindness. Quite the reverse, usually.

Iris attempted to sound disinterested, knowing the long pause had given her away. "Yeah, me, too."

"What are you going to do?"

"Do? What do you suggest—I drive to Colorado and put a stake through his heart to make sure he stays dead?" Iris's harsh laugh jarred the jay into flight.

"He never was dead."

"As good as."

When Jane didn't respond, Iris set her mug atop the birdseed can and pulled a velvet-covered box from her windbreaker's pocket. She crossed to Jane and opened the case, displaying the choker inside. "I finished the Nicholson piece."

"Put it on so I can get the whole effect," Jane commanded.

Iris fastened the necklace around her neck, the stones and semiprecious gems cold against her skin. The handful of faceted aquamarines the client had inherited in an antique setting glowed greeny-blue from the mesh of silver wire and tumbled quartz Iris had fashioned around them. A chunk of quartz abraded her neck, the slight discomfort the hallmark of an Iris Dashwood design. The largest aquamarine nestled in the hollow of her throat, warming, and she got the same sense of love and delight that always came over her when she worked with that gem. It had been given and worn with love, she was convinced, wishing she could keep it.

"Exactly what Letitia asked for," Jane said with satisfaction. "Thank goodness not everyone has jumped on the vintage bandwagon." Jane's gaze fell to the sleeping cat and she abruptly changed the subject. "The vet's worried about Edgar's kidneys." She stroked the long fur and the cat slitted his eyes with pleasure. "She's got him on a special diet. I could put him through college for what the special kidney food costs."

She spoke with asperity, but Iris recognized the worry beneath her words. "He's what? Nineteen? Twenty?"

"Twenty. I got him the year we met, remember?"

The now somnolent cat had been a frisky ball of orange fluff. Had she changed as much? "One of the two strays you adopted that year."

Jane cleared her throat and spoke briskly, as if to get them past the emotional moment. "You got an offer for another commission this morning. It's an award. A cup or sculpture of some kind—your discretion—to recognize the outstanding employee at Green Gables, an eco-green construction company. Materials and style up to you." She named a figure that made Iris whistle.

"Can't turn that down," Iris said, "and the project sounds intriguing. Not my usual."

"You can work on the new piece in Colorado. Maybe the change in environment will spark some new ideas."

"I'm not going to Colorado," Iris said, as if she hadn't been awake half the night, thinking about it. "Too much work." She listed half a dozen partially completed commissions, stacking them like bricks, creating a barrier between herself and a journey into her past. "I haven't even got a design yet for Jack Weston's emerald and he wants to propose—"

"Tell me you didn't come over here this morning knowing I'd poke at you to go." Jane cocked a near-invisible eyebrow.

"I can't go." Her eyes met Jane's. "What would I do if I went?" Her voice sounded thin, uncertain in her own ears, and she hated it. Still, she let the question stand.

Lowering Edgar to the ground, Jane reached for her glasses and put them on. The purple rectangular frames made her look less vulnerable, more like the savvy businesswoman Iris had known for two decades. "I don't know. See your family. Reconnect with your roots." Jane rose. "Disconnect the man's ventilator hose."

Iris laughed.

Jane gave her a serious look. "You can't go on like this, Iris … nonsensical forays into vigilantism, sleeping with men half your age—"

"Not half!"

"—and drifting around the country, aimless, rootless."

"My 'aimless drifting' netted me close to a quarter million last year."

Ignoring her sarcasm, Jane continued, "To use a gardening metaphor"—she gestured to their surroundings—"you've got to dig up your roots before you can transplant them successfully. Pack your trowel and get on a plane."

# THREE

## JOLENE

JOLENE BROZEK SAT AT the kitchen table after school Wednesday, the *Colorado Springs Gazette-Telegraph* spread in front of her, a pile of *Romeo and Juliet* essays to be graded at her elbow. Clove and baked ham perfumed the air. She'd decided to make a special dinner as a sort of celebration of her father-in-law's awakening. It would please Zach. The delicious smells competed with the less savory odors coming from the bird cage near the sliding glass doors. The canary hopped from a perch to his water dish and tried a brief trill, apparently unperturbed by a cage that was a week overdue, at least, for cleaning. Jolene wrinkled her nose, but couldn't seem to make herself move or even summon Rachel, whose chore it was.

Her right hand rested lightly on the article, the one detailing her father-in-law's virtually unheard-of return from minimal consciousness—doctor-speak for a coma—to full consciousness. Neurologists were flying in from around the country to study him, and the media was full of comparisons to an Arkansas man who'd awakened from a coma after nineteen years of being cared for by his parents. Zach and his sister had spent time with their father yesterday, and Zach had come home praising the Lord that he recognized them and had said a few words, although his speech and memory were garbled. Jolene was supposed to go with Zach when he visited tomorrow and the thought made saliva pool in her mouth. She swallowed. She knew in her bones that Pastor Matt's awakening would cause many more problems than his death would have.

A *thud-thud-thud* down the stairs warned of her daughter's approach. She drew in a deep breath and held it, resolving not to lose her temper again. A quick prayer gave her some hope of success. Looking up from the paper, she waited for Rachel to appear, to mention how long she'd be studying with friends, and maybe give her a kiss goodbye. Fat chance. The slap of a sandal on the small foyer's oak floor and the creak of the front door told Jolene that Rachel was hoping to sneak out unobserved. Never a good sign.

"Honey?" Jolene said. "Clean Waldo's cage before you leave, please."

The sound of the storm door opening pulled Jolene to her feet and sent her toward the front hall where she caught the heavy door before it closed. Snow still lurked in the shadowy spots beneath trees and shrubs, and it was brisk at almost three-thirty, despite the sunshine. Jolene shivered. "Rachel Mercy Brozek. Stop right there."

Reluctance in every line of her slim body, Rachel halted halfway down the stone walkway and turned to face Jolene. "I didn't hear you."

"Cage. Now." Jolene kept a tight rein on her temper. She'd tried to work on her anger during Lent, but since Easter had struggled more than ever, as if she had forty days of pent-up anger to release. She worried it might all come bursting forth at once, steam spewing from a geyser, and scald whoever was standing nearby. She counted slowly to three before saying in a gentler voice, "And make sure Waldo's got clean water."

Rachel shouldered past her mother and stomped to the kitchen, blond ponytail bouncing. Moments later, the sound of the cage bottom rattling out of its slot with more violence than necessary told Jolene Rachel was doing as told. She spoke affectionately to Waldo, though, and the bird responded with conversational twitterings. Jolene relaxed slightly. A fly buzzed against the glass storm door and she wondered where he'd come from this early in a Colorado spring. She cracked the door to shoo him out, thinking of all the other problems she'd like to solve by shooing them out the door: her daughter's rudeness, her son's rebellion against the Community, her sister-in-law's annoying saintliness, her mother's failing health, the way she felt edgy all the time.

Jolene latched the door, wondering if she should get the glass cleaner and give the panes a swipe, when she spotted Zach walking up the road, coming home from the church. Jolene felt something ease inside of her at the sight of his solid figure. He'd filled out a bit since they'd married, and his dark blond hair was a bit thinner, but the creases in his face spoke of kindness and concern for his flock and family. He wore glasses now, with tortoiseshell frames that made him look scholarly. She knew he secretly liked the way he looked in his glasses, even though he complained about having to wear them. She stepped onto the stoop.

As he approached, she sensed an inner tension or excitement and bit back her complaints about Rachel's lack of respect. They exchanged a light kiss and she asked, "Zach, what's happened? Is it your father?"

"In a way."

She looked a question at him, something in his voice stirring unease. "I'll get you some iced tea." She reached for the door, wanting to postpone whatever he was going to say.

"I'm not thirsty." He caught her hand and tugged her back. Looking with great earnestness into her face, he massaged his earlobe between his thumb and forefinger. "It came to me while I was praying, Jolene, that we should welcome my father into our home when they release him. It made sense that Esther should care for him before, and that when she got sick he should go into the care center, because we didn't have the room and you had all you could handle with the kids. Without a job or family, my sister was the obvious choice as caretaker. Besides, she wanted to. She might be a bit overbearing at times, but no one can deny her devotion to our father. But now, with Aaron moved out, we've got a spare room and you've got more time. Since he's awake and will be able to eat normally, his care won't be so difficult, and the doctors haven't ruled out the possibility that he'll learn to talk better and maybe even regain some mobility, with time and therapy." Zach beamed at her.

The world tilted under Jolene and she steadied herself with a hand on the door jamb. "Here? I'm not—I can't—" Revulsion rose in her and she wanted to shout that she wouldn't allow that man in their house. She closed her lips over the words, knowing she couldn't explain them to Zach. No more could she tell him she'd just begun to sight a kind of freedom on the horizon, with Aaron moved out and Rachel already taking her PSATs. She still had her students, and her wife-of-the-pastor responsibilities in the Community, but she'd begun to think about the benefits of life as an empty nester. The thought of caring for anyone new, much less her father-in-law, made her feel like someone had chained cinder blocks to her feet and tossed her into a lake. She could almost see bubbles drifting toward the surface far, far above her.

"We can't decide something like this on the spur of the moment," she said, trying to sound calmly rational.

"We'll need to discuss it with Esther, of course," Zach said, opening the door and standing aside for her to enter, "but I can't see why she'd object. The important thing is that he be cared for by family. Praise the Lord that we have the blessings of food and shelter and love to share." The door banged shut behind them.

"Praise the Lord," Jolene echoed hollowly, wondering how her husband could be oblivious to the tectonic plates shifting beneath the surface of their oh-so-placid and insufficiently-appreciated-until-just-this-moment lives. Why couldn't Matthew Brozek have had the decency to die twenty-three years ago?

# FOUR

IT STARTED TO DRIZZLE shortly before Iris left Jane's Wednesday afternoon and she biked home in a steady rain, compiling a mental list of reasons not to go back like Jane suggested. With rain and damp hair obscuring her vision, she coasted almost to a stop in front of her house before she saw the pickup parked at her curb. It was dark blue, heavy duty, with yellow script that read "Lansing Landscape" on the door. She disentangled herself from the bike, wondering if the landscaper had the wrong address. A man stepped from the cab holding up a familiar leather jacket and Iris relaxed her grip on the bicycle, which she had automatically swung in front of her.

"Greg. How did you know where I lived?" Lassie had told him, she realized.

"You forgot your jacket," Greg said, handing it over, clearly pleased with himself. His fingers brushed hers, transmitting warmth. He looked older in the daylight. The rain made his dark blond hair curl around his face and he smiled, inviting her to share in his pleasure that he was here, that he had been attracted enough to find her.

Iris realized she was chilled. She regarded him through wet lashes. He was a ready-made distraction from her thoughts. She'd planned to bring him home last night, after all. "I need a shower and then lunch," she finally said.

"I'm up for both."

His confidence surprised a small laugh out of Iris. "You may make sandwiches while I shower," she said, wheeling the bike up the sidewalk and unlocking the door. She maneuvered the bike into the small entryway and shoved it up against the wall. Tossing her wet windbreaker over the bicycle, she invited Greg to do the same with his jacket. His hip bumped hers as he draped the coat off the handlebars. His presence shrunk the hall, made it feel close, and the warm, spicy scent of him filled the cramped space.

"Kitchen's that way," she said, backing toward the hall that led to her bedroom. "Bread's in the—"

Greg's hand caught hers. She barely had time to register its size and roughness before he pulled her close. "Okay?" he whispered, hesitating just long enough to let her object if she wanted to, before locking his arms around her and kissing her with unexpected expertise. His body was solid, muscled, and she felt unusually fragile pressed against the length of him. Her head swam—low blood sugar, she told herself—so she clutched at his shoulders to steady herself.

Iris broke the kiss after long, blood-stirring minutes and drew back slightly to study Greg's face, not sure how she felt about him taking the initiative, and knowing she should at least find out his last name, if he liked the Trailblazers, had a job or a girlfriend, or preferred Thai to Italian. But the need to silence the memories that last night's news had aroused, to bury them in an avalanche of sensation was too strong. Her lips slightly swollen, she said, "You know this is only sex, right?"

"Whatever you say." Kissing her again, he lifted her so her feet just cleared the floor and walked her down the hall to the open bedroom door.

———

An hour and a half later, after a hot shower where the water pulsing against their bodies made the sex that much more urgent, and a leisurely and surprisingly intimate round of lovemaking on the bed, Iris rolled over, naked, to face Greg. He smiled and smoothed an index finger over her eyebrow. Rain pounded steadily against the roof.

"You are not twenty-four," she said.

He looked surprised. "No, I'm twenty-nine. What made you think I was twenty-four?"

"Lassie." Come to think of it, he hadn't actually said Greg was twenty-four. What kind of game was Lassie playing?

Greg laughed. "He and my sister are quite the pair. You'd think I was twelve the way they treat me sometimes."

"What's your last name?" That seemed like the bare minimum she ought to know about a man who'd taken her out of herself so completely she felt disoriented. She folded her fingers around the obsidian pendant at her neck to ground herself.

"Lansing. Gregory Allen Lansing."

Remembering the script on the pickup truck, Iris asked, "You own a landscape company?"

"Yep. I'm a landscape architect. I've owned the business since I got out of college, and I paid back my main investors—Mom and Dad—eighteen months ago."

Iris raised her brows but said nothing. His career explained the solid muscles, the farmer's tan, the callused hands. There was more to Greg than she'd expected when she set out to pick him up at Lassie's. The thought of Lassie's reaction gave her pause. "Does … your sister know you're here?" She winced as soon as the words left her mouth. What a stupid-ass question to ask an adult man.

"Does it matter?" Greg sounded amused.

Lassie's friendship mattered, but he had no right to pass judgment on who she slept with. With any luck, he wouldn't find out that she and Greg had spent a rainy afternoon together in bed. "You know I'm thirty-eight?" If he called her a "cougar," he was out the door.

"No one would take you for a day over thirty-six," he assured her, running his hand over her flat abdomen.

Momentarily taken aback, she slapped at his hand, and then laughed. "I guess I deserved that."

"What made you run off last night?"

His words stopped Iris mid-laugh. The newscaster's voice sounded in her mind, telling her that Pastor Matt had emerged from his coma. She rolled away from Greg, swinging her legs over the side of the bed. When she sat up, the sheet slipped to her lap, and a chill mottled her arms. Reaching for the green sweatshirt bunched on the wicker rocking chair, she pulled it over her head, then stood and found her discarded panties, stepping into them unselfconsciously. "Nothing. It wasn't about you. I didn't feel well." *Leave it alone.*

"Want to talk about it?"

Iris gave him a look.

"I'll take that as a 'not yet,'" he said, not one whit abashed. He interlaced his fingers behind his head and grinned sleepily at her, not taking the hint that he should be getting dressed.

His nose was crooked, like it had been broken, and Iris wondered if he'd been in a fight, or an accident of some kind. He needed a haircut, too. "I'm hungry, and I've got work to do," she said.

"Don't let me stop you," Greg said, rolling onto his side and closing his eyes. "I need a nap."

Iris stared at him. He was asleep. In her bed. Strangely, his tanned torso didn't look as alien as it should against the white of her sheets and comforter, the willow-patterned wallpaper the landlord's grandmother had probably chosen. It wouldn't hurt anything if he slept here while she ate and worked in her studio. But he'd have to leave as soon as he woke up. Her boy toys did not have spend-the-night privileges.

# FIVE

### IRIS

IRIS PADDED BAREFOOT INTO the kitchen. Scrambling an egg with chives and nuking it, she ate, standing over the farmhouse sink and gazing absently out the window onto what was probably the most out-of-control yard in the greater Portland area. Almost a foot high in spots, and studded with dandelions and weeds, the grass could have hidden a tiger. A jungle gym, abandoned by a previous tenant, rusted near the back fence, swings jittering to the raindrops' beat. Rose bushes rioted in a bramble of thorns, buds clenched. Lashed by the rain, it all looked even more depressing than usual, and Iris turned her back on it. She hadn't planned to stay this long, so it hadn't seemed worthwhile investing any effort in subduing the yard.

Maybe it was time to move on. She'd spent more time in Portland than anywhere else since washing up at Lassie's pub two-plus decades ago, hungry, bone-weary, and willing to put out for food. She'd been here ten years cumulatively, interspersed with years in California and Europe, apprenticed to metalsmiths and jewelry designers, and months-long stays in other parts of the U.S. and the

29

world, scavenging for stones or design ideas to incorporate into her jewelry. Santa Fe or Austin might spark new design ideas, lift her spirits. She was ready for a city with more sunshine.

The refrigerator hummed on, startling her, and she headed to the studio, the small spare bedroom she'd made into a work area. Tension eased from her shoulders as she crossed the threshold. Her tools—files and pliers, punches and scribes, Bezel rollers, clamps, mandrels, and others—hung in their places, ranged on a pegboard mounted above the counter she'd had installed when she moved in. The big drill press and the tumbler had their own table beneath the window. Semi-precious gems, wire, stones, and other materials lodged in clear plastic drawers. Design ideas seemed to flow more easily in an orderly space than in a cluttered one. Pushing aside the low stool, she crouched and dialed the combination of the wall safe set under the counter. Halfway through, she stopped. She was too jittery to work with the Weston emerald. She stood and picked up a half-finished cuff that lay on the counter. Hooking one foot around the stool's leg, she drew it toward her and sat.

The two-inch wide strip of hammered copper had a filament of silver wire soldered at one end. Iris pondered it, then tried twisting the wire into various shapes across the top of the bracelet. None pleased her. Pulling a length of gold wire from a plastic drawer, she twisted it this way and that, twining it with the silver wire, encircling the smooth arc of metal. With a *pfft* of disgust, she returned the wire to its bin. Her original vision had been of intertwined lengths of gold and silver wire crisscrossing the copper, perhaps studded with a piece or two of polished agate, maybe tiger's eye. Nothing faceted or sparkly. But it wasn't coming together. Iris set the cuff down and her gaze slid to the computer on the other side of the room.

She knew why she couldn't concentrate, why she couldn't hold a picture of the bracelet in her mind's eye, see the way metal and stones needed to come together. Pastor Matt's face kept getting in the way. Damn him for waking up. Pushing away from the worktop, Iris glided on the castored stool to the computer and powered it up. There couldn't be any harm in reading a news story or two about Pastor Matt's recovery. Maybe learning the details would let her push the whole damn thing from her mind, get on with her jewelry making and selling, with deciding where to go from Portland.

The search terms "Brozek" and "coma" brought up hundreds of articles. After only a brief hesitation, Iris clicked on one at random. Pastor Matt's face, unchanged from when she'd last seen him, filled the screen. He was smiling, the curve of his mouth pushing up the pads of flesh on his cheeks, squeezing crow's feet around his blue eyes. His blond hair swept back from its part near his left temple, thick and straight, disciplined with mousse or hairspray. Her clenched teeth made Iris's ears ache and she forced a yawn, assessing him from a distance of twenty-three years and two thousand miles. Unable to face his smile any longer, Iris scrolled down the page but didn't find a recent photo.

Keeping her eyes averted from the snapshot, she read the text. "Matthew Brozek, 72, awoke from a twenty-three-year coma yesterday morning, astonishing doctors and convincing family members that miracles happen. 'It's a miracle,' Brozek's daughter, Esther Brozek, 41, said with tears in her eyes. 'Our prayers have been answered. I always knew Daddy would come back to us.'"

Iris guessed Esther must never have married because she would certainly have taken her husband's name if she had. *Hunh.* She'd been sure Esther would be married by twenty-one, maybe even to Noah, although their mother had been against his dating a girl who was older than him. Iris skimmed the medical gobbledy gook that followed, but the technical terms meant little. She'd already gotten the gist: Pastor Matt's awakening after so long was a one in a bazillion, bona fide medical miracle. Yet another example of God's—not that there was a God—warped sense of humor. Surely there was a saint, or at least a war widow and single mother of four, who deserved a healing miracle more than Matthew Brozek.

Iris's hand trembled on the mouse as she closed the web browser and her fingers stroked the obsidian pendant at her neck. *I should visit Dad.* The thought had recurred a dozen times over the years, but she'd always pushed it aside. She hadn't undergone four years of therapy, working to come to terms with Pastor Matt's abuse and her family's reaction, making her way baby step by baby step toward healing and closure, only to jeopardize her progress by exposing herself to the forces that had ripped her life apart. She shoved herself away from the computer and back to the worktop where the cuff waited.

Jewelry-making had given her a focus and maybe saved her life years ago. She felt half-silly thinking that, but it was true. As soon as she'd started training with the goldsmith Jane had introduced her to, she'd felt a sense of purpose that made her think she could be more than a runaway, more than a drifter, more than a victim. When she was engaged with a piece she had a pure focus that pushed aside everything else, that walled out worry and anger and anxiety. Wrapping trembling fingers around the cuff, Iris willed herself to connect with the metals, to *feel* how the design should proceed. She would not not not let Pastor Matt take this from her, too.

# SIX

### IRIS

Two weeks later, Iris sagged on the stool in her workroom, half-drunk mug of coffee cooling at her elbow, discarded design drawings littering the floor where she'd missed the trashcan, and tools and supplies cluttering the counter. She bent her head to either side, trying to loosen the kink in her neck, and flexed her stiff hands. Scanning the counter, her gaze alit on her draw tongs, her loupe, her chasing hammer. Their shapes seemed alien today and she felt a moment of panic that she'd forgotten how to use them. Unconsciously, the fingers of one hand went to the bruise on her temple while the fingers of her other hand worried at the gem she'd removed from the safe an hour ago when she sat down to work.

She hadn't meant to get into a fight last night. She took a sip of lukewarm coffee. Okay, maybe she had. She'd spent two frustrating weeks unable to complete a design she liked or even finish the pieces she already had started. Every time she tried to work, something kept her from focusing, hijacked her creative process. Panic had set in after a week—she'd never experienced this kind of block before.

She had commissions due to individuals and a collection promised to Jane for a new opening. Even worse than disappointing customers and hurting her reputation and income, and letting Jane down, was the feeling—the *conviction*—that she wasn't herself, wasn't Iris Dashwood, if her brain didn't sizzle with ideas and her fingers itch to mold gold and silver and other metals into settings that brought stones and gems to life. She'd fought the empty feeling with frequent sex with the more than willing Greg, and punishing bike rides that left her too worn out to think about what might be disrupting her creativity.

Last night, with Greg on the coast for a landscaping convention, she'd reduced the copper cuff she'd been working on to a shapeless lump with her acetylene torch and set off to a bar temptingly near the bus depot. Dismayed by her lack of interest in any man who wasn't Greg, she'd been restless and frustrated and left after her usual two beers. It was midnight. Tossing her keys from hand to hand, she eyed her car in the bar parking lot, and then pivoted to walk toward the depot. She'd logged a lot of miles on buses before washing up in Portland, and the chug of idling engines and blasts of diesel exhaust brought a surge of old feelings: wariness, exhaustion, never-quite-extinguished hope that *this* town would offer something new and better.

Thrusting the memories to the back of her mind, Iris stood across the street and scanned the sidewalk outside the depot. Things hadn't changed much since she'd last done this almost a year ago. She knew what kind of people trolled bus stations preying on runaways: scum, exploiters, lowlife pimps. A man caught her eye almost immediately. In a black leather car coat and jeans, he leaned against the depot's wall, his shoulders and one foot propped against the brick. In the light shining through the glass doors, he seemed youngish, early twenties, maybe. He was smoking, the cigarette tracing a red arc as he raised it to his lips and lowered it again. A couple of people emerged from the depot, roller bags trundling behind them, and the man straightened and ground out his cigarette with his foot. When a young blond teen exited, looking around nervously, he headed toward her with a loose stride.

The burn began in Iris, starting in the pit of her stomach and moving through her limbs. The hairs on the back of her neck prickled and her vision seemed sharper. She'd been approached numerous times by pimps, had made the mistake of believing one once when he said he just wanted to buy her breakfast at a nearby diner. Remnants of fear and desperation, the headlong run through a strange city to get away from him when he tried to force her into his car, made her breaths come faster. When the leather-coated man put his hand on the teen's duffel and she jerked it away, Iris started across the street, dodging a taxi cruising for a fare.

She stopped three feet from the couple and made eye contact with the startled girl. She couldn't be more than fourteen, Iris thought, observing the braces. She swiped her tongue across her top teeth at the memory of twisting the braces from her teeth with a pair of pliers in a bus depot restroom in Topeka. The blonde looked clean and reasonably well-rested; she hadn't been running long. Maybe Iris could talk her into returning home and buy her a ticket back to where she'd come from. "You don't have to go with him, you know," Iris said, voice gentle and reasonable, holding the girl's gaze.

The man glowered at her. "What the fuck business is it of yours? C'mon." He tugged on the girl's arm.

"He's a pimp," Iris said. "Whatever he's told you about buying you a meal or helping you find a place to stay, he's lying."

The man swung toward her, anger darkening a face that was all long nose and cheekbones like blades. "What the fuck—?"

Iris widened her stance and brought her arms up slightly so she'd be ready if he took a swing at her. Adrenaline buzzed in her veins, headier than any drug. She willed him to do it, visualizing how she'd take advantage of his momentum to catch his arm and pull him in closer so she could maximize the impact of her knee in his groin. That would probably put him down. If it didn't, she'd—

"He's my brother."

It took a moment for the girl's words to penetrate. When they did, a flush warmed Iris's cheeks. "I'm so sorry," she stammered. "I thought—" She turned on her heel and walked away, hands pushed into the pockets of her jacket. *How did I get it so wrong?*

"Loony bitch," the man muttered behind her. "I told Mom not to let you take the bus. Too many weirdos."

Iris ducked her head as if the words were missiles and hurried toward the bar parking lot. She burned with humiliation and was so caught up in berating herself for her stupidity that she didn't notice the dark figure ooze out of the alley beside the bar until the man grabbed her arm and jabbed a gun into her ribs.

"Wallet and keys," he rasped.

The sickly sweet rot of his breath and the way he jittered told Iris he was a tweaker. Her years of self-defense training took over automatically, and she stamped on his instep while pivoting and bracing her right arm to sweep his gun arm away. Savage exhilaration swept through her. Something clanked on the asphalt. Iris followed through with a palm strike, glimpsing red-rimmed eyes and stringy hair as the heel of her palm crunched into his nose. His hand flailed upward, thudding against her temple, and he crumpled to the ground. She stood over him, breathing sharply, almost hoping he would get up. The too-brief fight had left her unsatisfied, like sex that was over too soon. A sound like a cow lowing issued from the mugger and she knew he wasn't getting up. Tension drained from her shoulders.

"Hey, you okay? I'm calling the cops." A man had emerged from the bar and was hurrying toward Iris as he punched in 911.

Iris turned toward him and her foot stubbed something hard that skittered away. She bent to pick up the mugger's weapon. Her fingers closed around smooth glass, not the heavy metal weightiness of a gun. A beer bottle. She huffed a laugh under her breath. She'd been held up by a damned Michelob bottle.

The ringing phone cut through her thoughts of last night. Iris eyed Jane's number on the caller ID and answered reluctantly.

"Jack Weston called again this morning to ask about the ring," Jane said, sounding carefully non-accusatory. Weston had inherited millions in lumber money and parlayed it into more millions with a gourmet donut emporium he franchised across the northwest. Landing the design commission from him was the ticket to doubling or tripling Iris's income, as Jane had pointed out more than once. "He's getting antsy. His girlfriend leaves for her Doctors without Borders stint next week and he wants to propose before she goes."

"I know that!" Iris heard the sharpness in her voice and took a deep breath. "I know," she said more moderately. "I'm working on it." She fingered the 4.2-carat emerald she'd been staring at half the morning, tracing its smooth facets. The gem, with remarkably few inclusions and flaws for an emerald that size, glowed greeny-blue from her palm. Jack Weston's beloved grandmother had given him the stone, set in a necklace, on her deathbed, and he'd kept it the twenty years since, waiting for the right woman to come along. Now almost fifty, he was ready to propose and he'd selected Iris to design an engagement ring setting worthy of the gem. It winked at her, having smugly rejected all her design efforts so far. She couldn't blame the emerald—the designs had sucked.

"Really?"

Iris sat up straighter and winced, hearing something in Jane's voice. "What's that supposed to mean?"

"I'm worried about you. Since you heard about—"

"Not necessary. I'm fine."

The exaggerated silence from the other end of the line said Jane didn't agree.

"Really." When Jane still didn't respond, Iris said, "Look, I'll have the ring done by close of business. All I've got to do is set the stone." *And hope that it doesn't look like total crap.*

"Good." Jane didn't sound convinced, but Iris didn't give her a chance to say any more, hanging up with a quick, "Gotta get back to work."

She folded her fingers around the emerald, wishing it would give her an inspiration as stones sometimes did. She wasn't surprised when it remained inert. With a sigh, she laid it on the counter and retrieved the ring she'd already made, finished except for the rectangular setting. The wide gold band had tiny leaves of gold, rose gold and platinum layered across the top. It was a variation on a design she'd used before and, thus, unsatisfying, but she couldn't make any new ideas work. She'd fashioned the gold frames for the setting yesterday, cut spacers, and soldered the two frames together. Now, she cut strips from a 22-gauge gold sheet, scored grooves down their centers and bent the metal inward to form the prongs. She sanded the edges smooth and gold filings drifted to the countertop. Becoming aware that she was wielding the file with anger rather than joy, she set the tool and the band on the counter and pressed the heels of her palms to her eyes. She hated feeling angry and frustrated with her materials. Part of her worried that her negative feelings would fuse with the metal and the gem. *Silly. Superstitious nonsense.* Taking a deep breath, she resumed filing more gently.

Time unspooled in a taut ribbon of concentration and precision as she worked an intricate design along the base of the setting and soldered it carefully to the band. The bitter tang of heated metal filled the workroom. She was vaguely aware of hunger, but felt like she was almost in the zone for the first time in weeks and didn't get up for fear of dispelling the moment. Trimming the prongs, she soldered them into position and then attached the setting to the band. Done. Taking a deep breath and swiping her hair back, she picked up the emerald and lowered it toward the setting. Her hands shook slightly—low blood sugar, she told herself. Even as her fingers drew away from the unsecured gem, she knew it didn't work. The setting looked cumbersome; it obscured the pure beauty of the stone, rather than enhancing it. Disappointment socked her, hollowing her stomach. The emerald deserved better than this.

*Maybe in the sunlight.* She lifted the ring carefully and started toward the window, hoping the play of natural light would spark the stone to life. Halfway there, her foot caught against the edge of the acetylene tank strapped to the work bench's leg and she jolted forward. The emerald sprang free and arced toward the window. Iris lunged for it, palm cupped, but it smacked against the glass and fell to the ground. *Oh, no! Nonononono.*

Iris sank to her knees and reached for the gem. Her fingers felt the conchoidal fracture blooming from one corner of the emerald before she could see it. Sickened, she stood and examined the snail shell-like whorls marring the stone. Rubbing her thumb across the roughness, she bit down hard on her lower lip, grieving for the emerald's former beauty. It felt like a tiny death. It's a gemstone, she told herself, a happenstance combination of beryl, aluminum, silicon and oxygen, not a friend or even a pet goldfish. It didn't help. She sniffed back the tears that clogged her sinuses, picturing Jack Weston's face when she told him that his family heirloom, the emerald his great-grandfather had earned by performing some service for an Indian maharajah, was ruined. She tasted blood. Her insurance would pay Weston the monetary value of the stone, but its sentimental value was beyond price. She dreaded telling him what had happened.

Trying to summon language that would convey her sorrow and repentance to Weston, Iris let the truth seep in. Her problem wasn't low blood sugar or carelessness or a temporary loss of inspiration. It was Pastor Matt. She wasn't going to be able to focus, to work, to design the way she needed to until she'd confronted the bastard and told him he deserved to roast in hell with the devil ladling sulfuric acid sauce over him while turning the spit. It was time to take Jane's advice. Feeling like herself for the first time in two weeks, she placed the fractured emerald in its cotton nest, rolled the stool to the computer, and logged onto an airline website.

———

Iris returned home late that evening, after a hideous meeting with Jack Weston, whose eyes had dampened at her news and whose quiet had been much harder to bear than rage and accusations would have been, and an almost as difficult session with Jane, who grieved with her for the emerald and reminded her in no uncertain terms that completing the piece for Green Gables on time and making it "brilliant" were now crucial to her future as a jewelry designer.

"Weston won't keep quiet about this," she'd said, eyes weary behind her glasses. "You can bet none of his friends will be asking you to design their engagement rings or anniversary presents. And it's my reputation on the line as much as yours."

Iris knew that and it made the burden of her failure that much harder to bear. As she got out of her car, drained, Greg Lansing pulled up. Dinner. She'd forgotten.

She greeted him with a light kiss and invited him into the kitchen, scuffing off her shoes at the door. "Look, I can't do dinner tonight. I'm leaving for Colorado Springs in the morning. I've got to pack."

Greg's brows soared. "This is sudden, isn't it? Was it something I said?"

Iris had to smile at his look of exaggerated concern. "It's not all about you, you know."

He mimed shock. "Hm. Then what is it about? The same thing as the night we met?"

She didn't answer. Keeping her gaze locked on his, Iris grasped her sweater's hem and pulled it over her head. She could spare half an hour for goodbye sex. She was conscious of an unusual twinge of regret.

Greg's gaze flicked over her partial nakedness and then returned to her eyes. He didn't move toward her as she expected. "What is this? One for the road?"

Iris re-donned the sweater, embarrassed and disappointed, and irritated with herself for both emotions. "Apparently not. As we established at the beginning this is sex. S-E-X." A draft drifted across her toes, chilling them, and she curled them under. A car with a defective muffler rumbled past the house.

"Can't it be more?" He crossed to her then, stopping two feet in front of her. He looked down into her face but made no attempt to touch her.

"No." The word was out before Iris gave it any thought. One of the reasons she preferred much younger men was that they were no more interested in long-term relationships than she was. She shed herself with record speed of the ones who thought they were falling in love with her.

"No," she said again, conscious of annoyance that Greg wasn't playing by the rules. She started past him, but he didn't move. Rather than shove him aside, she dropped back a step, bumping against the fridge, and gave him a stony look.

"I like you, Iris, and I think you like me. Can't we give this some time, see where it goes?"

His gentleness startled and scared Iris. "There's nowhere for it to go. Now, I've got to pack, so if you'll let me by—"

Greg backed off and Iris passed him, headed for her bedroom. She went straight to the closet, knowing Greg had followed her. The closet held the slight wet wool smell it always got when it rained. She yanked a pair of jeans from a hanger so it clinked against its neighbors. Closet music. Grabbing her weekender suitcase, Iris carried it to the rumpled bed and threw the lid open. She layered the jeans with undies and sweaters while Greg watched.

"Doesn't look like you'll be gone long." He nodded at the small suitcase.

Iris didn't respond, retrieving socks from her drawer. The suitcase bucked as he sat on the bed. She didn't look up, fetching the open box of condoms from her bedside table and tossing it into the bag.

Greg actually laughed. "Subtle."

His healthy self-confidence grated on emotions left raw by her failures. She faced him, arms stiff at her sides. "Look, I picked you up because I thought you were a hot twenty-four-year-old who could scratch my itch for a night or two. Well, itch scratched."

"So—wham, bam, thank-you-sir?"

Iris flung a pair of sneakers into her bag. When she started for the dresser again, Greg stood and put a hand on her arm. "Don't you think you owe me—"

"I don't owe you anything." Iris moved away from his touch. "We've known each other—what?—two weeks?"

His brown eyes held her gaze steadily.

"Don't," she whispered. She couldn't have told him what she meant, and he didn't ask.

After a long moment, he turned and walked out. Iris stayed still, listening to the fading footsteps, the squeak and clunk as the front door opened and closed. When he was gone, she unballed the T-shirt she'd unconsciously mangled, smoothed it, and laid it in the suitcase, blinking back tears. Her stomach felt all hollow, like it had when she'd fractured the emerald. Stupid. The emerald was unique, irreplaceable; men were a dime a dozen. Returning to the closet, she gazed blurrily at her meager selection of "good" slacks and blouses, wondering if the prison had rules about visitors' attire. As long as she was going to be in Colorado anyway, she'd make time to visit her father.

# SEVEN

**IRIS**

THE ARID COLORADO SPRINGS climate sucked the moisture from Iris's mouth and skin when she stepped out of the airport Thursday morning. *We're not in Portland anymore, Toto.* She downed half of the bottled water she'd bought on the concourse, and paused on the sidewalk, considering returning to the terminal and scurrying onto a flight back to Portland ... or anywhere that wasn't here. No. She would do what she'd come to do. Pikes Peak dominated the skyline and, despite herself, she felt an unwanted sense of homecoming. There was something so purple mountains majesty, so immutable and somehow benevolent about that peak which sheltered the city from the worst of winter's storms and created a safe zone in summer from tornadoes which violated ranches and towns farther east on the plains.

With a purposeful stride, she headed across the street to the rental car kiosks. Accepting the keys to the Ford Focus, she loaded her suitcase, laptop, and the jewelry-making supplies she rarely traveled without into the trunk. Then she sat. Visiting days at the prison were Fridays, Saturdays, and Sundays the website said, so she couldn't see her father until tomorrow. That left only one other destination. The thought of seeing Pastor Matt made her fingers icy. They were stiff as she turned the key. *He can't hurt me anymore.* She thought about the fractured emerald. *What a lie.* She could drive out to Lone Pine, instead, see how the town had changed, maybe go by the hospital tomorrow. *No.* She'd come here to confront Pastor Matt. Putting it off would only make it harder, like removing a Band-aid bit by bit instead of just ripping it away. She'd face him now, get it over with and get on with her life. She gulped half her water, wishing it was a martini, and set it back in the holder with a trembling hand. Depressing the accelerator, she headed for the airport exit and drove into the past.

Only it wasn't the past, Iris realized almost immediately, confronted by a highway dotted with big box stores, restaurants and traffic where she'd known pronghorn-dotted prairie. She missed seeing the antelope, but had to admit she was relieved by all the changes; she wouldn't be confronted with uncomfortable reminders at every turn. For the first time, she let herself ponder the changes that almost a quarter century might have wrought on her family and friends, the Community. Her mother would be fifty-seven now, her brother forty. Had the Community grown in her absence, or had it disbanded when Pastor Matt never returned? And Jolene ... had her best friend gone to Juilliard and then Broadway as she'd always dreamed? The Community had frowned on that dream, regarding actors as a drug-raddled, immoral lot prone to divorce. Iris had Googled Jolene's name a couple of times, but never gotten any hits. She probably used a married name, or a stage name, she'd thought.

Steering the car onto Woodmen Road, she focused on the hospital complex just ahead where an on-line article had said Matthew Brozek was. The hospital, like so much else, hadn't existed when she lived here. A Flight for Life helicopter sat on a pad out front and its blades began to whir. Within seconds it was lifting off, rotors beating the air into submission, to airlift someone from a rollover car crash, Iris imagined. With that sober thought, she parked, entered the hospital and strode to the information desk. She'd never spent much time in hospitals—only the once after the incident in Ames, Iowa, days before her eighteenth birthday. Three days. That had sparked her move to Portland, taking the self-defense classes, and her meeting with Jane, made her realize that drifting from city to city, bunking with whoever had a spare bed, was too dangerous. This hospital was bigger, newer, and didn't smell like much of anything, thankfully.

Iris conned a very young volunteer into supplying Matthew Brozek's room number by claiming to be his niece. She got into the elevator, but as the doors started to close she stuck out her arm with a mumbled excuse to the three other occupants and got off, suddenly unable to face a confined space, especially since one of the passengers had a phlegmy cough. At least, that's what she told herself as she hunted for the stairs. She suspected that she was also delaying the moment when she'd stand face to face with Pastor Matt. She couldn't afford to do that: she knew she wasn't going to be able to design again until she'd had it out with him.

A slight burn in her thighs and shortness of breath as she reached the fourth floor reminded Iris that she wasn't used to the altitude anymore. Pausing to breathe and finish her water, she scanned the area. With a start that made her grip the plastic bottle so hard it crinkled, she realized she was directly across from the room she sought. Before she could find an excuse not to, she approached the half-open door, knocked once and entered.

Her breaths came fast and shallowly, and a dizziness that had nothing to do with the altitude made her grab the door jamb for balance. Sunlight blared through the blinds, striping the floor and making the room too warm. The confined space held a chair, a TV mounted from the ceiling, a potted plant bound with a yellow bow, and a six-foot-high medical gadget or monitor pushed against the wall, silent. A privacy curtain concealed the bed. Could Pastor Matt sense her presence through the thin fabric, hear her breathing? Did he think she was a nurse assistant coming to take his blood pressure? *Not even close.* Two steps brought the curtain within arm's reach and she rattled it back with a sweep of her hand.

The bed was empty.

Putting a hand across her mouth to stifle the combination gasp and giggle that threatened to erupt, Iris stared at the rumpled bed as if the intensity of her gaze would cause Matthew Brozek to materialize. He couldn't be checked-out gone, out of her reach. Not when she'd come all this way.

A footstep warned her of someone's approach before a voice said, "Who are you and what are you doing in my father's room?"

Iris whirled. A grossly fat woman stood in the doorway. A pale green garment Iris could only think of as a muumuu covered most of her bulk, and a large silver cross on a heavy chain lay on an outcrop of bosom. Her moon face, cushioned by half a dozen chins and framed by an expertly blonded bob, was smooth and pale and flawlessly made-up, with red lips and mascara-fringed eyes of marine blue that glittered within deep pockets of flesh. They gazed at Iris with a mixture of suspicion and anger. Iris would never have recognized her except for those eyes and the clue of "my father's room."

This woman had to be Esther Brozek, but it didn't seem possible that the slim teen Iris had known was buried in the mausoleum of flesh that confronted her. The changes she'd imagined had run along the lines of a few wrinkles or gray hairs ... surface changes. Yet, these layers of fat spoke of a wound as deep as Iris's, of changes as profound. Esther was like an oyster that had added coats of nacre to an irritant, year after year, making it unrecognizable. A quick flush of embarrassment made Iris grip her lips together. Her fantasies about confronting Pastor Matt seemed juvenile in the sterile glare of the hospital room.

"You don't belong here, whoever you are," Esther said, surging forward. "This is a private room. All requests for interviews are supposed to come to me. I'll have to talk to the hospital administrator again."

"I'm not a reporter," Iris said. Even though Esther had obscured her once slim figure, her bossy and condescending attitude still shone through.

"Oh. Well, it's still not appropriate for you to be here, dear." Her tone had altered, now carrying a disconcerting hint of the unctuousness that had characterized Pastor Matt's speech. "I know it can be comforting to stand in the presence of the miraculous, of a great healing, but my father is still recovering and I'm afraid he needs rest when he returns from his tests. Are you ill? We can pray." Esther closed her eyes and held out a hand, clearly expecting Iris to grasp it.

Iris clasped her hands behind her back. "Esther, it's me."

As the sound of her name, the fat woman's eyes flew open. She studied Iris for a long moment before saying with certainty, "I don't know you."

"Pretend you're throwing stones and then maybe my name will come to you." Iris stood rigidly, her chin jutted forward.

Esther's mouth dropped open, jiggling her jowls, and her eyes widened. She stood frozen, only the hem of her muumuu fluttering in a stray draft. "Mercy Asher."

"It's Iris Dashwood now."

A flush of color stained Esther's cheeks. She exhaled heavily and moved toward Iris, an imposing wall of flesh. "Get out. It is *profane* for you to be here, for you to pollute my father's room with your presence after what you did to him. Get out!" Her voice was a low growl.

"What *I* did to *him*?"

"Your lies."

"They weren't—"

"Your filthy, baseless lies! They tore him apart." Esther thrust her face toward Iris until their noses were mere inches apart. Her breath smelled of mouthwash. "Then your father tried to kill him, and gave my mother a heart attack, all because of what you'd said." She drew back slightly. "You knew that, right? You heard your father went to prison for what he did? I hope he rots there! No prison could be as awful, as inhumane as the prison my father's lived in these past twenty-three years, trapped in his own head, unable to walk or talk or communicate in any way, with us but not with us. If your father has been beaten and sodomized repeatedly, it is still less than what he deserves."

Esther's words and fury battered Iris. Instinctively, she widened her stance and shifted her balance onto the balls of her feet. If Esther attacked, she'd be ready. Although she was taller and fitter than Esther, she wasn't going to underestimate the advantage the other woman's fury and weight gave her.

"Is that what passes for compassion in the Community these days? I guess not much has changed." Iris would have been happy to sink a punch into the angry woman's gut, feel the fat close around her fist like bread dough deflating, watch her stagger back. Even as the thought flitted through her mind, she dropped her fists, knowing she couldn't make Esther the proxy for Pastor Matt. She retreated to the window on the far side of the bed and gazed unseeingly at the mountains.

"You shouldn't have come back, Mercy Asher," Esther said, now more weary than spiteful. "You were as good as dead to the Community—some thought you *were* dead—and you should have stayed that way. Nothing good can come of stirring up the past."

"I'm here to see my father and yours," Iris said, turning, "and I'm not leaving until I've done that. I'll come back at a better time." *When you're not here.*

"There's no point," Esther said. She moved to the bed and smoothed the pillow. "You can't talk to him."

"We'll see about—"

Esther shook her perfectly coifed head. "No. He can't talk. Not really. He hears, because he responds if you say 'Open your mouth' or 'Turn over on your side,' but his speech and memory are garbled. He seems to think I'm my mother. He's awake, but he's not *back*."

For a fleeting second, Iris wondered if Esther could be lying to make sure she didn't return and confront Pastor Matt, but Esther's frame drooped with defeat as she lowered herself slowly into a chair to await her father's return. Her thighs spilled over the chair's sides and her meaty forearms enveloped its arms. She looked up. Her sparrow-bright eyes glittered as she observed, "I guess you came all this way from wherever for nothing."

*No. I am going to make him **see** me and acknowledge what he did.* Without a word, Iris edged around the bed and past the seated woman. The door leading to the hall promised escape, but Iris hesitated on the threshold. She looked over her shoulder, flashing on an illustration of Lot's wife from her childhood Bible, to see Esther had opened a book and was determinedly reading it, her stiff posture giving Iris no opening for ... what? An apology? Hardly. A request to start over? Maybe. A brief rundown of what she'd missed the last twenty-three years? Iris stepped into the hall and strode toward the elevator. Whatever she'd come for, she wasn't going to get it from Esther Brozek.

# EIGHT

### JOLENE

Jolene set down the phone with a shaking hand, and returned to the piano. The news that Mercy was back unsettled her even more than her father-in-law's unexpected awakening. Matthew waking up was startling; Mercy reappearing was like a ghost materializing, a fictional character taking on corporeal form and interacting with readers. Hamlet's father or Banquo's ghost. She sifted through the sheet music she was considering purchasing for the choir, but couldn't distract herself from the news about Mercy. Why come back after all this time? She must have heard about Pastor Matt waking up; otherwise, the timing was too coincidental.

"Who was that, Mom?"

Aaron slouched into the living room, lean and almost frail looking in jeans and a University of Colorado at Colorado Springs T-shirt. His hair was a darker blond than his sister's, brushing his collar in the back and falling over hazel eyes. A scruff of goatee softened the strong chin that was so very Brozek. Zach, his father, and even his sister had that same square jaw. Aaron's fingers trilled the top two keys on the Baldwin upright and Jolene made a mental note to call the tuner.

"Your aunt."

"What'd she want?" Aaron's voice had tightened; he was ready to take issue with pretty much anything Esther had said. Since declaring himself an agnostic during his freshman semester at UCCS, he had gotten into it more than once with Esther, who defended God and the Community with a zeal that would do an Old Testament prophet proud. For some reason, Aaron didn't often argue with his father, who had taken over pastorship of the Community ten years ago, but Esther's pronouncements about God's will and his revelations to the Community acted on Aaron like a red cape on a bull.

"To let me know she'd seen an old friend of mine."

"Who?"

"Mercy Asher."

Aaron stared at her. "Asher? As in—"

Jolene nodded. "As in."

"Did I know he had a daughter?"

"Maybe not. She left the year before you were born. I haven't heard from her since…" *Since the punishment. Since she ran away. Since the spring that changed all our lives.*

# NINE

*Twenty-Three Years Ago*

THAT SPRING, JOLENE FARRADAY fell in love twice, with Zachary
Brozek and Shakespeare, not necessarily in that order. She'd never
heard of Zach, and had never read any Shakespeare when her family
moved from Ohio to Colorado three years earlier; now, they were
the center of her life. Getting off the high school's activity bus which
dropped her a mile from Lone Pine, still high from play practice, she
whispered her lines as she started down the path through the close-
packed lodgepole pines. Birds twittered, seemingly entranced by her
performance.

"'Things base and vile, holding no quantity, love can transpose
to form and dignity. Love looks not with the eyes but with the mind,
and therefore is winged Cupid painted blind.'" She recited all of Helena's monologue on the walk home several times, shifting the accent
to different words and infusing varying degrees of dolor and frustration into the lines, but remained unsatisfied. During rehearsal,

54

she'd asked the drama teacher why Helena would try to help the man she loved, Demetrius, hook up with another girl.

"Helena's a dumbshit," Noah Asher, the play's Lysander, said in an undertone heard only by the students grouped loosely on the stage. "She should give the dude a BJ that pops his eyeballs and he wouldn't be chasing that Hermia anymore." He exchanged high fives with a hooting senior who played Theseus.

Jolene heaved a sigh, wondering how her best friend's brother could be such a moron. Mrs. Asher would have a coronary if she heard him talking about blowjobs. She looked forward to sharing the incident with Mercy and wished they could walk home together, but play practice kept her late and Mercy was helping with something at the church that ate up a lot of her time. Mrs. Asher was pleased that Mercy was devoting more of her time and talent to the Community instead of doing extra-curriculars at the high school.

Thank heaven her own parents weren't quite so into the Community as Mercy's. They'd moved from Ohio to become part of the Community, drawn by Pastor Matt's charisma and a religious philosophy that revolved around simplicity, service, and living Biblically, but her mom worked for the utility company—the only woman in the Community who worked outside her home. She insisted on the modest dress the Community prescribed, but she let Jolene wear a little makeup and didn't object to her being involved in the high school plays, as long as they weren't anything lewd. Jolene sometimes wondered if it was her mother's job that allowed her to be more ... independent-thinking than most of the Community's women, to not kow-tow to Pastor Matt quite as much as Mercy's mom, for instance.

She had reached the house-sized boulder that crowded the path where it turned and sloped toward the Community. It had landed there two years earlier when a minor earthquake triggered a landslide that sent thousands of tons of rock thundering from the far side of the canyon, filling the ravine and creating a bridge of sorts from the Lone Pine side to the north rim. The tumbling boulders had uprooted whole trees, some of which had adapted to their new locations and now grew there, lonely bursts of green in the rocky landscape. Her gaze settled on the small white cross a third of the way up the slide and she said a prayer for Penelope. She was thinking ahead to the evening's homework and chores when a scraping sound gave her a moment's warning. Still, she gasped when Zach dropped off the boulder onto the path in front of her. He grabbed her and tried to kiss her.

She pushed him away. "You'll break your leg one of these times."

"You were daydreaming again." His blue eyes, so like his father's, smiled down into hers. He leaned in to kiss her again and this time she let him. After long moments, she turned her head, breaking the kiss to look past his shoulder. "We shouldn't."

"There's no one to see." His hands caressed her back, pulling her tightly against him, and her body reacted to the proof of his arousal pressed against her.

"Your dad would say that's not the point. In last week's sermon he said chasteness—"

"But we love each other." Zach's hands roamed her body and he drew her off the path. Within feet, the trees embraced them and the path disappeared. A breeze stirred the pines and their scent filled Jolene's nostrils, blending with Zach's soap and perspiration smell to make her dizzy. His lips found hers again and she moaned as he sucked her bottom lip into his mouth. Her backpack thudded to the forest floor and Zach's nimble fingers popped the buttons on her blouse, then slid under the fabric of her bra. She arched against him, the sensations he roused overwhelming her.

"Your parents won't be home for an hour," he mumbled against her ear, his warm breath making her shiver.

The implication thrilled and scared her. Was she ready? "I've got … geometry homework," she said between kisses.

"I love you, Jolene."

He'd said the words first, last week, and they still made her catch her breath. She brushed a leaf from his collar. "I wish we didn't have to hide our … us. I hate it."

"Me, too, but not near as much as we'd hate having everyone spying on us, snitching to my dad if we kissed or held hands or disappeared at the same time for a couple of hours, whether or not we were together. Dad's given me and Esther the speech about how everything we do reflects on him and his fitness for 'shepherding the sheep' so many times, I could puke." He mimed the action.

"Romantic," Jolene observed drily.

"Let me come over and I'll show you romantic." Zach grabbed for her, tickling, and she giggled.

"Okay, okay!"

"Okay?" Zach quit tickling and studied her face.

"Yes. Really okay." Feeling shy suddenly, she peeped at him through her lashes.

His face lighting up, Zach seized her hand. She pulled it away. "No. I'll go home like usual. Alone. You come around through the woods"—she traced an arc in the air with her finger that indicated the path he should follow behind the Community's homes—"and I'll let you in the back."

"Ten minutes." Zach pressed a quick kiss on her lips and jogged away, disappearing almost immediately in the trees.

Jolene waited a long moment, filled with expectancy and fear, a sense of life plunging off in a whole new direction, and then started down the path to Lone Pine, no longer feeling the weight of her backpack as she hurried toward Zach.

# TEN

### IRIS

EXITING THE HOSPITAL, IRIS grimaced as a radio talk show yammered out of a van idling near the door. Her rental car, nondescript and anonymous as it was, seemed like a haven and she settled into the driver's seat and relaxed her head against the headrest. Matthew Brozek might have awakened, but he couldn't communicate, probably wouldn't know who she was. The lights were on, but no one was home. He was a cup and saucer shy of a place setting, two knights short of a crusade. Iris grunted a humorless laugh. Her chest muscles constricted, like someone had dropped a lariat over her torso and jerked sharply and she breathed deeply to dispel the tightness. All for nothing. She'd lost her one and only chance to force Matthew Brozek to hear her, to acknowledge what he'd done twenty-three years ago. *No.* She refused to believe that. If it were true, she might never get past the block that was keeping her from designing and making jewelry. She'd come back and look him in the eye and search for a flicker of consciousness, of shame.

And she still had the appointment to visit her father at the prison. That wasn't until tomorrow ... what should she do now? She could drop in on her mother ... *Right. If I'm in the mood for an emotional milkshake of guilt, resentment, and disdain.* She could check into a hotel, or cruise through the Community to assess the changes. Maybe it had a Starbucks now. Iris snorted and pulled out her phone. Dialing Jane's number, she considered telling her about the run-in with Esther, the frustration of not being able to challenge Pastor Matt once she'd worked up the nerve to return, her reluctance to visit the Community and see her mother. Instead, when Jane picked up, Iris asked, "How's Edgar?"

Jane laughed her throaty laugh. "Hello, Iris. His highness is doing well, thank you, eating his weight in cat food that might as well be caviar and Kobe beef."

"Good. That's good."

Silence fell. Indistinct voices came from Jane's end of the line and Iris assumed she had customers in the gallery.

"Want to tell me about it?" Jane asked after a long moment.

"I'm at the hospital."

"And—?"

"And nothing. He wasn't in his room. Tests." Why didn't she tell Jane that seeing Brozek might be pointless? Because it felt, irrationally, like failure.

"Inconsiderate of him," Jane said. "Excuse me a minute."

The phone clunked down and a conversation ensued. "... bring my husband back to see the piece," and "I'll put a hold on it" filtered through the phone before Jane picked up again and said, "I'm back. Sorry. Customers."

"We can talk later—" Iris half regretted phoning, not sure what she wanted to tell Jane, if anything.

"So what's your next step?"

"See my mother." Iris hadn't known that's what she was going to do; the words popped out unbidden in response to Jane's question. "Then check into a hotel, get a good glass of wine, and..." And a young stud to drive it all from her mind. The memory of Greg's laugh sounded in her head and she shook it away.

"You're strong enough to do this, Iris. It's the right path."

Iris wasn't so sure, but Jane's faith warmed her.

"Say 'hi' to your mom for me." With a laugh, Jane rang off.

Iris turned the key and pointed the car toward Lone Pine before she could change her mind.

———

Driving fifteen miles into what used to be virtually uninhabited woods, Iris noted how strip malls and housing development had encroached on the Black Forest north and east of Colorado Springs, boxing in the tiny town of Lone Pine. She wondered what the Community thought about no longer being so isolated. Did the elders like the convenience of having a 7-Eleven with gas pumps a couple miles down the road, or did they resent having a tattoo parlor and sports bar within walking distance? She'd bet the latter, would also bet that Lone Pine's more adventurous youth regularly hiked the distance to the sports bar to buy a soda and watch forbidden TV.

Stopping the car on the verge where the school bus used to pick up and drop off Noah and her, the Brozek kids, Jolene, and a couple of others, Iris got out. A dump truck laden with gravel blasted past, dusting her with dirt and rock bits. She squinched her eyes against the draft and opened them when the truck was safely past to study the path that still bisected the brief apron of meadow before disappearing into the stands of pine and aspen beyond. It was fainter than when she'd lived there. She could just see the outermost boulders of the rockslide. Tempted to walk the mile-long trail into Lone Pine, Iris decided she might want to make a quick getaway and having her car nearby would be handy. Dredging up sentimental memories of giggling her way home from the bus stop with Jolene, or the time she watched bobcat kittens play from atop Big Boulder, was not on the agenda.

Back in the car, she folded her lips in, drove the last half-mile, and made the turn at the 1960s era motor court with the tacky neon sign spelling out SLEEPYTIME MOTOR INN, with only the SL, the Y and the last N illuminated. Did the Welshes still own it? The road, still unpaved, ambled slightly downhill as she passed the motel. A new sign at the town's outskirts announced LONE PINE, CO. POP. 346. So, the Community had almost doubled, despite the scandal and Matthew Brozek's inability to shepherd his flock. Iris couldn't count the number of times she'd heard him use that phrase. Who was leading the flock now, or had it dispersed?

The sun, sinking toward the west, was just high enough to illuminate the town, like a spotlight on a set. Iris tried to view it with as much detachment as she would a movie. Still vaguely horseshoe-shaped and hemmed in by high forest walls, the town now bulged to the south. Most of the houses were simple ranches, but several had brick or stone facades, or doors painted aubergine or garnet. Chicken coops squatted in many yards, and a field on the north held containers Iris thought might be beehives with a small barn or shed beyond them. The spring-fed pond, almost lake-sized, glinted bluely from the field's far end. What wasn't there was just as telling: no satellite dishes clinging to the eaves like fungi, no fences between the houses, no RVs or boats or third cars parked alongside the houses.

The downtown area—Iris didn't know how else to refer to it, even though that gave it more importance than it merited—looked busier, with more storefronts than she remembered, in addition to the café and the tiny library/post office. Four-way stop signs at the intersection near the general store testified to increased traffic. Center Street still dead-ended at the church of God's Community of Believers and Disciples, set at the closed end of the horseshoe, and the low building gleamed whitely from a cocoon of barbered shrubs and yellowing tulip leaves. Iris struggled to identify the feeling that itched at her and realized sheepishly that she was affronted that the town had apparently grown and flourished in her absence. It had had the temerity to change. Well, so had she.

Iris angled into a parking spot in front of what had been the general store. Her mouth felt dry; she'd get another bottled water in the store before seeking her mother. As she mounted the two plank steps, a sleek tourist-type bus rumbled out from behind the store and paused, belching diesel fumes. Middle-aged and elderly women and a few men jostled Iris as they streamed out of the store. Almost all of them carried bags marked "Lone Pine Traditional Crafts" in coral on a pale blue background. Hunching her shoulders inward to let the horde pass, Iris raised her brows at what appeared to be an organized shopping expedition, maybe for a senior's center. She helped one frail woman down the shallow steps and saw a cranberry wool sweater peeping from a nest of tissue paper in her shopping bag. *What in the world—?*

Crossing the store's threshold, Iris found herself in an unfamiliar space. Gone were the chest-high shelves that held cans of Campbell's soup, Wonder bread, Kotex, and matches. Gone were the sputtering fluorescent light fixtures, the whirring fan on the counter, the air of homey shabbiness. In their place was a stylish sales space with up-scale lighting glowing on stacks of sweaters, racks of scarves and hats, and baskets of yarn advertised as "Organic Alpaca Wool." Shallow refrigerator chests on the far end of the store featured local cheeses. Pyramids of honey, candles, and other beeswax products gave off a pleasant, waxy scent. Iris's eyes got round. She spotted a salesgirl behind a counter, her fingers skimming through the contents of a wallet, like she was looking for a stamp or receipt.

"Hi," Iris said.

The girl's head came up and she dropped her wallet. "Oh! I didn't hear you come in. Welcome." She stooped for the wallet, tucked it behind the counter, and came around to greet Iris.

Iris was ready to ask what had happened to the general store, whose brainchild this crafts boutique was, but choked on the words when she got a good look at the blond girl standing in front of her. Jolene! A lump lodged in her throat and she swallowed hard. A mere second's thought made her realize it couldn't be Jolene; Jolene was approaching forty, just like she was, and this girl was no more than sixteen. Jolene was still here, then. She hadn't escaped. Sadness—no, something more like regret—sifted through Iris as her fantasy of Jolene playing Nora or Major Barbara off-Broadway evaporated. This girl was a Jolene clone: petite, blond, hazel-eyed, with the same uptilting eyebrows and slightly sticking out ears. She wore a calf-length skirt and Peter Pan-collared blouse, the kind Iris had eschewed ever since leaving the Community. Something about the girl's posture told Iris she hid a pair of jeans in her backpack and put them on in the high school restroom, probably topping them with a cami or T-shirt the Community's elders would condemn as immodest. A tag clipped to her collar said "Rachel."

As Iris hesitated, unsure what to say, Rachel broke into a rehearsed spiel: "Lone Pine Traditional Crafts is a cooperative that celebrates the arts that made our pioneers self-sufficient. We have wool from alpacas raised in this community, and wool products hand-spun and knit by award-winning local artists. The cheeses are made by our citizens from goats and cows never treated with hormones of any kind. The honey comes from our hives. Here." The girl handed Iris a tri-fold brochure with a photo of alpacas grazing in front of the church.

Iris slid her fingers across the slick paper. "How long has the store been ... like this?"

"We've been open eight years," Rachel said, apparently happy to have someone to chat with since the shoppers had left. "The Community has always been big on being self-sustaining"—she said it with a sniff, like having a Walmart down the block beat self-sustaining every day of the week—"and eight years ago, our elders decided we should share our bounty with others."

*Rake in some tourist bucks, you mean,* Iris thought, but didn't say. She wondered whose brainchild the store really was, unable to imagine the stodgy group of elders she had known, all middle-aged men, coming up with a concept like this.

"You work here?" Iris groaned inwardly at the stupidity of her question.

"We all do," Rachel said. "We have to. It's part of our service to God and the Community."

Iris suppressed a smile at the resentment lurking in Rachel's voice. Clearly, the girl would rather be stalking boys at the mall with her friends, or working some place a bit more happening than this senior citizen shopping Mecca in the woods. The phone rang and Iris examined some hand-drawn note cards on a revolving carrel as Rachel answered it.

A door opened somewhere in the rear of the shop and a young man appeared behind the counter, bringing the scent of outdoors with him. With collar-scraping light brown hair, a willowy build, and finely drawn features, he seemed almost delicate, a little like the blond elf in *Lord of the Rings*. At first, Iris thought he might be Rachel's boyfriend, even though he looked too old for her, but his tone dispelled that idea.

"Chloe's sick and can't work her shift today," he told Rachel when she hung up. "Mom says you have to stay until six tonight and close up."

Rachel flushed angrily. "Abby and I are … we have plans."

"Not any more you don't."

Her tone turned pleading. "Aaron, you could do it. It'll be quiet … you could get some studying done."

"Not happening. I'm meeting friends at The Thirsty Parrot."

The revolving stand creaked as Iris turned it and the man noticed her for the first time. "I didn't see—. Sorry." He smiled apologetically. "I didn't know we had customers."

"No problem." Iris realized that Aaron must be Jolene's son, even though he didn't much resemble her. If he was as old as he looked— twenty-two or -three—Jolene must have had him within a year of Iris leaving the Community. She hadn't even been dating anyone, as far as Iris knew, so who was his father? She studied him, trying to think who he reminded her of.

"Do I have a smudge on my face?"

He sounded half-prickly, prepared to take affront, and Iris gave him the slow smile that rarely failed to win men over. "Sorry. I didn't mean to stare. It's just that you remind me of someone."

Aaron's stiffness melted under her smile and he asked, "Who?"

Iris started to shake her head, but then said, "Orlando Bloom."

Aaron looked pleased and Rachel snorted. "Shakespeare's Orlando, maybe, mooning through the woods after Rosalind."

Iris arched her brows.

Correctly interpreting her expression, Aaron said, "Our mom teaches Shakespeare."

"Ah." The idea of Jolene teaching took a minute to sink in. Iris had been so sure she'd follow her passion for performing. Aaron, she thought. His birth had trapped her here. Iris eyed him, surprised to

66

find she was half angry with him on Jolene's behalf. She shook off the feeling.

"I'm Aaron, by the way," Jolene's son said, gazing at Iris with more interest now that his sister had moved away to swipe a sleeve over a smudgy handprint on the refrigeration unit. He reached over the counter to shake hands.

"Iris. Do you live here?"

Aaron shook his head. "My folks do. I've got an apartment near UCCS. I'm working on my psych master's. How'd you find us, anyway?"

"I used to live around here." *Damn.* Iris regretted the truth the minute it was out of her mouth. Now he'd want to know when she'd lived here, if she'd known Jolene's family, the Ashers, Pastor Matt.

The phone on the counter rang and Aaron answered it, lifting a "just one moment" forefinger. He listened for a few seconds, covered the receiver, and called, "Hey, Rach, did you find a brown, fake alligator wallet? One of the ladies—"

Iris seized the opportunity to escape. Opening the door, she let in a chilly breath. "Thanks. I might be back," she said, slipping through the door without waiting for an acknowledgement.

Walking away from the co-op without a conscious destination, she realized she was headed toward the house where she'd spent her first fifteen years. Toward her mother. She drew a few sidelong looks, possibly because she was a stranger, or maybe because she was the only woman wearing jeans rather than a skirt. Clearly, a lot of the Community's restrictive rules were still in place: modest dress and long hair for women, no TV (if the lack of satellite dishes was anything to go by), simple living. Probably four elders and the pastor still ruled with iron rods, requiring the men to tithe and the women to be homemakers, meting out punishment to members who strayed from the path the elders had narrowed even more than Jesus intended. She brought her knuckles to her lips, feeling the ruler's sting from when she'd stumbled over the words of Galatians 2:20 during a Sunday school recitation. Alcohol, tobacco, gambling, and sex outside marriage had been strictly forbidden while community service, Bible study, and church attendance had been required. She'd bet the elders were still all men.

Nodding at one girl who gave her a shy smile, Iris left Center Street for the road her former home stood on. She continued the length of a football field to the house that used to be almost at the edge of Lone Pine, but which now had a buffer of newer houses between it and the line of trees which had been cut back to accommodate the Community's growth. Her footsteps slowed as she drew level with the house, smaller than she remembered, painted blue instead of gray, the maple sapling grown up to tower over the roofline. Blurring her peripheral vision so she didn't see the additional homes and streets, she experienced a chill of déjà vu. It felt like time travel must, like she'd walked out of her Portland life and into the 1990s. She could almost hear Noah bouncing his basketball on the driveway, and her mother sweeping the front stoop, her broom *whisk-whisking*. Iris's mouth went dry; she'd forgotten to purchase water at the store. Suddenly reluctant to approach any closer, to knock on the door she used to bang in and out of at will, to speak to her mother, she stopped halfway up the drive.

*I don't need to do this.* The thought blossomed. She had returned to confront Pastor Matt and to see her father. Her mother ... she didn't need to see her mother. She turned away on the thought, the tightness in her chest easing slightly. She had taken one step when the door behind her creaked open and a pleasant voice asked, "Can I help you?"

Reluctantly, Iris turned and found herself facing a stranger, a young woman with long reddish hair, a toddler balanced on her hip, and an enquiring expression. Having expected to see her mother, Iris was momentarily at a loss. She tucked a strand of hair behind her ear. "No, I, um ... I was looking for Marian Asher."

"Oh, she hasn't lived here for years, not since the tragedy," the woman said.

Iris didn't know if she was referring to the tragedy of her own disappearance, Pastor Matt's incapacitation, or her father's imprisonment. "I didn't know."

"Marian is the church's caretaker now ... has been since before we came to the Community," the woman said. "She lives in the cottage behind the church. We call it Outback Cottage because, well, it's out back of the church. You can find her there. I'm sure she'll be happy to see you." She smiled goodbye and closed the door as the toddler began to make unhappy noises.

Controlling an urge to jog back to her car, Iris kept her pace to a brisk walk and her eyes straight ahead. If she'd needed another reason for not seeking out her mother, the news that she lived in Outback Cottage provided it. It would take a team of draft horses to drag her through that door again.

# ELEVEN

**MERCY**

*Twenty-Four Years Ago*

OUTBACK COTTAGE ORIGINALLY BELONGED to the house, the out-of-place Victorian built by a fanciful settler in the late 1800s who prized both isolation and ostentation. His only surviving son, an early Community member, had willed the house and cottage to the Brozeks. Pastor Matt's mother-in-law, Zach and Esther's grandma, had lived in the cottage until she died the summer before Iris started eighth grade. Pastor Matt declared that he was donating the cottage for the use of a caretaker who would be responsible for janitorial and maintenance work at the church, but when no candidate stepped forward, the cottage stayed empty. The first time fourteen-year-old Mercy Asher stepped over the threshold, she thought it smelled like an unemptied cat litter box mixed with the kind of floral perfume that made her think of Nana Asher. She sneezed. She couldn't imagine why Pastor Matt wanted to meet her here, instead of in his office or one of the worship center's meeting rooms, but he'd said something about an important project.

A gilt-framed mirror hung over a narrow table in the tiny entry hall and a two-foot tall iron cross, thin but heavy looking, hung across from it. Fusty old people furniture and knick-knacks—lacy doilies over faded brocade upholstery and porcelain figurines and glassware—made the cottage feel like old Mrs. Wellington had just stepped out. Mercy felt uncomfortable, like an intruder, even though the woman had been dead for a year. She almost expected one of Mrs. Wellington's six or seven cats to come wind about her ankles, but they were gone, too.

"Pastor Matt?" When there was no answer, Mercy poked her head into the kitchen, dim with the shutters closed. A gleam caught her eye and she traced a forefinger over the spout of a delicate china teapot painted with forget-me-nots. It sat on a ledge that ran at eye level around the attached dining area.

"No one saw you come in, did they?"

Pastor Matt's voice sounded behind her, and Mercy whirled, long braid whipping. "No, sir. You told me to keep it a secret."

He smiled, big white teeth out-gleaming the fine china. "Good."

Mercy relaxed a tick, happy to have earned his approval, and wished she could open a window to let in some light and air. The stuffy rooms felt smaller somehow, now that Pastor Matt was here, even though he wasn't that tall. He gave the impression of being bigger than he was. Partly, it was his squared shoulders and thickening torso, but mostly it was his personality. He had a kind of presence that enveloped you, that draped itself over you, Mercy had thought more than once, that made people feel good about themselves and him. Not like her mom who too often made people feel smaller with the way her eyes cut away from them, or that little sniff she gave to signal contempt or disappointment, or the way she was all the time cleaning, cleaning, cleaning, like her family tracked in more dirt and left more grubby fingerprints on the walls than any other family in the Community. Mercy remembered she had yet to dust the base-boards and blinds; she wouldn't get dinner until she'd done her chores.

Pastor Matt interrupted her thoughts. "You know the church's twentieth anniversary is coming up and I want to do something special. With your artistic talents, I think you're just the girl to help me. What do you say?"

Half flattered and half confused, not understanding what sort of project he meant—a mural of some kind, maybe?—Mercy said, "Thank you. I'd be happy to help."

"Let me show you what I have in mind." Gesturing toward the table, Pastor Matt unrolled the tube of paper he carried and spread it out, anchoring the curling corners with cat-shaped salt and pepper shakers and a yellow sugar bowl that still held dusty cubes. He explained his plan for a triptych of banners featuring Biblical scenes. "It'll go behind the altar, floor to ceiling. There are plenty of women in the church who can do the needlework, Mercy, but we need a sketch, a drawing they can use as a blueprint or pattern. And what with you winning first place in the state fair art contest—. I thought maybe Samson in the temple for one panel, Saul on the road to Damascus for the middle one, and a scene from Revelation for the third. What do you think?"

Flattered at having her opinion asked, Mercy shifted slightly away from the heat of Pastor Matt; he stood so close their hips touched. "I could do that," she said, her mind fizzing with possibilities. "Maybe for the Old Testament scene you could have Ruth and Naomi in the field, or Esther pleading with the king to save her people? Having a woman in one of the scenes would be good, someone besides Mary, that is." To look at most of the paintings and sculptures Mercy's art teacher was so fond of, you'd think there hadn't been any women in the Bible besides Jesus's mother. Mercy wanted to break new ground and draw a Biblical woman with more *personality* than Mary seemed to have had.

"My daughter would like it if we used Esther," Pastor Matt said, tugging on his underlip with his thumb and forefinger. "Or the dogs tearing Jezebel apart would make a powerful scene."

Mercy couldn't imagine looking at something like that every Sunday and said, "I don't know if I can draw dogs so good. How 'bout I do a few different scenes and you decide what you like?" Lot's wife turning to salt with Sodom and Gomorrah exploding into a fireball in the background would be dramatic, or David slingshotting Goliath, although that was almost as overdone as Mary . . . .

"Great idea." His hand absently kneaded her shoulder as they studied his rough sketch laid out on the table. "I can't wait to see what you come up with, Mercy—you're such a talented girl. Creative. Remember, though, that this is our secret. Don't want the whole Community knowing about it before the anniversary!" He squeezed her shoulder one last time and let his hand drop. It brushed her rear as it fell to his side. An accident, surely.

"Absolutely," Mercy said, her mind working on the composition and content of possible scenes. "Our secret."

# TWELVE

### IRIS

Weary from her sleepless night, early departure, travel, and the emotions whipping through her like debris sucked up by a tornado, Iris returned to her car and drove slowly out of Lone Pine, wishing she'd pre-booked a hotel room. The Sleepytime Motor Inn came into view and, on impulse, Iris pulled into its small parking lot. Frost heaves in the asphalt made walking difficult as she crossed to a small A-frame building whose roof sloped almost to the ground. A sign on the door said "OFFICE." She pushed it open and a bell tinkled.

"Minute!" a voice called.

Standing on decades-old indoor-outdoor carpeting that had faded from blue to brownish-gray, Iris faced a short counter that hinged to allow the innkeeper access to the small reception area. Old-fashioned keys with plastic tags hung from hooks numbered 1 to 8 behind the counter, and a rack of colorful brochures advertising local activities ranging from cog rail rides up Pikes Peak to tours of the U.S. Air Force Academy, stood by the door. She was already regretting the impulse that had made her stop at this dumpy motel, but a woman she recognized as Mrs. Welsh emerged from the room behind the counter before she could duck out.

Petite and graying, she wore a corduroy dress with clogs and the worn-down expression of many small business owners in the tough economy. Small pearls graced her neat ears, her only jewelry. When she said, "You'd like a room?" in a hopeful voice, Iris didn't have the heart to head for the nearest Embassy Suites or Hyatt as had been her original plan.

"Yes, please." Iris pulled out her credit card. "I don't know how long I'll need to stay." *As short a time as possible.*

"That's okay. We're not too busy yet. Our busy season is the summer. Tourists." She passed Iris a registration card and a pen. "It's $28.99 a night."

Iris found it hard to imagine that flocks of tourists found their way to this out-of-the-way corner, but the cheap rooms probably attracted some families trying to stretch their vacation dollars. Mrs. Welsh drew the card across the counter and studied it. "You look familiar," she said, a line between her brows, "but I don't recognize the name. Iris. That's pretty." She turned and unhooked a key from the pegboard, sliding it across the counter.

Iris almost denied any connection. But, then, a spark of anger crept in. She'd done nothing wrong, nothing to be ashamed of. Why should she skulk around and lie about her ties to the Community? "I used to live here," Iris said. "Penelope was a couple years ahead of me in school. We played together sometimes. Model horses."

Before she could tell the woman her former name, Mrs. Welsh took a half step back. "Mercy Asher. We thought you were dead."

"Iris, please. Alive and well and living in Portland, for the moment," Iris said, determinedly cheerful, even though Mrs. Welsh was now looking like she regretted giving Iris a key. Was she remembering

Iris's accusations against Pastor Matt, or thinking about Neil Asher, in jail for beating the pastor and causing his wife's death?

Apparently, the thought of income outweighed whatever scruples she was battling with because she said stiffly, "Number two's around back. Nice and quiet."

*As if any of the rooms would be noisy, out here at the intersection of Nowhere and Back of Beyond.*

"You can park right in front of the door. I'm afraid we don't fill the pool until Memorial Day." She gave Iris an apologetic smile, and then, as if curiosity had trumped her discomfort, she asked, "What brings you back? Marian didn't mention that you were coming."

"I'm really here to see my dad," Iris said, "but maybe I'll stop in and surprise her."

"Oh, you'll do that, I'm sure," Mrs. Welsh said dryly. "There should be towels in the room, but if you need anything, we're in the blue house just past room one."

"Okay. Thanks." Iris considered asking about a wi-fi connection, and decided it would be a waste of breath. The bell tinkled again as she left the office.

The motor inn was arranged with the office nearest the road and the rooms in two blocks of four with the pool in a small courtyard between the two rows. The house Mrs. Welsh had mentioned was kitty-corner from the office on the far side of the motel and Iris spotted an overalled man—Mr. Welsh?—hoeing in the garden. He paused and leveled a stare at her for a long moment, and then returned to hacking at the ground when she got in the rental car. Driving around the building, she found her room at the far end, butted up against a strip of scraggly trees.

The lock yielded reluctantly to the key after Iris jiggled it, and she discovered the room was not as dreary as she'd expected. A yellow comforter and ruffled shams on the double bed offset the effect of clunky, mismatched furniture that looked like it had come from a variety of thrift shops and garage sales. It was sturdy, though, and gave off a pleasing odor of beeswax. She could work on the award design at the desk. She rattled open the drapes. Light poured in and she found herself facing the pool, a rectangle covered with a heavy tarp that sagged toward the middle. Not unlike the bed, Iris thought, eyeing it dubiously.

Leaving the door open, she returned to the car to retrieve her weekender and the case containing her jewelry-making tools and supplies. She'd probably only be here one night, maybe two, she told herself as she unzipped her bag, so it didn't matter that the Sleepytime Motor Inn wasn't exactly on par with the Ritz. She'd visit her father tomorrow, find a way to have it out with Pastor Matt in the afternoon or the next day, and return to Portland ready to create the best damned award the Green Gables company had ever seen. She picked up her drawing pad and flipped it open, thinking she might start on the design. Pencil poised, she hesitated, and then flipped the pad closed. She needed a shower. Marching nude into the bathroom, she hoped the water heated up quickly.

# THIRTEEN

**IRIS**

THE ARKANSAS VALLEY CORRECTIONAL Facility loomed on the horizon. About fifty miles east of Pueblo on State Highway 96, it was suitably isolated, rising from the prairie like a pop-up against the flat pages of a children's book. With the sun almost directly overhead, it cast no shadow, enhancing the two-dimensional effect. Iris hadn't known what to expect—the closest she'd ever been to prison was the overnight stay at the Baton Rouge jail when she'd been picked up for shoplifting—but she'd anticipated something more sinister, more *Shawshank Redemption*, than these rectangular buildings with flags. It looked like a community college campus or the headquarters for a mid-sized, light industrial corporation that got a tax break to locate in this barren county. If the corporation needed double twelve-foot fences topped with concertina wire to keep its employees in.

Only a handful of visitors suffered through the check-in procedures in the small reception area, a space about the size of Iris's bedroom. They were a motley lot ranging from an octogenarian trailing an oxygen tank to a wailing two-year-old. Most of them seemed to know the drill. Iris tried not to think about how depressing it would be to see your son, brother, or husband only in this environment. When she'd filled out the paperwork, listing Neil Asher as the "offender" she was there to see, Iris waited her turn in the inspection line run by a slender Hispanic guard. A class ring with a central peridot winked from his pinky. He made her open her mouth and curl up her tongue—what weapon did he think she could hide there?—and fan her long hair. Even though she was only a visitor, could walk away whenever she wanted, she found herself tensing her muscles until her stomach ached. The search was a violation, an indignity. She'd never complain about TSA again.

Once siphoned through double gates that made her think of the airlocks in sci-fi films, Iris found herself on a 200-foot-long path through a sea of rock studded here and there with lonely cacti and other plants. The open air was a huge relief after the claustrophobia-inducing reception area. An ornamental bridge, weathered and with a railing, arched over a faux creek of round river stones. It seemed like the bridge to nowhere, an ironic statement about the facility, and Iris wondered if it was intentional. Probably not.

Once she handed her paperwork to the corrections officers in what looked like a command center, Iris found herself in an L-shaped room ringed with vending machines, waiting for a guard to fetch her father. A young couple sat as close as they could without touching, the girl weeping softly. The family with the crying toddler occupied the table next to Iris's. *Tears seem to be the theme of the day.* She resolved not to add to the waterworks. It wasn't until the muscles in her forearms started to ache that she realized she was clenching and unclenching her hands. Consciously stretching her fingers wide, she inhaled the room's pine cleaner odor.

She hadn't found out about her father's imprisonment until a year after she left. She'd been almost seventeen by then and living in Virginia. When she'd left Lone Pine, she'd made a clean break, foresworn contact with her family and former friends. They'd all believed Pastor Matt, so she was through with them. Even her parents. Especially her parents. Then she'd learned from an old *USA Today* article that her father had been convicted of aggravated mayhem against Matthew Brozek and of felony murder in the death of his wife, Glynnis Brozek, who suffered a fatal heart attack upon witnessing the assault. Iris had zeroed in on her father's name, on the news that he'd beaten Pastor Matt so brutally he was still in a coma. She'd read the paragraph three times before she took in the fact that her father was going to spend the rest of his life in prison.

He'd believed her after all, even though he hadn't stood up to her mother, or spoken out against the reckoning stones. Tears had pricked her eyelids. The surprise of it had left her unsettled, unsure if she should try to contact him. She'd found the name of the prison easily enough, but didn't know if he was allowed phone calls or if she could stand to hear his voice. Finally, after two days of thinking about it, she'd mailed him a one-word note—"Thanks"—and immediately moved to a new state for fear someone might trace her.

Now, she didn't know what to feel. She was nervous, her palms sweaty, but maybe that was because she was trapped behind bars and razor wire with murderers, rapists, and violent offenders who would as soon carve your heart out with a spoon as pass you by. She felt guilty that she hadn't tried to get in touch with her father after that one-word note. She'd denied his existence for more than two decades. And, she realized, she was still angry. Pissed off that he hadn't proclaimed his belief in her, saved her from the reckoning stones and the scorn of the whole community. Pacing two hasty strides in each direction, she caught the guard's eye and made herself sit down. Sure, he'd pummeled Pastor Matt after the fact, but that hadn't done her much good, had it? She didn't hear the door open, but a change in the air made her turn.

Her father stood on the threshold, blinking like a bear just awakened from its winter hibernation. She jumped up as if goosed and looked at him. He'd been tall and on the thin side when Iris left home; he'd packed on both muscle and fat in prison, managing to look bigger and yet softer. The skin on his face sagged to jowls, and his fleshy ears seemed more prominent against his bald head. The green uniform of trousers and a short-sleeved pullover turned his skin sallow. The sad smile she remembered split his face, showing coffee-stained teeth. He made his way to the table she'd been assigned.

"Mercy? God has returned you to me, Mercy." He held out his arms tentatively, as if afraid of a rebuff, and Iris hugged him awkwardly, and then with fervor. Years of missing him formed tears that she refused to let fall. He felt frail, despite his seeming bulk, like a puff pastry. He smelled of soap, and fabric burned in an industrial dryer, and sausage.

She tried to say, "Dad," but couldn't force words or air through her closed throat.

"Let's sit." He pulled out one of the chairs. She sank down, but held onto his hand for a moment before releasing it. Choosing a chair across from her, her father stared as if trying to memorize her every pore and eyebrow hair. "You've grown up beautiful. I see a lot of your mom in you."

"Only on the outside."

Her father pulled back at the sharpness in her voice and Iris regretted letting the bitter words out. She didn't know what to say. The possibilities seemed either too flip—"What have you been up to?"—or, strangely, too personal. He might be her father, but they hadn't communicated in more than two decades. She finally said, "I've missed you," realizing that it was true.

"I've thought about you and prayed for you every day of these last twenty-three years."

"I'm sorry." What a pitiful, inadequate phrase.

Her father took a moment to absorb the words and finally accepted them with a tiny nod. "Your going was hard on your mother."

*She should have believed me, taken my side.* Iris didn't want to argue with her father within minutes of seeing him again, so she said nothing and his words hung between them until her father leaned forward to scratch behind his knee. The movement brought on a cough that wracked him for almost a minute. When it was over, he slumped in the chair, breathing cautiously, looking exhausted. He shook his head when she asked if she could get him some water. "Had the flu at the end of February and I haven't been able to shake this cough."

"What's it like?"

"This? Prison?"

She regretted the question. What could he say? Prison had to suck.

"I've adjusted. I won't deny it was hard early on, when I was in Bent County, partly because I could see my being a convict was hard on Marian. Partly because ..." He paused and scratched behind his ear. "I can't explain prison to you. Some of the men are animals— truly evil and I've witnessed things ... Enough of that. Most are lost, confused—they've got substance abuse problems, or were abused as kids, and they made mistakes, sometimes horrible mistakes, and those mistakes will define them forever, in or out of prison. And it's boring. You can't imagine how boring, how draining and demoralizing that boredom is. Prisons are full of hopeless people, for the most part, just taking up space."

Iris listened in growing horror. The thought that her gentle father was trapped here forever was like bees buzzing inside her head.

"Since they moved me here…" He twiddled a shirt button. "I make cubicles. You know, for offices. Fitting, right, that inmates make the prison walls for corporate jails? That's what we say, anyway." His gaze strayed to the window. Iris could see nothing through it except light. "I get three squares a day, and plenty of time to read my Bible. Jesus is a lot more present to me here than he ever was on the outside. It is in our weakness that God's strength is made plain, and nowhere is that truer than here."

The Jesus-words smothered Iris, who had long ago thrown off the illusory comfort of her childhood beliefs. Right about the time the Community saw fit to punish her for speaking the truth. Despite the way his words slid under her skin and made her itch, she didn't want to argue with her father, to undermine whatever comfort he might have found.

As she searched for something neutral to say, he touched her hand lightly. "Tell me about you. Where did you go that night?"

"Kansas." The single word loosed a torrent of memories and Iris found herself telling her father about dying her hair in the bus station and choosing her new name. "Iris" because she'd always loved the lavender flowers that grew alongside their house, and "Dashwood" from a Jane Austen paperback someone had left on the bus. She told him about drifting from town to town and working odd jobs or stealing to feed herself, avoiding the pimps who hung about bus stations, looking for runaways, who would have prostituted her. She skipped some of the harder and more sordid episodes, not wanting to re-live them or inflict them on her father. Fetching them each damp, plastic-tasting sandwiches from the vending machine, she told him about meeting Lassie, who introduced her to his godmother, Jane Ogden, when he saw her sketchbook one night, and how Jane had given her a job at the gallery, awarded her "scholar-ships" for art classes, and introduced her to a goldsmith who took her on as an apprentice.

"She saved my life," Iris said. "She helped me discover that I was meant to design and make jewelry. She suggested I take self-defense classes so I'd feel safer. Without her—" She choked to a stop. Clearing her throat, she said, "I do pretty well. People like my designs. I'll bring you some photos next time I come, if they'll let me." She nodded sideways toward a guard. The words "next time" had slipped out unconsciously, but she knew she'd visit her father again. She could afford to fly back a few times a year. *I can't make up for lost time, but I can damn sure be here for him now. He's only in here because of me.* The thought made her swallow hard.

"You always were artistic," he said. "We were so proud when your painting won the ribbon at the state fair that time. Remember?"

Ice wormed its way down Iris's spine. She remembered what that prize had led to. "I decided I preferred stones and metal to paint," she said. Noticing with surprise that the clock was ticking its way toward the end of visiting hours, Iris reached for her father's hand. "Look, Dad, I always wanted to say … thanks."

"You sent me a note."

"You got it?"

He nodded. "Made it worth it."

Iris folded her lips in and blinked back tears. "You don't know what it meant to me," she said, "to realize you believed me. When Mom accused me of lying, and the whole Community … Well, when you didn't stop it, I figured you didn't believe me either. It wasn't until a couple of years later, when I saw the article about your sentencing, that I knew you'd believed me after all. You punished Pastor Matt for—"

"What?" His brow wrinkled, pulling his ears slightly forward.

The young couple were hugging goodbye within earshot. "You beat up Pastor Matt," she whispered. "You beat him into a coma. For what he did to me."

His mouth dropped open and he snapped it closed, a look Iris couldn't interpret settling on his features. "I didn't attack Matthew Brozek, Mercy," he said finally. "I told the police I did so they wouldn't go after you."

"You—" Iris stared at him. His words didn't make sense.

"I thought you did it." He looked as stunned as she felt.

"C'mon, Asher," a corrections officer said, putting a heavy hand on her father's shoulder. Another coughing fit seized him.

"Can we have a couple more—" Iris started, desperate to continue the conversation, to seek clarity. Surely her father hadn't meant—. Did he mean he hadn't done it, hadn't beaten Pastor Matt, that his confession was a lie? No way. The impossible thoughts whirling in her head weighted her down like a lead apron, rooting her to the chair.

"Sorry, miss. Time's up." He started to lead her father away. He went easily, accustomed to following the rules, acceding to the guards' authority, not drawing attention.

Iris wrenched herself out of the chair and ran after them. A beefy guard blocked her way, expression stern. "Settle down, miss—"

She craned her neck to see around the officer's bulk, getting a sour whiff of chewing tobacco as he breathed open-mouthed. Her father paused at the door, looking back at her over his shoulder, his expression equal parts confusion, desperation and hope. "I don't belong here, Mercy. I'm not—. Get me out."

"Dad—" But he was gone.

———

At least he hadn't said "God works in mysterious ways," Iris thought savagely, pushing the rental car past ninety miles an hour as she drove away from the prison. Dun-colored prairie flashed past. A pronghorn bounded away. Traffic was light. The inside of the car felt too warm, like a mohair blanket wrapped around her, and Iris rolled down the window, preferring the slash of cool air against her face and bare arms. He hadn't believed her, after all. No one had believed her. Tears pricked behind her eyelids. Talk about ironic, or a comedy of errors. One of the Greek playwrights must have written something like this. A man takes the blame for something he didn't do, thinking he's saving his daughter, while the daughter makes a hero of the man for doing the thing he didn't really do. Iris shook her head violently to clear the confusing thoughts, and the car swerved onto the shoulder. The wheels juddered over fractured asphalt and weed clumps before she swung the car back on the pavement. The speedometer inched toward one hundred.

An hour later she was almost back to Colorado Springs, forced to slow by clotting traffic, when the shock drained away enough for her to look at her father's actions in another light. He might not have believed her, but he'd gone to prison for what he thought was her crime. Her lungs burned and it was hard to breathe through the toxic mix of anger and grief that swelled within her at the realization that he thought her capable of beating a man, even Pastor Matt, into a coma. She coughed and breathed deeply, her chest expanding against the seatbelt. He'd spent twenty-three years locked up to protect her. Twenty-three years for a crime he didn't commit. Resolve tightened Iris's grip on the steering wheel. She had to get him out.

It was only mid-afternoon when she got back to the motel, but Iris was tempted to head for the nearest bar, slug back a couple of beers, and see what the local action looked like. The melancholy anonymity of the motel room had a calming effect, however, and by the time she'd showered off the probably imaginary prison stink and changed into faded jeans and a Henley shirt, she'd plotted her next step. She needed an Internet café to find the name and address of her father's lawyer. Giving her jewelry-making tools a wistful look, Iris slung her computer bag over her shoulder and closed the motel door firmly behind her. Maybe she'd try to sketch some designs for the new commission this evening, after energizing her father's lawyer for a new appeal or whatever it took to free him.

# FOURTEEN

## IRIS

THE LAW FIRM OF Weber and Parrish was located on Tejon Street in downtown Colorado Springs. Beyond noting brown stone and tinted glass, Iris gave the building little thought as she fed the meter, checked the lobby directory, and headed for the elevator. It spit her out on the seventh floor, and she found herself facing a travertine counter behind which sat a male receptionist talking on the phone. When the man hung up and gave Iris an enquiring look, she stepped forward.

"I'm Iris Dashwood. I'd like to talk to Susan Tzudiker about the Neil Asher case. I don't have an appointment."

The receptionist's brows twitched together. "I'm afraid Ms. Tzudiker is no longer with the firm. She's gone over to the other side."

Iris hated coy references to death. "She died?"

The receptionist permitted himself a prim smile. "She joined the DA's office. Lawyer joke."

"I'm really not in the mood for jokes," Iris said. "Just hook me up with whoever took over Neil Asher's case when Ms. Tzudiker moved on."

"What is your interest in the case?" the receptionist asked, clearly miffed by Iris's tone. He picked up his phone and pushed an intercom button.

"I'm Neil Asher's daughter." She'd been avoiding talking about her family for so long that claiming the relationship out loud felt strange.

The receptionist's brows soared and he turned away from Iris to murmur into the phone. "Someone will be with you in just a few minutes," he said more cordially, gesturing toward a small sitting area.

Too restless to sit, Iris prowled the reception area, inspecting the artwork on the walls, the predictable magazines on the glass-topped table, the array of plaques that extolled the firm's contributions to the city. She'd looked at them all twice over before a man's footsteps sounded behind her. She turned.

"My God, it is you. Mercy Asher. I thought you were dead."

The man standing there, immaculate in a suit and tie, was still recognizable as the eighteen-year-old she'd last seen in jeans and worn leather jacket the night of her humiliation. There were crow's feet around his brown eyes now, and silver strands in the black hair, but he still wore it in a low ponytail. The establishment suit dimmed the electric charge he used to give off; he'd been a wire thinly wrapped in leather and denim, apt to burn through at any moment. They'd met in Spanish class when Cade was a senior and Iris a sophomore. The attraction was mutual and violent. She knew her parents would never let her hang out with a friend who wasn't from the Community, so she used to sneak out to meet him in the woods, on the rockslide, or in his car. She'd gotten good at lying to her parents about her whereabouts when she was meeting Pastor Matt—oh, irony—and she put the training to good use to steal an hour here and there with Cade.

The faint odor of cigarette smoke clung to him. Iris's lips tingled, as they had when he'd kissed her for hours on end, making her flush with heat, and she put two fingers against her mouth. Like Pavlov's dogs, she thought, annoyed with her body for its instantaneous re-action to the stimulus of her former boyfriend's presence. "Cade? What—?"

"Let's go into my office, Ms. Asher," Cade Zuniga said with a meaningful glance at the curious receptionist.

"Dashwood. Iris Dashwood." Without another word, Iris trailed him through the carpeted hallways to a corner office guarded by a secretary's desk, currently empty. "A lawyer, huh? I'd never have guessed. You've done well for a boy who wasn't sure he'd graduate on time," she said, glancing at the Pikes Peak view from the window before her gaze caught on the photos of a dark-haired boy and girl, maybe four and six, on the desk. She swallowed hard.

"The DWI conviction didn't help, either," he agreed, closing the door. An expensive watch gleamed from his wrist and a band of white on his ring finger testified to the recent presence of a wedding ring.

"I didn't know about that."

"The night you left." He didn't move, but his gaze flicked over her before returning to her face. "You're looking well. Beautiful."

"And you. Well, I mean."

"It's good to see you. Really good. I worried about you." He paused and the tip of his tongue moistened his lips. "I would have gone with you, if you'd told me you were going."

Exactly why she hadn't told him. "You couldn't. Your sister, your grandfather—. How's your grandmother?" Cade had been raised by his grandparents after the courts took him and his sister away from their parents. Cade's mother had later kicked her drug habit, but Cade and his sister had remained with their grandparents.

"Still kicking. Still the church secretary, even though she's pushing eighty. The fathers make noises about her retiring now and then, but the parish would fall apart without her and they know it."

Iris smiled at her memories of the four-foot-nine dynamo, her thick hair pulled into a low bun, laying down the law to her husband and Cade. She could easily imagine her bossing the priests around. "Say 'hello' to her for me."

"Aw, hell." Cade rubbed a hand down his tanned face and moved toward his desk. As if the movement had snapped him back to the present, his voice assumed a professional overtone, less raw, more distant. "Bernard said you were asking for Susan Tzudiker, so obviously you didn't come here looking for me."

"I did if you're my father's lawyer. How did you end up representing him?" Without waiting for Cade to ask her to sit, Iris settled into a squashy blue chair positioned in front of the desk. She shifted it so she wasn't gazing directly at the photos of Cade's children. Reaching out, she let her fingers trail along the smooth bird's eye maple of the desk before dropping her hand back in her lap.

"When Susan left, his file came over to me."

She fixed her gaze on Cade's face. "He didn't do it."

"He told you that?"

"He thought I did it."

Cade didn't express the surprise she'd been expecting. "Even though he confessed, I had trouble thinking of your dad as the violent type."

"He wasn't. He's not. I—we—need to get him out of prison."

"It's not so easy, Mer—Iris."

"Can't you file an appeal or get them to re-open the case or something?"

"Not without new evidence."

"But he said—"

Cade was shaking his head. "Retracting his confession at this stage isn't going to make a difference." He depressed a button on his phone. "Lib, bring me the Asher file, please." Leaning back in his chair, he tapped a pencil on the desk. Iris well remembered his inability to be still; he was always pacing, or fiddling with something. "Where have you been?" he asked, his gaze settling on her.

"Around. Early on, I moved a lot. I finally put together a life, my Iris life, soon after I turned twenty. In Portland mostly. I design and make jewelry. I've been in Oregon the last couple of years, but I've been thinking that it's time to try someplace new again." Iris wished the paralegal would show up with the file, and end the awkwardness.

"All that moving around must be hard on your family." Cade's dark eyes never left hers and she knew what he was asking.

"No family. Well, except Jane and Edgar. Her cat."

"Sounds lonely."

She slanted a self-mocking smile. "Not so much. I don't have any trouble finding companionship when I want it." Before he could respond, she added, "You've got kids."

He fingered the photos and smiled. "Stephen and Elena. We—"

A brief knock heralded the entrance of a middle-aged woman. "Here's the Asher file, Cade," she said, shooting a curious look at Iris. Handing over a two-inch-thick expandable folder, she left reluctantly when Cade thanked her.

"I can sum this up for you in twenty-five words or less," Cade said, slapping a hand on the file. "The vic's daughter called 911 to say Matthew Brozek was injured and needed an ambulance. The police arrived before the EMTs and found Neil standing over Brozek in a cottage on the property, covered in Brozek's blood. They snapped the cuffs on him. He originally said he walked in and found Brozek injured and tried to help him, which is how he got the blood on himself. Hours later, though, he confessed to beating Brozek, but wouldn't say why. There were plenty of folks in Lone Pine, however, quick to tell the police about your accusations and what happened to you. The cops figured that added up to motive and labeled the case 'closed' before the week was out."

Iris wrinkled her brow, trying to piece together the order of events. "What about Mrs. Brozek?"

"The cops found her a bit later, in the kitchen. The 911 call only mentioned Brozek and the beating, so they didn't go looking for a second vic. Your father didn't know she was there, either. She was dead when they found her."

Iris shivered, picturing Mrs. Brozek, who had been an inoffensive woman, lying in pain on the kitchen floor, maybe hearing the commotion, but unable to call out. Iris hated to think that if she'd been found a few minutes earlier, the EMTs might have saved her. Then she could have named her husband's attacker, presumably, and Iris's father wouldn't have spent twenty-three years in prison. What a difference those ten or twenty minutes might have made for so many people: her father, obviously; her mother; Esther and Zach, who had essentially been orphaned...

Cade interrupted her thoughts. "The perp used something like a tire iron or fireplace poker to beat Brozek. The weapon was never found. Your dad refused to say what he did with it when he confessed."

"It doesn't make sense that he would beat Pastor Matt, go somewhere to dispose of the weapon, and then come back," Iris said heatedly.

Cade shrugged. "The prosecutor suggested he'd had an attack of conscience and returned to render aid. At any rate, they found plenty of fingerprints in the house and cottage. Half the Community apparently

93

hung out at the Brozeks'. There were the prints you'd expect—the family's—plus your mom's and dad's, Jolene Farraday's, a dozen others from the Community, another half-dozen unidentified"—he paused—"and yours."

Iris nodded, unperturbed by the searching look he gave her. "I was there. That night."

"You were?" He leaned forward, his eyes fixed on hers.

Was she imagining it, or did he look slightly wary? She faced him, deliberately expressionless as she remembered the short walk from her house to the Brozeks' home in the darkness, cold weighing down the air, the spooky hoot of an owl launching for a hunt. "I went there to confront Pastor Matt. I'd been crying pretty much non-stop since the ritual the night before. I'd already made up my mind to go. But I needed to see him, to tell him that he was evil, that even if the Community didn't see it, I did. God did. And I was never, ever going to forgive him. That would show him." She smiled bitterly at her fifteen-year-old self's naïveté.

Cade came around the desk and laid a hand on Iris's shoulder. The warmth seeped into her skin, into her muscles. She resisted the urge to lean her cheek against his forearm. "What did he say?"

She shook her head, shrugging his hand away. He stepped back, hitching one buttock up on the desk and crossing his arms. Uncomfortable with him standing over her, Iris stood and crossed to the plateglass window. "Nothing," she said, watching a woman on the sidewalk below try to fold a stroller into the back of her car. "I chickened out." The shame of it bowed her head, even now. "I got to the house, put my hand on the doorknob, and even knocked. Before anyone could answer, I lost my nerve. I imagined Esther or Mrs. Brozek opening the door, looking at me like I was dog dirt on their shoes, believing, like everyone, that I'd falsely accused him. Or him standing there, pretending I was a troubled soul he was saintly enough to forgive, yet with that look in the back of his eyes that said he remembered what the crook of my neck smelled like, how the old couch squeaked—"

"God, Iris."

She turned to face him, leaning back against the window, letting its rigidity and coolness strengthen her. The sun streamed around her, casting her face in shadow. "I took off. Scrammed. Vamoosed. Ran like a frightened bunny."

"Of course you did. You were fifteen! You can't blame yourself for not facing him down. Damn!" Cade pounded a fist on his desk and a stapler shivered off the edge, spewing staples when it hit the floor. "I wish *I'd* beaten him to a pulp."

They stood for a moment in silence, neither making a move to retrieve the stapler. Finally, Cade spoke softly. "Is that why you came back? To confront him?"

Iris nodded. "Silly, huh? After twenty-three years—"

"Not silly at all."

Cade's phone buzzed and he punched a button with an apologetic look at Iris. His paralegal's voice came over the intercom; she'd been with him for some time if the note of reproof in her voice was any indication. "Stephen called. He said he's waiting at soccer practice?"

"On my way. Thanks, Libby." Facing Iris, he said, "I've got to pick up my son. Look, we need to talk more. Tomorrow's Saturday—I can make some time to work on this." Pulling some documents from the folder, he passed them to Iris. "This is the police report and some interviews our PI did—nothing privileged. Read through it tonight— maybe it'll spark something. We can discuss the options first thing tomorrow."

She stopped him with a hand on his arm. "Tell me what it would take to get him out."

He looked at his watch and spoke quickly. "Significant new evidence, emphasis on *significant*, that would give the parole board cause to parole him, or the DA reason to enter a motion to vacate the judgment of conviction. An eyewitness coming forward to say he saw someone else beating Brozek—unlikely. An unimpeachable source giving Neil an alibi—not gonna happen since Neil was on the scene. The murder weapon, depending. The parole board's meeting later this month, by the way—we don't have much time. I've got to go—we'll talk about it tomorrow."

Iris preceded him out the door and toward the elevator, aware of the secretary's gaze following them. Saying he was taking the stairs, Cade left her at the elevator door with a swift kiss on the cheek. "Damn, it's good to see you again, Mercy."

Up close, he smelled earthy, warm, like he always had, and she caught her breath, fighting off the memories. Her skin tingled where his five o'clock shadow had grazed it. "Iris," she said to his departing back. "It's Iris now."

He raised a hand in acknowledgement and kept going as the elevator door dinged open and Iris got in.

# FIFTEEN

### IRIS

Iris returned to the motel, her emotions whirling from the encounter with Cade, to find her room as overheated as a sauna. She fiddled with the thermostat, but the system kept blasting out hot air. Exasperated, beginning to perspire, she dialed the office. No answer. Putting her father's file on the desk, she marched over to the office, enjoying the evening's cool breath, only to find it deserted and locked. It was almost six, she realized, and she couldn't much blame the Welshes for not staffing the office round-the-clock when she seemed to be the only guest. With a resigned sigh, she headed toward the blue house on the corner of the motel property.

She rapped on the newish storm door, inhaling the scent of fresh-turned earth from Mr. Welsh's garden. There was something about the smell of loam. It had lowered her blood pressure a couple points by the time the door swung inward and Mrs. Welsh stared out at her. She had a housecoat wrapped around her and wore slippers on her feet. She looked worn down and Iris wondered how much of the motel maintenance and cleaning the woman took on. Even in the off-season, with not too many customers, there was probably a lot to do to keep the old place standing.

"I'm sorry to disturb you, Mrs. Welsh, but the heater in my room is broken," Iris said.

The woman sighed and pushed the door open. "Come in, Mer— Ms. Dashwood."

"Iris."

"Let me find my husband. It does this sometimes."

Iris stepped into the small house, hearing a teakettle whistle. Mrs. Welsh disappeared down the hall and Iris drifted into the living room that opened off the small foyer. Nineteen-eighties-era wallpaper patterned the walls in mauve and teal, and a velvet-covered sofa and loveseat of the same vintage faced a brick fireplace. It was the photo portrait above the mantel that caught Iris's attention, however. Sixteen by twenty, with a gold frame, it showed a doe-eyed, brown-haired teen with a shy smile. Penelope Welsh. Tendrils of sadness twined through Iris as she approached the fireplace, her eyes never leaving the fixed gaze of the girl in the photo. Lost in the rockslide.

A pair of half-burned candles sat at either end of the oak mantel, and various items cluttered the space between them: bronzed baby shoes, a Breyer model of an appaloosa mare, a round music box that Iris knew held a pop-up ballerina, and more. It was a shrine to Penelope, Iris realized. She stroked a finger down the horse's slick resin back, remembering the hours she and Penelope, and later Jolene, had spent playing with the model horses. Penelope had been a couple of years older, but had stayed friends with Iris until her last year of middle school. Then she'd drifted away, pursuing new interests and friends. Her two years of distance made it kind of weird that she'd slipped a note into Iris's locker, saying she needed to talk to her that last day, only hours before a minor earthquake triggered the rockslide.

Iris had kept that last reminder of Penelope for months until it went through the wash in her jeans pocket and dissolved. She could still see Penelope's neat, rounded letters: *Meet me at 4. Usual place. I have to tell you something IMPORTANT.* The word was capitalized and underscored three times. The note was signed simply, *Penny*, with the tail of the Y curled up to form a heart. The usual place was in the ravine, beneath a huge spruce whose branches dipped almost to the ground and formed an enclosed room that smelled of pine and dust. Iris had had to take a make-up test after school, though, and by the time she was done, millions of tons of rock had sheared away and swept into the ravine, burying everything in it, including the magnificent spruce and Penelope. Iris told her mother she was supposed to have been with Penelope, and it was one of the few times she could remember when her mother had pulled her into a tight hug and held her close for long minutes.

Iris's gaze fell on Penelope's favorite bracelet, half-hidden under the music box. It was a chunky nugget of turquoise on a braided leather band with a lobster-claw hook. Smiling sadly, Iris slid it out from under the music box, meaning to prop it against the box's satiny wood. When she touched the stone, though, a sense of panic, of mounting terror filled her. Her fingers tightened involuntarily around the bracelet and she began to shake, unable to control the sudden rush of fear. Iris looked around the room wildly, searching for a way out, and felt her vision blur until all she could see was blue and more blue through a murky film. *Can't breathe.* What was happening to her?

"Get away from there."

The harsh voice cut through Iris and she dropped the bracelet, which clinked against a brass stand holding fireplace tools before landing on the carpet. Iris felt her pulse returning to normal and took a deep breath, swinging around to see Mr. Welsh approaching, anger clouding his craggy features. He stooped in front of her and retrieved the bracelet, placing it carefully, gently, on the mantel, centered between the horse and the music box.

"You've got no business in here," he told Iris, looking at her from under unruly brows. The grooves in his forehead and bracketing his mouth were deep, gouged by the sharp chisel of time and tragedy.

He topped her by at least six inches and Iris thought she caught a whiff of bourbon on his breath. "I'm Ir—"

"I know who you are." He stepped forward, as if intent on herding her toward the door and out of the house.

His truculence pissed her off but she tried to sound reasonable. "The heater in my room isn't working. Your wife told me to wait here." When he didn't respond, she added softly, "I didn't mean to pry. I remember Penelope wearing that bracelet. She loved it."

"We found it. On the rockslide. The rocks, the stones—they ripped it off her." The words emerged with an effort. "That's all we ever found of my little girl. Those uncountable tons of rock ... there was no way. No way to shift them, find my little Penny." He turned his back on her, his gaze uplifted to the photo of his dead daughter.

Unable to think of words that would begin to touch this man's sorrow and anger, Iris stood awkwardly, wondering if she should just leave. Before she could decide, Mrs. Welsh reappeared, dressed, metal toolbox in her hand. She stopped abruptly on the threshold.

"Quentin. I didn't hear you come in. The heater in Ms. Dashwood's room is stuck again."

"I'll take care of it," he said, holding out his hand for the toolbox. Mrs. Welsh handed it over with a look of relief and he headed for the back of the house.

"I'm just making some tea—?" Mrs. Welsh started, giving Iris an uncertain look.

Iris could tell the woman would prefer it if she left, so she said, "I think I'll wait outside. I could use the fresh air after spending the day in prison." She wasn't sure why she'd added that last bit, but she felt faintly satisfied when Mrs. Welsh drew in an audible breath.

"Your father," the woman said after a moment. "You visited your father."

Iris nodded. Encouraged by the lack of animosity in Mrs. Welsh's voice, she added, "I'm going to get him out of prison. He didn't . . . he's not the one who hurt Pastor Matt."

Mrs. Welsh blinked several times fast, but her expression didn't change. "How do you know?"

"He told me."

Silence stretched between them and Iris became uncomfortable under the weight of Mrs. Welsh's suddenly knowing gaze. "You'd think he would have mentioned his innocence before, unless he had a really good reason not to," she observed. "I knew a woman once who carried her own grandbaby to term because her daughter's womb was malformed, even though she had breast cancer and needed chemo treatments. Fact." Before Iris had time to wonder about this seeming non sequitur, she added, "It's wonderful what parents will sacrifice for their children."

"I didn't—!" It hadn't occurred to Iris that the Community would think exactly what her father had. "I'm going to find out who really did it." The words crystallized the thought that had been floating through her brain since her talk with Cade.

"I don't suppose that'll be easy after all this time. People won't like it." Mrs. Welsh's voice held a note of warning.

By "people" she meant the Community, Iris knew. She didn't try to hide her contempt. "'People' won't like seeing an innocent man freed?"

Mrs. Welsh squinted, as if trying to peer through smoke or fog. "People never do, do they? Like having their truths shown up as falsehoods."

The woman's acuity took Iris aback and she stared at her. "I guess not," she said slowly.

"It'll be good if you remember that. My tea's getting cold." Without a word of farewell, she turned and followed the hallway her husband had taken, leaving Iris to show herself out.

After a final glance at Penelope, Iris left the house, taking a deep breath on the front walkway. The cold silk of night wrapped around her. The temperature had dropped a good five degrees in the half hour she'd been inside. Hugging her arms around herself, she took a single step and almost bumped into Quentin Welsh. He was a shadow in the darkness, looming over her.

"Oh!" She couldn't prevent the startled gasp.

"Heater's fixed."

"Great. Well, thanks." She edged around his bulk.

As she did, he caught her upper arm with a hand that circled it easily. She twisted free and stood poised for flight.

"It'd be best if you moved on soon. You're not one of us anymore." Before she could respond, he lumbered away, toolbox clanking, leaving her staring after him with indignation and a touch of uneasiness.

She strode toward her room, stumbling once or twice in the darkness. *Damn right I'm not one of them anymore. They couldn't pay me to be part of the Community again.* But under no circumstances was she leaving until she was good and ready. Pushing open the door of her room, blessedly cooler, she laughed at herself. An hour ago she'd been counting the minutes until she could leave; now, she was determined to stay, just because someone told her to scram. Shaking her head at her own contrariness, she thought back to the brief moments with the turquoise bracelet. She had long ago accepted that she had an unusual connection with stones, that something embedded in them sometimes, but not predictably, spoke to her. She'd never felt anything as strongly as when she'd held Penelope's turquoise, though. She shivered and wondered, as she did less often as the years passed, what Penelope had wanted to tell her that last day. She'd never know and the not knowing bothered her. Deliberately pushing the question away, she reached for her cell phone to call Jane, but then noticed her father's file didn't seem quite as she had left it. A couple pages peeked out and it sat nearer the edge of the desk. She was almost certain.

Looking around, suddenly wary, she crossed the room to peer into the bathroom. Nobody. Telling herself that she was being ridiculous, that Mr. Welsh must have brushed against the file when he came in to fix the heater—*but the desk was nowhere near the radiator*—she looped the chain across the door and drew the drapes. Even if Mr. Welsh had given into curiosity and looked at the file, so what? Most of it was probably a matter of public record. Despite her logic, she felt violated and carefully tucked the errant pages back into the folder. Suddenly unable to face an evening alone in the cramped room, she put the file under her arm, grabbed her purse and phone, and headed for her car. She'd find a cheery place to have dinner and go through the documents, maybe the sports bar down the road, and check out the local action.

# SIXTEEN

### JOLENE

JOLENE GAZED AT HER daughter, lithe and beautiful as she sat at the kitchen table with her feet propped on a chair, knees pushed toward her chest, the scent of the tangerine she was peeling brightening the air. Half-dressed for the college fair at the Colorado College campus, she wore a white blouse over a pair of panties, even though Zach was after her all the time to dress more modestly around the house. Her hair was only a couple of shades darker than the maple tabletop and it shone in the morning sun pouring through the butter-colored sheers veiling the window. The indiscreet sunlight also illuminated the scratches on the laminate countertops, the dings in the refrigerator door, and the cracked floor tile where Zach had dropped her favorite mixing bowl last December. Sliding one bare foot into the sun path on the floor, Jolene expected to feel warmed, but it was too early. Her expression troubled, she opened and shut her mouth twice before saying, "Rachel."

The girl looked up.

Jolene took a deep breath. "The woman who lost her wallet at the co-op came by to pick it up. She said there was fifty-five dollars missing. She was very distressed."

Rachel dug her thumb under the tangerine's skin with a spritz of juice and began to work it around so the peel spiraled over her hand. She bent her head as if engrossed in the task, and Jolene couldn't read her expression. "She's too old to remember how much she had in there, Mom. She probably bought a couple books, or new slippers, and forgot. Want some?" She separated a section from the tangerine and offered it to Jolene.

"Thanks." Jolene popped the fruit into her mouth, grateful for an excuse not to respond right away. The tangerine was unusually tart, but she found it refreshing. "Could be." She forced herself to continue. "But this isn't the first incident. It was just ten days ago that that other woman said her wallet was stolen at our store."

"Puh-leeze, Mom. They'd been to the mall before coming out here. She probably left it at Penney's or in the food court. She's got no way to prove that something happened to it in our store."

The woman, though probably over ninety, had seemed sharp as a tack telling Jolene that she'd bought a bracelet at the mall, and that she distinctly remembered placing the boxed bracelet and the wallet back in her purse before boarding the bus to come to Lone Pine Traditional Crafts. She hadn't seen anything she wanted at the Community's store, but had missed her wallet on the return trip to the nursing home when she dug through her purse for her antihistamines. "The pine pollen always gets me," she'd said.

"Or maybe you think I'm a klepto," Rachel said. Affront widened her eyes.

"I don't think you're a kleptomaniac."

Rachel stood and dumped the tangerine peel into the sink. "Thanks for the ringing vote of confidence. Not a klepto, just a garden variety thief."

"I didn't say that."

"You didn't have to. The fact that we're having this conversation says it all." Rachel faced Jolene, head tilted back so her jaw jutted forward. "If that's what you think, maybe I shouldn't be allowed to work in the store anymore. I'll stay away. When another wallet goes missing, you can apologize." She stomped out of the kitchen in a way intended to advertise how aggrieved she was.

Stuffing the tangerine bits into the grinder, Jolene turned on the water and flipped the switch, letting the harsh gargle of the grinder drown out her thoughts. It was painful and almost impossible to think of Rachel as a thief, but the evidence was mounting. Rachel was the only common denominator. Chloe had been working with her when the first wallet went missing, and Aaron had been with her last night, at least part of the time, but Rachel was the only one who was in the store both times. Was it possible Rachel had stolen the money to get out of working at the store? Would she risk being branded a thief, putting her own and the Community's reputation on the line, to avoid contributing her time and talent to the co-op? Surely she couldn't be so selfish. Anger simmered at the thought.

There had to be another explanation, Jolene told herself. She shut off the grinder, realizing it had been chirring emptily, tangerine peel long washed away, for thirty seconds. Maybe those women really had misplaced their wallets, or miscounted their money. Unlikely. She was going to have to discuss it with Zach.

"Are you going like that?" Rachel had reappeared, purse hanging from one hand, wearing the rest of her school uniform: mid-calf navy skirt and black loafers. She cast a pointed look at Jolene's bare feet. "Aren't you the one who wanted to get to the fair early, so I could talk to the recruiters before it gets too crowded?"

Wanting to slap the self-righteous look off her daughter's face, Jolene fisted her hands, and said a prayer. The thought of Rachel interviewing with college recruiters was stressful enough. It hardly seemed possible her baby would be gone in just over a year. Praying the day would get better, she stepped into a pair of low-heeled pumps, and hurried to the car where Rachel sat with a posture that said she'd been waiting for hours, pointedly staring out the passenger window.

# SEVENTEEN

**IRIS**

IRIS ROLLED OVER IN the motel bed, reluctant to open her eyes and let in the spear of sunlight she could feel probing her eyelids. She checked the clock through one slitted lid. Ten-twelve. She needed to get moving. Her head ached even though she'd limited herself to her usual two beers, and the sheets smelled like sex and a musky cologne. The altitude might have enhanced the alcohol's effect. Thank goodness the kid—Jared? Jermaine?—had had the decency to leave after their second go-round so she didn't have to face evicting him this morning. He'd been cute and brash, allowing her to pick him up easily at the sports bar, Bumpers, just down the road. There'd been two teams worth of softball players in the bar, young twenty-somethings still wearing their uniforms and dirt. It'd given her a brief moment of satisfaction to walk out with him in the teeth of girls his own age, the pretty ones working their white smiles, pert breasts, and glossy hair to get the result she'd gotten with a half-lidded glance and feigned disinterest.

Actually, Iris thought, dragging herself from the bed to the bathroom, her disinterest wasn't so feigned. She peed, and got into the shower, letting the cold water sluice over her. The game had lost its edge. She found it harder to lose herself in the sex, harder to conceal her eagerness for her partner's departure when they were done. The thought of having a conversation over eggs or waffles with Jared-Jermaine or any of his counterparts made her teeth ache. A disturbing question wiggled its way into her brain: if she was getting too old or too weary for the one-night stands, where would she find release when that restless, itchy feeling came over her? Wrapping a towel around herself, she dripped to the dresser to retrieve her jeans and noticed the red light blinking on the bedside phone. *Huh.* She must have missed the message indicator when she came in with Jared— she was almost sure it was Jared.

She hit the button to retrieve the message, expecting to hear one of the Welshes checking to make sure the heater was still functioning correctly. Instead, a tinny, unrecognizable voice startled her. "Go home before you end up like Glynnis."

Glynnis who? Iris's first impulse was to laugh at the teen slasher flick nature of the message, but something about the metallic voice worked its way beneath her skin and made her shiver. Or maybe she was cold because she was naked and wet, she told herself, scrubbing at goose-pimpled skin with the towel as she hustled back to the bathroom. It must be a wrong number. Or stupid teens calling hotels, giggling as they left their oh-so-spooky message. That's all it was.

Before hooking up with Jared, she'd spent an hour reading through her father's thin file. It appeared the police hadn't done much in the way of investigating or interviewing once her father confessed to the crime. Practically every able-bodied inhabitant of Lone Pine was a suspect, as far as Iris was concerned, since the police hadn't checked alibis. Needing a place to start, she'd reluctantly decided on her mother. Marian Asher had initially told the police her husband was home with her all evening, but then changed her story when Neil confessed. Iris wanted to get the truth from her first, before talking to others in the Community. Dressed in jeans—sure to annoy her mother—and with her damp hair twisted into a messy knot, Iris nodded once at her reflection. With a flick of mascara and a slick of lip balm, she exited the room to find Mrs. Welsh standing a few feet away, a pile of clean towels in her arms.

"Good morning," Iris said, sticking the key in the stiff lock, more focused on getting coffee than on exchanging pleasantries.

"You had company last night."

"Excuse me?" Iris lifted her head and stared at the woman, reading condemnation in the way she flared her nostrils in and out.

"We couldn't help but hear the car."

Torn between wanting to say "You're spying on me?" or "What the hell business is it of yours?" Iris bit down hard on her lower lip. She wasn't going to give the woman the satisfaction of reacting to her near-accusation. She bent to wrestle with the key again.

"Don't bother with that," Mrs. Welsh said. "I'm on my way in to clean." She jangled a key at her belt, indicating she'd lock up when she finished.

Iris nodded her thanks. Reversing the car, she watched Mrs. Welsh push her way into the motel room. Suddenly glad she had her father's file locked in the trunk, she punched the gas, wishing she didn't have to see her mother and determined to get the "reunion" over with.

Minutes later, Iris pulled up beside the ancient Volvo parked in front of the church of God's Community of Believers and Disciples, hoping she'd find her mother working there and wouldn't have to look for her at Outback Cottage. She'd called Cade on the way and asked him to meet her there. A little moral support wouldn't hurt, and he'd be able to tell them what they needed to do to get her father a new trial, or a commutation, or whatever. She got out of the rental, leaving the door open. *Like I'm planning a quick getaway*, she thought, making herself slam it closed. She faced the church. She wanted to be able to think that the building was nothing special, a rectangle of wood painted white, one story with a steeple, reminiscent of the churches she'd seen on postcards from New England where Matthew Brozek was raised, but the building had a certain grace she couldn't deny. Aspen and cottonwood trees dappled the roof and sides with leaf shadows, and the hum of bees from the nearby field could have been a hymn drifting from the building's barely open door. Iris found herself relaxing slightly.

Taking a deep breath, she headed into the church.

# EIGHTEEN

**MERCY**

*Twenty-Three Years Ago*

MERCY ASHER SAT WITH her family near the rear of the church, eyes fixed on the wooden beams of the ceiling. A flutter of movement betrayed a sparrow perched on a shallow ledge, breathing hard. Mercy watched it, sorry for its distress. It hopped the length of the ledge fronting one of the narrow rectangular windows inset high above the pews, and then flapped to the next window back, closer to the door. Mercy turned her head to follow the bird's progress, but her mother elbowed her and she faced forward. Her mother preferred to sit in the front pew, but in recent months Mercy had become adept at dawdling as she readied herself for church, changing her dress or rearranging her hair until her family was among the last of the Community to arrive for the Sunday morning worship service. She wanted as much distance between her and Pastor Matt as possible; her stomach hurt at the thought of sitting where his gaze could rest on her as he stood in the pulpit, at having to take his soft, damp hand during the passing of the peace. Even the thought made her swallow hard and look at Noah for distraction.

Her brother, nineteen months older, was drawing Spiderman figures on the small pad he'd smuggled into the service. The stubby pencil slashed across the page, Noah's deft fingers bringing the superhero to life with only a few lines. He was good—better than she was. Her envy of his talent was wrong and she asked forgiveness in a silent prayer, eyes open and glued to the pencil as it defined the muscles in Spiderman's thigh.

Her gaze went from Noah's page to her banners behind the altar. They'd been installed three weeks ago, during the twentieth anniversary celebration, and every time she set eyes on them she felt a confusing mix of pride and shame. Five of the Community's older women and Gabrielle Ulm, a quiet seventh grader who always sat by herself on the school bus, had spent weeks working Mercy's design onto the banners with various fabrics and embroidery. The colors set the small church alight, and the cloth-of-gold they'd used for the wheat in the Ruth and Boaz scene glowed, backlit by the sunlight pouring through the windows set high on the walls behind the altar.

Finally, Pastor Matt wrapped up his sermon and Esther moved forward to sing while the offertory plate was passed around. She had a light, sweet soprano and Mercy caught Noah craning his neck to get a better view of her. Oh, no! Surely he didn't have a crush on Esther? She was pretty—slim and dark-haired, with truly startling blue eyes—but she was so, so … Mercy couldn't come up with a word to describe Pastor Matt's daughter. Holy. No, not holy. Wanting people to think she was holy, which was a whole different thing.

After the service, Mercy burned to escape, to meet Cade who would be parked in his car near the bus stop on the main road, but her father blocked the exit from the pew, exchanging greetings with the couple in front of him. Noah escaped from the pew on the far end, wriggling rudely around Mrs. Lees who was trying to maneuver her walker into the aisle, and wove his way to where Esther stood accepting congratulations on her singing. Mercy caught her mother staring after him, anger and dismay stiffening her face, and figured she must have seen him almost deck Mrs. Lees. Noah was in for it when he got home, if their mother's face was anything to go by.

Joining the trickle of parishioners headed out the back of the church, she glimpsed the sparrow, eying the open doors as if waiting his turn to exit. "I know the feeling," she whispered. As she watched, he swooped toward the door, but veered away at the last minute, frightened by a tall man who turned abruptly, and flew away from the crowd toward the altar.

Circling the worship space twice, the bird then flew toward the brightness of the floor to ceiling picture window beside the pulpit. He gathered speed, and Mercy knew he thought he was headed for freedom, the sky, and the pine trees framed by the window. She could do nothing but watch as he sped toward the pane, lovingly polished with ammonia and newspaper by her mother and a handful of other women who kept the church spotless, so not a streak or smudge marred its clear surface. Mercy thought she heard a small thud as the sparrow hit the window, although, surely, his lightweight, feathery body hadn't made much sound. She winced. He fell straight down, leaving a bird-shaped blur on the glass, wings upraised and fanned out, like illustrations of the Holy Spirit descending as a dove.

Mercy walked up the center aisle, hoping to find the bird merely stunned. Before she was halfway to the window, her mother swept in from the left, bent, and picked up the bird by one wing, holding it between a thumb and forefinger. He dangled from her hand, clearly dead.

"Mercy, find a plastic bag, a trash bag," she said unemotionally. "There's a stash of old grocery bags in the kitchen, under the sink." Studying the window, she shook her head. "It'll take some elbow grease to get this mark off the window."

Near tears and not sure why—it was only a sparrow—Mercy did as directed, descending to the church basement which held the Sunday school rooms, the kitchen, and a large gathering area. She came off the last stair and turned the corner. A flutter of blue skirt and flip of dark hair disappeared into the first-grade Sunday school room with its Noah's ark poster on the door. More sad about the bird than curious about why someone was in the deserted classroom area, Mercy made her way to the kitchen, not bothering to turn on the lights. Finding a flimsy grocery bag, she stuffed it with a handful of paper towels to make a nest, and returned to the hall.

A heavy tread on the stairs warned of someone's approach, but she still gasped when Pastor Matt stepped into the dimly lit hallway. Her heart beat like the panicked bird's and she backed up a step. She hadn't been alone with him for months, not since she told him she wouldn't anymore, that she'd tell if he tried to touch her. Now, his scent, a mix of deodorant and warm wool, activated by the heat he generated preaching, wafted over her. Swallowing back a mouthful of bile, she froze, hoping he wouldn't notice her.

She must have made some sound, though, crinkled the grocery bag, because Pastor Matt turned toward her, surprise and a hint of consternation on his broad face. "Mercy! What are you doing down here?"

She stuttered something about the dead bird and held up the plastic bag. "My mom sent me for this. I'm just taking it to her. She's waiting for me." *She'll miss me. She'll come looking for me.*

"Then you should go," he said calmly, stepping away from the stairs. Grateful that she didn't have to brush past him, touch him, she crumpled the bag in her fist and fled up the stairs.

# NINETEEN

## IRIS

Determined not to let memories from the past derail her, Iris shoved the door wide and stepped into the church. She meant to walk straight on through the worship area and find her mother, but she paused. The sanctuary looked the same, exactly the same. Same airy, sunlit space with high windows. Same wooden pews. Probably not the same deep blue runner on the aisles, but identical to the old carpet. Same—her banners were gone. Iris had barely noted their absence, when a movement made her slew to the right. Her mother, just as slim and upright, hair gone gray, stood at the window by the pulpit, running a squeegee down its length as if still trying to remove all traces of the dead sparrow from years ago.

Iris watched for a moment in silence, admiring her economical movements, her focus on the task. Her concentration reminded Iris a little bit of the way she got when she was working on a jewelry project. Wearing an apron over a shirtwaist dress that could well have been in her closet when Iris lived at home, she had cut her hair.

Gray and silver strands framed her face in a sort of pixie. Maybe some things *had* changed.

Taking a deep breath, Iris started up the side aisle.

Her mother turned her head and stilled when she saw Iris. Then, the squeegee dropped into the bucket, the only sign of her surprise.

"Mercy. No, I understand it's Iris, now. Iris Dashwood. Mercy wasn't good enough for you." Marian's voice was measured, almost toneless, betraying no surprise, no anger, no joy or even mild pleasure at seeing her daughter after twenty-three years.

*So that's how it's going to be.* Iris was surprised by the wave of desolation that rushed over her. Swallowing hard, she came within hugging distance, or hand-shaking distance, of her mother and stood awkwardly. Neither moved.

"I like your haircut." *Stupid. As if she cares what I think of her hair.* Iris fumbled for something more meaningful to say, but there weren't words to bridge a twenty-three-year gap. "I guess you heard I was in the area."

"Your father mentioned it, and Esther. The whole town knows you're back, although some of them moved in after your time, so it doesn't mean much to them."

*Does it mean anything to you?* Iris wished she had the nerve to ask the question. "No, it wouldn't." She cast around for a safe topic. "The Community's grown. I like the new store, the co-op. Whose idea was it?"

Marian retrieved the squeegee and drew it down the window. She gestured to the stack of newspapers at her feet and Iris obediently picked one up, formed it into a pad, and began to polish away the thin streaks. "Esther Brozek's. When the Community selected Zachary as the new pastor, they made her the senior elder." She looked thoughtful. "She'd been working with the alpacas for some years by then, on top of caring for Pastor Matt, and she came up with the idea of doing more than just selling their wool. She persuaded some of the women to learn to spin the wool into yarn and convinced others to knit it into sweaters, gloves—well, you saw the place. When Howard Hecht suggested we get some beehives, she researched it and hives popped up in the Community's fields faster than anthills after a rain. It's been good and bad for the Community."

"How so?" Iris was content to let the conversation drift along on this non-confrontational current.

Marian shrugged a bony shoulder. "We're not as tight knit anymore. Too many tourists traipsing through Lone Pine, calling our religion a cult, talking about us like we can't hear them. Why, a couple of them even tried to take photos in the worship service until Pastor Zachary stopped them. You'd think we were one of those churches juggling rattlesnakes or something." She sniffed.

*Or something.*

"Too much of a focus on materialism," Marian continued, "even though the co-op's profits go to our outreach programs for the poor." She picked up the bucket and gestured for Iris to collect the crumpled newspaper from the floor. "I remember when the Community was about serving God and your fellow man, living simply and obediently."

Iris followed her mother down the stairs to the kitchen, reflecting that she never would have guessed their reunion would involve window washing. Scrubbing the newsprint off her hands at the sink, she turned off the tap and glanced around at the sparkling counters and stove so clean it looked unused. "So, I guess you're the caretaker, now?"

Marian nodded, a small smile stretching her lips. "For almost twenty years. I clean, mow, do small repairs. I'm surprisingly handy."

Iris could believe it. "It's never looked better."

Marian accepted the compliment as her due.

"So ... Dad."

Marian stiffened, but raised her brows for Iris to continue.

"I saw him yesterday, in the prison."

"You could hardly see him anywhere else."

"He … it turns out he was under a misapprehension, that he confessed because …" Iris didn't know why she was finding it so difficult to spit out. "He didn't attack Pastor Matt or cause Mrs. Brozek's death."

"Of course not." Marian emptied the bucket of sudsy water into the sink and rinsed it out. "He thought you did."

Iris gaped at her mother's back. The silence lengthened and her mother turned around with raised brows. "Surely you didn't think I didn't know? Neil was my husband; he wasn't capable of such an act."

"Then, why—"

"I couldn't talk him out of it. I begged him not to do it, but he felt he had to. For you. He was—is—my husband. I gave in to his wishes. Ephesians tells us that wives must submit themselves unto their own husbands, as unto the Lord."

For the first time, Iris sensed resentment. Drawing herself up, she said, "It wasn't my fault."

Marian flicked her a scathing glance and then attacked the stainless steel sink with cleaning powder and a sponge. "If you hadn't run off, your father would not be in jail right now."

"If you hadn't called me a liar, I wouldn't have left. The least you can do is look me in the eye." When her mother didn't budge, Iris started to grab her shoulder, but stopped herself mid-reach. She backed away two steps, coming up against a pantry door whose pull dug into her spine. Her whole body shook and she stilled her hands by shoving them into her jeans pockets. "I'm going to get Dad out of prison. If it takes me six months"—*God forbid I have to spend half a year here*—"I will find the truth and get him out."

"He confessed, Iris."

Her mother's ease with her new name was almost unsettling when everyone else she'd talked to had slipped up and called her Mercy at least once. It was like Mercy had died. No, had never existed. As if Marian had been introduced to a new person, Iris, and accepted her at face value. Like she didn't even find Iris particularly interesting, not someone to get to know better over coffee or lunch.

"Don't you want him back?"

Her mother's silence filled the kitchen. It infiltrated every crevice—the sliver of space between the refrigerator and the wall, the wells beneath the coils on the range, the toaster slots. It was like a heavy gas, weighting the oxygen to the ground so Iris found it hard to breathe in. "You don't. You don't want him freed."

Marian whipped around, water arcing from the sponge she held and splotching Iris's shirt. Her voice, though not loud, thrummed with anger. "You don't get to come back here after a quarter century of running away and pass judgment on me. *I* saw my husband through the trial—a trial he underwent because of you—and I have visited him faithfully twice a month since he was wrongfully imprisoned. *I* spent what little money we had on lawyers, trying to get him out and failing because he wouldn't tell the truth. *I* bore the burden of this town's hatred because of what you and Neil did, but I couldn't up and leave like you two—"

"Dad didn't—"

"—just walk away from my responsibilities as if they didn't matter. I couldn't be so damned selfish."

"Stop! I wasn't even sixteen. Pastor Matt—"

"*I* undertook to care for this church when no one else would, bec—"

A clunk interrupted Marian's tirade and Iris turned to see a girl of five or six, glossy dark hair slicked back with a red headband, standing wide-eyed in the doorway. "Nana, why are you mad at this lady?" she asked. Her wide-eyed gaze traveled slowly from Iris to Marian and back again.

Marian stopped mid-word and placed the sponge in the sink. When she turned back, her face and voice were smoothed of emotion. "Angel, this is your Aunt Iris."

The words jolted Iris, although she didn't know why she was so surprised; she'd speculated about Noah having children.

"I don't have any aunts," the girl announced. "Mommy doesn't have any sisters and Daddy's sister is dead."

*Ouch.* Iris shot her mother a look and got a slightly malicious smile in return.

"I'm not dead," Iris said, sinking so she was eye-to-eye with the child. Brown eyes with ridiculously long lashes stared into hers. "I just live a long way away. In Oregon. Do you know where that is?"

Angel looked doubtful, but then said, "The capital of Oregon is Salem, and the capital of Colorado is Denver, and the capital of Idaho—"

"Wow. You know your capitals already. How old are you?"

"Five and a half. I'm the smartest one in my class."

Iris had no trouble believing that, but Marian said, "We've talked about boasting before, Angel, and how it does not become us. All our talents and skills come from the Lord and we use them to reflect glory back on him."

"Yes, Nana," Angel said, bobbing her head, "but I wasn't boasting. I was just *saying.*"

Iris stifled a chuckle and Angel beamed at her.

"What are you doing here, anyway, young lady? Did you quarrel with Ruthie?"

"She has to go to her soccer game, so I came home. Can we Skype with Daddy?"

"Later."

"Where is Noah?" Iris asked.

"Afghanistan," Marian and Angel chorused.

"You're kidding!" The words leaped out before she could stop them, but Iris had trouble seeing her obnoxious, slightly rebellious brother as a soldier. He must have changed a lot. Well, why not? She certainly had. "How long—"

Marian's frown stopped her; obviously, she didn't want to discuss the war in front of Angel. Iris nodded her understanding and vowed to find out more later. Had Noah joined the military out of a desire to serve his country, or to escape from the Community? She didn't know him as an adult; she couldn't begin to guess.

"I'm hungry," Angel announced, standing on tiptoe to pull a jar of peanut butter from a cupboard.

"Hands," Marian said, letting a breath of refrigerated air into the room as she handed Angel some grape jelly. The little girl obediently washed her hands before returning to her sandwich-making, the tip of her tongue poking from the corner of her mouth as she spread the peanut butter evenly onto some bread.

"Sorry I'm so late." Cade's voice came from the doorway and Iris turned toward him with relief. He represented stability in this world gone topsy-turvy. He smiled and held up two coffees, handing her one. "Good morning, Mrs. Asher."

Marian's gaze slid from Cade to Iris and back again. "I suppose I shouldn't be surprised to see you now that Mercy's back. How long have you been married now? Must be going on for sixteen years." She stared at Cade's ringless left hand wrapped around the cup as she accepted the coffee.

"Fifteen in August," Cade said levelly.

"Do you know Angel?" Iris asked hurriedly.

"I don't believe I've had the pleasure." Cade shook hands with the little girl, who giggled again, and engaged her in a conversation about Polly Pockets and *Jake and the Neverland Pirates*. Iris looked on semi-wistfully, wondering how she'd gotten so out of touch with that segment of the population under the age of legal consent and their favorite activities, music, and TV shows. The glimpse of Cade's family life also left her feeling ... untethered. She couldn't think why that word came to mind, but it would do. She was untethered by family or even a job since she could take hers with her anywhere. She'd always appreciated what she thought of as her flexibility, her ability to pick up and go on the spur of the moment, but right now it felt more like homelessness.

Iris squashed the thought. She was living the dream, a free, untrammeled life full of adventure, creativity, and casual sex with hot men. Cade was trapped by a mortgage, the need to fund his kids' college educations, and his wife's expectations. He probably had to spend every Christmas with his in-laws—whoever they were—listening politely as his father-in-law droned on about the Avalanche, and every vacation at a kid-friendly Howard Johnson's Hotel with a waterpark. As for her mother ... Marian was so much a prisoner of the Community, of the church building itself, that she might as well be locked in. Poor Marian. Poor Cade. Iris's gaze lingered on him as she sipped her coffee, and when he looked up and smiled at her, she scalded her mouth with a too-big gulp.

Finishing her sandwich, Angel said a sunny goodbye to everyone, gave Marian a hug, and said she was going to see if Janelle could play. The adults looked at each other as Angel's footsteps faded. Without a word, Marian retrieved the sponge from the sink and began to wipe the table, gray head bent over the task. Iris continued to lean against the pantry, and Cade, subtly elbowed aside by Marian, backed up against the windowsill so they made an awkward, lop-sided triangle.

"We need to get Dad out of prison so he can spend time with Angel," Iris said. She didn't know where the words had come from, but she felt the truth of them in her bones. "She deserves to know him. He deserves to know her. 'Children's children are a crown to the aged,' it says in Proverbs." Iris was surprised that she could still dredge up the Bible verses she'd been forced to memorize in Sunday school.

Marian stilled, and then straightened, table half-wiped. Her gray eyes dwelled on Iris's face for a moment before she said, "Don't quote the Bible at me like it's a weapon. It's God's sacred word."

Although the words seemed combative, Marian spoke quietly, without hostility, and Iris heard acceptance in her voice. She expelled a breath she didn't realize she'd been holding. "Okay, then. He's innocent. We need to prove that. Every day he spends in prison is—" *Is flaying me with a whip.* She couldn't say that—Marian and Cade wouldn't understand the guilt she felt, the responsibility she had to free her father. "Where do we start? I'm going to investigate, ask some questions," Iris said defiantly when her mother remained silent. "There's a limited suspect pool. We know I didn't do it and Dad didn't do it … it shouldn't be that hard to figure out who did."

"Do what you want," Marian said, pushing back from the table with a scraping sound. "You always did."

"Oh, for God's sake!" Iris stood so rapidly her chair would have toppled over if Cade hadn't caught it. "You—"

"Don't take the Lord's name in vain."

Iris saw her mother through a veil of anger, like the multi-hued light dots that popped behind her eyes if she knuckled them hard. "Is that all you can do? Spout the Ten Commandments? Maybe if you'd ever actually *listened* to me, had a conversation, instead of falling back on Scripture every time I tried to talk to you, tried to tell you——. Maybe everything would have turned out differently. Ever think of that?"

Marian drew her mouth into a tiny knot, sucking in air with a thin hiss.

Cade put a hand on Iris's arm. "Walk me out, Iris. Mrs. Asher, I'll be in touch soon."

Iris turned and banged through the nearest door, instinctively taking the half-flight of stairs that led to the churchyard, rather than the ones that opened near the worship area. Cade caught up with her as she marched down the path leading to the columbarium where engraved stones memorialized the people whose ashes were interred below them. Yellow forsythia frothed over a stone wall and a robin tugged at a worm in a manicured patch of lawn that, Iris imagined resentfully, her mother trimmed by hand, probably blade-by-blade with a pair of nail scissors.

"Iris, wait."

Iris halted but didn't turn, realizing with fury and chagrin that she was close to crying. She never cried. She pressed the heels of her palms to her eyes, and then wiped her sleeved forearm under her nose before turning. "Well, on a scale of one to ten, I'd rate that reunion as a minus two," she said, with an attempt at lightness. Her muscles wouldn't respond when she tried to force a smile.

"Iris." Cade pulled her into his arms and hugged her tightly.

"She doesn't care. She's sorry I came back."

Cade made soothing noises and rubbed her back. It was several minutes before she relaxed under the spell of his hand stroking her spine. Her face rested on his shoulder. If she angled her head just a bit, her lips would press against his neck … She pulled away, wiping moisture—not tears—from her eyes with the hem of her shirt. Cade's gaze rested on the expanse of tight abdomen she exposed.

"Sorry for falling apart on you," Iris said, working hard to make her voice sound normal. She met his gaze and smiled faintly. "I usually cope a little better."

"It's an emotional time."

Iris smiled wider at the understatement, and brushed away a wisp of hair caught at the corner of her mouth.

Cade said, "Look, I've got an appointment I can't blow off. Meet me later? Drinks at Nosh? It's on Tejon."

"Remember when you introduced me to beer? I'd never had alcohol before."

"You didn't like it."

From the look in his eyes, Iris knew he was remembering what came after her first half-bottle of Coors. "I like it better, now."

"Six thirty?"

"Won't that make you late for dinner?"

"Lila and I are separated."

"But still married."

Cade nodded, his gaze skimming the sharp line of her cheekbones, the way her dark hair sprang back from her temples, the indention above her upper lip. "Maybe not for long. She cheated on me. With an intern at the firm."

Although he tried to hide his pain by delivering the words dispassionately, Iris could almost feel the hurt and anger and betrayal seething inside him. "That sucks."

He barked an unamused laugh. "Understatement."

"Do you still love her?"

Running a hand down his face, Cade said, "I love my family." He forced a smile. "But that's neither here nor there. What about that drink? I promise not to bore you with the sordid details of my marital troubles. I want to hear about you."

Iris forced herself to shake her head, feeling an almost tangible pain, like yanking a chunk of hair from her scalp. She knew what would happen if they met for drinks. Alcohol plus her emotionally charged state plus the lingering desire rippling between them would add up to bad decision-making. She didn't sleep with married men. It was a line she didn't cross. "Drinks are a bad idea," she said baldly, "and I don't want to be revenge sex."

Cade put out a hand and cupped her chin, his thumb moving lightly along her jaw and then across her mouth. "It wouldn't be like that. I don't think I ever stopped loving you."

She turned her face away from his hand with a pinch of anger. "Stop it, Cade. We're not teenagers anymore."

His hand dropped. "No." He sounded so sad, Iris wondered what the last twenty-three years had brought him besides a cheating wife, two kids, and a legal career. For the first time, she noticed the hint of pouches beneath his eyes that seemed to drag them down at the corners.

It would be so much easier if they were still teenagers, Iris thought as he turned and walked away, instead of adults with a minefield of experiences and mistakes, memories and false expectations, booby trapping the space between them. She opened her mouth to call him back, but shut it and let him go.

# TWENTY

### IRIS

Iris watched until Cade disappeared around the corner of the church, his pace increasing the farther he got from her. Almost like he was running away. She could have met him at Nosh, had a beer, and let him pour out the story of his failed marriage. That, in her experience, was the only thing newly divorced men wanted to talk about once they downed a martini or three. If she and Cade ended up in the sack, his not-quite-ex-wife would be right there with them. No wonder she stuck with younger men, Iris told herself, kicking at an acorn on the path. The bed was a lot less crowded.

With annoyance, she realized she hadn't even asked her mother the questions she'd come to ask: Where were she and Neil that night and what had they been doing? What time had her father left the house? The acorn dribbled to a stop on one of the granite blocks marking the site of a buried urn. The date of death made her curious: the day she ran away. Using the toe of her shoe, Iris lifted the rambunctious crocus that arched over the name. She had to cock her head and bend forward to read through the shadow that made the letters hard to make out. G, L ... Glynnis Brozek.

"Oh, my God." Iris spoke the words under her breath. How had she forgotten that Mrs. Brozek's first name was Glynnis? Probably because children in the Community back then called adults Mr. or Mrs. Whoever, not "Miss Heather" or "Mr. Jim" like kids did today. Her phone message from the morning no longer felt like a wrong number. Someone was warning her that she might end up like Glynnis Brozek: dead.

Suddenly feeling creeped out despite the sunshine and a swallowtail butterfly gliding toward a daffodil, Iris hurried toward her car. Her boots scuffed dully against the paving stones and the sound of a door closing carried. Iris looked up to see a man locking the church office. He straightened. On the short side, he carried himself tall with shoulders squared. Even at a distance, Iris could feel a sense of purpose about him. As she drew closer, she recognized him. His light hair had darkened to an indeterminate brown and receded, but the long nose was the same, as was the smile. Glasses gave him a professorial air.

"Zach." She held out her hand. She'd always liked Zach Brozek better than his sister, Esther. She smiled, surprised by how nice it was to see him. He had matured into what had always been a precocious seriousness, a level-headed way of viewing his peers and his circumstances.

"Mercy." He unexpectedly swept her into a bear hug, squeezing her against the doughiness of a slight paunch. He smelled like deodorant soap and coffee. Releasing her, he smiled and said, "No, it's something else now. Starts with an I. Irene?"

"Iris."

"That's right. Esther told me. It suits you."

"Thanks."

He slid keys into his pockets and said, "Walk with me. I'm off to visit old Mrs. Dorfmann. Remember her? She's blind now and I read to her a couple of times a week."

Falling into step beside him, Iris said, "Wow. I thought she was ancient when we were kids. She must be what—a hundred and twelve?"

Zach laughed. "Ninety-seven last month. She hardly leaves the house now, but people are kind. Her son Steve and his wife have tried to talk her into moving in with them, but she wants to stay at home."

Iris had no reply to that and a silence fell. A barbed-wire fence, new since Iris's time, bounded a field two feet from the dirt path. Tufts of brown and tan hair clung to some of the barbs and Iris puzzled over them before the sight of an alpaca in the field clued her in. It gazed at them, blinked once, then trotted toward its brethren drinking from the wind-riffled surface of the pond. Bees burrowed into the clover dotting the verge and buzzed, pollen-laden, to the hives hunched in the middle of the field. Their hum reverberated inside Iris, helping her relax.

Zach paused and turned, studying her face. "Why did you come back, Iris?"

She got a sense that he didn't approve of her return or, at least, that he had reservations about her presence. "I wanted to see your father, now that he's awake," she said baldly. "And mine."

"Esther said she found you in his room."

Iris nodded. "You don't seem quite as opposed to my presence"— *as out of your gourd hostile*—"as your sister."

"This was your home. It could be again." When she made a slight gesture of denial, he continued, "I've always been sorry that you were driven away from it, that you left without the ritual of reconciliation. It's not too late."

"Oh, yes it is." Iris had no intention of reconciling with the Community in the service that welcomed back sinners after they'd been punished with the reckoning stones. It was supposed to occur one month after the stones, to give the sinner time to truly repent in the face of being banned from the church, shunned by friends and neighbors, cast into social purgatory. Mr. Carpenter had eagerly embraced reconciliation, eyes streaming with tears of joy, at the ceremony a month after young Mercy watched him disappear into the woods. Even at fifteen, Iris would rather have eaten glass than accept reconciliation, let the Community pretend they were good and generous to welcome her back to the fold. The idea was equally repulsive now.

Zach resumed walking. "It's a miracle that my father woke up," he said, not ducking the topic as Iris had thought he might. "God must have a purpose. I don't presume to know what it is, but perhaps it's the opportunity for healing and forgiveness."

"I didn't come to forgive him," she said.

Zach stiffened. "I meant that *you* could receive *his* forgiveness for what you said about him. Accepting forgiveness can lead to healing and spiritual growth." He paused. "You might be able to offer forgiveness as well. Although my father was a righteous man, he could be ... harsh on occasion when meting out punishment. Since the Community made me pastor, we haven't used the reckoning stones."

His last words were clearly an afterthought, meant to appease her. She strode several steps ahead, stopping shy of Mrs. Dorfmann's house, and then turned, arms crossed over her chest. There was no point in reiterating her innocence and Pastor Matt's guilt. "I don't believe in that—in God, in prayer—anymore." She wasn't sure she ever had. Her childhood prayers and church attendance had been no more than obedience to her parents and the Community, a reflex. Answered prayers were coincidence; unanswered ones were not

God saying "No," as her mother would have it, but simply the universe going about its business unheeding of individual pleas, hopes, and desires. To stop him from arguing the efficacy of prayer, she added, "My father didn't do it."

Zach looked grave. "He confessed, Mercy."

She let the name slip go. "He lied to protect me, but I didn't even see your father"—so much easier to think of him that way, as having no link, not even that of "pastor," to herself—"that night."

"Mercy—" He put a hand on her shoulder, his face a mask of understanding and pity.

*That's how he'd look at someone who told him she'd been abducted by aliens*, Iris thought. "Iris."

"Right. Sorry." He squeezed her shoulder and reminded her so much of Pastor Matt in that moment that her stomach lurched.

She stepped back, and his arm fell. "Where were you that night?" she asked, to cover her distress. "Did you see anyone at your house?"

Turning away from her, he mounted the single step to Mrs. Dorfmann's porch and rapped on the door. He glanced at her over his shoulder. "We all doubt, Iris. Now and then. Sometimes for long, dark periods. But God, in his mercy, shines bright enough to dissolve the doubts, or, at least, to thin them so we can see him through them."

What the hell did that have to do with her question? Her brows twitched together. Was he deliberately refusing to tell her where he'd been that night, or was he so accustomed to using pastor-speak, that he couldn't respond straight-up? Another thought occurred to her. "Are you saying you have doubts about what happened to your father?"

Zach sighed and knocked louder, not looking at her. "Don't go digging up the past. We've all come to peace with what happened. There's no point to—"

A thin voice called "Who is it?" and Zach broke off to answer. "It's Pastor Zach." Looking down at Iris, he said, "You haven't been reconciled."

It took her a long moment to realize he was saying she couldn't enter Mrs. Dorfmann's house, that she was no more welcome in the Community than sewage in a pristine river. The exclusion stung more than she'd expected.

"Damn, Zach. Rigid much?" She considered forcing the issue, pretty sure Mrs. Dorfmann would be delighted to see her, but then decided it would be unfair to put her on the spot. She started to leave, but turned back to say, "I'm surprised you spoke to me. Weren't you afraid of being contaminated?"

A slight flush colored the tops of his ears, but he said levelly, "Jesus went among tax collectors and prostitutes in order to save them."

"Well, I've never been a tax collector, at least." Not waiting to see how he took that, she walked away as the door squeaked open behind her.

"Who was that, Pastor Zach?" Mrs. Dorfmann's quavery voice asked.

"A stranger," he said. "Lost. So, are we going to read another chapter of *The Secret Life of Bees* today?" The screen door banged shut.

# TWENTY-ONE

### JOLENE

TRUNDLING A SHOPPING CART around the King Sooper's after the college fair, Jolene scanned her list, moving away from the chill of the frozen foods aisle. She enjoyed grocery shopping, taking pleasure in the orderly rows of stacked cans and boxes, the sense of plenty in the meat section, the international foods aisle with the products she kept meaning to try, but never did. What did one do with garam masala or fish sauce? The store smelled of baked goods and flowers from the florist department and, on impulse, she stuck a bunch of sunflowers atop the groceries in her cart. Their zingy yellow made her happy. *Produce section, and then check-out.*

She was gently palpating avocadoes when a woman's voice said, "Hello, Jolene."

Marian Asher stood there, shopping basket filled with leafy greens and a baguette. Her short hair and shirtwaist dress were crisp and Jolene felt limp by contrast, like the romaine leaves a store employee was ripping off and tossing in a cardboard box. She forced a smile. "Marian. How are you? Where's Angel?"

The older woman's face tightened. "At ballet. Nothing I could say convinced Noah that dance classes are a waste of time and money. He's gotten spiritually lax since he joined the Army and married that Methodist. If it were up to me … However, when he deployed, I promised I'd try to stick to her routine as much as possible, so I haul her over there twice a week." Her tone suggested she was leaving her granddaughter in an opium den.

"It's hard on you, having a five-year-old around. You're not used to it. Rachel would be happy to babysit, you know, take Angel off your hands any time you need a break." Rachel would be resentful, not happy, but serving others would be good for her.

"I'm perfectly capable of caring for my granddaughter." Before Jolene could respond, Marian added, "I suppose you've heard Mercy is back. I saw her today. Calls herself 'Iris' now." Marian sniffed her disapproval.

"She's a jewelry designer."

"Is she?" Marian looked uninterested.

Jolene eyed her, wondering if the disinterest was a pose. "Yes. She's won lots of awards."

The website had captivated Jolene, drawing her into a world of sparkle and glamour that was totally foreign. She'd pored over the sparse biography, the single headshot of Iris Dashwood looking beautiful and intense, the photos of her jewelry. Iris led a creative life, free to join some handsome man for a weekend in Fiji or work with her gems and gold into the wee hours. Jolene led a mother's life, a wife's life, constrained by faculty meetings, Community events, her children's needs, her husband's expectations. She gripped and released the cart's handle. "Did you get her phone number?" Jolene said, surprised to realize just how intensely she longed to see Mercy again.

"No. She'll be around the Community, though. She's set on proving Neil innocent and getting him released from prison."

"Really? She thinks he didn't do it?"

"Of course he didn't do it."

"He confessed."

"Be that as it may, Iris intends to free him."

Jolene's hand clenched and her fingers dented the avocado. "Who does she think did it?"

"I don't know, but I wouldn't bet against her finding out. She always was determined, that girl. It led her to set up her will against mine and her father's sometimes, which I tried to discipline out of her. Overall, I thought it was a good thing, her working so hard when she wanted something, that the Lord could use her to accomplish a lot. But she turned her back on him, on us, and ran away and hid like Adam and Eve after they ate of the forbidden fruit and lied to the Lord about it."

Anger bubbled in Jolene. "*Iris*"—she deliberately used the new name—"was never a liar. Maybe if we, the Community, hadn't been so quick to assume she was .... Who knows how things might have turned out?" *If I had spoken up, would Mrs. Brozek still be alive? Would Iris still be Mercy, still be part of the Community?* The questions had haunted her for twenty-three years. She turned away to hide the tears that sprang to her eyes and put the damaged avocado into a plastic bag.

"When I see her again, I'll tell her you'd like to see her," Marian said, shifting the basket to her other arm. "I've got to run or I'll be late picking up Angel. The way that child babbles on about toe shoes and sequins and wanting to be a princess—*tch*. Noah and Keely actually allow her to watch TV and it's clearly had a negative effect. Did you know there's apparently a show about girls her age being in beauty pageants? Wicked."

Jolene nodded noncommittally and let out a relieved breath when Marian headed toward the cash registers. She appreciated Marian and all she did for the Community, but couldn't like her. She knew it wasn't fair, but she found the woman cold. Even when she was expressing outrage, like against the television show, she spoke in a colorless tone, never getting loud or excited. *It's unnatural*, Jolene thought, bending to lift groceries onto the moving belt. A memory stirred, of her and Mercy as teenagers discussing Marian's lack of passion, with Mercy saying she and Noah had probably been conceived by artificial insemination.

"I mean, can you see my mom *doing it*?" she'd asked. They were sitting cross-legged on the floor of Jolene's bedroom, ostensibly finishing their World Lit homework.

Jolene wrinkled her face. "Gross."

"'Neil,'" Mercy said, putting on her mother's clipped voice, "'I've scheduled precisely ten minutes this evening for marital relations. Please ensure you've showered beforehand and be prompt. I've got good deeds and housecleaning to accomplish when we've finished.'"

Jolene put a horrified hand to her mouth but couldn't stop the giggles from erupting. "Mercy! You shouldn't talk about your parents that way."

She was smiling faintly at the memory of their uncontrollable laughter when the cashier asked, "Paper or plastic, ma'am?"

# TWENTY-TWO

**IRIS**

Unaccountably hurt by Zach calling her a stranger, Iris walked to Debby's Café; it was more or less on her way back to the church where her car was parked, anyway. Half of her wanted to beat feet out of Lone Pine, but the other half argued she should take the opportunity to check some people's memories of the night Pastor Matt was beaten and Glynnis Brozek died. If they were going to get her dad out of prison, she'd have to prove someone else committed the crimes. The only way to do that after all this time, she figured, was to talk to people, to sift what they said, compare it to what others said, and find discrepancies. She wasn't going to find a smoking gun or bloody tire iron after twenty-three years.

A bell over the café door announced her entry. Half-expecting to see one of the Ulms, who owned the café, Iris was greeted by a young woman she didn't know and followed her to a window table. She ordered a glass of iced tea and a tuna salad sandwich, liking the way a fern half-blocked the light coming in the window, and the soothing neutrality of the taupe and cream décor. No more red-checked gingham curtains. The pies displayed under glass domes on the counter looked the same as when she lived here, and Iris ordered a slice of apple pie when she finished her sandwich.

"Apple's the best," the waitress said, sliding a plate in front of Iris.

"Looks like it," Iris said. Thank goodness she'd caught herself before she'd said, "I know" and invited all sorts of questions. Taking the first bite of the tart apples in cinnamony goo and flaky pastry, Iris pulled out the small sketchbook she always carried. Flipping past several pages with half-finished drawings of bracelets and necklaces, she found a clean page and began to list the people who might know what really happened the night she left Lone Pine. The list wasn't too long... Matthew and Glynnis Brozek, Esther and Zachary Brozek, Jolene Farraday, her parents, Noah.

She couldn't talk to Matthew or Glynnis Brozek, for obvious reasons, and Iris drew a line threw their names. After a second, she erased the line through Pastor Matt's name and traced over the letters. Was it possible Esther had lied about how uncommunicative he was? Or that he might respond in a new way if confronted with something unexpected, like her? Circling his name, she studied the rest of the list. No way was she tackling Marian again today, and Neil was unreachable without another trip to the prison, so that left the Brozek siblings and Jolene, since she had no idea how to get hold of Noah in Afghanistan.

She should have asked Marian how much longer he was going to be overseas. She should also, she realized belatedly, have asked about his wife, Angel's mother. Who had Noah married? Flipping through a mental Rolodex of the girls she'd gone to school with, she came up with no one who felt like a good fit for Noah. Last she knew, he'd been crushing on Esther Brozek, but he clearly hadn't ended up with her. Thank God. Iris found herself thinking that when the situation with her dad was resolved, when he was freed, hopefully, she'd ask

Marian if she could sit in on a Skype session with Noah. She was curious about the man he had become, and found herself wanting to reconnect with him, even though they hadn't been particularly close growing up. But that had to wait. She had more on her plate emotionally than she could handle at the moment without adding another estranged (and possibly angry or resentful) family member to the mix.

Becoming conscious of someone at her elbow, Iris looked up, expecting to see the waitress. Debby Ulm stood there, looking not much older than when Iris had last seen her, even though Iris figured she must be sixty or sixty-two, at least. Her hair was still a glossy brown with only a few silver strands, and her eyebrows, curiously straight, dominated a face that belonged on a cameo. The apron she wore with "Debby's Café" embroidered across the bib showed off her slim waist and hid most of her simple blouse and denim skirt. Her eyes were fixed on Iris's notes, and Iris instinctively covered them with her hand. Her expression clearly said she'd recognized Iris.

"Mrs. Ulm! Is Gabby here?" She'd thought of Gabrielle Ulm off and on over the years, wondering how the girl had turned out.

"Gabby lives in Denver," Mrs. Ulm said, not returning Iris's smile. Her voice was pitched low for someone so petite and she bit the words off in a way that let Iris know Gabby's departure from Lone Pine had hurt or angered her. "Has done for almost twenty years now."

Iris lifted her brows. Gabby must have ditched Lone Pine two seconds after she graduated from high school. Before she could comment, Mrs. Ulm continued, "We heard you were back. You're not welcome here, Mercy Asher. The Community passed judgment on you for your lies and you chose to run off rather than repent and be reconciled." Her hand snaked out to snatch up Iris's half-eaten pie and held the plate close to her chest. Ropy veins mapped the back of her hand and twined across her thin wrist, almost the only sign of aging Iris could see. Mrs. Ulm took a step back, clearly commanding Iris to exit the booth.

Iris shouldn't have been so surprised, not after her conversation with Zach, but she was. Astonished, angry, and a little embarrassed, she glanced around the café to see if anyone was witnessing her eviction. A pair of women two booths away stared openly and then leaned toward each other to whisper when Iris looked at them. The waitress hovered near the espresso machine, apparently entranced by its hissing and gurgling. She didn't look up. Mr. Ulm, instantly recognizable, emerged from the kitchen and started toward them. No taller than Debby, he had a wiry build and rusty hair flecked with gray. His face had the leanness Iris associated with marathon runners, and he moved with the vigor of someone fifteen years younger.

Iris stood and gathered her notes, slapping a ten dollar bill on the table.

"We don't want your money," Mrs. Ulm said. "Just go."

Mr. Ulm put a hand on his wife's arm and gave Iris an apologetic look. "Now, Debby—"

She shook off his hand, not looking at him. "She doesn't belong here."

Leaving the money on the table, Iris walked toward the exit, trying to make her stride nonchalant. She resisted the urge to slam the door. On the sidewalk, she let the rising breeze cool her flushed face. *Coming back was a rotten idea.* She'd known it, but had come anyway. If her mother and Debby Ulm thought their rudeness was going to chase her away, they had another think coming. Iris wondered if either of them was responsible for the threatening phone call. Surely her own mother wouldn't—

On the thought, a nondescript sedan passed her and made a left off Center Road. Almost certain the driver had been Jolene, Iris started across the street on impulse, trying to catch up. As soon as she reached the corner, she saw the car pull into the driveway of a lemon-colored house a quarter mile away. Delight had flashed through her when she glimpsed her old friend, and she'd started after her instinctively, but her footsteps slowed as she approached the house. The yellow house was farther than it looked and Jolene had almost finished unloading her groceries when Iris reached the mailbox at the end of the driveway.

Her former friend had always been several inches shorter than her, and now she carried an extra ten or fifteen pounds on her hips and abdomen. Her hair was still blond and looked natural, caught up in a loose chignon. Wisps curled alongside her cheeks. She had on a peach-colored blouse and a challis skirt that skimmed her ankles. Her face wore its nearly forty years lightly, with only enough smile lines around her mouth and eyes to make her look adult, give her credibility in the classroom. Iris could suddenly see Jolene as a teacher and knew she was a good one. Catching her upper lip with her teeth, Iris wished she'd prepared something to say other than, "Let me help."

Jolene spun, skirt belling out, and an orange popped out of the bag she grasped, rolling to within a foot of Iris. The two women stared at each other, the silence seeming to expand, pushing them apart. Iris noted that the white rock chips in the beds edging the lawn were grimy, Jolene's engagement ring was a small sapphire rather than the traditional diamond, and the sedan had rust patches and a loose bumper . . . all signs that her family lived with the simplicity the Community had always endorsed.

"I don't know what to say," Jolene finally said, breaking the silence bubble and seeming much closer.

"Me, either. It's good to see you, I think."

Jolene half-smiled. "Ditto."

Stooping to retrieve the orange, Iris held it up.

"Grab a bag," Jolene said, nodding toward the open trunk. She headed through the one-car garage into the open door. Looping her fingers through four bags, Iris followed her, relieved that her former best friend didn't seem to think that her unreconciled presence would permanently pollute her house. The kitchen continued the theme of reasonable austerity without deprivation with its plain oak cabinets, Formica-topped counters and tiled floor. Iris knew if she peeked in the cabinets she'd see Martha Stewart stoneware from Kmart, or the like, and a mish-mash of glasses and cups. Photos cluttered the refrigerator and Iris recognized younger versions of Rachel and Aaron from the co-op.

"Tea, water?" Jolene offered.

"I could use a beer." Three-thirty wasn't all that early for an adult beverage and Iris was about reunioned-out. Alcohol might make conversation with Jolene flow more smoothly.

"We don't drink."

Iris felt faintly reprimanded, even though Jolene's tone was, if anything, apologetic. "Ah, well, a glass of water would be great. I'd forgotten how dry it is here." Unable to just sit, Iris began emptying the grocery bags, stacking canned goods on the table and putting produce near the sink.

"You don't have to do that," Jolene said, plopping a couple of ice cubes in the water glass and handing it to Iris. As Iris took a long swallow, she continued, "Sooo ... you're Iris Dashwood now and you design jewelry. I like some of your pieces. Why do you make them so they irritate the wearer?"

At Iris's arched brows, she said, "I Googled you at school after Esther told everyone you were back."

"My pieces are wearable art." Iris gave the answer she'd delivered many times before. "I didn't want them to be ignored, treated like mere accessories."

"You want to control people's reactions."

Jolene's observation was a new one and it took Iris by surprise. She sidestepped it. "I met your kids yesterday. At the store."

"Do you have any—?"

"No."

"Well," Jolene sighed, "I wouldn't trade them for anything, but there's no denying life is very different once you have kids. Full of love, but hectic and tiring and emotionally draining, especially once they get to be teenagers. No Broadway openings or jetting around the world getting ideas for jewelry designs."

Surprised by the note of dissatisfaction—even jealousy?—in her former friend's voice, Iris said, "I've never been to a Broadway show and jewelry-making is more painstaking than glamorous." She held up hands burned and scarred from working with sharp tools and solder.

"My goodness." Jolene inspected Iris's hands. "I didn't mean to imply—. I'd like to watch you work sometime."

"You'd be bored." Silence fell and Iris felt compelled to break it. "You must have had Aaron about ten minutes after I left. I didn't even know you were pregnant." Aiming for a tone of mild interest, she was proud of herself for not sounding aggrieved.

"I found out the day before you left," Jolene said, her voice muffled as she stowed orange juice in the refrigerator. Cold, vaguely strawberry-scented air drifted out. She straightened and gazed directly at Iris. "When I told Zach, we—"

"Zach? Zachary Brozek? You married Zach Brozek?" No wonder Aaron looked familiar. "I didn't even know you and he were . . . I was your best friend!" Iris could hardly have been more shocked if Jolene had admitted that George Clooney fathered her baby.

"Well, I guess we both had our secrets, didn't we?" Jolene's face closed down and she thrust a bottle of salad dressing into the refrigerator with more force than necessary. The open fridge door brought the photos closer to Iris and she now saw that several were of Jolene and Zach together and with the kids and Esther, and one featured a smiling Zach with his arm slung across the shoulders of a slighter, darker man who might've been a cousin.

"You are not comparing dating a guy your own age with my being molested by his father, are you?" Iris asked, tired of dancing around the elephant in the room all day. Irritated as she was, it was a relief to say the words aloud. She held up a bottle of cumin and Jolene pointed toward a narrow rack beside the stove.

Her jaw tight, Jolene bit out, "I'm sure you got some ... satisfaction out of the relationship." She looked appalled by the words the minute they left her mouth. "Iris, I'm—"

Iris spun, the spice bottle slipping from her suddenly nerveless grasp to shatter on the floor. The aroma of cumin made the kitchen smell like a Delhi bazaar. "What the *fuck* do you mean by that?"

"We don't use that kind of language in this house," Jolene said, retreating behind primness.

"Well, good for fucking you!" Iris's chest ached with the strain of holding back tears and rage and confusion. Seeking an outlet, her hand closed over another bottle on the spice rack. She hurled it at the floor and it exploded in a cloud of glass splinters and cinnamon. It felt good.

Jolene let out a tiny shriek.

"I was fourteen when your father-in-law seduced me. Did you know that? Fourteen. He lured me to Outback Cottage, praised my drawing abilities, and talked me into working on a project with him.

Those altar tapestries. You know the ones. He was always standing too close, rubbing up against me, but he was Pastor Matt, so I shoved aside my reservations. During our third rendezvous, he kissed me. He told me I was beautiful and talented. Classic pedophile technique, I've since learned." She spit the words bitterly. "Isolate a child who feels ugly or unappreciated and make them feel special. Loved. Well, by our fourth meeting his tongue was in my mouth and his hands were down my pants. He—"

"Stop!" Jolene's voice cut through Iris's words like a shrilling teakettle. "Stop. Please."

Iris clutched at the counter behind her to still her shaking hands, gazing at the mess on the floor. She felt ashamed about losing control and herded the bigger chunks of glass into a pile with her foot. Raising her eyes, she fixed them on Jolene. "Your daughter's, what, sixteen? You should give thanks every day that her grandpa has been in a coma for twenty-three years, and not free to do to her what he did to me."

"Oh, no!" Jolene looked as if the idea had truly never crossed her mind. "He wouldn't—"

"Pedophiles don't stop with one. I got too old for him, after all. He was losing interest by the time I got up the nerve to tell him if he touched me again I'd tell. I'm pretty sure he was doing Gabrielle Ulm by then. Where's a broom?"

"Little Gabby?" Jolene swayed. Her mouth opened slightly and her face twisted in a way that made Iris think she was going to reveal something important.

When she closed her mouth again without saying anything, Iris said, "What?"

Jolene shook her head. "I think you should go. I can clean this up."

Iris hesitated. "Look, I'm sorry." *For making a mess, for telling the truth, for upsetting your perfect life.* "This isn't the way I wanted things to go. I really came over to ask you about the night Pastor Matt was hurt. My father didn't do it. He doesn't belong in prison. I—"

"I can't do this right now, Iris," Jolene said, pulling a broom from the pantry and wielding it so wildly that the spices tornadoed up. She coughed. "Not now. Rachel will be back any minute."

"When?" Iris's tone said she wasn't budging until she had a commitment.

"Monday," Jolene said. "I can meet you during my planning period."

# TWENTY-THREE

### JOLENE

JOLENE SHUT THE DOOR behind Iris, and looked at the brown film of spices coating her kitchen with dismay. Tears leaked as she broomed up the mess. What a disaster! It had started out so well, the two of them talking civilly, like strangers meeting at a party. "What do you do?" "Do you have any kids?" But then … history intruded. Pastor Matt had come between them again. She'd made that stupid remark and Iris had, with some justification, gone through the roof. She'd wanted to hear what Iris's life was really like, what had drawn her to jewelry design, whether she'd gone to college, who the important people in her life were. Instead—

Rachel came in through the garage door and Jolene hastily wiped her eyes. "Whoa! Did I miss an earthquake?"

"Some spices fell off the rack while I was putting the groceries away," Jolene said, stooping to whisk the anthill of powder into the dustpan. "No earthquake. Don't walk through it, though," she said, as her daughter walked through the spice dust, leaving athletic shoe imprints.

149

"Sorry," Rachel said. She grabbed an apple from the crisper, polished it on her sleeve, and took a bite. "Homework. Later." She disappeared down the hall and up the stairs.

"Sure, later," Jolene sighed. She considered reminding Rachel that her chores were still undone and her shift at the co-op started in an hour, but she didn't have the energy. She had long suspected that good parenting was ten percent wisdom, ten percent patience, and eighty percent energy—enough to play with the kids when they were little, take care of their physical needs, listen to them, and make them toe the line with chores and manners and behavior and values. Exhausting. Now that Aaron and Rachel were older, it took a different kind of energy than the physicality required to lug strollers and change diapers—it took emotional energy—but it was still draining.

She had mopped the floor, finished putting the groceries away, and was chopping onions to make black bean soup for dinner when Zach came in.

"Mm, smells good in here," he said, kissing the back of her neck.

She closed her eyes for a moment and let the feel of him against her back stabilize her. His solidity was reassuring, comforting. Why did she sometimes find their domesticity and routine so confining? She said a prayer of thanks for her blessings and turned to kiss him on the lips, holding her oniony hands down and away. They pulled apart, both of them saying, "Guess who I saw today?"

"Mercy Asher," Zach said.

"You mean Iris Dashwood. Let me finish this, you change, and we can talk on the deck. I'm getting a headache from the smell."

Zach kissed the top of her head and went upstairs to change. She could hear him greet Rachel, but couldn't make out what Rachel said. With the soup simmering, she washed her hands, smoothed on the grapefruit-scented lotion that was one of her few indulgences, and poured two glasses of iced tea. Zach clomped down the stairs and they settled into the chairs on the deck. Jolene tried to let the peace of the evening sink into her, but found she couldn't relax. While Zach filled her in on his time with Iris, she refilled the birdfeeder attached to the deck rail.

"She wanted to know about that night, but I put her off," Zach said, after describing their talk on the way to Mrs. Dorfmann's. "I didn't feel it was respectful of your privacy to tell her—"

"I told her I was pregnant," Jolene said, clanging the metal lid onto the birdseed can. She drifted back to her chair, picked up her tea, and swallowed. She didn't sit.

"Where did you run into her?"

"Here. She dropped by."

Zach's brows drew together. "You invited her in, talked to her? She was never reconciled, Jolene—you know that."

He spoke in the condemnatory tone that frequently made her itch to do the opposite of what he commanded. Suggested. She fought down the disloyal feeling. "I'm sorry. It didn't even cross my mind." Before he could say more, she changed the subject. "In all these years, we've never really talked about what happened that night."

"What's to say?" Zach gazed at her from beneath lowered brows, the vein at his temple throbbing as it did when he got tense. "Neil Asher apparently believed what Mercy said and came looking for my father. He went after him with the poker. I'll grant that it was probably a crime of passion; I don't think he planned it. He let rage drive his actions and the consequences were tragic for all of us."

"What would you do if someone had ever molested Rachel?"

"Pray."

He hadn't even thought about it, hadn't let himself see a grown man's hands caressing Rachel, just come out with the church-approved answer to any crisis. "Oh, come on." Jolene looked at him with open skepticism.

"I'm a man of God, Jolene."

She turned back to him, breathing in the scent of grilling meat from the neighbors' house. "Last I knew, that didn't mean you'd had your feelings surgically removed."

"Don't be flip."

"I'm not. Iris brought it up today, told me I should be grateful your father's been in a coma all these years, that he wasn't up to—forgive the pun—abusing our daughter. I haven't been able to get that thought out of my head since she left."

Zach rose, and the heavy step he took toward her made the deck tremble beneath her feet. "Are you saying you think—? That you believed Mercy back then? That my father—? It's not possible." He made a gesture that brushed away the repulsive idea.

The truth hovered on the tip of her tongue. She swallowed hard, paused, and then said, "I was at your house that night you know, looking for you."

He stilled. "You never said."

She looked down, noticing that the silvered wood of the deck needed refinishing. She worked at a splinter with the toe of her shoe. "I heard you fighting. You and your father. You both sounded angry enough to … What was it about?" She looked up and met his eyes.

Zach's lower lip jutted and he bit out in the voice of a man goaded past discretion, "You. He wanted to have you punished for the sin of fornication. Apparently your mother went to him for advice when you told her about the baby."

"Did you tell him it was yours?"

His silence answered her. She should have felt like crying, but something cold and steely was seeping through her blood vessels, freezing her emotions, and she gazed at him dry-eyed. "So … what, then? Did you at least try to talk him out of the reckoning stones?"

"Of course I did! After seeing Mercy—I told him it was barbaric, un-Christian. He recited First Corinthians to me, about the congregation needing to chastise the sexual sinner. I told him there were better ways. He reminded me of my duty to honor him as my father. I … I told him I was leaving, that I couldn't be part of the Community anymore. He roared at me to stay, but I ran out." Zach looked sickened by the memory, his face pale.

Jolene felt a flicker of pity but stopped herself from going to him. He had denied her and Aaron by not owning up to his paternity. "Did you hit him?"

"Jolene!"

She stared him down.

"I have never raised my hand in anger against another human being. You should know that's not who I am."

The hurt on his face brought her to him. She stroked his cheek. "I *do* know. I'm sorry. It's just—"

"I thought I heard you back here." Esther Brozek's voice cut into the still night and Zach's sister maneuvered her bulk through the sliding glass door onto the deck. It quaked.

Jolene had a sudden vision of the deck collapsing beneath their combined weight, the three of them plunging through jagged boards to the concrete pad below. She and Zach drew almost imperceptibly closer, the two of them closing ranks against Esther. A glow rose from the neighbors' barbecue coals and Jolene realized the afternoon had edged into dusk while she and Zach talked. She rubbed her upper arms, conscious of the chill. There'd be no getting around asking Esther to stay for dinner, she thought resignedly.

"I hear Mercy Asher's been stirring up trouble and I wanted to talk to you, Zachary, about what we should do about it." Without being asked, Esther settled into the chair they kept for her, an armless chair of sturdy wood that could bear her weight.

"She's Iris Dashwood, now," Jolene said, ignoring the inner voice that told her not to needle her sister-in-law.

"She was born Mercy Asher and she'll always be Mercy Asher to me," Esther said.

"We're all different people than we were twenty-three years ago," Jolene said. "We just don't all have new names to reflect that." *And wouldn't it be lovely if we did, if we chose different names at ten, eighteen, thirty-five, to reflect who we'd become?*

"Not me." Esther shifted in the chair and arranged her caftan to cover her calves.

"I don't think we need to 'do' anything about Iris," Zach said, and Jolene knew his use of Iris's new name was a way of siding with her. "I haven't given up hope of persuading her to be reconciled."

Esther snorted. "The sins of the father get visited on the children for generations."

"Don't be so Old Testament, Esther," Jolene said.

Esther's eyes slid her way. "It's our duty and privilege to obey the Scriptures. Mercy has shown time and again that the Lord's will is nothing to her. She was too prideful to accept the Community's discipline twenty-three years ago, and I sense that she hasn't changed. We need to convince her to leave the Community before her example corrupts our youth."

Jolene sensed Esther's measured words concealed a burning desire to have Iris run out of town by an old-fashioned mob wielding torches and farm implements. "What did you have in mind, Esther?"

A tiny smile cut into the woman's fat cheeks. "Oh, I think Mercy Asher will choose to move on before too long. She might find that memories can be … painful."

Jolene bit back the verse about offering hospitality that came to mind. There was no point. She crossed to the sliding door, wanting to get away from the almost physical aura of self-satisfaction that pulsed from Esther. "The soup smells done. You'll stay for dinner?"

"Of course."

*Of course.* Jolene sighed, and entered the house, calling for Rachel to set the table.

# TWENTY-FOUR

### IRIS

Iris emerged from the motel room Monday morning after a restless night, determined to buy a large coffee before meeting Jolene. She needed the caffeine. She'd tried to work on designs for the new commission Sunday, become frustrated with her lack of progress, and been pleased when her cell phone rang. Jane, she thought, picking it up. She hadn't recognized the number that came up and answered warily: "Iris Dashwood."

"Mercy, is that you?" A phlegmy cough followed.

Momentarily astonished to hear her father's voice, she learned he was allowed to make daily calls and had gotten her number from Cade. "Have you made any progress?" he asked, the hope in his voice squeezing her heart like a vise. "Found out who attacked Pastor Matt? I heard he's awake now—praise the Lord. Has he said anything about what happened?"

"No, he, uh, his memory is messed up." Iris couldn't admit she hadn't been able to make herself try to see him again. Feeling her father's disappointment in his silence, she hurried on, "But I'm talking to people and I've been through the police reports. Did you see or hear *anything* that night that I can follow up on? Walk me through exactly what happened."

He told her about discovering that she wasn't in her room and immediately setting out for the Brozeks.

"I did go there," she admitted when he petered out, apparently embarrassed at having thought she'd harm Pastor Matt. "Keep going."

"You were so *angry* after the ritual," he apologized. He'd noticed the cottage door hanging open and gone there instead of the main house, finding Pastor Matt just inside, beaten and bloody. "I felt his pulse—he was still alive. That's how I got his blood on me. I was about to go for help when Esther showed up and set up a screech. I told her her father was still alive and she ran out, up to the house to call for help. I stayed with him, praying, wishing I knew something about first aid, until help arrived."

"You didn't see or hear *anything*, sense someone in the house or on your way over?" Iris tried to keep her frustration out of her voice.

"No, I—wait. I heard a car. I thought it was the ambulance arriving, but then no one came for another five minutes. I'm sorry."

"It's okay." It wasn't much.

He cleared his throat and Iris heard other conversations going on in the background. "You know, I thought I was resigned to dying here, to living out the rest of the years God grants me in this place, but now ... Now, this place itches at me like a wool sweater. Things I was used to—the routine, the boredom, the complaining, the food—they rub at me like they haven't done in years. I've been reading Job and taking hope because even though God let Job live in misery for years, took away his health and his family and all that mattered to him, he restored it in the end. Twice as much as he had before, the Bible says."

Iris closed her eyes, feeling the burden of her father's hope. What if she couldn't prove someone else had done it? What if she had gotten her father's hopes up, only to dash them? He'd be so much worse off than if she'd never come back. She made reassuring noises into the phone and was relieved when he said his phone time was up and that he'd try to call tomorrow.

Giving up on the design she'd been working on when he called—it wasn't worth the piece of paper it was drawn on, anyway—she'd gone to bed early and alone. The gremlin in the heater had begun working overtime again around midnight and she'd had to turn it off to avoid being roasted, leaving a message on the motel office's answering machine since she was reluctant to wake the Welshes. As a result, she'd ended up shivering by four in the morning, and had slept fitfully the rest of the night, finally turning the heater back on, but opening the windows.

Now, wearing a fleece jacket over a light sweater, she noticed the grass was frost-tipped. April in Colorado was a tricky month weather-wise, she remembered, with temperature swings of sixty degrees in a twenty-four-hour period and conditions ranging from icy fog to snow to pounding rain and hail. She glanced at the rental car, hoping she wouldn't need to scrape ice off the windows, and stopped.

Red slashed across the windshield. Four letters in drippy red spray paint almost obscured the glass: "LIAR." A slow burn started in Iris. She circled the car, gripping her purse so tightly her knuckles whitened, and read the same word written on the driver's side and the rear window. On the passenger side, only the letters "L" and "I" marred the car's finish. Like someone or something had scared the cowardly vandal off. Maybe she'd spooked him when she got up to mess with the heater. The thought of someone out here, defacing her car, not twenty feet away from where she slept, made her suck in a deep breath.

Fanning her anger to chase away the pang of worry, she marched toward the office, stiff-arming the door open and setting the innocent bell jangling. Mrs. Welsh looked up from a computer and pushed reading glasses atop her head at the sight of Iris. A cream cheese–smeared bagel sat on a napkin beside the keyboard and the aroma of coffee wafted from a steaming mug.

"I got your message about the heater," Mrs. Welsh began. "Quentin will—"

"It's not about that," Iris said. "Someone vandalized my car last night. I want you to call the police." She could do it herself, of course, but the police might take the incident more seriously if the motel's owner called.

"Oh, dear. Vandalized?" She blinked several times and approached the counter.

"Spray painted it. I don't suppose you heard anything?"

Mrs. Welsh gave it a moment's thought. "I don't believe so."

"Of course not. You only hear my guests coming and going."

Pursing her mouth into a tight knot, Mrs. Welsh said, "If they didn't use a car, we wouldn't have heard anything."

Lone Pine was less than a half mile away. Someone could easily have walked it, Iris realized. Of course whoever did it was from the Community that had condemned her as a liar when she accused Pastor Matt. She took hold of her temper. "You're right, of course. I'm sorry. Please call the police. I want to report this."

"There is no Lone Pine police," Mrs. Welsh said. "The county sheriff has jurisdiction out here, but we mostly prefer to handle things ourselves." She made no move to place a call.

"I've had experience with that," Iris bit out. "This time, I want the police. If you don't call them, I will."

Reluctantly, Mrs. Welsh made the call after looking up the number in a phone book.

The chunky blond sheriff's deputy who arrived twenty-five minutes later held out little chance of catching the perpetrator. "Probably kids," she said, strolling around the car and making notes. "That's gonna be a real bitch to get off. You got any idea what it means?" She jabbed a finger at the words.

"It means someone's afraid of the truth," Iris said, thanking the officer for her time and taking the report number the woman offered. She'd already called her insurance company and the rental car company while waiting for the deputy.

"We don't get many calls from Lone Pine," the deputy said, standing behind the open door of her cruiser with her freckled forearms resting atop the door. Garbled voices crackled from her radio. "Fact, other than a heart attack once, this is the only time I've responded to a call out here. I got my dad a sweater at the co-op last Christmas, though. They make some high-quality wool goods. Use alpaca hair. Raise the alpacas themselves, turn the hair into yarn, and do all the knitting right there in Lone Pine. Talented ladies."

From her admiring tone, Iris couldn't tell if the deputy was more likely to question the town's inhabitants about the graffiti, or take advantage of the opportunity to do some shopping. She supposed it didn't much matter; no one in the Community was going to rat out anyone else.

A car pulled off the road. Eager to sign for the replacement rental car, identical to the one she'd been driving, and get on the road to Jolene's school before she missed her chance to talk to Jolene, Iris thanked the deputy again and hurried to meet the rental company rep. It was going to be another coffee-free morning.

———

Parking at Jolene's school half an hour later, Iris was determined to get some hard information. She was ready to tackle her and anyone else who might know what had happened the night she left town. Fingering the obsidian pendant hanging around her neck, Iris pressed her thumb against the stone's pointed edge, hard enough to dent the skin, but not hard enough to draw blood. She let the pendant drop to her chest and marched into the school.

When Iris asked for Jolene Brozek at the office, the secretary dispatched a student to show her to a storeroom where Jolene was inventorying costumes. Rolling racks of dresses, uniforms, coats, and menswear crowded the room. Shelves were stacked floor to ceiling with shoes, hats, umbrellas, and large hollow animal heads, including a panther that seemed to gaze at Iris with malevolent green eyes. Bagheera from *The Jungle Book*, maybe? The room smelled a bit like a locker room and Iris wondered how the animal heads got cleaned inside after students wore them for a couple hours on stage. She decided not to ask.

"We'll have more privacy here," Jolene said in answer to Iris's raised eyebrow when the student left. "I've got to find another Juliet costume. The play opens this weekend and our Juliet broke her arm last night, horsing around on the balcony with Romeo after rehearsal. Her understudy's half a foot taller."

"You're the director?"

"Assistant. The school has a full-time drama teacher. I help out when I have time."

Drifting toward one of the racks, Iris fingered the lace frothing at the neckline of a medieval gown. She let it fall when Jolene said, "I guess you want to talk about what happened to Pastor Matt. I don't know that, but I was there that night, at the house, around seven. I was looking for Zach. I'd found out I was pregnant the day before and I needed to tell him." She laughed bitterly. "Little did I know his father had already told him. When I got close to the house, I heard them fighting, both yelling. I didn't know then that it was about me."

"What did you think it was about?"

Jolene shrugged, and pulled a blue velvet gown from the rack, holding it against her torso. "Zach and Pastor Matt argued a lot that spring. Zach was tired of being under his father's thumb, of always being reminded that what he did or didn't do reflected on Pastor Matt. I guess I figured they were fighting about college. Pastor Matt wanted Zach to go in state, and Zach had applied to schools in California and Texas. He wanted to get away."

Iris nodded. "So, you heard them arguing and then what?"

"I hung around for maybe five minutes, hoping Zach would come out, but he didn't, so I left."

"Zach and his dad were still going at it?"

Jolene nodded unhappily.

"Any idea where Esther and Mrs. Brozek were?"

"No."

"Did you see anyone else around the house?" *Please don't say my dad.*

Jolene started to shake her head, but then stopped, an arrested look in her eyes. "I saw Cade Zuniga's car parked by the church, but I didn't see him."

Iris remembered that car, a blue hatchback that showed all of its two hundred thousand miles. It stank of its previous owner's hound, despite Cade shampooing the upholstery and carpets numerous times. Iris found herself scrunching the cheerleader's costume she'd been examining into a ball and consciously relaxed her hand. Was this why Cade had been reluctant to put an investigator on the case? He'd never mentioned being in Lone Pine that night.

Iris cleared her throat and asked, "Where did you go?"

"Up on the slide." Jolene's voice fell to a whisper. "I was really scared, Iris. I sat up on the rocks and tried to think, but no amount of thinking or praying made me not pregnant. I came back to the Community, oh, about forty-five minutes later. It was scary dark and I almost broke my ankle, like, a dozen times on the way down. I went by your house, but you were gone. I didn't know then that you were gone gone. I thought maybe you were out with Cade." She smiled ruefully and Iris felt a twinge of guilt for having abandoned her best friend in her time of need, even though she hadn't known about the pregnancy.

"I'm sorry," Iris said. "I should have been there for you. I should have stayed in touch, at least. You were the only one who didn't shun me after I accused Pastor Matt. You might not have believed me, but you were still my friend."

Tears welled in Jolene's eyes and she dabbed at them with the sleeve of the yellow gown she had draped over her arm. Squaring her shoulders, she faced Iris. "I did believe you."

Something in Jolene's tone warned Iris. The hairs on her arms stood up. She stayed silent, gaze fixed on Jolene's face.

Taking a deep breath, Jolene blurted. "I saw you together. You and Pastor Matt. In the cottage. We needed a throne for the play, for *A Midsummer Night's Dream*. I'd seen a chair I thought would work in there once, when I visited Mrs. Wellington and I asked Mrs. Brozek if we could use it. She gave me the key. You were on the couch. You didn't even hear me come in. You were naked and Pastor Matt was ... was ..."

Iris knew perfectly well what Pastor Matt was. New humiliation erupted within her at the thought that Jolene had actually seen them together. She couldn't look at Jolene. Time seemed to slow and the air to thicken. Iris felt detached from her body, separate from the flesh and blood form that was standing statue-still. If she nudged it, her body would topple over and explode on impact. Dust. The real her was hovering up, up by the ceiling which, she noticed in an impassive way, was high, at least twenty feet with small square windows protected by wire mesh set higher than any basketball could bounce. Maybe the storage room had been carved out of a former gym. She let her gaze rest on a pair of ruby sequined slippers and the refrain from "Somewhere Over the Rainbow" played in her head. She could float over to Oz, like Dorothy—

"Iris? Say something."

Jolene's plea grabbed her and slammed her back into her body. She blinked. Then, anger crept in. "You knew. You witnessed him raping me and you didn't speak up when—"

"It didn't sound like rape."

The words disappeared almost immediately, swallowed by the acres of fabric in the room, but they rang in Iris's head. "I was fourteen the first time. Fourteen."

"I know that now," Jolene cried, struggling past a rack of costumes to reach Iris. The yellow dress's hanger snagged on something and she dropped it. "I know it was rape, I mean. But I didn't understand then. I'm so, so sorry. I've felt horrible about not speaking up every day since you left. Every. Single. Day. I know I don't deserve it, but please forgive me."

Iris held both arms at shoulder height, palms out, to keep Jolene from coming closer. "You could have stopped it. You could have stopped it all, but you didn't. You want me to forgive you?"

Jolene nodded miserably, tears streaming down her face.

"Well, I don't. I do not forgive you. Do you want to know what happens to a fifteen-year-old runaway? A girl? I can tell you about the hunger, the fear, the shoplifting and pickpocketing to eat, the sex."

Jolene started to put her hands over her ears, but then lowered them, as if she owed it to Iris to listen.

"Oh, yes, there was lots of sex. Some of it for money. I was beaten up a couple of times, knifed once, raped. When I started to make some money, I took self-defense lessons because I was never going to be at someone's *mercy* again." Shards of memory sliced at her and the sick fear she'd felt when the knife slashed toward her made her stomach lurch. She kicked at one of the rolling racks and it shot across the floor, banging into the wall. "You could have stopped it. Could have told the Community I was telling the truth, but you chose not to."

"He was Zach's father! I was so afraid of hurting Zach, of how he'd react . . . But that's no excuse."

Iris's gaze raked Jolene. She didn't look pretty now, with her eyes and nose reddened from crying, her hair in disarray. "I've had enough therapy to know Matthew Brozek was—is—a criminal. You're his accomplice."

"No! I—"

Iris strode to the door and flung it open, letting light and the sound of clanging lockers and students changing classes into the dim room. She was going to explode if she didn't get out of here. Pushing through the tide of high-schoolers that hemmed her in and buffeted her with backpacks and sharp-cornered books, she forced her way toward the exit, a square of light from the window of a door marked "FIRE EXIT ONLY." Moving faster and faster as she neared the door, she slammed both hands against the bar.

# TWENTY-FIVE

**IRIS**

IRIS BARELY MADE IT through the door before she was running flat out, uncaring of the startled looks she got or the harsh pulsing of the fire alarm. Her speed *whanged* her into the side of the new rental car and she paused a moment, gasping, before wrenching the door open and peeling out of the lot with a squeal of tires. *Jolene knew, but never said*—She shook her head to dislodge the feelings of betrayal and embarrassment and anger that caromed inside her like a pinball. She hadn't thought about where she was going, but she was unsurprised when she found herself pulling into the motel parking lot fifteen minutes later. A cluster of cars were parked near the Welshes' house and she wondered if Mrs. Welsh was hosting a Tupperware party or a coffee klatch. She didn't want to be here.

Reversing the car, she pulled away from the motel, took a deep breath, and dialed Cade's number. She was in the mood for confrontation and she wanted to know why he hadn't mentioned being in Lone Pine that night. He came on the line as she was passing the lay-by where the bus used to pick them up, and she skidded into it.

"Top of the rockslide in forty-five minutes," she told Cade when he said he could meet her for lunch. "Bring lunch and water—we'll have a picnic." She hung up, hoping the climb would give her enough time to figure out what to say to him.

She'd often climbed the slide her last couple of years in Lone Pine, after the cliff had birthed the river of boulders and stones that slid into the ravine, burying Penelope Welsh under millions of tons of rock. All the kids had loved the climb which made the canyon rim on the far side accessible from the Lone Pine side. She knotted her boot laces, locked the car door, and started down the path, blocking the memory of Jolene saying how she had climbed the rocks to ponder her options when she learned she was pregnant. Iris jolted to a stop. Jolene had admitted to being alone that night, on the slide, when the police report said Jolene and Zach had spent the evening together, studying at Jolene's house. If Jolene was telling the truth now, neither one of them had an alibi and they both had reasons to be mad at—and afraid of—Pastor Matt.

Iris resumed hiking. Trees and shrubs had grown up among the boulders since she last climbed it and the slide looked less barren. She wanted barren. Stark. Unforgiving. Leaving the path that led to Lone Pine, she started up the slide, having to concentrate to avoid getting a foot stuck between two rocks or skidding on scree. She was grateful for the need to pay attention. She didn't want to think. After only ten minutes of climbing, her breaths came heavily and she paused to suck in air, cursing the altitude. Bicycling the streets of Portland, she decided, did not adequately prepare one to go rock climbing at better than six thousand feet. Acres of rock stretched around her, soaking up the sun. Dark clouds slunk over the mountaintops, promising shade and maybe rain later. The giant spruce tree with its cool circle of shade used to be just about here ... A frisson shivered up Iris's back. The tree, and Penelope's skeleton, might be directly below her, buried on the ravine floor, two hundred feet down.

Starting off again, she conserved her energy by moving more slowly, taking care where she planted her feet. The canyon wall was only two-tenths of a mile away, and she was only gaining a hundred and fifty or two hundred feet in altitude, Iris figured, but the instability of the rocks worked all her muscles. On the thought, a rock twisted beneath her foot and she fell forward, catching herself with a hand on a basketball-sized rock. She got an immediate impression of water, and of the shadow of something swimming overhead. The sensation was so strong she leaned forward and touched her tongue to the rock, expecting to taste salt. Only grit and dust. Scraping her tongue against the roof of her mouth to clean it, she remembered Colorado used to be an inland sea. Maybe Penelope's turquoise had also been underwater, millions of years ago, and that's why she had gotten such a strong sense of water when she held the stone. That didn't explain the terror she'd felt, however.

Ten minutes later she reached her arms over the canyon's lip, searching for purchase. Before she could lever herself over the edge, strong hands gripped her wrists. She squeaked with surprise.

"Got you." It was Cade's voice and she let him help her over the edge.

Flopping onto her back, she lay for a moment, staring straight up into the blue. Then Cade's upside-down face moved into her field of view. He grinned and handed her a bottled water. She swished some in her mouth to loosen the dirt that clung to her tongue and teeth, and drank. Cade handed her a second bottle without comment. He looked incongruous in his suit slacks and button-down shirt, his wingtips filmed with dust. She thanked him, stood and dusted herself off as best she could. "So, what's for lunch?"

Clouds scudded the sky by the time they finished the burgers Cade had brought, a towering anvil-shaped mass promising thunderstorms. Iris had forgotten how quickly the weather changed in Colorado and wished she'd asked Cade to bring her a heavier jacket. Wind gusted fitfully and the temperature had dropped several degrees.

"I hadn't planned on this," Cade said, biting into an oversized oatmeal cookie.

"What had you planned?"

"An exciting sandwich at my desk, working on a workman's comp case. This is better."

She didn't know if he meant the cookie or being out of the office, picnicking on a canyon rim with her. The lines on his tanned face relaxed as he chewed, making him look younger, more like the man she'd dated so many eons ago. His black hair, tied back in its short ponytail, gleamed, looking barbered rather than rebellious. Zipping her jacket to her neck against the chill, Iris bit into her peanut butter cookie. He'd remembered her favorite.

"Remember when we used to come here?" Cade asked, staring out over the ravine. He lit a cigarette, making sure the smoke drifted away from her.

"Of course." Looking west, they had watched magnificent sunsets over Pikes Peak, content to sit with hands linked as the sky turned from pink to mauve and then inky blue. They'd brought a blanket and spread it out, and lain kissing for hours, until Iris's lips and cheeks were chapped and red from beard burn. They'd made love here, too, not their first time, but once when an electrical storm sent sheets of lightning ripping from cloud to cloud and the air was fresh with the scent of ozone and birds' calls. The lightning had ensured their privacy as sane people sheltered inside, and its electricity had charged the air. From the look Cade slanted her, Iris suspected he was remembering their lovemaking.

She wondered if he thought that's why she'd asked him to meet her here. Maybe he thought she was interested in reprising that evening. Was she? There was still a chemistry between them, even though it was muted, like the scent from an empty perfume bottle not properly stoppered. Mostly evaporated, but still lingering. She imagined his hands caressing her bare skin and shivered. She was suddenly certain he had a blanket in his trunk.

Reminding herself that he had lied to her, by omission if nothing else, she stuffed the uneaten half of her cookie into the bag and weighted it with a rock so it wouldn't blow away. "I talked to Jolene. Did you know she married Zach Brozek?"

Cade propped himself on his elbows, canting his body toward her. "I heard."

"They've got two kids. She teaches." Taking a deep breath, Iris added, "She said she saw your car that night. In the church parking lot. You didn't tell me you were there, Cade. I think that's strange." She kept her voice as neutral as she could, not wanting to sound like she was accusing him of anything.

His mouth tightened and he looked away from her to the west and the approaching clouds. "You want to know why I was there?"

She nodded, but he didn't see it. "Fine. I'll tell you." He stubbed out the half-smoked cigarette and faced her, a strand of black hair swinging forward where it had come loose from his ponytail. His face was stony. "That bastard chased you away. That predatory, megalomaniac fuck abused you and punished you and chased you away from your home. And me. Your parents let it happen, didn't lift a finger to help you. I wanted to punish *him* for what he did to you. And us."

170

Iris stirred, uneasy with Cade's intensity. He was no longer the detached lawyer; he'd morphed into the enraged eighteen-year-old he'd been a quarter century earlier. "I wanted to beat him to a pulp."

"You didn't—" Iris was surprised by how much she didn't want to hear Cade admit to the crimes.

He nodded. "I downed a six-pack and drove to Lone Pine, determined to fuck him up. I knocked on his door and when he opened it, I socked him before he could even say 'Good evening.' Landed a punch on his jaw." His right hand rubbed his left fist, and he rotated his shoulder as if feeling the punch vibrate all the way up his arm again.

"He fell on his ass." Cade smiled savagely. "I stood over him, feeling almighty and powerful, and a bit dizzy from the beer. I told him to get up, but he wouldn't. Coward. I kicked him once in the thigh, to try and get him up, but he stayed on the floor, saying something about turning the other cheek. I yelled at him, told him I knew what he'd done to you, called him a sicko, a pervert, every name I could think of. He didn't budge. I couldn't bring myself to punch a man who wouldn't even try to defend himself, and I was feeling sick and thought I heard someone moving around upstairs, so in the end, I just left. Not one of my finer moments."

He finally met her eyes and Iris realized he was embarrassed by what he saw as his failure to protect her or avenge her, even after the fact.

"Cade—" She laid a hand on his thigh. His muscles tensed beneath her fingers, and then his hand covered hers and squeezed hard.

"I capped off the evening by vandalizing the church, whacking at things and breaking windows with the baseball bat I had in the car, and then driving off and wrapping my car around a tree. Lone Pine almost became No Pine that night." His laugh was strained. "I was in the hospital for a couple of weeks and added a few hundred thousand dollars of hospital bills to my grandma's money problems. Leg broken in two places, ruptured spleen, cracked vertebra, and a host of lesser injuries."

"Ouch." Cade's was probably the car her father had heard.

"Yeah, well."

"That's why you didn't want another investigation."

Cade nodded, watching closely to gauge her reaction. "Yes. My fingerprints weren't on file back then, and no one thought to print me, so my prints on the door, in the house, got labeled 'unknown.' No one knew I was there. I straightened myself out after the accident, Iris. I went to the community college for a couple of years, pulled up my grades, and graduated from the University of Colorado. Then, law school, passing the bar, getting married, having kids. I'm in line for a judgeship in the next election."

"Congratulations."

"I don't need questions coming up about that night and my presence at the Brozek house."

Iris plucked at a tuft of grass, yanking up each blade individually, then offered them to the wind on her palm. They blew away. She pinned Cade with her eyes. "So, it was okay for my father to continue to rot in prison for a crime he didn't commit, as long as things continued to be smooth sailing for you? Don't they call that conflict of interest, counselor?" The wind whipped hair into her face, and she pushed it back. Digging in her pocket, she found an elastic and secured her hair, gaze never leaving Cade's face.

"That's not fair." Cade leaned in, face tight. "It's not my fault he's in prison. I didn't put Brozek in a coma or cause his wife's heart attack. I didn't make your dad confess. By the time I was coherent in the hospital and heard about what happened, Neil had confessed and the case was closed. Admitting I'd been there would have served no useful purpose."

Iris gave him a stony look. "You could have told me."

"Right. You show up in my office after a twenty-three-year absence, wanting to re-open the case, and I'm supposed to bare my soul, open myself up to prosecution. I don't think so."

His words hurt. There'd been a time when they'd bared their souls to each other. At least, she'd bared hers. He was the first person she'd told about the abuse, the one who'd urged her to speak up. *And look how well that turned out.* "It's going to rain. We should go." She started to gather up their trash, but his arm on her wrist stopped her.

"Do you ever think about what might have been?"

She gazed into his eyes, brown, liquid with wistfulness or maybe even longing. If she hadn't spoken up, hadn't run away, would they have transformed their hot, desperate, first love passion into a solid marriage? Or would they have drifted apart, finding new loves and paths? Or worse, would they have damaged each other, with Cade settling for some meaningless job and never graduating, while she spiraled into the darkness that Pastor Matt's abuse inclined her to? Pointless questions.

She didn't move away and he leaned in until their lips met. Iris lost herself in the sensation of his mouth opening under hers, the familiar rasp of his stubbled jaw against her skin. He smelled like warm skin and fabric softener, and tasted of smoke. She closed her eyes and let the heat rise between them, even as the air temperature dipped and the first drop of rain splatted against her cheek.

Cade's weight pressed her into the ground and sharp-edged pebbles dug into her back and shoulders. His hand, warm and smoother than she remembered, slipped inside her shirt and cupped her breast. His thumb teasing her nipple, and his erection pressing against her thigh triggered her body's usual responses. As she kissed him, though, she felt sadness welling up, the way water seeped into a sand castle moat at the beach, not displacing the passion, but making it incongruous. A distant rumble of thunder warned of lightning, but it was far enough away Iris didn't see the flash. After another half minute of kissing, as Cade's hand worked the button at her waist, she pushed at his shoulders. He pulled away so readily that she wondered if he felt the same way she did. Or maybe he was thinking about his wife.

"It's going to rain," he said, gazing down into her face with the sort of melancholy look people sometimes got when flipping through childhood photos.

Iris pushed herself to a sitting position and re-buttoned her jeans and blouse. She couldn't find the elastic she'd used to corral her hair. To the west, a solid sheet of rain advanced toward them, curtaining the view. She fought a sudden boxed-in feeling by swiveling her head to the east, but the clouds had lowered to meet the treetops of Black Forest and she found no relief there. She stood and walked to the brink of the ravine.

Cade spoke from behind her. "I'll give you a ride to your car."

Iris studied the advancing clouds. "I can beat it." She wanted time alone, didn't want to be cooped up in a car with Cade right now. She kissed his cheek and he made no move to hold onto her. "I'd better get started."

She started down the rocks, hearing Cade's car start up behind her. Descending the slide took all her concentration; it was much trickier than climbing up. As the wind whipped her hair into her eyes, she told herself she was grateful the broiling sun was behind the clouds. Grabbing saplings to steady herself, or putting a hand down to catch her balance, Iris was a bit more than halfway down and could see her car clearly when something made her glance back. She scanned the canyon's rim and caught a flicker of movement. A bird's shadow? She looked up at the hematite sky, but no birds flew overheard; they'd all gone to roost to wait out the coming storm.

Maybe a tumbleweed. The wind had picked up enough to send tumbleweeds bowling across flat places. The faintest tremor beneath her feet felt like the vibration from a passing train. At first, she thought it was thunder. Then, the stones sang a warning.

# TWENTY-SIX

**IRIS**

A BOULDER TORE FREE from the rim and hurtled downhill, gathering dirt and other rocks until a virtual avalanche of stones surged toward Iris. If they hit her, she was dead. She threw herself sideways toward a gnarled pine. Leaping, she caught hold of the lowest branch, knobby and sap sticky, and levered herself up, using all the power in her shoulders and back. Her feet scraped the trunk and then she was clambering higher, praying the tree would stand fast as the first rocks slid into it. Pebbles bounced up, peppering her bare arms where they clutched the tree trunk. She ducked her chin to her chest and squinched her eyes closed.

The tree shuddered and swayed with the force of the avalanche. Iris pressed herself against the trunk so tightly the rough bark imprinted on her torso and legs through her clothes. After what felt like a long time but was probably less than a minute, everything went still. A cloud of dust hung in the air and Iris blinked. Waiting long moments to see if the rocks would shift again, she forced her stiff fingers open. It began to rain, a mist that streaked her dusty limbs with mud. Gingerly descending the tree, which seemed to have shifted several feet, but was still upright, she patted the trunk and laughed weakly. She broke off mid-laugh when she thought of the figure she'd seen just before the avalanche. Someone had pried the first boulder loose—she was sure of it. Delayed reaction set in and she started to shake. Had someone tried to kill her? No, that was silly, paranoid. Scare her maybe, or hurt her.

Iris sank to her haunches until the shaking stopped. Then she stood, wiping damp hair off her face. The rain had picked up, slicking the rocks and drenching her. She ducked her head. She wanted to dash pell-mell down the hill toward the rental, but knew that would result in a twisted ankle or worse, so she forced herself to descend cautiously, gaining confidence as the landscape remained stable. A gentle susurration puzzled her, until she realized it must be rainwater forming rivulets beneath the rocks, coursing downhill unseen.

The memory of the movement she'd seen tugged at her. Someone had pushed the boulder down on her. She didn't want to think it, but her mind latched onto Cade. She'd heard him drive away, but he might have come back. The possibility that he might have tried to hurt her made her limbs heavy and she stubbed her foot against a rock. *Ow.* Regaining her balance, she skidded down the last twenty feet to the dirt path and turned onto it with relief. She couldn't think why he might want to hurt her, but who else knew she was here?

She lifted her head and peered through the rain wall to locate her car. The car! Anyone could have driven past and spotted her rental parked in the lay-by. Relief washed over her at the realization that anyone could have followed her, or seen the car and taken advantage of the opportunity to try and injure her or scare her away—it didn't have to be Cade. She broke into a jog and reached the car moments later, opening the door just wide enough to slide in. Wringing her hair out over the passenger seat, she started the car and watched the windows fog, chilled, bruised and aching in muscles she didn't even know she had. She tilted the rearview mirror down and looked at herself, pale and with a scratch on her forehead, hair clinging to her cheeks. Her eyes hardened. Whoever thought a rock avalanche would scare her away before she got her father out of prison had another think coming.

———

Although she'd planned to visit the hospital again and assess Pastor Matt's condition for herself, Iris let the lure of warm, dry clothes pull her to the motel room. Once inside, she spent twenty minutes in the shower before the hot water petered out, then dressed and sat at the desk to call Jane, wishing she were at an anonymous luxury hotel with room service so she could order a bowl of hot soup. She hadn't allowed herself to think about her scrape with death, but now her finger shook as she punched in Jane's number.

The sound of Jane's no-nonsense voice cheered her immediately.

"It's about time you checked in," Jane said by way of greeting.

"Your phone dials out, too," Iris pointed out.

"Hmph. What's going on out there?"

"Not much. I got a threatening phone call and my car was vandalized, found out that my brother's a soldier and I'm an aunt and that my best friend knew all along about Brozek abusing me." She left out the bit about a rock avalanche. She didn't want to worry Jane too much. "Oh, and I almost slept with my high school boyfriend."

"Almost?"

Just like Jane to key in on the sexual element. Iris smiled. "Almost. The tingle was still there, but the connection wasn't. Besides, he's married. Separated, but married."

There was silence from Jane's end while she processed that. She apparently decided to let it lie, because she asked, "What threatening phone call?" When Iris filled her in, she said in a sharper tone, "You told the police, of course."

Iris's silence answered her.

"Iris! The police have ways to trace calls now, even after the fact. The NSA probably records every conversation we have."

"That's paranoid, even for a dyed-in-the-wool liberal like you." Iris twiddled the wand that controlled the blinds, opening and closing them so light striped the floor and then disappeared. The rain had stopped.

"Whatever. The point is, you've been threatened and you need to get the police involved."

"I called them when someone painted 'liar' all over my car. So far, they haven't hauled anyone off to jail." *And weren't likely to any time soon. The Community protects its own.*

As if reading Iris's mind, Jane sighed. "And your friend?"

"Jolene."

"She knew all along that Brozek was molesting you?"

"Apparently." Jane's outrage pleased Iris, but the wound was too raw; she didn't want to touch it and regretted mentioning it. "How's Edgar?" Through the window, she watched a young family tumble out of a van and gaggle toward the motel office, mom cradling an infant, dad towing a toddler, and twin boys racing ahead. She hoped they didn't get the room beside her.

"Doing better." Jane sounded relieved.

They said their farewells and Iris got dressed. Talking to Jane had reminded her that she needed to work on the award piece, so she picked up her sketchbook with trepidation, worried that the ideas wouldn't flow. The pencil felt as ungainly as a shovel between her fingers, but she forced herself to draw. Nothing worked. Increasingly frantic, she ripped out page after page, some with no more than two or three lines on them, and flung them toward the trash can. Flipping the pad closed, she dropped it on the desk and lowered her forehead to her clenched fists. Wherever her creativity came from, it was dammed up like the ravine, choked off by her emotions, her history, Pastor Matt. She hoped it was merely blocked and not gone forever. Feeling desperate, she got out some of the rocks and gems she had with her, feeling them cool and round in her palm, looking for inspiration. Nothing nothing nothing. When she gave up and shoved them aside, it was dark. The bedside clock read 8:30.

Surprised by the lateness, she put away the sketchbook and her supplies, feeling not tired, but restless and itchy. When her stomach gurgled, Iris traded her work boots for a pair of peep-toe pumps, grabbed her leather jacket and headed out.

———

One hour and one margherita pizza later, Iris strode through downtown Colorado Springs, headed toward Weber Street and the Greyhound bus station. She knew it was foolish—it was still too early to go looking for trouble—but the thought of lost girls arriving at the station she had left from, threading their way past drug dealers and pimps, con artists and sickos, drew her away from the busy downtown. She considered calling Jane, but slid her phone back in her jeans. Jane wasn't her sponsor in some sort of twelve-step addiction program. As she crossed Tejon Street, a large neon parrot standing guard over a bar called The Thirsty Parrot caught her eye. The name was familiar and it took her a moment to remember that it was the one Aaron Brozek had recommended.

She hesitated, part of her leaning toward the bus depot and the possibility of a fight, her saner half arguing that sex would do the trick, would scratch her itch and restore her equilibrium. She wrenched herself off the sidewalk and into The Thirsty Parrot. The bar felt and smelled and sounded familiar, even though she'd never been there before. It could have been any one of a dozen bars in any one of a dozen cities. The crowd looked to be part college kids, part military, and part professional. Easy pickings. She wound her way to the bar, still fighting the urge to stake out the bus station. Swinging herself onto a barstool with a scowl, she ordered a Laughing Lab.

"Someone's had a bad day," the man on the stool to her left said jovially. Gray hairs sprouted above the neckline of his purple silk T-shirt and tangled in the heavy links of a gold chain. A gut spilled over the waistband of his slacks. He winked when he caught Iris's eye.

Iris gave him a "drop dead" look and turned her back on him. On her other side, a young couple were kissing and feeling each other up like they were alone in a bedroom instead of standing in full view of a couple hundred people. The man's hand had shoved the woman's short skirt up far enough that Iris glimpsed lacy black undies. She rolled her eyes and faced front again, drinking half her beer. Maybe she wasn't really in the mood for sex. She'd drink two beers and go. Back to the motel, maybe, or to the bus depot. She'd see how late it was when she finished her beers.

Halfway through her second beer and a friendly conversation with the female bartender, Iris felt someone wedge his way between her stool and Mr. Winker's. The voice that ordered a martini was familiar and she looked up to see Aaron Brozek standing beside her, casual in jeans and a button-down shirt with sleeves rolled to his elbows.

"Hey, I know you," he said, catching her eye as he picked up his beer. He smiled. "The co-op."

"Thanks for recommending this place," Iris said. "You're Aaron, right?"

181

"And you're Iris." He put down his beer to shake her hand.

He didn't say her name like he knew about her, and Iris gave him a brilliant smile. Mr. Winker chose that moment to belch and slide off his stool, headed for the bathroom or home, and Aaron seized his seat. "Do you mind?"

"Not at all." Iris flipped her hair over her shoulder and rested her elbows on the bar. The movements reminded her of Greg Lansing and she felt an inexplicable pang. "So, you're working on your master's. In what?"

"Psychology."

"So, is a cigar ever just a cigar?"

"Sometimes." He laughed and she caught hints of Jolene in the way his eyes crinkled at the corners. "I'm not a Freudian."

Iris half-listened as he explained the research he hoped to turn into a dissertation topic. Her hand brushed his where it lay near hers on the bar, and her knee rubbed his thigh when she swiveled her stool. He jumped like he'd been hit with an electric current, then leaned in closer.

"It's loud in here," he said, his lips mere inches from her ear. She nursed her beer for half an hour, flattering him and teasing him and asking interested questions about his studies. He was nice, if a bit pretentious about his intellectual attainments. He'd be better looking than most of the men in the bar if he lost the soul patch. She suspected he affected it to make himself look older and more serious. Licking her lips, Iris realized that she was only going through the motions, that she wasn't in the mood for sex anymore, that her calculated seduction of Jolene's son had drained her of randiness, rather than stoking it. She wanted to sink into her bed, alone, and sleep until noon. The thought surprised and un-nerved her. *This is a hell of a time to get scruples.* College-age men had always been self-absorbed and ever so slightly boring, so why was that putting her off Aaron and, for that matter, every man in the bar?

She let anger rise to displace the anxiety that threatened to derail her, and defiantly ordered a martini, despite her long-standing rule of no more than two beers. Sucking the olive between her lips when the drink arrived, aware of Aaron's gaze glued to her mouth, she let her body sway to the grinding bass beat of the music pulsing through the bar. It seemed twice as loud as it had. Desire stirred within her again and she fanned it by downing the rest of her martini. She immediately felt buzzed and welcomed the feeling. When her glass was empty, she slid off her stool, standing close enough to Aaron to feel his chest expand with each breath. "I'm going," she said, her tone a take-it-or-leave-it invitation.

His response was instantaneous. "I'll walk you to your car."

Tamping down the sadness that threatened to swamp her, Iris linked her fingers with his and followed him out of the bar.

They ended up at the motel when Aaron admitted to having a roommate in his thin-walled apartment near the university. His body was slim and his chest almost hairless, and his lovemaking was thoughtful and considerate when Iris wanted raw and unconstrained. Her short nails raked his back and bruises bloomed along his neck where she tasted him. In the end, he seemed to catch some of her fury and drove himself into her, expression almost savage as he strained for his orgasm. He left her technically satisfied, but writhing with an unfulfilled need she couldn't name. She rolled away from him almost as soon as he was done and pulled up the sheet. Aaron flipped over on his back and let out a long breath.

"I've never had sex in a motel before," he said, surprising a laugh out of Iris.

"Really?" She thought about it and realized he'd probably confined his sexual activities to the back seats of cars, and hurried trysts in apartments or dorm rooms when his or his partner's roommates were out. Unless he was bedding married women, he'd have no need of a hotel's anonymity. Iris felt old. "Well, now you have. Was it any different?"

She meant the question as a joke, but he took it seriously. "You're different. I've never made love with an older woman."

"You haven't yet." When he looked puzzled, she added, "That was sex, not lovemaking."

His fingers explored a bruise where his neck met his shoulder. "Whatever you want to call it, it was great." He grinned. "It's my good luck that you have control issues."

Iris sat up, uncaring that the sheet slipped to her waist. "What?"

"The whole cougar thing is about control," he said in a didactic voice, like he was reading from a journal article. "Older women want to be in charge of their romantic relationship, so they seek out younger men. The media treats the cougar phenomenon like it's a new thing, but so-called 'cougars' have been around for thousands of years. It's a recurring theme in the mythologies of several cultures where goddesses like Isis, Ishtar, and Aphrodite all fell for men who were younger, weaker, and mortal. You see, it's a power thing, a role reversal thing. It's not just because younger men have more stamina and hotter bodies."

He flexed a slender bicep in a way Iris would have found endearingly self-mocking if his words hadn't pissed her off.

"Don't get me wrong," he said, apparently misinterpreting Iris's expressions. "I'm all for it." He reached for her, but she rolled off the bed, taking the coverlet with her. Her nudity felt more vulnerable than powerful all of a sudden.

"Is that what you learned in Psych 101?" she asked, a dangerous edge to her voice.

"I've done some reading." He seemed uncertain now. "Look, if I hurt your feelings by calling you older, I'm sorry. You're by far the hottest—"

Iris turned her back on him and stalked to the bathroom, closing the door with immense gentleness. She wanted to throw pillows and yell at him to get out, but that seemed petty and might make him think she was mad at him for calling her old. She sank onto the toilet, coverlet pooling at her feet. Her breaths came in shuddering exhalations and she realized with surprise that she was on the verge of crying. Turning on the shower so Aaron wouldn't hear her, she rattled some toilet paper from the roll and blew her nose. Steam billowed, bringing with it a scent of lavender soap. *What is wrong with me? Why the hell do I want to bawl like a baby?* She stared at the ghostly reflection of her face in the fogged mirror. It had been an emotional few days, she reminded herself. She'd found out her father was innocent, her mother indifferent, that her best friend had betrayed her, and that the great love of her life had fizzled like a firecracker doused with too much water under the bridge. No wonder she was blinking back tears.

"Iris? Are you okay?" Aaron tapped at the door.

She cleared her throat. "Fine," she called. "I'll be out in a minute." She also had to admit that Aaron's words had pricked her. Oh, she didn't mind being called older—she wouldn't trade her "older" for his callow "younger" any day of the week. But what he'd said about control issues ... Was he right? Did she zero in on younger guys because she wanted to call the shots, decide when they ended up in bed and how long the relationship lasted, whether hours or a couple of months? She had a sneaking suspicion there was something to Aaron's analysis and it galled her that he'd found her so easy to dissect with his Psych 101 bullshit. She'd always thought psychologists were a wonky lot. She wouldn't want any son of hers majoring in psychology. Poor Jolene.

As steam blotted out the mirror completely, she faced another ugly truth: she'd seduced Aaron, in part, to get back at Jolene. It might have felt like she'd walked into The Thirsty Parrot by accident, but Iris didn't believe in accidents of that kind. She'd gone there hoping to run into Aaron, planning to fuck Jolene's baby boy. She imagined Jolene's reaction if she knew and got no satisfaction from it now. Jolene had been sixteen when she refused to tell the truth that would have spared Iris. Iris was thirty-eight, way more than old enough not to let herself be driven by hurt and anger. She dropped her head into her hands and let the tears come. She stayed like that, hunched over on the toilet, crying silently, until Aaron had knocked twice more.

Finally, she got into the shower and let the water drum on her face, sluicing away tears and snot and makeup. It didn't do such a good job with her guilt and confusion. She thought about praying, but dismissed the alien idea. Re-donning the damp clothes she'd hung on the back of the bathroom door to dry earlier, she opened the door, letting a cloud of humidity into the bedroom. Her sodden hair soaked her shirt between her shoulder blades. Aaron, dressed, sat on the edge of the bed, hands resting on his thighs. He looked worried. She was too exhausted to feel anything but grateful that he, apparently, wanted to go as much as she wanted him to leave.

"I didn't want to leave without saying goodbye," he said, rising.

Iris kissed him on the cheek. She wanted to warn him not to say anything to his mother, but knew that would only alarm him and make him curious. She had to be content with knowing that twenty-something men did not routinely discuss the details of their sex lives with their moms. Wishing she could think of something to say that wouldn't sound totally lame or condescending, she finally said,

"Thanks." *Thanks for slapping me upside the head with an unpleasant truth. Thanks for leaving. Thanks for being a basically nice guy that your mom can be proud of.*

He nodded uncertainly, and opened the door. His throat worked. "Will I see you again?"

"I've got to go home soon. To Portland."

Aaron nodded again, as if she'd answered his question rather than ducked it. "Well, I … uh … It was special. For me, anyway."

Iris closed her eyes, pained, and when she opened them he was gone.

# TWENTY-SEVEN

### IRIS

IRIS KNEW SHE WAS dreaming, but couldn't wake up. She was in a bar, dressed provocatively in a dress she'd never buy, but she was only ten or eleven years old. Garish makeup rendered her young face hideous. "Mary Had a Little Lamb" played from the jukebox, over and over. Lounging on a stool, her back to the bar and her elbows propped on it, she directed come-hither looks at a man across the room. When the man approached, smiling with anticipation, she saw it was Pastor Matt and awoke, heart pounding.

Wouldn't Aaron have a field day analyzing that nightmare, she thought, getting out of bed at 4:02 to use the bathroom and shake the dream from her head. She crawled back into the sex-scented bed, afraid of sinking back into the dream, and awoke Tuesday morning with a headache, and a resolve to give celibacy a try. A long-ago therapist had told her she needed a prolonged period of celibacy to help sort through her mixed-up motivations for sex and she'd laughed the idea off. Now, it felt right. She showered and called Jane, knowing her friend would get a kick out of her new celibacy resolution, but got no answer and no guidance. She felt a strong urge to talk to Greg. On impulse, she dialed the first three digits of his phone number, but then broke the connection.

She pondered her options. The only person close to the case she hadn't talked to was Esther. The thought of confronting the bitter woman made Iris grimace, but she might well have seen or heard something that would help her discover what really happened.

Iris drove into Lone Pine determined to get a coffee from Debby's Café whether Debby wanted her there or not. The mood she was in, she'd be just as happy if Debby tried to kick her out. Iris pushed into the café, setting the bell to ringing, and approached the counter. The smell of bacon made her tummy rumble. A quick survey of the space showed Mr. Ulm working behind the counter, several couples and families breakfasting on hotcakes or eggs, and the young waitress zipping between tables and the kitchen. No sign of Debby. Mr. Ulm, in jeans and a maroon Henley shirt that clashed with his rust-colored hair, approached Iris with a smile that showed a gap between his two top teeth.

"You look like a woman who needs a coffee."

"Yes, please." Iris returned his smile. "Extra large, extra hot, extra caffeine."

"Coming up."

He returned in moments with an orange stoneware mug. Iris sniffed the steam rising from it, sure she could absorb some of the caffeine. "You're a lifesaver, Mr. Ulm."

"It's Joseph," he said. "Some eggs and bacon to go with that brew?"

Iris hesitated.

"Don't worry about Debby," he said, guessing her thoughts. "She was in a mood the other day. Of course you're welcome here."

"In that case ..." Iris sat and ordered scrambled eggs and toast.

Joseph Ulm left to ring up a customer. When he returned, Iris asked, "You wouldn't happen to know where I could find Esther Brozek, would you?"

He gave her a thoughtful look. "I don't suspect she wants to see you." At Iris's questioning look, he added, "Esther blames you for her father's condition," he said. "She's been trying to get folks to run you out of town ever since you came back, saying you undermine the Community, that you're only here to make trouble, that you mock us."

That might explain the phone call and the spray-painted car, maybe even the rockslide. Iris leveled a look at him. "And you're telling me this because—?"

He swiped a cloth over the counter and said, "Maybe because I think this town is a little too insular, that we need some shaking up. Or, maybe"—he grinned—"because Esther Brozek rubs me the wrong way with her bossiness and holier-than-thou attitude. This town has always been too Brozek-centric, if you ask me." A ding from the kitchen window got his attention and he returned moments later to slide a plate of fluffy eggs in front of Iris.

She tucked in and cleaned her plate, listening to the conversation and laughter from the tables behind her. Joseph didn't reappear and it was an unsmiling Debby Ulm who showed up with her check. Whatever Joseph had said to his wife kept her from ejecting Iris, but it didn't make her chatty; she didn't respond to Iris's "good morning," and accepted her money without comment, unless one counted the way she slammed the cash register door closed. She turned her back on Iris to seat newcomers before she could ask where Esther lived now.

Rather than try to pry the information out of Debby, Iris went next door to the co-op and mounted the steps to find the place full of shoppers. The press of bodies made the room too warm and Iris hovered by the door as she searched for a clerk who might be able to point her toward Esther's house. She hoped Aaron wouldn't be there—heaven knew how he would interpret her turning up—and figured he was probably in class at the university. To her surprise, Rachel was helping one of the customers select some cheese. Shouldn't the girl be in school?

"Teacher work day," Rachel said, smiling, when Iris followed her to the counter and asked. "Mom had to go for half a day, but I didn't." She rang up two sales while Iris waited, reminding the customers that their bus would be leaving in five minutes. They began to trickle out.

"But you're stuck here."

"Only till noon." Rachel's eyes shone with anticipation. "Then Abby and I are headed to a concert in Denver. Casting Crowns." She named the Christian rock group hastily, as if Iris might think she was going to a Marilyn Manson concert.

"I don't suppose there might be any cute boys you know going?"

Rachel looked momentarily alarmed, but then grinned. "I have no control over who buys tickets to a public concert, do I? And if we happen to run into some kids we know, we wouldn't want to be rude." She put on an angelic expression that made Iris laugh.

"Can you point me toward Esther Bro—"

"Oh, no!" a woman with permed gray hair said, staring into a cavernous tote bag. "My wallet's gone missing. It's been stolen."

Something in Rachel's stillness caught Iris's eye. She studied the girl's suddenly motionless profile, and saw her gaze dart to the underside of the counter. Before Iris could say anything, Rachel was moving around the counter, ostensibly to help the distraught customer. With everyone's attention on the moaning woman, Iris slipped behind the counter unseen and let her fingers glide along the shelves beneath it. They closed over smooth leather the general bulk and length of a stuffed wallet. Damn the girl. Why in the world was she stealing? Easing out from behind the counter, Iris approached the knot of people clustered around the woman who was insisting that everyone in the room be searched for the wallet before being allowed to leave.

"Call the police," she ordered Rachel. Her tote bag, a straw monstrosity embroidered with faded raffia flowers, lay unattended on a display case. Iris picked it up.

"Are you sure the wallet isn't in your bag?" Iris asked, handing it to the distressed woman who blinked at her from behind round, pink-framed glasses. "It's awfully big. I know I've thought I've lost my phone and keys and all sorts of stuff before and then found them in the wrong pocket or down at the bottom of my purse." She patted her brown leather shoulder bag.

"Why, I'm sure!" the woman said, nonetheless pawing through her tote. "I'm very careful about where—" She stopped, a strange expression coming over her face, and withdrew her hand from the bag with the wallet clutched in it.

Iris kept her gaze on Rachel as the woman's friends congratulated her, joshed her, and prodded her to hurry out to the bus before it left without them. After catching Iris's eye for one swift, astounded moment, Rachel busied herself carrying an awkward package to the bus for a woman using a walker. Iris waited.

"Oh, you're still here," Rachel said in a markedly less friendly voice when she returned and found Iris leaning against a counter, arms crossed over her chest. She didn't meet Iris's eyes, but hurried toward a sweater rack. "I'm sorry, but I've got to inventory—"

"We need to talk, Rachel." Iris crossed to the door and flipped the "Closed" sign toward the street, locking the door.

"It's none of your business!" The girl whirled, her elbow knocking a stack of cardigans to the floor.

Iris went on as if Rachel hadn't spoken. "You can start with, 'Thank you for saving my thieving ass from jail,'" she suggested pleasantly.

"I'm not a thief."

Iris cocked a skeptical brow.

"I wasn't going to get caught." Rachel's chest heaved as she took several deep breaths, apparently trying to decide what to say next. "How did you do that?" she finally asked.

"I used to be a thief, too." Iris nodded when Rachel's eyes widened. "I ran away from home when I was about your age and if I wanted to eat it was sometimes a choice between whoring and pick-pocketing. I got pretty good at it—the pick-pocketing, I mean. It's even easier in reverse."

Her unemotional confession silenced Rachel. "It sounds awful," she said after a long moment.

"It was. But not near as awful as landing in jail. You don't want to end up in jail, Rachel."

"Have you—"

Iris nodded. "Once. Briefly." She could see Rachel wanting to ask why she'd been in jail, but the girl bit back the question.

"The money's not for me," Rachel said.

"The cops won't care."

Fear darkened the teen's eyes. "You won't tell them?"

"I should. Or I should tell your mother." Iris's tone invited Rachel to give her a reason not to.

"I have a friend," Rachel started. As if uncomfortable meeting Iris's eyes, she dropped to her knees and began to fold the scattered cardigans. Her fingers shook. "She really needs the money."

Iris eyed the girl, wondering if the "friend" was hypothetical. "For?"

"She needs to leave here."

"She wants to run away?" Iris shook her head. "That's not the—"

"She has to. Her father beats her. He's going to kill her!"

The fear in Rachel's voice convinced Iris the girl believed what she was saying.

Words tumbled out of Rachel, like she'd unplugged a dike. "She's scared of him. She wants to go to her sister in California, but her sister's barely getting by and can't afford to send Je—her money for a plane ticket, or even bus fare. She's desperate. I just want to help her, but I don't have any money of my own. Neither does she. The Community won't let us have real jobs, like at Subway or something. What we earn here goes straight into a communal fund for feeding the homeless." She sneered the words. "The homeless don't need help any more than J—my friend does. It's not fair!"

"But you weren't stealing from the Community," Iris pointed out. "You were stealing from some little old lady who might be living on a fixed income."

"If that were the case, I don't think she'd have bought two sweaters at $120 each," Rachel retorted.

Realizing that she'd let the conversation wander down a side path, Iris wrenched it back. "How much money she does or doesn't have isn't the point. Stealing is wrong."

Rachel stuck out her lower lip and slapped the last sweater back onto the rack. She stood. "You sound like my mother."

"Good for me."

"What are you going to do?"

"You need to tell your folks, about the stealing and about your friend's problem."

"I can't! They won't believe me."

Her anguished words struck a chord in Iris. She remembered working up the courage to tell her parents about Pastor Matt's abuse. She'd only spoken up because she suspected he had moved on to Gabby Ulm and she couldn't turn her back on Gabby and whoever might come after her. She'd waited until her father came home from work, convinced he would take her side, even if her mother was difficult. Noah was at football practice when she asked both her parents to sit down in the kitchen. She was so nervous that sweat ran down her sides and tickled behind her knees, even though it was a cool evening. To this day, the scent of sautéing onions made her feel ill. When she finally got her mother away from the stove and seated with Neil at the kitchen table, Marian studied her face for a moment and said, "You're pregnant. I knew that Zuniga boy was no good. This is what comes of taking up with a boy who's not part of the Community. He—"

"I'm not pregnant."

"He doesn't respect you, doesn't respect the Community's values. Catholics are all about sinning, thinking that confession gives them a 'get out of hell free' card. They don't understand about self-control and self-discipline and abstention. But you do. How could you give into his lusts, Mercy? You know what the Bible says about fornication: 'Flee from sexual immorality. Every other sin a person commits is outside the body, but the sexually immoral person sins against his own body.'"

"I'm not pregnant!" Mercy had to shout the words to make her mother shut up. "And if I were, it would be Pastor Matt's baby, not Cade's."

The words seemed to fall individually, toppling slowly like Stonehengean monoliths shoved by a gargantuan force, gathering momentum as they thudded to the ground. Pastor. Matt's. Baby. Mercy was mildly surprised the words hadn't dented the linoleum. That wasn't at all how she had planned to tell her parents. She'd wanted to walk them through events, starting with his invitation to meet in Outback Cottage. Instead, she'd blurted the gist in ten words.

Marian stared blankly for a long moment. Neil's brows snapped together and he started to get up, but Marian's extended arm blocked him. "You wicked girl," she said. "How dare you tell such lies about a holy man like Pastor Matt!"

"Marian, maybe we should listen to what Mercy has to say." Neil's deep voice cut across his wife's.

"I'm not lying." Mercy's sobs garbled the words. "He made me … we … I didn't want to! It was in the cottage, when we were working on the tapestries. I made him stop last year, told him I would tell, but now—"

"I've heard enough." Marian stood, smoothed her apron across her thighs, and crossed to the stove to stir the sautéing onions. Mercy thought she glimpsed tears in her mother's eyes, but that was probably from the onions.

Her father put his arm around her shoulders and squeezed tightly. She gazed up into his face, searching for some sign that he believed her, and saw grief. His free hand grabbed at his cheeks and compressed them, slid to his chin, and then fell helplessly to his side. "Mercy-punkin, you're upset. We need to talk this through. I don't know what happened in that cottage—"

She wiggled away from his arm. He didn't believe her either. Not really. He was going to side with her mother like he always did. A cold fury filled her, chilling her feet and migrating up her legs to her core and finally to her torso and head. When she spoke, her voice was icy calm. "Do you want the details? Do you want to hear about how he made me suck—"

"Mercy!" Marian's hand slammed down, clipping the pan's handle, and the sizzling onions and oil flipped off the stove, spattering Marian, the wall, and the floor. "Oh!"

Neil rushed to his wife's side, guiding her to the sink and turning on the cold water. Mercy ran out of the back door, unnoticed.

The echo of Rachel's "They won't believe me!" hung in the store when Iris pulled her thoughts out of the past.

"Why not?" Iris asked. The power of her memories had chilled her and she rubbed her arms.

"Because ... because her father is an elder. No one in Lone Pine will ever believe he beats Jenny." Rachel paced three steps toward the window and three steps back. The girl bristled with nervous energy. "But I've seen the bruises. I've *seen* them. She had a broken arm last year and he made her say it was from falling downstairs. And a few months before that he broke three of her fingers and made her say she slammed her hand in the car door." The words tripped over each other, running together.

Iris held up a hand to stop the flow. "I believe you."

"You do?" Rachel paused her pacing and blinked back tears. "So you won't tell?"

"I can't promise that." Part of Iris wished she'd never come into the co-op, that she'd gone door to door in Lone Pine instead, asking for Esther Brozek. She cut off Rachel's protest with an upraised hand. "First of all, you've got to stop stealing."

"I will."

The words came too glibly and Iris gave the teen a pointed look. "And you've got to tell your folks about Jenny."

Disgusted, Rachel turned away, but Iris caught her shoulder and forced the girl to look at her. "You have to, Rachel. Does she have younger siblings?" At Rachel's reluctant nod, she said, "Do you really think he's only hitting your friend and not her brothers and sisters?" Iris blinked away an image of Gabby Ulm's slight figure. "You're a good friend. You're trying to help. But the only way to really help, to stop this man, is to tell. If not your parents, then the police."

"I promised Jenny I wouldn't." Rachel sounded less sure of herself.

"This is one of those cases where it's better to break a promise than to keep it," Iris said.

A knock sounded on the door and an irate face peered around the "Closed" sign. Iris cursed silently. She'd been on the verge of convincing Rachel.

The teenager moved away from her toward the door. "I'll think about it," she said. She flipped the dead bolt and the sign, inviting the woman into the store with a smile and an apology.

# TWENTY-EIGHT

### IRIS

AFTER FINDING OUT THAT Esther still lived in the old Brozek home, despite its being way too big and hard to maintain for a single woman, Iris left the co-op. She stood on the steps outside the store, grinding her teeth. Irrationally, she was mad at Jolene. Both her children were causing Iris heartburn, within hours of each other. Aaron was an adult and made his own decisions, so Iris wasn't going to spend a lot of brainpower worrying about him. Rachel, on the other hand ... Rather than staying uninvolved when she caught Rachel stealing, Iris had slipped the victim's wallet back into her purse and saved Rachel from the consequences of her actions. Iris had learned valuable lessons from the school of hard knocks—why the hell had she intervened to keep Rachel from learning one of them? Then, she'd compounded her idiocy by demanding an explanation. She should have walked away. Once Rachel had told her the truth, she'd assumed an obligation.

Iris growled deep in her throat and started down the street toward the Brozek house. She'd give Rachel twenty-four hours to speak up, she decided. If the girl hadn't told her parents by then, Iris would have to tell them about the thefts. And wouldn't that go over well with Jolene and Zach? Iris tried to imagine the conversation but couldn't get past, "Hello, I caught your daughter stealing a wallet." They'd be furious, disbelieving, and inclined to shoot the messenger. They might even think she was out for some twisted kind of revenge, still upset because Jolene hadn't spoken up years ago.

Her angry stride took Iris to the Brozek house in short order and she was up the six shallow wooden steps and ringing the doorbell before she had time to think. While waiting for Esther to answer, she glanced to her right, at Outback Cottage, and wondered if her mother was inside. The sight of the little building made her queasy and she faced the double doors again, swallowing hard. Although lovely windows of original leaded glass framed the doors, the slender columns supporting the porch's overhang had been gouged by woodpeckers, hints of peach showed through the house's chipped lavender paint, and strips of caulking curled away from the window frames. The signs of deferred maintenance made Iris wonder about the Brozeks' financial situation.

A slight vibration and heavy footfalls warned of Esther's coming before the door swung open. Esther stood there, veiled by the hallway's gloom, ash-blond hair frozen in place and her body swathed in a men's over-sized plaid shirt over loose-fitting denim pants. Narrow-plank wood floors that needed sanding and refinishing stretched across the foyer behind her, and a brass chandelier hung too high to illuminate the space. A gracious staircase wound upward. A clock ticked loudly from a nearby room and the odor of fresh paint drifted down the stairs. The signs of shabbiness made Iris think for the first time of how much Pastor Matt's care must have cost.

"Mercy." Esther's tone and expression were unwelcoming. "I wasn't expecting you."

"It's Iris, now."

"You'll always be Mercy to me."

Iris didn't know what to make of that. Was Esther just being disobliging, or was she trying to say something? "May I come in?"

"I'm busy." Esther set her lips into an unaccommodating line.

"What are you painting?" Iris was beginning to feel silly, hovering on the threshold while they talked.

"How did you—? My father's room."

"He's coming home? Here?" Iris arched her brows.

"Eventually." Esther's face softened at the thought of her father's return. "He was here for nineteen years, you know. The first year and a half he was in the hospital, back when they still hoped he might come out of the coma. When it became clear he had sunk into a minimally responsive state—that's what doctors call it—they moved him here. When I got pneumonia a couple of years ago, Zach and Jolene insisted we had to move him to the nursing home." She sounded genuinely grieved. "They said that caring for him was killing me."

"You cared for him here for almost twenty years?" Iris tried to keep the astonishment out of her voice, but suspected she hadn't succeeded.

Esther clearly knew what Iris was thinking. "Yes. It's even more grueling than you might imagine: feeding tubes, catheters, cleaning him up after bowel movements, shifting him every couple of hours so he won't get bedsores, and more."

No wonder the woman ate. No wonder she got sick. It was enough to kill anyone. Iris felt the burgeoning of real respect for Esther, even as her flesh crawled at the thought of giving Pastor Matt a sponge bath. Sure, the woman was no picnic, but Iris doubted she would have had the fortitude or love to care for one of her parents at home if something similar had befallen one of them.

"I had help, of course, from Medicaid and state agencies. Zach and Jolene spelled me, as well, as did Aaron once he got old enough. He's my father," she said simply. "It was my honor to care for him, and I'm happy to do it again as soon as the doctors say he can come home. It will be easier now that the Lord has answered all our prayers and he is recovering."

"Look, Esther," Iris said. "You love your father and taking care of him is important to you. I respect that. Can you respect the fact that I'm trying to help my father, to honor him as the Bible commands?" She played the commandment card shamelessly, hoping it would sway Esther. "I just want to know what you remember about the night your father got hurt. Where were you?"

Esther's knuckles whitened on the door. "I should have been here. Then it wouldn't have happened. I was in the church basement cutting out construction paper whales for my Sunday school lesson. I didn't hear a thing." Her fleshy face sagged, pulling her small mouth into a red-rimmed O. "I walked past Outback Cottage on my way home and saw the door was open. I knew something was wrong—I just felt it. I ran in." She stepped out the door, brushed past Iris and lumbered down the steps, heading toward the cottage. Iris followed, thinking how sad it was that the obese woman Esther had become wouldn't be capable of running like her slim, eighteen-year-old self had.

Iris was relieved when Esther stopped halfway between the house and the cottage and pointed. "He was lying just past the entryway with Neil Asher standing over him. There was blood. Oh, dear God, there was blood."

"It must have been horrible for you," Iris said over the grousing of a flock of grackles searching for seeds nearby.

"I ran back to call 911—there was no phone in the cottage—and returned to Father, but he was gone. I thought he was dead. Neil didn't even try to run off."

Iris almost said, "Because he hadn't done anything wrong," but knew that antagonizing Esther would serve no purpose. "Where was Zach?"

Esther shrugged and returned to the porch, laboring up the steps. "Out looking for Jolene. I didn't know that then. I screamed for him, for my mother, but no one came. It was only after the EMTs took my father, and the police arrived that we found my mother in the kitchen, dead. At first, we thought Neil had killed her, too, somehow, but the autopsy revealed she'd had a heart attack. We think she must have been with Dad when he was attacked, and run back to call the police. It brought on the heart attack." Esther settled onto a bench by the porch rail, as if the effort of standing any longer was too much. The bench groaned. Inches of fabric got caught in the folds of flesh created by her overlapping stomach and thighs. "Can you imagine what it's like to be eighteen and lose your mother?"

Esther meant the question rhetorically, but Iris answered. "Yes, I can. I lost mine, too."

"Marian's next door!"

"She might as well have been dead." Her mother had not spoken a single word to her in the twenty-four hours between when the ritual had ended and when she left. Not one. Iris sometimes wondered, if she'd stayed, how long her mother would have subjected her to silence.

As if the interchange had reminded her that she hadn't wanted to talk to Iris in the first place, Esther heaved herself to her feet. "I've got to get back to work. You're not staying in Lone Pine much longer, are you?"

"Your spirit of hospitality is astonishing, Esther," Iris said dryly, descending the steps. "I'm staying until I discover the truth and get my father out of prison."

"Don't you think it might have meant a lot more to your father if you were here for him the last twenty-three years?" Esther asked, the very reasonableness of her tone meant to needle Iris. "If you'd been here to visit him and comfort him, to bake for him and bring him books to read? You swoop in a quarter century after the fact to orchestrate this ridiculous effort to free him. Is this some belated attempt to make up for what you did? For the lies you told that led your father to attack mine? Well, you can't make up for it. You can't bring my mother back, or repair the damage to my father. You can't free your father from the consequences of his sin, or give your mother back her husband and family." A wing of blond hair fell across her cheek and she tucked it behind her ear. "I don't know where your pretensions of saviorhood have come from, but I'm not buying it. *We're* not buying it. We all see through you, Mercy Asher."

Iris wanted to bat the words away, to keep them from penetrating, but they wormed their way under her skin, stinging and itching. The truth of much of what Esther had said reverberated through her. Maybe she should make everyone happy and leave Lone Pine. *The real attacker would appreciate that.* She wasn't going to quit. Esther might be right on some fronts—Iris couldn't change the past— but she was wrong, too. Iris had no delusions of being anyone's savior, but she was the only one working to free her father and she was damned if she'd give up on him now.

Esther's eyes glittered with triumph and she leaned forward, almost crowding Iris off the porch. "You keep saying Neil didn't do it. If that's true, then the only possible reason I can see for his saying he did is that he was protecting someone. You." She jabbed a finger into Iris's chest. Iris angrily swatted it away. "You hated my father. You made up lies about him. You disappeared that night. If Neil didn't do it, then he knows you did." Esther's eyes narrowed and her words came more slowly. "You did it, didn't you? You brought a shovel or a poker with you and you beat my father because he showed you up as the liar you are. Then you ran away and let your father take the blame."

"That's ridic—" Iris couldn't say it was ridiculous; it's what her own father had thought.

Drawing back as if sickened, Esther waddled to the doorway. "I'm calling the police. If you're determined to get your father out of prison, you'd better be prepared to take his place." She gently closed the door.

A wind gust rattled the loose gutters and Iris jumped. She descended the stairs and retraced her steps to where she'd left the car in front of the co-op. The woman was pure poison. Would the police listen to her? Of course not—they had their man safely locked up. She reached the rental and pulled out her keys.

"Miss Iris!"

She turned to see Rachel holding the store's door open. A breeze fluttered the girl's butter-colored hair and her eyes beseeched Iris.

"I've been waiting for you to come back." She sucked in a deep breath. "I'm going to tell. Will you … will you come with me?"

# TWENTY-NINE

**JOLENE**

JOLENE HAD BEEN HOME from the half-day workshop at school for only thirty minutes and was happily raking last year's mulch out of the flower beds, enjoying the sun's warmth on her bare shoulders, when the sound of a car pulling up at the curb made her turn. Her smile faded when Iris stepped out of the car. The sight of her former friend sent a toxic mix of guilt and anger pulsing through every blood vessel. When Rachel got out of the passenger's seat, she puckered her brow and hurried toward the street.

She acknowledged Iris with a cool nod, and asked Rachel, "What's wrong? I thought you'd already left for the concert."

"Abby's picking me up in half an hour. We'll still be there in plenty of time." Rachel clipped off the last word and gave Iris a beseeching look.

Jolene's grip on the rake tightened. She looked from her daughter to Iris, confused.

When Rachel didn't say anything more, Iris said, "Rachel has something she needs to tell you. Maybe we should sit down?"

Thoroughly worried now—What could Rachel have to say that involved Iris?—Jolene led the way around the house to the deck. "I just mopped," she explained.

"This is fine." Iris brushed a twig off the aluminum chair and sat. Jolene joined her, clasping her hands together on the table. Rachel remained standing. The air was uncharacteristically still for Colorado and Jolene heard the far-off drone of an airliner overhead.

"What is this about?" Jolene said in the voice she used to coax students into admitting plagiarism or other infractions, the voice that said she knew they really wanted to confess and atone.

"I ... it's about ..." Rachel trailed off. "I can't," she told Iris.

Iris gave the girl an encouraging smile. "Rachel has a friend ..." she started, and then paused, waiting for Rachel to leap in.

"Jenny. It's about Jenny," Rachel said. Then the story poured out of her, details about how her father beat Jenny, about her injuries, about Rachel trying to raise money to help her friend escape.

Jolene felt bombarded, shell-shocked, when Rachel fell silent, watching her anxiously. She couldn't imagine mild-mannered Leland Naylor beating his children. Surely Rachel had gotten it wrong. Where had Rachel said she was getting money to give Jenny? Those details had been fuzzy. And why, oh why, had Rachel confided this story to Iris of all people? A hot, caustic feeling surged like bile in Jolene's throat. Rachel was *her* daughter, not Iris's. Iris had no right to her daughter's confidences. She found herself gripping the edge of the patio table, the wood biting into her palm. Iris had put Rachel up to this, hoping to embarrass the Community somehow. Jolene thrust her chin out and said stiffly, "I'm not—"

Iris's voice, soft, but with an undertone of warning, cut across what she was going to say. "You have to believe her."

Jolene bit her lip, her gaze flying to Iris who leaned forward a little bit, opening herself to Jolene's scrutiny. In Iris's vulnerability,

Jolene suddenly saw her friend trembling in the church twenty-three years ago, where she stood accused of lying. With her back to the altar, she had faced the Community, her features twisted with desperation as she searched for help from those who loved her, her gaze lighting on her parents, her brother, Jolene. Her face had gradually hardened in the jumpy candlelight, smoothed itself into blankness, as she realized she had been abandoned. Sacrificed. Jolene couldn't stand the thought of her daughter's face going all waxy like that, of her pupils shrinking to pinpricks so it looked like she had left herself. She reached for Rachel's hand.

"You did the right thing telling me, honey," she said. "It was very brave of you."

"You believe me?"

The combination of hope and doubt in her daughter's voice brought tears to Jolene's eyes. "Of course I believe you," she said strongly, willing at that moment to accuse Leland Naylor and anyone else in the Community of terrorism or devil worship if that's what it took to reassure Rachel that she always and forever had her back. "We'll talk to your father tonight and see what our next step should be. We'll need to call the police." The thought almost made Jolene hyperventilate—the Community members would be scandalized, disbelieving, and Esther would be furious, saying that such things should be handled within the Community—but if Rachel was right, they had a duty to protect Jenny and her siblings.

Rachel squeezed her hand hard enough to make Jolene wince.

"I guess my work here is done," Iris said mock-seriously, pushing back from the table.

"Thank you," Rachel said, flinging her arms around the taller woman. Jolene gasped at how much the affectionate gesture stung. When was the last time Rachel had hugged her like that?

The hug clearly took Iris by surprise and she stood stiffly for a moment, before hugging Rachel in return, her dark hair contrasting sharply with Rachel's bright hair. "Happy to help," she said, "although you did all the hard work. Just remember, no more of you-know-what." She wagged a finger at Rachel.

"Thank you, Iris," Jolene called as Iris rounded the corner of the house. She smiled at the uplifted hand she got in return, and then turned to Rachel. "What is 'you-know-what'?" she asked.

# THIRTY

## IRIS

Iris drove away from the Community, headed for the hospital, feeling something almost like affection for Rachel. Despite her errors in judgment, her heart was in the right place and she'd had the courage to do the right thing…with a little prompting. Jolene and Zach had done well with both their kids, she had to admit, the thought of Aaron making her wince. She had used him last night, like—The unspeakable thought that popped into her head made her swerve onto the verge. She guided the car back onto the road, a plume of dust streaming behind it, and let the thought re-enter her brain. She'd used him like Pastor Matt had used her. Her muscles clenched and she found it hard to breathe, her lungs shutting down like a faucet had been turned off.

A moment's thought told her that she was over-reacting. She was not like Pastor Matt. Aaron, and all the young men she slept with, were legally adults, not vulnerable teens. She was not in a position of authority over them. Quite the contrary, actually; she was nothing to them. She breathed shallowly, testing her lungs, and then more deeply. She stilled owed Aaron an apology and she called him, leaving a voice message inviting him to breakfast the next day. Breakfast was a nice, safe meal with no sexual overtones, unlike dinner that looked ahead to darkness and beds. Iris pulled into the hospital parking lot, dismissing the idea that she owed any of her other sex partners apologies. She wasn't entering some damn twelve-step program that would have her saying "I'm so sorry for having hot, mutually gratifying sex with you" to dozens of men around the country. Her celibacy, going cold turkey with sex, was about her, not about the men she'd slept with.

As if to contradict herself, she pulled out her phone and dialed.

"Lansing."

The single word sent a spiral of warmth curling through her and it took her a moment to find her voice. "I've decided to be celibate."

A long pause made her wonder, agonizingly, if he recognized her voice.

"Permanently?"

His humorous undertone, free of judgment, let her relax back against the seat with a small laugh. "Maybe."

"Okay."

"Okay?"

"Whatever you need, Iris."

"Things are a little more complicated here than I anticipated, so it might be another week or two before I get back. Maybe we could get together, have dinner?" The beeping of a delivery van backing up cut through her last words.

"I'm not going anywhere."

"Good to know."

"Thanks for calling."

She swallowed around a lump in her throat. "Thanks for answering."

She hung up with a feeling of well-being, a fragile sense of connection, that entering the hospital obscured but didn't destroy. Not giving herself time to re-think the visit, Iris hopped on the elevator and wound her way through the halls. She heard voices as she approached Pastor Matt's room, and let them stop her short of his door. Deciding to retreat and return again another day, she was startled when a compact, lab-coated figure shot through the door and almost collided with her.

"Oh, so sorry," the woman said, pushing black-rimmed glasses up her pointy nose. The nose made her look like a fox, an impression her henna-red hair, pulled back in a loose knot, reinforced. She had the muscled build of a gymnast and exuded an energy that suggested she mainlined caffeine. A gold chain made up of oval links thick as a pencil looked too heavy against her thin neck. "Dr. Valeria Shaull" was embroidered over the white coat's pocket.

Thin brows arched up, wrinkling her forward as she studied Iris. "Have you come to visit Mr. Brozek? I don't think I've seen you before?"

Her voice was enquiring, not suspicious, but a lie came immediately to Iris. "I'm his niece," she said. "From Portland. I couldn't get here before now. My job," she said vaguely. "Uh, how's he doing?"

Dr. Shaull nodded rapidly. "It's a miracle," she said, "a medical miracle. I can only think of two, three other cases in medical history of a patient emerging from a minimally responsive state like this after more than ten years. It's mind-boggling how the brain sometimes heals itself, given time. Medical science can't explain it. Not yet. It's early days, of course, but we can already see huge improvements in his cognition and speech, although speech is still difficult for him and he sticks to short phrases and struggles to find the right words. He recognizes his children now, although of course he thinks it's still 1991."

"Of course," Iris said, although she'd given the matter no thought. *How weird.* What must it be like to fall asleep in 1991 and wake up to a world with Internet, terrorism, cell phones, e-books, and who knew what other medical and scientific advances? The first Gulf War had barely happened when Pastor Matt fell into his coma, and Ronald Reagan was still alive. He'd never heard the name Monica Lewinsky or seen the Twin Towers collapse.

"Does he remember the attack?" Iris asked. If he did, maybe Pastor Matt's testimony could free her father.

Dr. Shaull shook her head. "He suffered a lot of head trauma, including to the temporal lobe and the hippocampus. He appears to have no memory of the attack itself or the week preceding it. He may re-gain some of those memories as he heals, but he may not. Many of his other memories seem disjointed, non-sequential, or displaced in time, according to your cousins."

It took Iris a moment to realize she was referring to Esther and Zach.

An orderly in striped scrubs wheeled an elderly woman past them, greeting Dr. Shaull. "Let's see if he recognizes you," Dr. Shaull said, startling Iris.

"I don't think—"

The doctor re-entered the room, confident Iris was following. "This is an unprecedented opportunity to study the human brain, you know," she said over her shoulder. "We're doing MRIs, studies. For a neurologist like me, this is a once-in-a-lifetime opportunity. No, even rarer than that. Studying Mr. Brozek could do more to advance our knowledge of how the brain heals itself, re-wires itself, than decades of lab work. Mr. Brozek," she said, "you've got a new visitor." She beckoned impatiently at Iris.

Swallowing hard, Iris lifted a leaden foot and put it down on the threshold. Her body followed and she found herself staring into the well-lighted space, her gaze resting on the seams in the linoleum and the way the sun coming through the blinds striped the bed … anywhere but at the man in the bed.

"Do you recognize her, Matthew?" Dr. Shaull asked.

Iris forced herself to look, to let her eyes drift up the expanse of white sheet to a hand held awkwardly at shoulder height, palm outward, fingers curled. Blue veins twisted from the back of his wrists to large, prominent knuckles. His fingernails were too long, thickened and ridged. Iris stared at them, fascinated.

Following Iris's line of sight, the doctor said matter-of-factly, "Contractures. The muscles contract when a patient is essentially immobilized for as long as Mr. Brozek was. Come closer so he can get a look at you."

Fighting an almost overwhelming urge to turn and run, Iris moved closer, her feet dragging. Her peripheral vision grayed out when she reached the foot of the bed and she realized she wasn't breathing. She sucked in a long audible breath. Then, she closed her eyes briefly and opened them to look full into Pastor Matt's face.

He was old. She supposed she should have expected that—he was in his seventies, after all. Buzz-cut hair stubbled his skull, and what there was of it was white. He was clean-shaven, but his eyebrows were long and bushy, a few wiry hairs poking forward. It looked like no one had thought to trim his brows in years. He was thinner than he'd been, parchment-like skin covering broad cheekbones and sinking into the hollows with no trace of the ruddy glow he'd had. His skin was relatively unlined for a man his age and Iris realized that must be because he'd quit smiling, frowning, and squinting almost a quarter century earlier. Blue eyes so like Esther's it was uncanny, gazed into hers from rheumy corneas as viscous as egg whites. Pastor Matt stretched out one of his restricted arms and said, "Mercy."

Iris jumped back a good foot and Dr. Shaull raised her brows questioningly.

"My name's Iris," she managed to whisper.

"Not to worry," Dr. Shaull said, patting Pastor Matt's hand. "You'll remember in time. It's possible he's reliving the attack," she said in a low voice to Iris, "asking for mercy like that. He gets agitated sometimes and says it over and over again: 'mercy, mercy, mercy.'" A *beep* sounded from her waist and she checked a pager. "I've got to run. You two enjoy a good visit. Don't expect much," she told Iris. With a brisk nod, she hurried from the room and Iris was alone with Pastor Matt.

"Mercy," he said again, his blue eyes locked on hers. The way he said her name, the slight over-emphasis on the sibilant, slammed her back into Outback Cottage, where his weight pressed her into the sofa as he whispered her name over and over again through lips that grazed her ear.

"You bastard," she bit out. "You *bastard*."

He didn't react to the word or the fury in her voice, and his eyes never wavered from hers. In them, she read knowledge. Knowledge of her flesh, of her most intimate corners, of the way she expelled her breath with a little *heh* when he brought her to orgasm. His memories, smothered by the coma for so long, were alive again. He was remembering her acquiescence, her complicity, her eagerness ... she could see it in his eyes and hear it in the way he said her name. Taking a step toward him, she latched onto the metal guardrail that rimmed the bed and rattled it. "You bastard!"

She didn't realize she'd screamed the word until a nurse ran in. "What are you—?"

The bed shuddered from the force of Iris's shaking and Pastor Matt's head bobbled. He slid sideways. The nurse grabbed her around the waist, trying to pull her away from the bed. An orderly arrived moments later, summoned by the nurse's cries for help, and pried Iris's whitened fingers up one at a time. Detached from the bed, she staggered backward in the nurse's arms and they thudded against the wall. More people appeared in the doorway and Iris stared at the concerned and angry faces. Staggering to her feet, she offered the nurse a hand. "Are you okay? I didn't mean—"

"I've called security," the orderly cut in.

The nurse ignored Iris's hand, struggled to her feet, and went immediately to check on Pastor Matt. Aghast at her behavior, and weakened by the flood of emotions that had thundered through her, Iris stumbled toward the door. The orderly moved to block her, then hesitated, looking to the nurse for guidance, but she was strapping a blood pressure cuff around Pastor Matt's arm. Iris reached the door and wedged through the small crowd of patients and visitors, most of them aged or infirm and disinclined to stop her. Agitated whispers and speculation followed her down the hall. Her feet thwapped the floor and the sound of the thwaps coming faster and faster told her she was running. She hurtled down the stairs and past startled faces in the reception area, barely registering Esther's presence, and burst through the doors into the sunshine.

She was three miles down the road with no memory of getting into the car or starting it when she began to shake. She pulled into a grocery store parking lot and parked on its fringe, far from shoppers. Tears pushed against her eyelids but she scrunched them back. She had vowed long ago that Pastor Matt would never again have the power to make her cry. Instead, she struck the steering wheel with her palm and the impact vibrated up her arm, making her elbow ache. She did it again, knowing she'd bruised her palm, but welcoming a pain that had nothing to do with what had happened in Outback Cottage.

# THIRTY-ONE

### JOLENE

BRAIDING HER HAIR TUESDAY night, Jolene watched from the bed as Zach stepped out of his slacks and draped them over a hanger. His lightly furred belly protruded a bit more than when they married, but he was still an attractive man. He stepped into the bathroom and the dental floss rattled as he snapped off a length. She'd never slept with anyone else and hadn't felt the urge to in many years, not since she'd had a crush on Nicholas Eccles, the geometry teacher, not long after Rachel was born. She cringed to remember how she used to time her visits to the teacher's lounge for when he was likely to be there, how she'd tingled if she bumped into him unexpectedly in the halls. They'd shared nothing more than some intimate conversations, but still she felt like she'd betrayed Zach. She'd put it down to postpartum hormones and the seven-year itch, and eaten lunch in her room for the rest of the year to avoid him once she'd recognized how foolish and sinful she was being.

Now, she got out of bed, eased the door closed and locked it. Zach would take that as a signal that she wanted to make love, but she wanted to tell him what Rachel had said without Rachel over-hearing. She had flat-out refused to repeat her story about the Naylors to Zach, saying he wouldn't believe her, and Jolene had agreed to bring it up first. Zach emerged from the bathroom, wearing the lightweight flannel pajama bottoms he always wore to bed, and smiled when he noticed the closed door.

"We need to talk," she said, patting his side of the bed.

His weight dented the mattress, rolling Jolene slightly toward him as he got into bed. He reached for her, smelling of toothpaste, and said, "I thought maybe we could—"

She batted his roving hand away, annoyed, and told him about Leland Naylor beating his children. He lay beside her, not interrupting, for the ten minutes it took her to relay what Rachel had said and how she'd come to say it.

"Rachel told you that Leland Naylor hurts his daughter and that she was stealing from the co-op to help finance Jenny's running away?"

She hated it when he did that—repeated what she'd said back to her, a habit he'd picked up from some counseling course he'd attended. She knew it was supposed to assure her that he'd been listening, but somehow it frequently came out as slightly disbelieving.

"Yes. Well, she told Iris and Iris talked her into telling me." It still grated that Rachel had chosen Iris as a confidante.

Zach thought for a moment and then said, "There's no proof that Leland's been overly harsh with his daughter." He massaged his ear between his thumb and fingers. "He's a good man. He's served the Community well for many years. He's been an elder, and our treasurer and—"

"Rachel has seen Jenny's injuries."

"We're supposed to take the word of a teenager who is a self-confessed thief?"

Zach was using what Jolene thought of as his heavy voice, the one that sagged with disappointment, that said someone had let him down. She tried to get him focused on the Naylor problem, rather than on Rachel. "The hospital will have records." Once she'd started thinking about it, Jolene remembered the times Jenny had worn a cast or a sling, far more than her peers. The girl had always referred to herself apologetically as a klutz. "We have to believe Rachel," she added, unconsciously parroting Iris's words.

"I'll have a conversation with Leland—"

"We have to tell the police."

"I'll decide after—"

"I'm a mandatory reporter," Jolene said, already disgusted with herself for not picking up on the clues and helping Jenny sooner. "I'm talking to the police tomorrow. Jenny's well-being has to be our first concern, not how the Community will react." Her fingers plucked at the thread tufts patterning the ecru bedspread.

Zach struggled up from his supine position, supporting his weight on his elbow as he faced her. A throw pillow got in his way and he tossed it off the bed. "I am responsible for the spiritual guidance and the welfare of the Community. As my wife, you share in that responsibility."

Jolene shook her head from side to side, watching anger twitch a muscle in his jaw. "Not this time. My responsibility is to our daughter. I am not going to let what happened to Iris happen to her. God has given me a second chance, Zach, a chance for redemption, and I'm not going to throw it back in his face." Jolene hadn't known that thought was in her until she heard the words come out of her mouth, but she knew they were true. She'd failed Mercy, failed to speak the truth, and the consequences still haunted many people. She wasn't making the same mistake a second time.

"I am your husband. We are one flesh."

"Now and always, Zach." She reached up to stroke his cheek, filled with compassion for his confusion and hurt, but he jerked away from her hand. She let it fall, grieved by his response, even though she'd known he might react this way, might force her to choose between supporting Rachel and him, between Rachel and the Community. He'd grown too apt, of late, to conflate himself and the Community, talking sometimes like they were one and the same. She suspected she'd be unable to convince him she hadn't sided with their daughter against him, but had chosen to speak the truth aloud, rather than remaining silent.

"This is Iris's fault," he bit out.

"It's not about Iris," she said, surprised. "It's about protecting Jenny and her brothers and sisters."

"Before Iris returned, you respected me, and shaped your will to mine, as the Bible commands." He plumped his pillow too roughly. "Now, within days of her return, unmarried, un-churched, living a life that is about no one and nothing but herself, you turn against me. I don't think it's a coincidence." Turning his back, he socked the pillow again and then laid his head on it, facing the door. His shoulders were stiff and unyielding.

Anger pushed out the compassion Jolene was trying to hang onto. "This isn't about you, Zach," she said to his back, "or the Community. Not everything is." She got out of bed and unlocked and cracked the door so she'd hear if Rachel needed her during the night, then slipped under the covers, her back to Zach, and tried to fall asleep.

# THIRTY-TWO

### IRIS

WEDNESDAY MORNING DAWNED WITH loud knocking on Iris's door. She sat straight up in bed and checked the clock. Eight. She'd returned to the motel after seeing Pastor Matt, and gone for a punishing run, wishing every step of the way that she had her bicycle. After an alcohol-free dinner at the sports bar up the road, she'd gone to bed early but lain awake until after four a.m., unable to shut her brain down. If there'd been a "Privacy, Please" placard, she could have put it on her door so Mrs. Welsh wouldn't be rousting her so early.

"Come back later," she called, collapsing back against the pillow and snuggling the coverlet up to her chin.

"Iris?"

Her eyes popped open. Aaron. Breakfast. She'd forgotten. She slid out of bed and opened the door, glad she'd worn actual pjs to bed now that the heater wasn't acting up. He wore a tentative smile and his eyes were uncertain. His goatee was slightly scruffed, as if he'd been plucking at it.

"I got your voicemail about breakfast and tried to call you back," he said. "I left messages?"

"I turned off my phone," Iris said, not confessing that she hadn't wanted to talk to anyone, not even Jane, after the day's events. "I overslept. Give me ten minutes." Leaving the door open so he could come in or not as he chose, she grabbed yesterday's jeans and a clean shirt and panties and disappeared into the bathroom to shower and dress.

She had slid one leg into her jeans when there was a soft knock on the bathroom door and Aaron said, "Iris, the police are here. They want to talk to you."

She almost fell over, but caught herself with a hand on the sink. "Be right out." *Esther. Esther called them and told them about me, that I attacked Pastor Matt and caused his wife's death.* She hadn't thought the woman would really do it, or that the police would pay attention after so long. Bracing herself, she zipped and emerged from the bathroom.

Two men in suits stood facing her, one Asian and slim, the other white and stocky. Neither smiled. They were not uniformed, as she expected, but wore suits. She looked a question at Aaron, who sat at the desk, and he shrugged. "I'm Iris Dashwood," she said, offering her hand to the Asian cop.

"Detective Ko," he said, shaking her hand briefly and releasing it. "This is Detective Harrison. We're with the Colorado Springs Police Department." They displayed their badges.

Raising her brows, Iris silently invited Detective Ko to state his business.

After a pause, where he seemed to be waiting for her to say something, he continued, "What was your purpose in visiting Matthew Brozek yesterday evening?"

"Why?"

"Just answer the question."

Iris shrugged. "I was a member of his church years ago. I went to see him."

Detective Harrison puffed his cheeks out and then let out the air with a disbelieving *pft*. "Various staff members allege that you attacked him."

So it wasn't about the attack twenty-three years ago; it was about yesterday. "I didn't *attack* him. I didn't even touch him." *Surely, shaking someone's bed isn't a federal offense?*

"We've got more questions for you. At the station. Please come with us."

Aware of Aaron staring at her open-mouthed, Iris fought down a flare of panic. Could Pastor Matt have died? He couldn't be dead. If he was, she'd never get the opportunity to confront him rationally and calmly, get him to admit what he'd done. She'd squandered her chance yesterday, letting her emotions get the best of her. Her fingernails bit into her palms. She might never be able to design again, to make jewelry, if—

"Now," the detective prodded her.

"Of course." She gave Aaron a thin smile. "Take a rain check?"

Aaron nodded and followed her and the cops out of the room. The last thing Iris saw as she got into the waiting car—unmarked, she noted with relief—was Mrs. Welsh staring from the office doorway, mouth open and eyes wide.

It was almost one by the time the detectives let Iris leave the police station. They'd grilled her about why she went to the hospital, what she and Pastor Matt had said to each other, and why she'd shaken his bed. Having already discovered that her father was in prison for the original attack on Pastor Matt, they made ugly insinuations about Iris trying to finish the job he'd started.

"No one would blame you for wanting to take the guy out permanently," Detective Harrison said, thumping a folder that lay in front of him on the interview room's small table. He'd mentioned that it contained her father's court transcript. "Not after what he did to you. Guy's a perv. Deserves to die."

Sickened by the knowledge that details of her abuse had apparently come out in her father's court appearance, and that these two strangers knew what had happened to her, Iris could only repeat that she hadn't meant to harm him and that shaking the bed had been a spur-of-the-moment reaction. When she asked why she was being questioned, the detectives refused to answer. After enduring their repetitive questions for an hour, she'd called Cade Zuniga. It'd taken him twenty minutes to get to the police station, and another hour to effect her release. He'd managed to get Detective Harrison to tell them what had happened.

"He relapsed into the coma, the docs say. He's unresponsive. Brozek's daughter put us on to your client." Harrison jerked a thumb at Iris. "We checked with the hospital staff and they confirmed that Ms. Dashwood attacked Brozek yesterday afternoon. His doctor says it's possible that the injuries he suffered during her assault caused his relapse."

"I rattled his bed," Iris said before Cade could shush her. "I didn't lay a finger on him."

"Let's go, Iris," Cade said. "The DA isn't going to go near a courtroom with this. I'm no doctor, but I know enough to realize that there're probably half a dozen reasons Brozek could've ended up back in a coma. No way can they prove that anything you did caused it. This is frivolous," he told the detectives.

From the looks they exchanged, Iris got the feeling they agreed with Cade. A *whoosh* of relief blew through her.

It was short-lived as the four of them stepped out of the interview room to find a seething Esther Brozek waiting in the corridor. It was linoleum-floored and so narrow that Esther's bulk blocked it entirely. A black skirt and jacket with a white blouse gave her a funereal aspect. Low-heeled pumps cut into the fleshy tops of her feet. Tear tracks through her makeup and a red nose testified to an earlier crying jag, but she had composed herself. She looked like she had aged overnight, Iris thought.

"Murderer." Esther spit the word at Iris who shrank back involuntarily until she bumped into Cade's warm chest. His hand at her waist steadied her.

"That's enough, Ms. Brozek—" Detective Ko started.

Esther's eyes traveled from the detectives to Iris and Cade. Realization hardened her features. "Wait. You're letting her go?"

"We're still looking in—"

"She tried to kill my father! She killed his mind, pushed him back into the darkness, away from me." Esther's voice rose and a couple of uniformed officers appeared at the end of the hall. "You can't just let her go! She tried to kill him twenty-three years ago and now she's finished the job. It wasn't her father, it was her. It was her all along. Murderer!"

"Let's get out of here." Cade maneuvered Iris past the detectives and started to hustle her down the hall in the opposite direction.

"I'm sorry," Iris whispered over her shoulder to Esther as the detective stepped between them to keep Esther from following.

"You will be," Esther said through clenched teeth, craning her neck to glare at Iris over Detective Ko's head. "You most definitely will be."

Iris was shaking by the time she and Cade exited the police station. They stood in a parking lot from which Iris could see a baseball stadium and unending blue skies stretching to the east.

"What if I—" she started. The thought that she could have caused Pastor Matt's relapse sickened her, even though it was nothing more than he deserved. She tried to hold onto her anger, but it slipped away in the face of her probable culpability, harder to grasp than fog.

"Ssh." Cade put his fingers across her lips. "You didn't. There's no way to know. Don't torture yourself." His hands went to her shoulders and he gave her a little shake, peering into her face, his brown eyes full of concern. "I'm missing my son's soccer game. You okay?"

She nodded tentatively, then more firmly. "Yes. Go. And thank you." With a grateful kiss on Cade's cheek, Iris watched him leave. Realizing she didn't have a car since she'd ridden into town with the detectives, she flagged a taxi and settled into the back seat, too mentally drained to try and think through the morning's events. She tried to call Jane, but her friend didn't answer. She left another message as the cabby pulled up in front of her motel room.

There was no sign of either of the Welshes and no eviction notice on her door, which she'd been half afraid there might be, given the way Mrs. Welsh had looked when the police carted her away, so she inserted the key in the lock and was surprised when the door yielded immediately. Maybe she'd forgotten to lock it in the confusion of being hauled off by the cops. She stepped across the threshold and immediately stopped, catching her breath.

The room reeked of violence. Downy feathers coated every surface, stripped from the eviscerated quilt. The sheets were flung on the floor and her few clothes were strewn about the room. The words "Liar" and "Murderer" and "Leave" were written in what looked like red Sharpie or magic marker on the wall behind the bed. The thinness of the letters didn't take away from their potency. Shock held her still for a moment, but then she stepped into the room and reached for a sweater which had landed on the radiator. She held its fuzzy warmth against her cheek. Stepping carefully over the debris, she approached the bathroom door and pushed it inward with a stiff finger. A litter of broken glass and the scent of lavender shampoo greeted her. The intruder had smashed all her toiletries and squeezed toothpaste and shampoo and lotion over the walls and sink. She turned away. Worst of all, her jewelry-making tools and supplies lay twisted, broken, and scattered around the room, faceted semi-precious stones twinkling inappropriately in the light from the open door.

Tears started to her eyes and she pressed the heels of her hands into her eyes to thwart them. What was the point of such wanton destruction? Theft, she could understand, but this? If it was meant to scare her away, it was not going to work. Other than the sweater, she had touched nothing, and she backed toward the door, determined not to disturb anything so the police would have the best chance of catching whoever had done it. *They'd better hope the cops catch them first, because if I get my hands on them…*

"Oh, my."

The soft syllables came from behind her and Iris whirled to see Mrs. Welsh standing in the open doorway, peering in with rounded eyes.

"Who did this?" Iris demanded.

"I don't know," Mrs. Welsh said, sounding genuinely upset. She twisted her hands together. "I don't know. I took Mrs. Dorfmann to a doctor's appointment today. I only just got back myself fifteen minutes ago and was about to start cleaning the rooms. Maybe Quentin saw something. Someone." She faced her house, where her husband was once again working in the garden plot, jabbing a pitchfork into a wheelbarrow and shaking mulch in neat rows. He seemed to feel her gaze on him for his head came up, he made a visor of his hand, and looked their way. She beckoned to him and he leaned the pitchfork against the wheelbarrow and started toward them.

"Quentin, look," Mrs. Welsh said when he drew near, bringing the scent of loam and cedar on his overalls and work boots. She stepped aside so he could see into the room.

He stared at the destruction and the thin red words for a long minute, not attempting to enter. When he finally turned around, Iris could read nothing on his long face.

"I guess you'll be wanting to leave us then, Miss Dashwood. Mary, make out her bill."

Astonishment held Iris still for a moment, but then anger moved her forward. "What I want," Iris said, blocking his way when he would have walked off, "is to find out who did this. I think you know."

Quentin Welsh scratched a spot behind his ear. "You'd be wrong," he said. "I don't."

Iris narrowed her eyes. "Maybe not for sure, but you've got a good idea, don't you?" Mrs. Welsh made a bleating sound, but Iris kept her gaze pinned on Quentin. His large hands hung at his sides, grime caked under his nails, and he made no attempt to push her aside.

"I went to visit your father once," he said, voice low, red-rimmed eyes fixed on Iris's. "Not long after they put him away."

"You did?" Iris had figured that the Community had shunned her father after he was convicted of attacking Pastor Matt. "Why?"

"I know what it's like to lose a daughter," he said. "I thought maybe I could help him with that. He'd committed a terrible crime against the Brozeks, yes, but a man shouldn't have to cope with losing a child all on his own. We talked—about you, not about what he'd done—and we prayed. I know that man prays for you every day, just like I pray for my Penelope."

Too stunned to respond, Iris finally said, "He didn't 'lose' me … not in the way you're talking about. I didn't die. I'm back now.

I'm trying to help him, to free him. Someone's obviously trying to stop me." She gestured toward the destruction.

"Only God's forgiveness can free us from the weight of our sins." With a nod, Welsh stepped past her, headed back to the garden.

Frustration rose in Iris as she watched his back. Could no one in the Community do anything except mouth religious platitudes? Welsh knew something. He might even have wrecked the room himself. To make her leave? To punish her for causing her father grief? Before she could puzzle through all the angles, Mrs. Welsh reclaimed her attention by saying in a resigned voice, "I suppose you want the police again?"

"Don't you?"

Mrs. Welsh twitched her brows together and then said, as if surprised, "Why, yes. Yes, I do." She marched in the direction of the office and the phone.

# THIRTY-THREE

### JOLENE

THE RESIDUE OF JOLENE and Zach's argument coated their Wednesday evening. Zach had left for the church before Jolene was up, and there was still constraint between them as Zach prepared to make the pancake supper he cooked every Wednesday. Jolene offered a "How was your day?" which he ignored by pulling the griddle out from amidst the pots and pans with a painful clanking. The uplifting aromas of vanilla and butter sizzling did nothing to diffuse the tension in the kitchen. Rachel was uncharacteristically silent, accepting her pancakes with a muffled "Thanks," and eating them quickly, darting glances at her mother and father. Jolene declined pancakes, helping herself to leftover ham and scalloped potatoes. She knew she was only doing it to needle Zach, but she couldn't seem to help herself. He accepted her refusal without a word, merely adding her pancakes to the stack on his plate and drowning them in syrup.

A sharp rap was followed immediately by the creak of the front door opening. Jolene gripped her lips together. Esther. Just what the evening needed. Her sister-in-law hurried into the kitchen, looking more unkempt than usual with hair flat and beginning to show dark roots, her black suit jacket unbuttoned over a white blouse with a stain on the collar. "I should have called you, but—Did the hospital call?"

Jolene and Zach exchanged puzzled looks and shook their heads.

"What's wrong, Aunt Esther?" Rachel asked.

Esther took a deep breath, expanding her already formidable bosom, looked at each of them in turn, and said, "Your grandfather's slipped back into his coma because of her, that . . . that Mercy Asher. She attacked him and she's going to get away with it, even though she's taken him away from me—us—again."

Zach stood statue-still, and then swallowed hard. "He's gone?"

"I don't believe it," Jolene gasped. "Iris? Attacked your father? What happened?" Sensing Zach's pain, she moved to him and rubbed his back. He seemed to lean into her hand for a moment, but then stepped toward his sister.

"Sit down, Esther," Zach said, pulling out a chair. He returned to the stove and dolloped batter on the grill to make more pancakes.

Holding the table to steady herself as she lowered onto the chair, Esther shot Jolene a condemnatory look. "I might have known you'd side with her over your own family."

"What happened?" Jolene asked again, keeping her voice level and resisting the urge to shout that Matthew Brozek was not related to her by blood.

"She attacked him. Last evening. She went to the hospital, lied to Dr. Shaull, and shook his bed so hard it jarred something in his head. He's unresponsive again." Esther covered her mouth with a cupped hand and blinked rapidly.

Conscious of a feeling of relief that Iris hadn't actually struck Pastor Matt, Jolene put a comforting hand on her sister-in-law's shoulder, sympathizing with her very real grief.

"The police questioned her, but they let her go." Esther's cheeks quivered. "They told me the DA will decide whether or not to press charges, but I could see they're just going to sweep it under the carpet. Well, I'm not going to let her get away with it. It was her all along, not her father." Seeing their confusion, she added impatiently, "Neil lied about attacking Father to cover up for Mercy. She needs to pay."

Jolene exchanged a surreptitious glance with Zach and knew he was as troubled as she was by his sister's delusional accusations. Trying to reason with her wasn't going to work when she was so wrought up. Dismayed by the way Esther's eyes glittered, Jolene stepped back and busied herself by clearing the dirty dishes from the table. Behind her, Esther wheezed several heavy breaths, and then said, "I'm going to visit Father this evening, Zachary. You'll want to see him, too."

"I can't go with you," Zach said, putting a plate of pancakes in front of his sister. "I'm counseling Mary Lee and Seth. Their wedding's next Saturday, remember? I'll drive out to see Father tomorrow."

"I'll go with you, Esther," Jolene heard herself say.

Esther shot her a look, but then smoothed her face into a mask of gratitude. "Thank you, Jolene." She slathered her pancakes with butter.

Unable to watch her sister-in-law eat because it made her sad, and already regretting her offer to visit Pastor Matt, Jolene rose to scrape off her plate and put it in the sink. *At least this gives Zach something to think about other than Rachel's thefts and our argument.*

On the thought, Zach said, "Rachel, I need to see you in my study as soon as you've done the dishes."

When Jolene moved to speak, he directed a look at her that she couldn't ignore. Rachel would have to face her father alone.

"Yes, Father," Rachel said, her voice trembling slightly. Brushing past Jolene with an armload of dishes, Rachel put them on the counter. The set of her mouth told Jolene she felt betrayed. Rachel wouldn't meet her eyes or absorb the message of reassurance she was trying to send her. Zach wouldn't be overly harsh. He'd lecture their daughter, express his disappointment and sorrow, take away some privileges, and assign her extra duties, like reading to Mrs. Dorfmann or taking meals to old Silas Billings. Even though they hadn't discussed it, Jolene fully agreed that their daughter's stealing, no matter the motivation, deserved heavy punishment.

Picking up on the tension, Esther glanced from Zach to Rachel. "What's going on? What's Rachel done? Did something happen at that concert? I was against letting Community youth attend from the start, as you know. Rock concerts stir up all sorts of unhealthy urges."

Irritation flared in Jolene and she snapped, "It's none of your business, Esther." Even as the words left her mouth, she knew they were a mistake.

Zach, who otherwise might have gone with a dignified silence, gave her a minatory look and explained in measured tones, "Rachel has admitted to stealing."

Esther's fork clattered to the table. Her mouth dropped into an O, her multiple chins sagging one atop the other to her collarbone. "Stealing! A member of the Brozek family?" She glared at Rachel's stiff back. "For shame, Rachel. Your sinfulness reflects badly on all of us, and as shepherds of the Community flock—"

Rachel whirled, showing a tear-stained and angry face. "I don't see how my sin of stealing reflects any worse on us than your gluttony." Without waiting to see how her words went over, she rushed out the back door, leaving it swinging. The canary's happy evening song trilled into the room.

The disastrous truth of Rachel's words lingered. With precise movements, Esther folded her napkin and tucked it under her plate, leaving half her pancakes uneaten. She scraped back her chair and rose, tugging down the hem of her jacket. "I trust," she said, addressing her brother and not Jolene, "that you will convene the elders to mete out the appropriate punishment. You cannot be lax because Rachel is your own daughter. She has broken a commandment—she must submit to the reckoning stones."

"No!" Jolene gasped. "We don't do that anymore. Not since—"

"Brother, you know what must be done." Esther's pious expression was belied by the gleam of malice in her eyes.

Jolene wanted to dig her thumbs into the woman's glittering blue orbs and pop them from their sockets like peas squeezed from a pod. She'd never experienced such an urge to violence and it made her shake. She caught her breath on a sob and folded her fingers around her thumbs as if to control them. "Zach—"

Zach held up a hand to silence both women. "I will discuss it with the elders."

# THIRTY-FOUR

## IRIS

BY THE TIME THE police had come and gone—the same deputy eyeing Iris askance and asking her what she'd gone to make herself so "unpopular"—and Iris had taken photos of the damage to send to her insurance company, and moved what she could salvage into the room next door, it was coming up on seven o'clock. She had just finished locating the last of her gems and stones by getting on her hands and knees and patting every inch of the floor in her old room when her cell phone rang.

"Cade called," Marian said when Iris answered. "He wants to interview me and Neil together about that night, see if we can come up with anything he can use to get Neil's case reviewed. Tomorrow. At the prison, of course. If only Neil had let me tell the truth at the time …" She spoke in her usual phlegmatic way and Iris couldn't read her state of mind.

It was a good idea. Discussing that night together might bring up something neither one had thought to mention before. "I'll go with you."

"I can't drag Angel out to the prison. I need you to watch her."

Her mother was asking her to *babysit*? "Tomorrow? All day?"

"Yes."

"Isn't there someone else—"

"You're her aunt."

Iris got it then. Her mother thought she should want to get to know her niece. A bit to her surprise, Iris realized that she did. "I don't know anything about what five-year-olds need or want," she warned.

Marian laughed and Iris smiled at the sound, realizing she hadn't heard her mother laugh since she returned. "Don't worry. Angel will let you know."

———

It wasn't until Iris drew level with the co-op store Thursday morning that she realized that taking care of Angel meant spending the day in Outback Cottage. No way. Her mind raced to find alternatives as she drove slowly down Center Street and parked in the church lot. Her mother emerged from the cottage as Iris came around the church. Angel peeped from behind her, eyes big with curiosity and a little worry.

"It's about time," Marian said. "Angel's had breakfast, so all you have to do—"

"I thought we'd go to the zoo," Iris interrupted. She vaguely remembered visiting Cheyenne Mountain Zoo on a field trip in elementary school and hoped it was still in business. "Do you like animals, Angel?"

The little girl rushed out from behind Marian, clapping her hands. A small red purse with Tweety Bird on it swung from her shoulder. "Can we see the bears and the elephants and can I pet Tiger Lily?"

"What's Tiger Lily?" Iris asked, unwilling to make blind commitments.

"A skunk."

"We'll do it all," Iris said, swept away by the girl's eagerness. "When will you be back?" she asked Marian.

"Hopefully, by five. You can go back to the cottage and—"

"I'll take her out to dinner after the zoo," Iris said, refusing to take the cottage key Marian was trying to hand her. "I'll put her down at the motel when she gets tired, if you're running late. Just call my cell when you're half an hour out of town."

The three of them walked to the parking lot and Marian opened the door of an old station wagon and pulled out a booster seat. "This is a good opportunity for you, Iris," she said, as if she was conferring a favor.

Maybe she was doing Iris a favor. "Angel and I are going to have fun."

"No ice cream or candy. She's not allowed sweets between meals." With that, Marian got into the station wagon, and drove off. Angel and Iris waved until she was out of sight and then Iris led the girl to her car and opened the front door. Angel gave her an appalled look.

"What?" Iris asked.

"I can't sit in the front seat, Aunt Iris. The airbag will kill me when we crash."

At the zoo, Angel immediately towed Iris up a steep hill to the giraffe enclosure where she demonstrated the proper technique for feeding the prehensile-tongued creatures with lettuce Iris bought from a vendor. Having no interest in getting slimed by a giraffe's tongue, Iris gave her share of the lettuce to Angel and mentally sketched the asymmetrical spots from the giraffes' coats into a bib-type necklace. Heavy links could connect irregularly shaped enameled disks ...

"Come on, Aunt Iris!" Angel headed uphill toward the tapirs and elephants. Iris followed, the altitude making her momentarily dizzy. Built on a mountainside, the zoo sloped steeply and trolleys clattered as they carted the less fit visitors from exhibit to exhibit. Iris decided she might be grateful for a ride herself by the end of the day.

While Angel scrunched up her nose against the odors of the elephant house, Iris, feeling uncomfortably sneaky trying to elicit information from a child, asked casually, "So, Angel, who's your daddy married to?"

The girl gave her an incredulous look, apparently dumbfounded by her stupidity, and said, "Mommy, of course!"

Duh, Iris thought, realizing she didn't know squat about a five-year-old's thought processes. Angel darted across the street before Iris could reformulate the question, and Iris found her with her nose pressed against the glass of the lion exhibit. Bouncy music drifted from an out-of-sight but nearby carousel.

"That lion's sad," Angel announced, pointing to a tawny lioness who seemed lazily, contentedly asleep to Iris.

"You think so?"

"Uh-huh, cause her babies got taked away. One went to a zoo in New Mexico and one went to California. That's what the lady said when my class came."

A field trip, Iris figured. "You must be sad that your parents aren't—"

"Let's ride the tram," Angel said, her eyes pleading with Iris. "Please? Can we?" An aerial tram let the more adventurous get an eagle's eye view of the zoo and surrounding landscape.

"Why not?" Iris said and held Angel's hand as the girl skipped all the way to the tram station. The feel of the sturdy little palm against hers, damp with what Iris hoped was sweat and not giraffe spit, gave her a lump in her throat. She cleared it and said, "We have to save time for the hippos, though; they're one of my favorites."

From the swinging tram car, Iris looked down on the zoo enclosures, and then out across Colorado Springs, spread far below. The air was so clear and sharp it seemed brittle, like if she breathed too deeply, she'd suck in jagged particles. So different from Portland's gentle, moist air.

"They have wolves here, too," Angel said, pointing toward a wooded area. "They're my mommy's favorite."

As they exited the tram car and stood aside so a bevy of mothers with strollers could pass them, Iris took advantage of the opening Angel offered. "Where is your mommy?" she asked casually, hoping the girl wouldn't say "dead" or "living with my other daddy."

"In Qatar. That starts with a Q, even though it sounds like a G. Nana showed me where it is in the atlas. It's yellow."

"She's a soldier, too?"

Angel's head bobbed yes. "Like my daddy, only she wears a blue uniform. I like daddy's better."

Iris didn't know why she was surprised that her brother had married someone in the military. Noah had always had a thing for strong women—witness his infatuation with Esther Brozek. "I'll bet you miss her."

That got a tiny nod. "We Skype with her, too. She told me about finding a scorpion in her boot." Angel's eyes lit up, as if finding a poisonous arachnid in her sneaker would make her day. "We never Skype with Grampa," she added after a moment. She kicked at a pebble that dribbled two feet. "He's in jail because he's a bad man."

Iris's hand tightened on her cup and Coke splooshed over the side. "Who told you that? Your nana?" If Marian was denigrating Neil to his granddaughter...

"Uh-uh. She doesn't talk about Grampa. Sarah said so. She sits beside me in school and is really good at math."

Iris wanted to slap the uber-smart Sarah. "Well, Sarah's wrong." She didn't know where her anger had come from. Neil had confessed, after all. Having his granddaughter think he was evil was part of what he'd signed up for, even if he hadn't known it at the time.

Angel gave her a doubtful look. "He murdered somebody. That's against the Commandments. So he has to stay in prison until he dies."

"Don't let anyone tell you your grampa is bad," Iris said, "and don't you say it." When Angel pulled away, looking uncertain, Iris spoke more gently. "Your grampa didn't kill anyone," she said. "I'm going to make sure everyone knows that so they let him out of prison and he can come home to live with you and Nana. Would you like that?" She hunched down so her face was level with Angel's.

"Look, that grizzly bear is swimming!" Quick as a hummingbird, Angel darted away.

Iris flinched from the melancholy that threatened to sneak up on her. Angel's seeming indifference to Neil wasn't her problem. Putting aside all thought of learning more about the family she'd cast off, Iris concentrated on enjoying the afternoon. Time was Angel's laughter, bright and unconstrained, passing in a whirl of ice cream eating, skunk patting, and lion roar imitating, as they ran, skipped, or hopped from one end of the zoo to the other. Iris was exhausted when they finally headed for the car at three o'clock. She carried the worn-out Angel, who had her arms wrapped around Iris's neck and her legs around her waist. The girl's head slumped heavily on Iris's shoulder.

Although she enjoyed her niece more than she would have anticipated, Iris welcomed the silence as she plodded toward the parking lot. Her thoughts returned to Angel's remarks about Neil and a realization crept up on her. She cared about more than freeing her father. She cared about his happiness, about his having a relationship with his granddaughter so she'd know he wasn't a "bad man." She rested her cheek briefly on the sleeping Angel's head and wondered if Neil would ever have the opportunity to stroke her sleek hair and inhale the scents of sweaty scalp and coconut after a hard day's play.

Iris had just made the turn-off of Woodmen Road when her cell phone rang. It was Marian, saying she was half an hour from Colorado Springs.

"I'll see you at the cottage," she said, sounding weary.

"We're about to have an early dinner at Bumpers," Iris said. "Why don't you join us?"

"Dinner! Yay!" Angel crowed from the back seat, apparently refreshed from her forty-minute nap and starving since she'd had nothing but ice cream, a hot dog, peanuts, and animal crackers, Iris suspected, since lunch.

Marian agreed, sounding too tired to argue, and Iris hung up, relieved she was going to be able to avoid Outback Cottage.

———

The restaurant was busy on a Thursday evening, the celebrating sports teams replaced by families with young children. Angel accepted a placemat with a scene to color and a cupful of crayons. They both ordered burgers and fries before Marian walked in, wearing a slight frown and an air of weariness. Iris waved. Angel leaped up to greet her nana with a hug. "We saw meerkats. I think their babies should be called meerkittens." She giggled.

"You look tired," Iris observed.

"I am." Marian ran a hand through her short gray hair and sat. "It's a long drive."

The psychic distance from freedom to caged was even further, Iris thought. "Food might help." She beckoned the server and waited while Marian ordered a grilled cheese sandwich and tomato soup.

"So, what happened?" she asked, dipping a fry in ketchup and taking a bite. "How's Dad?"

Marian moved her head slowly from side to side. "You've got his hopes up, Iris. He thinks you're going to get him out, but I don't see how. Cade took us round and round about that night, but it always came out the same: We were together at the house, cleaning up after dinner, until Neil went to check on you. When you weren't in your room, he stormed out without telling me where he was headed. But I knew. It was only minutes later that the ambulance went past—he didn't have time to do … what was done to Pastor Matt." She shook her head again.

Making sure Angel was focused on her coloring, Iris asked, "Where was Noah? Surely he could testify that—"

"He spent the night at Tony Gray's, went over there before dinner."

Iris and her mother sat in silence for a moment, pondering the difficulty of freeing Neil Asher and watching Angel color. Finally, her mother said, "Cade gave us some time alone. We read the Bible together for a long time, and prayed. 'Find rest O my soul in God alone; my hope comes from him. He alone is my rock and salvation; he is my fortress; I will not be shaken. My salvation and honor depend on God.'" Marian fell silent, her gaze on Angel, but Iris didn't think her mother really saw the girl. "My hope comes from Jesus," she almost whispered, "but days like this it's thinner than air."

Caught by something in her mother's voice, Iris studied her face. What must it be like to be married but alone, to have a husband who shared his days and his thoughts with inmates who had killed and swindled and battered, rather than you? She was living a type of widowhood, but with her husband still alive and without the option of remarrying. Iris hadn't thought she could feel sorry for her mother, but she did. "I'm sorry, Mom," she said.

Marian reached a hand halfway across the table, but then let it fall. "Our Lord Jesus is with Neil," she said.

"I'm going to visit him again before I go."

Pushing aside her half-eaten sandwich, Marian asked, "Are you … have you found out anything about that night? Anything that might allow Cade to make a case for Neil, to get the conviction overturned?" Although she tried to sound casual, Iris heard the piano wire tautness in her voice.

"Nothing definitive." Iris hated to admit it. "No one has a real alibi for the whole time. I knocked on the Brozeks' door but left before anyone answered. I didn't see anyone. Jolene was at their house briefly, and heard Zach arguing with Pastor Matt. She saw Cade's car. Zach admits the argument but says he left to find Jolene. They never hooked up, so technically they're both unaccounted for. Obviously, I don't know where Mrs. Brozek was or what she was doing. Esther was in the church. Cade was in the house long enough to belt Pastor Matt—"

"What!"

"He wanted revenge for my sake." Iris kept her voice level, but hoped her mother heard the unspoken, *"Someone believed me."*

"He must be responsible," Marian said, latching onto the idea of Cade's guilt with the relief of a drowning swimmer grabbing a life preserver. "He struck Pastor Matt! How does he know the blow didn't kill him?" In her agitation, she bumped the table and it wobbled.

Iris grabbed her tea glass before it could fall. "He says Pastor Matt was fine when he left, talking about turning the other cheek, which sounds like something he would say because he always talked the holy talk, even though he didn't walk the walk."

"Iris—" Marian sounded like she was going to rebuke her, but she stopped. After a pause, she asked, "How do you know Cade isn't lying to you? That boy always did lead you around by your hormones. I was sure you'd come to me one day and tell me you were pregnant."

For one brief second, when Marian didn't launch into her about Pastor Matt, Iris had a spark of hope that her mother might have come to believe her. But, no. She just wanted to accuse her of screwing around with Cade. She forced herself to let go of the glass she was in danger of cracking, and to say in a falsely upbeat voice, "You didn't need to worry, Mom. Rubbers are cheap and easy to come by. Pastor Matt taught me that."

Marian flushed an ugly red, shoved her chair back and said, "Angel, hop down. It's time to go."

The girl blinked. "But I'm not done with my drawing, Nana. Can't we stay a few more minutes?"

"Is it respectful to argue with your elders?"

"I'm not arguing. I'm just asking."

"Get up. This. Minute."

The little girl burst into tears.

"She's over-tired," Iris said, signaling the server to bring a box for the remains of Angel's burger and fries. "We walked a lot at the zoo and it was hot. It's my fault. I'm sorry for—"

"It *is* your fault," Marian said, a tremor in her voice, whether of anger or something else, Iris couldn't tell.

Iris wasn't sure exactly what her mother was referring to, but she didn't take her up on it. "Come on, punkin," she said, lifting Angel down from the chair.

"My daddy calls me that," she said.

"My daddy called me that, too," Iris said, a lump in her throat. "I had fun today. Thanks for going to the zoo with me."

"You're my best aunt," Angel said, flinging her arms around Iris and giving her a hug. The solidity of the girl's warm body pressed against hers raised a lump in her throat. She stroked Angel's hair and thought how strange it was that she'd been hugged by girls twice in two days. She couldn't remember the last time she'd hugged a female, since Jane wasn't exactly the touchy-feely sort.

"You're her only aunt," Marian pointed out dourly. She took the girl's hand. "Let's go."

"The car's not locked—you can get Angel's booster."

Marian ignored her, pretending to listen to Angel chattering away at a mile a minute pace, presumably telling her all about the baby gorilla they'd seen, and the kestrel named Marty McFly who got weighed while they watched, and feeding budgies off a popsicle stick with a glob of seeds on the end. For a brief moment, Iris wondered what it would be like to have children, a family. *No point to thinking like that*, she told herself, paying the bill and ignoring the "Hey, baby" smile of an attractive man dining solo. *My biological clock must be winding down and I'm not mother material anyway.* Leaving a generous tip, she walked into the cool night alone.

# THIRTY-FIVE

### IRIS

RELUCTANT TO HOLE UP in her room, Iris dragged the desk chair out to the sidewalk to make phone calls after returning from the restaurant. The evening air was cool and clean; she pulled a sweatshirt on and curled one leg under her to keep warm. She tried Jane's numbers, both the gallery and her cell phone, but had to leave messages again. She twisted her mouth to the side as she hung up, wondering why Jane hadn't returned her last calls. It wasn't like her. She hoped nothing had happened to the cat and that Jane hadn't sequestered herself out of grief. That would be just like her, Iris thought, to refuse to burden her friends with her pain. The thought of a world without Edgar made her sad. She hesitated for a moment and then dialed Lassie's number. When he answered, she asked him to check on Jane.

"You worry too much," he said.

"She's not getting any younger," Iris pointed out, "and she doesn't have anyone there if—."

"If home invaders should break in, or a serial killer," he said, making fun of her fears.

She didn't bother to tell him she was more worried about Jane taking a tumble and not being able to reach a phone. She could hear concern under his flippant words.

"I'll drop by," Lassie promised. "You doing okay?"

"Just ducky. Never better," she said.

"Liar. Come back soon, will ya? We miss your smiling face at the pub. Greg's pining."

She snorted a laugh, surprised by how much it pleased her that Greg was apparently thinking about her. "I thought you didn't want me hooking up with him."

"He's a big boy," Lassie admitted.

She disconnected and dialed again, getting Cade's voicemail. After leaving a message asking him to call her, she snapped the phone shut and tapped it on the chair's arm. Damn. The parole board hearing was days away; she was running out of time. What more could she do to discover the truth? Short of a séance to contact Glynnis Brozek to find out what really happened that night, she was out of options unless or until Pastor Matt awoke again and his brain worked its way around to disgorging who attacked him. If that ever happened, it was likely to be too late to help her father.

Thinking of Mrs. Brozek brought Iris's brows together. Was it possible that Mrs. Brozek had beaten her husband and then died of a heart attack from the exertion? Maybe Mrs. Brozek knew what Iris knew about Pastor Matt: that he liked young girls. Could something have caused her to snap that night and take a poker to her husband? Had she tired of being the properly submissive pastor's wife, or had guilt at her complicity finally driven her over the edge? Iris bit her lip. Maybe she hadn't been complicit all along, but had learned something that night that drove her to kill her husband.

Iris's excitement about the idea subsided as quickly as it had come. She'd better hope Glynnis Brozek wasn't the guilty party, because if she was, Iris would never get her dad out of prison. There was no proof, and no judge was going to overturn the conviction based on Iris's convenient and completely unprovable theory. A car ground its way up the gravel driveway. She looked up. An old sedan pulled in beside her rental and Jolene got out, slamming the door. Hard.

Iris's instinctive reaction was pleasure, but then she remembered how they had parted, and set her face in a neutral expression. Jolene strode straight toward Iris, skirt flapping around her calves, and stopped three feet away. She planted herself, arms akimbo, and glared at Iris.

"Did you sleep with my son?"

*Oh, damn.* Iris's stomach lurched. "Did he tell you that?" she asked, looking across to the Welshes' house to see if Jolene's arrival had drawn them out. No one emerged; Iris's guilt must have made Jolene's words sound louder than they were.

"Not in so many words. He called to say that you'd been arrested for trying to kill Zach's father—"

"I wasn't arrested. The police only wanted—"

"—and when I asked him how he knew that, he hemmed and hawed and said he was here with you. In your room. Early yesterday morning. Did he spend the night?"

"No," Iris answered. The literal truth was a dodge, she knew.

For the first time, Jolene's face lightened, and she sounded uncertain. Her arms relaxed to her sides. "Oh, I thought—" She gave an embarrassed laugh. "I'm sorry. I—"

Momentarily tempted to let Jolene apologize and avoid the scene, Iris couldn't do it. She blew air through her lips and said, "I did sleep with him. Not last night, but the night before. He was here yesterday for breakfast because I wanted to apologize for … for taking it all too casually. It's a bad habit."

Jolene seemed to be standing still, but Iris could see tiny vibrations in her hands and jaw. "You could be his mother," she finally said. "It's obscene." The car's engine ticked as it cooled behind her.

"He's twenty-three—an adult."

"Did you do it to hurt me, to get back at me?" Jolene lifted her chin to look straight into Iris's eyes. "Is that it?"

"Don't be ridic—" Iris cut herself off and squared her shoulders. "Maybe partly." The relief of admitting it turned quickly to regret as Jolene looked at her with loathing.

"It makes me sick to think of it … you stalking my boy, getting him drunk, seducing him into your bed."

"It wasn't like—"

Jolene clapped her hands over her ears. "I don't want the details. This is hard enough."

"I wasn't going to tell you—" Exasperated, Iris cut herself off. She stood, prickles stabbing the foot she'd had tucked beneath her. "I'm sorry," she said, facing Jolene.

Her apology was apparently unexpected, because Jolene opened her mouth but then shut it again. "I'm sorry for Aaron and I'm sorry for disappearing on you twenty-three years ago. I'm not sorry I left Lone Pine, but I should have let you know I was going, should have kept in touch."

She *was* sorry, she realized. Sorry for things she couldn't even articulate. After Jolene's revelation at the school, she'd thought she hated her, but she couldn't seem to grab hold of that anger anymore. Part of her still thought Jolene should have spoken up back then, but it wasn't like she'd been a beacon of honesty and openness, either. She hadn't told Jolene about Pastor Matt, hadn't told anyone until it was too late for Gabby. She'd been so caught up in her own turmoil that she hadn't even noticed that Jolene was in love with Zach, that she was pregnant. *I don't have the moral high ground. Maybe there is no such thing, or not in a friendship anyway.*

Iris cleared her throat. "I don't have a lot of friends, Jolene, and meeting you again has made me realize that maybe it's because I'm not a very good friend."

Jolene collapsed onto the hood of her car. "Aaron might be twenty-three, but he's young for his age." When Iris didn't respond, she gave a strangled laugh, "I don't suppose he'd be happy to know I was here, having this conversation with you. I shouldn't have come. It's none of my business. He's an adult—I know he's an adult—but I still see him crouched over his Legos when he was three, tongue poking out of the corner of his mouth, or coming out of the bathroom when he was fifteen, little pieces of toilet paper stuck to his face after his first attempt at shaving. He's … he's … it's hard to let go." She expelled the last words on a rush of air.

"I won't tell him."

"Are you and he—? Will you—?"

"No."

"Thank God."

"What? You don't want to be my mother-in-law?" Iris smiled at Jolene's almost palpable relief that there wasn't going to be an ongoing relationship.

"No. I want to be you." Jolene half-whispered the words, but Iris caught them.

"What?"

Jolene flapped her hand, clearly embarrassed. "Oh, I don't want to *be* you—I just want your life. No, not even that. I just want to be more than a wife and a mother." She twisted an engraved silver bangle round and round her wrist.

"You're a teacher," Iris offered, unsure what to say.

Waving her hand again, Jolene dismissed her career. "I fell into that because it meshed well with the whole wife and mother thing. I could teach—a job Zach approved of, by the way—and still be home for the kids after school. I don't usually *dislike* teaching, and there are moments when I like it, but it feels like something I *do*, not who I *am*. I know I'm not making any sense."

"No, you are," Iris said. "Making jewelry is more than what I do. It took me a long time to realize I had to be an artist—art doesn't pay well usually, especially at first, and I had to live—and longer still to discover that rocks and metal were my medium, but I'm at peace when I'm working on a design. It's where I get my joy. If I still believed in God, I'd say it's why he put me on this earth." *But now my gift is gone.* Her hands ached to work with metal again and she curled her fingers in.

"I need that," Jolene whispered. "Rachel's going to be gone in a year, and I don't kid myself that she's ever going to settle in Lone Pine, maybe not in Colorado—and then what will I have? If I'm not 'mom,' who am I?"

Iris bit back the platitudes about Jolene still being mom and wife and friend. "It's never too late to find out," she said.

"Yeah, well." Jolene stood, dusting off her skirt. "I'm a little long in the tooth for Broadway."

"Oh, I don't know. Maybe they're casting a revival of *Arsenic and Old Lace* or *Driving Miss Daisy*."

Jolene giggled, suddenly sounding very much like the sixteen-year-old Iris had known. The sound seemed to surprise her because her eyes got big, but then she let the giggles come until she was laughing uncontrollably. Iris joined her and pretended not to notice when her friend's laughs turned to sobs. After a moment, she joined her on the hood of the car, the metal groaning at her weight, and put an awkward arm around Jolene's shoulders. When Jolene stopped crying long minutes later, Iris edged away, embarrassed, and asked, "What's it like having Esther as a sister-in-law?"

"Oh, my." Jolene choked out a sound between a laugh and a groan. "That woman has been my cross to bear." She started talking, describing Esther's attempts to stop Zach from marrying her, and then moved on by stages to describing her life in Lone Pine, having children, and her recent unsettled feelings that she wasn't living her life so much as letting it zoom past un-noticed. Iris took over when Jolene's voice grew tired, relating some of her experiences before she washed up in Portland, and telling her about Jane and Edgar.

"You never married?"

"Never found the right man, I guess," Iris said. *Never let the right man, any man, get close enough.* "Went out of my way, in fact, to hang out with men who thought marriage was something for the far distant future, like colonoscopies and prostate trouble."

Her words brought them dangerously near the subject of Aaron and they fell silent. Full dark cloaked the courtyard and the light bulbs over each motel room door attracted moths who hurled themselves ineffectually at the frosted glass domes. The large family straggled out of their room in the other wing and piled into their car, probably going off in search of dinner. A bat swooped past, close enough to make Iris duck.

"Zach will be worried about me," Jolene said finally, walking around to the driver's door. She paused before opening it. "It's good to have you around again, Iris."

"Not everyone seems to think so." Knowing she was holding Jolene up, Iris gave her a quick version of the vandalism to her car and destruction of her room.

"That's awful! Have the police found—"

"Nothing."

"Who do you think did it?"

"Someone from the Community. Someone who doesn't want me to clear my dad's name, I'd guess."

"Is that why you asked about Esther?" Jolene asked with the quickness Iris remembered so well. Not waiting for an answer, she continued, "I can't see Esther prowling around the parking lot in the middle of the night with a can of spray paint, but she might well have incited someone to do her dirty work for her. She wields a lot of power in the Community, by virtue of being a Brozek and the senior elder. A remark from her might have goosed someone into trying to scare you away, like Henry II and Thomas à Becket."

Iris gave her a blank look.

"You know, 'Who will rid me of this pesky cardinal?' or whatever the king said to get someone to assassinate Becket in the cathedral."

"Cheery thought."

"Oh, I can't think anyone in the Community would go so far as trying to kill you," Jolene said, getting in the car.

Iris's only response was a wave as Jolene reversed the car, but she couldn't help thinking about the movement she was almost certain she'd seen on the canyon rim before the boulder broke loose.

# THIRTY-SIX

**JOLENE**

ZACH DIDN'T ASK WHERE Jolene had been when she arrived home, hours later than usual, bringing a King Sooper's deli chicken and sides for dinner. He sat on the loveseat near the gas fireplace, apparently engrossed in a book on Paul's biblical letters. He didn't look up, even when she let the deli bag plop noisily to the counter and rattled the glasses setting the table. Fine. If he was so uninterested in her admittedly uninteresting life, she wasn't going to volunteer an explanation of what she'd been doing. Come to think of it, she didn't want him to know that Aaron had slept with Iris, anyway. She wasn't sure who he'd be most infuriated with, but couldn't stand for him to be angry with Aaron.

Warming the macaroni and cheese in the microwave, she *wang*ed the door shut with extra energy when she removed the dish. It struck her then, with Rachel's fate in regards to her thefts undecided, that it was a bad time to engage in silence one-upmanship with Zach. She came to the archway that separated the kitchen from the living room and hesitated. A lamp cast a gentle glow on her husband, making his hair seem blonder and diminishing the lines in his face. Despite that, he looked as worn out as she felt. Maybe it was the way his shoulders slumped forward, as if he were carrying a heavy weight.

When Zach still didn't look up, she asked in a low voice, assuming Rachel was upstairs, "Did you meet with the elders? About Rachel?"

His head came up then and he looked at her levelly. "Yes."

"Was Esther there?"

"She is the senior elder."

"What did you decide?" Jolene tried to keep all worry and judgment out of her voice, but she twined her fingers together tightly.

"I'm not prepared to discuss that now," said Zach, snapping his book closed. "There will be a special Community meeting tomorrow evening at five. Everyone will gather in the church." He clicked off the lamp and asked, "Is dinner finally ready?"

"But Rachel . . . You're not going to insist on the reckoning stones, are you? You didn't let Esther—"

Zach spoke sternly. "My sister is a godly woman who cares about the Community and its people. Look how she cared for my father all those years, and is prepared to care for him again. You would do well to emulate her, rather than casting aspersions on her. We need to tell her we're willing to spare her the burden this time around. We'll put him in Aaron's room."

His pronouncement struck Jolene with the force of a fall from a galloping horse. Even though he'd brought up the idea earlier, she'd assumed that Matthew would go back to the nursing home now that he had returned to a comatose state. She couldn't have him in the house. Before she recovered herself enough to object, Zach was calling up the stairs. "Rachel. Come down for dinner, please."

After dinner, eaten in near silence, Zach circumvented Jolene's plan to talk to him by placing his utensils on his plate and saying,

"You'll have to excuse me. I need to work on my sermon." He disappeared into his small study and closed the door firmly.

Rachel, scraping chicken bones into the trash, cut her eyes toward her mother. In a whisper, she asked, "Do you know what—"

Jolene shrugged helplessly. She felt impotent, unable to protect her daughter if she didn't know what was coming, and unwilling to vilify her husband, even in her mind. He would do what was right and just, she told herself, shooing Rachel upstairs and doing the dishes herself so she could have some time alone. A lemony scent drifted up from the dish soap as she squirted it into the sink. Despite the stony front he'd displayed the last couple of days, he was a loving man, a compassionate man. He spent hours each week reading to Mrs. Dorfmann or conversing with other lonely shut-ins. He had done all the cooking and cleaning for weeks after she lost the son between Aaron and Rachel midway through the pregnancy.

And Zach loved Rachel. She smiled faintly at the memory of him on all fours in the living room, letting Rachel pretend he was a unicorn and she a fairy princess. He'd tried to talk her into playing Ruth or Mary on a donkey instead, but agreed to be a unicorn when she insisted. Looking up quickly, Jolene caught a glimpse of a sadly smiling face in the sink window and dropped a spoon, thinking someone was staring in at her. After a confused half-second, she realized the face was hers.

Hastily wiping her soapy hands on a dishcloth, Jolene crossed the living room to the door of Zach's study and leaned her head against it silently. She stood there, the cool solidity of the wood pressing against her forehead. "I love you," she said softly.

She waited a beat, and when there was only silence, she stroked her hand down the door and returned to the kitchen.

# THIRTY-SEVEN

### JOLENE

FIVE O'CLOCK FRIDAY CAME too soon for Jolene's comfort. She'd been distracted all day by thoughts of the upcoming meeting and had not given her students the attention they deserved. Now, getting ready to walk over to the church, to gather with the Community, her stomach felt hollow and she dreaded that Zach would condemn their daughter from the pulpit, would announce that she must be punished with the reckoning stones.

Rachel emerged from the bathroom wearing a defiant expression, a white denim skirt that didn't quite reach her knees, and a peach cami and turquoise tank top, each thinner than a Bible page. "Might as well be hanged for a sheep as a lamb," she announced before Jolene could object, and stalked out of the house, head held high.

Caught between admiring her daughter's chutzpah and wanting to strangle her, Jolene sighed and followed her down the road to the church. The sun sat above Pikes Peak, an hour from sliding behind it due to daylight saving time, casting long shadows across the greening ground. As they neared the church, mingling with other

Community members making their way to the meeting, Rachel slowed, waiting for Jolene. When Jolene reached her, she slipped her cold fingers into her mother's hand. Jolene squeezed her hand and gave her a reassuring smile.

They settled into their usual pew, about one-third of the way back from the altar on the left, greeting neighbors. Esther sat in her usual front row seat, facing straight ahead, and Marian Asher and Angel sat across the aisle. Jolene knelt and tried to pray, asking the Lord to calm her spirit, but found herself wondering, midway through the prayer, what kind of punishment Zach would mete out to Rachel. At exactly five o'clock by Jolene's watch, the five elders rose from their places around the church and walked to the front, arranging themselves in a tight semi-circle facing the gathering. Esther stood in the middle, the only woman, and Zach was on the left end. Jolene clenched her hands into fists and felt Rachel stiffen beside her.

Esther clicked on the microphone and a hum filled the church. The door creaked open. Rachel turned to look and whispered, "It's Iris. She's wearing jeans."

Of course she was. Jolene smiled to herself. Iris might come to the meeting, but she'd do it on her own terms. Jolene knew suddenly, with absolute clarity, what she had to do.

# THIRTY-EIGHT

## IRIS

IRIS SLID INTO THE last pew, close to the door and escape, wondering what the hell she was doing at the Community's meeting. Mrs. Welsh had mentioned it to her, hinting that it involved Rachel, so she'd decided to come. She spotted the backs of Jolene's and Rachel's heads and focused on Zach in his dark suit, looking solemn as he stood beside his sister, Quentin Welsh, Joseph Ulm and a man she didn't recognize. The all-powerful elders. She tensed. Her hand absently traced the grain of the smooth wood and the texture under her fingertips took her back to that last night when she'd stood alone in the front pew, facing the Community, her hands clutching the back of the pew for support.

Candles, not fading sunlight, had lit the church and all the adults of the Community sat in their pews, punishing her with their gazes. Her parents sat in the row behind, but she steadfastly refused to meet their eyes. Only her father's entreaties had persuaded her to submit to the ritual.

"It would kill your mother if we got asked to leave the Community," he'd said, face sagging, eyes red from lack of sleep. She'd heard her parents arguing well into the night.

"You want me to lie."

"Your mother—I—want you to say you're sorry. Can't you be sorry?"

Oh, yes, she could be sorry. She hadn't stopped being sorry she'd told the truth since the moment she blurted it out. She knew that wasn't how he meant the word, but their refusal to believe her was a raw wound. It didn't much matter what the rest of the Community thought since her own parents didn't believe her.

The rough burlap robe scratched her nakedness, but she was barely aware of that discomfort as Pastor Matt denounced her.

"Mercy Asher has sinned against God and this Community by bearing false witness," he intoned. "She has told lies—ugly, vicious lies—that would rend the fabric that holds this Community together. Prompted by Satan, she alleged that I"—he laid a hand on his chest—"had unclean knowledge of her body, that I committed adultery against my wife." He gestured toward Glynnis, small and still as a mouse between Esther and Zach in the pew across from Mercy's. Mercy looked at the woman, but could read nothing on her face, veiled by the dimness. She returned her gaze to her hands where they clutched the pew back. The bones stood out strongly, highlighted by the candle flickering in the pew end holder. A small, perfectly round mole sat below the last knuckle on her right hand.

A gasp and angry mutterings rose from the congregation. "You know me better than that," Pastor Matt said. "You know me for a moral man, an upright man, dedicated to my God, my family, and this Community. I have been your leader for two decades now and I have never felt such sorrow as I do now." He bowed his head.

Mercy felt rather than saw the scornful, disappointed, and furious looks thrown her way. She raised her gaze from her hands and fixed it on the door. They would lead her through that door when Pastor Matt was done, and into the woods, to wherever they'd led Mr. Carpenter that winter night when she was eight. She tried not to imagine what would happen there. At least it wasn't snowing.

"Her parents have righteously turned her over to the Community's justice and mercy and submitted her for the ritual of the reckoning stones," Pastor Matt continued. Nods and agreement burbled from the congregation and Mercy hated them all. Every one. Well, except Jolene. Her eyes went to Jolene where she stood with her parents. In the gloom, she couldn't see her eyes, but thought she saw the gleam of tears on her cheeks. Jolene faced her for a moment, but then looked away.

Pastor Matt continued to say ugly things about her, to bemoan her wickedness, to talk about how pained and hurt he was by her lies. He talked about the yeast of sin leavening the whole loaf and she imagined them all trapped in bread dough, expanding, puffing out, and then falling back on themselves in a gluey mess. Her father made a sound and her gaze flitted to him, mere feet away. He tried to give her an encouraging smile, but it was a mere twitch of his lips and she couldn't bear to see the grief drawn into the lines of his face. The odor of smoke and hot wax clogged her nostrils as a candle guttered.

"The apostle Paul exhorts us to expel the wicked one from among us. 'When you are assembled in the name of our Lord Jesus and I am with you in spirit, and the power of our Lord Jesus is present, hand this man over to Satan, so that the sinful nature may be destroyed and his spirit saved on the day of the Lord,' he tells us in Corinthians. But this sinner is repentant and we may have mercy upon her. She is prepared, her parents say, to confess her lies publicly to this Community, and beg forgiveness from God and us."

He paused and bent an expectant look on Mercy. She swallowed hard and whispered something.

"You must proclaim your sin and repentance, Mercy."

Still looking down, Mercy said in a hoarse voice, "I sinned. I repent." She could feel his gaze upon her, working its way into her like his fingers had probed the slick, secret parts of her. She forced herself to continue, her throat so dry she coughed, "I am truly sorry and ask God's forgiveness for my sins."

For a moment, she thought Pastor Matt would try to force her to say more, to say she'd lied, to beg his forgiveness personally, but he seemed to think better of it. "I forgive you," he said, laying a heavy hand on her shoulder.

Mercy flinched away from him, from the hot weight of his hand pressing the ropy weave into her skin, wanting to yell that she didn't forgive *him*, that she'd never forgive him. His grip tightened.

"We will continue the ritual outside," Pastor Matt said, his hand propelling Mercy out of the pew and down the aisle. Two candle-bearers preceded them. Her feet felt heavy, larger than normal, and she stumbled. Recovering her balance without looking up, she hastened her step until she was on the heels of the acolytes, desperate to reach the now open doors and leave the smoky, close air of the church behind. It was a clear spring night with cool air verging toward chilly now that the sun was fully down. A breeze soughed through the pine boughs and filtered through the loose weave of her penitential robe, raising goose bumps. Her bare toes tried to burrow into the loose dirt as rustlings and footsteps told her the whole congregation had assembled behind her. Her gaze went to the spot where she had clung to the church's foundation almost a decade earlier, watching big-eyed as Pastor Matt led the snaking line of Community members into the woods. She almost expected to see a little girl there, watching, but there was no one.

Now, he lifted a candle high and they all followed him toward the narrow gap in the trees. The press of people herded Mercy along, keeping her just behind Pastor Matt as the path trended uphill. Pine needles and twigs pricked her feet. Bushy pine boughs and the thin pale arcs of aspen limbs, still unleafed, tangled overhead, denying the moonlight. Night creatures probably scurried and dug in the underbrush, but the tramp of dozens of feet drowned out their noises.

Mercy had no way to keep track of time, but she didn't think they'd gone too far—less than a mile, certainly—when they entered a small clearing. Ringed by trees in a rough oval, it was no bigger than the inside of the church. Pastor Matt led her to the clearing's center and, as people filed into the area and dispersed in a loose ring around her, she saw the three cairns and shivered. They stood knee-high, piles of rocks and shadows. Alien. The Community members clustered near them. She saw Noah reach for a stone and then exchange it for another, apparently not liking the feel or heft of the first one. Her eyes fixed on the nearest heap and she saw the stones were small, the size of grapes, maybe, and she remembered what her father had whispered as they made their way toward the church earlier that evening. "You'll be okay, Mercy," he'd said as her mother strode ahead. "It's about punishment, not hurting. I wouldn't let them really hurt you."

His words provided small comfort as he and her mother approached. Without looking Mercy in the face, they bent and lifted the hem of her robe. Rising as one, they pulled it up and over her head so she stood naked in the darkened clearing. She braced one arm over her breasts and her other hand went automatically to cover the soft triangle between her legs. Tears started to her eyes then as she felt the Community's gaze upon her. Her brother's. Her schoolmates'. Pastor Matt's. She was grateful for the darkness and was startled when the first stone struck her cheek.

It stung. It was followed by others as the dark, anonymous figures bent and straightened, flinging the pebbles at her with varying degrees of force. They peppered her buttocks and thighs, her arms and back and face. One clicked off her teeth. She gripped her lips together and shut her eyes tightly. A few landed hard enough to bruise and one or two had jagged edges that cut her skin. She hunched her shoulders in. She suddenly knew with fierce clarity why they only conducted this ritual at night. It wasn't to keep them from more clearly seeing the sinner being stoned, to preserve her modesty, but to keep them from seeing each other. Her eyes flew open with the realization.

She kept her eyes open and began to turn slowly, wanting them to know that she saw them. As she made eye contact with Noah, he slowly let the stone he held dribble from his fingers. Her eyes locked on her next-door neighbor and her Sunday school teacher. She thought she could make out a couple of classmates toward the back, and Mr. Welsh, whose daughter lay buried in the rockslide somewhere. Pastor Matt. Only Jolene stood apart, hands clasped behind her back, shaking her head back and forth as if saying "No" over and over again.

As Mercy turned, intent on letting each person know she saw him or her—*she saw them all*—the rock rain tapered off until one last stone landed short. Her breaths sounded labored in the sudden silence and she worked to breathe more shallowly. Without any conversation, the mob started to fade away, disappearing by ones and twos down the path or fading into the trees behind the clearing. Mercy turned, faster now, and saw she was alone. Even Pastor Matt had sneaked away without her seeing him go. She shivered. Spotting the robe in a crumpled heap, she hurried toward it, bruising her feet on the litter of stones surrounding her, and slipped it on. She welcomed its nubbiness and warmth now, even though the rough fabric rasped her welted and cut skin.

She wasn't injured—not go-to-the-hospital hurt—but a couple of cuts stung and her fingers touched a bruise on her temple. She was desperately thirsty and wanted to plunge downhill in search of water, but she didn't want to encounter anyone. She made herself wait. Once she was sure they were all gone, that she wouldn't run into any of them, she started back down the path. Humiliation hardened into resolve as she limped toward Lone Pine. She would return to her house now—she refused to think of it as "home" any longer—because she couldn't run away dressed in a burlap sack, with no money or clothes. But as soon as she had gathered together what she needed, she was leaving the Community. Tomorrow. Tomorrow she would go.

———

The microphone's squeal brought Iris back to herself and she looked around the sanctuary, intent on staying in the here and now. She focused on the pimple on the beefy neck in front of her, the way a sliver of light knifed through the crack where the doors came together and pointed up the aisle … anything to keep the memories of that night at bay.

# THIRTY-NINE

### JOLENE

Jolene couldn't rid herself of the notion that Esther was reveling in this moment. Her blond hair gleamed, roots newly touched up, contrasting with the cowl-necked black tunic she wore. It flowed over her elephantine bulk, hiding the individual ripples and bulges of fat, but not her immensity. For some reason, maybe the sight of Esther holding the microphone, a memory of Esther singing in church, her pure soprano floating to the rafters, evoking the voices of angels, came to Jolene and she realized she hadn't heard Esther sing in decades, not since.... Did the layers of fat weigh her down so she couldn't lift up her voice in song, Jolene wondered, or had she lost her desire to sing and turned to food for comfort? Chicken or egg?

Before Jolene could puzzle it through, Esther brought the microphone close to her red lips and said, "Thank you for taking time out of your evening to gather with us this evening. You have entrusted the elders and Pastor Zachary with the spiritual guidance of this Community. In that role, we must sometimes discipline members whose sinfulness threatens to undermine the way of life the Lord commands us to follow. We stand before you, sorrowfully, to pronounce judgment on one such sinner today." She paused. Her blue gaze briefly lighted on Jolene and then landed on Rachel. "Rachel Brozek, stand up."

Jolene could feel the slight tremors shaking her daughter's body as she stood. The congregation murmured and rustled. Jolene sensed uneasiness spiked with prurient excitement. The man on Rachel's far side edged away slightly. Jolene glared at him.

"Rachel Brozek," Esther intoned, taking a step closer to her niece. "You have confessed to stealing, to breaking one of our Lord's ten commandments."

Rachel's chin came up a notch, but otherwise she stood totally still.

"The elders have met, and even though we agree it is a sign of mercy that you have confessed your sin, we condemn that sin and command you to submit to the discipline of—"

Jolene stood. "I want to confess a sin to all of you."

Rachel turned, mouth slightly open, to stare at her. Jolene looked each of the elders square in the face, letting her gaze linger on Zach, and then turned her back on them. Facing the congregation and Iris, she said, "Twenty-three years ago, my father-in-law stood right there"—she pointed to Esther—"and shamed my best friend. He sentenced her to the discipline—No, let's call it what it is—the *punishment*—of the reckoning stones. Many of you remember that night." She let her gaze travel over the individuals seated in the church, some of whom averted their eyes or looked self-conscious. One woman turned so pale Jolene thought she might faint. "That night has haunted me for a quarter of a century," Jolene said, "because I could have stopped what happened, and I didn't."

She took a deep breath that sounded like a gulp. Jolene met Iris's eyes and felt strength—and maybe forgiveness?—flowing from her friend. "Pastor Matt made Mercy confess to lying. He made her say he hadn't molested her, and then we all walked behind her into the woods and stoned her." Total silence reigned in the church. "I could have told everyone that she wasn't lying, but I didn't. I let my friend suffer in unimaginable ways because I wasn't brave enough, or strong enough to do what I'm doing today: stand up in church and tell the truth.

"Mercy wasn't lying. Pastor Matt was. He molested Mercy. I saw them together. Naked. Having sex."

"You evil, lying—" Esther started, the words sputtering through the microphone.

"Jolene! That's not possible." Zach's voice. Jolene didn't look at him.

Now that the words were out, she felt limp. "I'm sorry, Iris," she said to her friend, who had left her pew and now had one hand on the door. "I'm so very, very sorry I wasn't brave enough for you." *Don't go*, she pleaded with her eyes. *Don't hate me*. She didn't think she could stand it if Iris hated her, even though she didn't deserve her friendship. Hadn't deserved it for twenty-three years.

Iris's face seemed to soften and she met Jolene's eyes for a long moment. Then, she turned her back on the congregation and pushed through the door, letting in a last blast of sunlight bright as a trumpet call.

Jolene's shoulders slumped, but then she straightened them again. She turned around to face the elders, "So, if you're determined to pass judgment on my daughter, you'd better do the same to me."

Murmurs bubbled around her, people whispering and wondering, condemning and second-guessing. Old friends avoided looking at her, inspecting her surreptitiously from the corners of their eyes or from under their lashes. *I haven't grown a second head*, she wanted to tell them, *or sprouted horns*. Maybe she should have followed Iris.

Rachel took Jolene's hand and gave it a gentle squeeze. "You're the bravest person I know," she whispered.

Surprised and touched, Jolene looked at her daughter, but Rachel had withdrawn her hand and was apparently lost in contemplation of her cuticles as she used her thumbnail to nudge at one. Jolene let herself feel a little bit better. She had done what she needed to do—confessed her sin of omission. She'd kept quiet all those years ago for fear Zach would hate her if she accused his father of something so vile, for fear the Brozeks would keep Zach from marrying her and her baby would be a bastard. Now, she met Zach's eyes, searching desperately for reassurance. *Do you still love me?* He looked stunned.

Esther attempted to regain control. "As to the matter we are here to—"

A voice quavered from the back. "I, too, want to confess."

Jolene turned to see Mrs. Dorfmann standing, hands clutching the pew back, her sightless eyes seemingly fixed on the window beside the pulpit. "I always disliked my daughter-in-law. I spoke badly of her to my son, and undermined their marriage. I sinned against both of them and I am sorry." Her neighbor steadied her with a hand to her elbow, and Mrs. Dorfmann sat.

"This isn't—" Esther began. Red flushed the tops of her cheeks and mottled her neck.

A man stood across the aisle from Jolene, looking determined. Jack Phillips, who owned an appliance repair business. "I've cheated my customers for years, talking them into purchases and repairs that weren't really necessary." Tears streamed down his face. "I ask your forgiveness, and theirs, and promise to try and make restitution."

"Jack!" His wife gaped at him. Jolene knew her well enough to suspect that she was more upset at the thought of her husband giving money away than she was about his sketchy business practices.

Two other people stood and confessed, one widower admitting to an affair before his wife died, and a woman Jolene knew slightly acknowledging that she was an alcoholic. Jolene thought Marian Asher made a move as if to rise, but she settled back against the pew, pressing into it as if nailed to it. Despite the pain of the confessions, a bubble of peace grew around Jolene. These people were standing with her and Rachel, building a human wall between Rachel and the reckoning stones, stripping themselves naked and daring the elders to stone them. Her throat tightened and her eyes brimmed with tears of gratitude. She sat, pulling Rachel down with her.

Zach stepped forward and removed the microphone from Esther's grip. For a moment it seemed she would wrestle him for it, but then she released it and stepped aside, her lips thinned and her eyes burning with fury. Jolene unconsciously raised her clenched hands to her lips. Would her husband support her or condemn her? She realized she wasn't sure, and marveled how you could be married to someone for twenty-three years, sharing all the conversations and intimacies that implied, and not know.

An expectant hush fell over the congregation. It seemed as if everyone leaned forward.

Zach cleared his throat. "Let us pray together the prayer our savior, Jesus Christ, taught us. 'Our Father …'"

As Jolene prayed the familiar words, her mind raced, worrying about Zach's reaction and whether she'd irreparably damaged her marriage with her impromptu and belated confession. It wasn't until they reached the phrase "forgive us our debts as we forgive our debtors," that tears streamed down her face. It seemed that Zach and everyone in the congregation put extra emphasis on those words.

Peace welled within her, as if the outflow of tears had made room for it, and she finished the prayer silently in her head, unable to make her lips form the words.

# FORTY

## IRIS

Outside the sanctuary, Iris drew in two deep breaths and tried to sort through her emotions. Across the church lawn, two squirrels zipped round and round a tree trunk in the gathering dusk, chittering, and she felt like they were inside her head. Anger and regret spiraled inside her. Her cell phone buzzed in her pocket, but she ignored it. On one level, she could appreciate Jolene confessing her lie of omission in front of everyone, exonerating her, but it was too damned late. She should have spoken up at the time.

Even as the thought darkened her mind, she put herself in Jolene's place and could understand how hard it would have been for her to speak up. Hell, if she herself hadn't been worried about Gabby Ulm, she might never have spoken up either. Needing a physical release, Iris headed into the woods as the uppermost branches clung to the last bits of sunlight, following the near-invisible path she'd walked barefoot so long ago. Semi-wishing she could punch someone, and regretting her celibacy resolution, she banged branches out of her way with a downward slash of her arm and hiked quickly, relishing the burn in her thigh muscles.

She reached the clearing in ten minutes, a little surprised by how close it was. It had seemed farther in the dark. New spring grass poked up and Iris scuffed aside the duff to give the little blades more light and look for the stones. There were no ghosts lurking in the clearing, and no stones, either. She swept her foot from side to side, dislodging layers of decayed leaves and plenty of acorns, but only a single quartzite rock the size of a crabapple. She picked it up, smoothed it with her thumb, and put it in her pocket. She wondered who had been responsible for collecting the reckoning stones and carting them to the clearing. She had trouble seeing Pastor Matt trundling them up the path in a wheelbarrow. They'd been stacked neatly in their three little cairns, not dumped haphazardly. Maybe her neatnik mother had arranged them.

Iris half-laughed at the thought, surprised that it didn't bother her. It didn't really matter how the stones had gotten there. She realized, suddenly, that she hadn't seen her parents after they removed her robe. They hadn't thrown stones at her, although she had a clear vision of her brother lobbing at least one. All these years and that realization had never struck her. She wondered at it. Did it make a difference?

Before she'd arrived at any conclusion, her phone buzzed again. Willing now to be distracted from her thoughts, Iris glanced at the display. Lassie.

"Jane fell, but she's all right now," he said in answer to her "Hello." "You probably saved her life by making me go over there."

Iris's head buzzed and she had trouble making sense of his words. She had to ask Lassie to repeat himself a couple of times before she fully grasped that Jane had fallen and broken her hip and not been found for at least a day and a half. She was in intensive care.

"I'll be there tonight some time," Iris said, already striding out of the clearing. "Tell her to hang on."

"She's right here," Lassie said. "Tell her yourself."

"Jane?"

"Edgar saved my life," Jane said, her voice breathy. Iris's hand tightened on the phone. "He curled up with me on the bathroom floor and helped me stay warm."

"Useless feline. I'll teach him to dial 911 as soon as I get there," Iris said, stumbling on a root.

Jane's laugh, though weak, reassured her somewhat. "Don't rush back on my account. Lassie and Karen are here and my son's on his way. A little surgery in the morning will fix me up right as rain. I'll be here when you've finished what you set out to do."

"But—" The urge to go to Jane, who felt more like her family, like a mother, than her blood relatives did, was strong.

"Your father only has you."

Sensing Jane's exhaustion and pain, Iris promised she'd do as she asked, and hung up. Before she could think about it, she said a prayer of thanks that Jane had been found in time and prayed that the surgery would go well so Jane could resume her normal life. The realization that she was praying made Iris fidget with embarrassment, and she walked faster, resisting the urge to tell God not to get used to hearing from her.

Dust had gentled into night when she emerged onto the church lawn. The meeting had apparently broken up. The last stragglers were making their way down Center Street and a car pulled out of the lot with a clang of loose muffler. Her rental was the only car left. She made her way toward it in the near dark, chilled and tired and cranky from the maelstrom of emotions she'd experienced in the past hour, including her worry about Jane, her doubt that she'd be able to engineer her father's freedom, and her confusion about Jolene.

She should seek out Jolene and acknowledge what she'd done today, but she didn't know what she'd say. Iris fingered her necklace. Her feelings about Jolene were all twisted up in her feelings about the stoning and she couldn't separate them instantaneously. They were like two delicate chains that had tangled at the bottom of a jewelry box. They need to be coaxed apart, separated link by link with a fine needle and a steady hand. She didn't have the time or energy to take on the task now. Opening the car's back door, she searched for the sweatshirt she thought she'd tossed there, unwilling to acknowledge that part of the reason she didn't want to find Jolene was because she was embarrassed by what Jolene might have seen.

Early on, Iris had met Pastor Matt with her gut twisting with anticipation, guilt, and fear. She'd felt a weird sort of power when his eyes lit with that greedy look when she unbuttoned her blouse, and it awed her that the most respected and beloved man in the Community was in love with her. She became more and more reluctant to meet him as time passed and the full horror of what they were doing worked on her conscience. By the end, it was only his threats that made her give him her body reluctantly and mechanically. Had Jolene seen the infatuated Mercy, or the reluctant Mercy? Iris cringed to think it might have been the former.

Her hand closed over the sweatshirt, inexplicably on the floor, and she pulled it out. As she did, something red tumbled to the ground. Stooping to fish the item out from under the car, Iris recognized Angel's little Tweety Bird pocketbook, the one she'd had with her on their zoo adventure. A photo and a change purse lay beside it and Iris slid the change purse back into the bag, and glanced at the photograph. It showed a dark-haired man with a military haircut, his arm around a curly-haired, olive-skinned woman with a wide smile. *Noah and his wife*, Iris thought, studying her brother's attractive face. She'd seen a photo of him somewhere else recently. She frowned, trying to remember, and when the memory came, it hit her with enough force to loosen her grip. The picture fluttered to the ground.

# FORTY-ONE

**JOLENE**

JOLENE LINGERED IN THE church after the service, unwilling to face everyone outside. She prayed for guidance, for patience, and for a calm spirit to replace the roiling one within that made her doubt her worth and the choices she'd made the past twenty-three years. Exhausted, she shifted off the kneeler and closed it with a clunk, and then sat in the pew until Zach came to find her. She didn't know how long it had been, but she couldn't hear voices from outside anymore, so the Community must have dispersed.

Zach had a heavy tread and she heard him approach, even down the carpeted aisle. He halted beside her pew and she could feel him looking down at her, and hear his exhalations. She shifted to her left in silent invitation and he sat beside her. She stole a glance at him. His face was somber and his shoulders sagged. Probably from carrying the weight of everyone's problems on them ... and she had added to his burden with her outspokenness and her unwillingness to any longer fill the role of pastor's wife the way she always had.

"I'm so sorry, Zach." She couldn't begin to list all the things she was sorry for—proclaiming his father a child molester was the least of them—but she knew that's what he thought she meant.

He didn't acknowledge her apology. "You mock me and my family in God's house," he said, anger and sorrow twining in his voice. "You accuse my father of unspeakable acts. You make a mockery of our one-ness, and hold me up for ridicule in front of my congregation."

"God's congregation." Jolene bit her lip. "I wasn't mock—"

"What congregation will follow a pastor who has no control in his own house, whose daughter steals, and whose wife—" He cut himself off.

"Whose wife what? Tells the truth? If anyone wants to condemn me, it should be for my years of silence, not for my honesty. I was not going to let Esther, you, me do to Rachel what we did to Iris. I wronged her, we all wronged her—"

"I never wronged her."

"You threw stones."

The flat accusation in her voice silenced him. He stared straight ahead, not looking at her. She didn't know if he saw the altar and the cross, or if he was looking inward. She put a hand on his thigh and the muscles flexed beneath her palm. He cleared his throat. "My father. Why didn't you tell me the truth?"

"I wanted to spare you. With Iris gone, and your father like he was, it didn't seem kind or necessary to make you see ... that side of him."

"He did a lot of good in this Community. He helped a lot of people." Zach sounded desperate, like a man trying to paddle a rowboat without oars. He blinked rapidly behind his glasses.

Jolene clamped her lips together and prayed for the strength not to say anything. The silence lengthened and she became aware of a faint buzz that probably meant the sound system hadn't been turned off, and the almost imperceptible ticking of Zach's watch. Dark had crept up the windows while they talked and only the topmost panes remained fog-colored, giving an ombre effect to the windows.

"I should have known." He bent his head and his shoulders shook. She scooted along the pew until their thighs touched and put her arms around him, resting her cheek on his shoulder. Jolene tried hard to imagine what it must be like to have to see a parent in a new and repellent, horrifying light. She tightened her grip on Zach and let him cry.

When he had recovered himself and they had broken apart, sitting side by side in silence again for ten minutes, she asked, "What about Rachel?"

He slewed in the pew to face her, his brows drawn together in an uncompromising line. "Rachel is my daughter and I love her, but I cannot condone stealing."

"I never asked you to—"

His upheld hand silenced her. The wedding band on his ring finger shone dully in the twilit sanctuary. "I prayed hard these past days and searched my conscience. I had decided that the reckoning stones do not accord with God's mercy and forgiveness and I tried to convince the elders of that, but I was out-voted." He fell silent. "My sister ... has had many crosses to bear, but she has the Community's best interests at heart. Still, after today, I think if our daughter contributes eighty hours to serving this Community righteously, and gracefully accepts being grounded for a month, that she will have ample opportunity to repent and atone."

A wave of relief washed through Jolene. "Oh, Zach, that's all I was trying to do: atone. I'm sorry if it felt like I was dissing you when—"

"'Dissing'?" A wry smile curved his lips and gave Jolene hope.

"Sorry. The kids' language is infectious. They say it when—"

"I know what it means."

He knew what she meant, but did he know who she was? The thought leaped, unbidden, into Jolene's mind. Her eyes lingered on her husband's face. She loved him, and yet that love seemed to eat away at her foundation, like waves sucking the sand from beneath a beach house. She had become one flesh with him, vowed to love him until death, and she was and would. Becoming aware that her nails were gouging her palms, she unclenched her fists. She could say she wanted a separation, but the very thought, the form of the word in her head, squeezed her lungs closed and made her gasp with pain. She didn't want to be separate from him; she just wanted to be different *with* him. Trouble was, she didn't know if he could accept, never mind embrace, the person she was becoming... had become. A doubter, not of God but of religion, a protector, a seeker, a voice. And if he couldn't? She wanted to shy away from considering either a future alone, like Iris was alone, or endless years of meeting other people's expectations.

"Jolene, I think we—"

"I want to act." She laid the idea down like a marker, stopping Zach mid-sentence.

Blank astonishment wiped his face clean of anger. "You want to—what?—run off to New York or Hollywood? At your age? You have responsibilities, Jolene."

"No, of course not," she said, ignoring the age comment. She wasn't even quite forty. "Here. At the Fine Arts Center, or Theaterworks, or that new center in Parker. I'm not talking about making it a career or anything. I just want to try, to have something to do for me. Maybe I won't get into a show, but if I do, it wouldn't take that much time... a couple hours in the evening for five or six weeks or so."

"I don't know if being on stage is appropriate for a pastor's wife..." His tone verged on disapproval, but he tugged at his earlobe and she knew he was thinking about it. Really thinking about it, not just pretending to like she sometimes did before denying Rachel permission to camp out on a sidewalk overnight to get tickets to a movie, or something equally outrageous.

"I'm not talking about doing burlesque," she said, standing. "I'm talking about Shakespeare, Chekov, Neil Simon."

He was silent for a moment. "I need you," he finally said. Despite his solidity, a trick of the light made him look somehow insubstantial in that moment, as if the mere thought of her leaving was enough to diminish him.

She leaned over until her face was inches from his and put her hands on his shoulders, the weave of his jacket imprinting into her fingers. "And I need you, and Rachel and Aaron, and the Community. I'm not leaving. I will never leave you, Zach, even if you are against this, against my finding a creative outlet, an activity that fulfills me in a different way than mothering and nurturing and *helping* all the times does. You can't tell me that always being available to your parishioners, always lending a hand or being a shoulder to cry on, doesn't wear on you."

"There's nothing wrong with helping." But he said it with a rueful look that told her he got it.

She let out a sigh of relief.

"I love you, Jolene. I can't remember not loving you."

"Good thing," she said in a voice muffled by the tears she was holding back, "because you're stuck with me."

Zach stood so suddenly she stumbled backward so his head wouldn't clonk her chin. He caught her waist and said, "I've been wanting to see the new exhibit at the art museum in Denver. Sunday, after the service, we can go up there, spend the night even."

Jolene opened her eyes wide. Spontaneity was not Zach's long suit and she couldn't recall another time when he'd suggested a spur-of-the-moment outing, never mind an overnight trip. "Really? What about Rachel?"

"We'll deal with Rachel and ... and all of it later. I'm sure Abby's folks will let her stay overnight. Right now ... well, I think we should just be Jolene and Zach and let our daughter, and my father and sister, and the whole darn Community muddle along on their own for a day or two." Anguish tightened his face when he mentioned his father, but was quickly erased.

He was trying so very hard to reach out to her that it made her heart ache. "I'll take a personal day Monday," Jolene said, happiness rising within her.

Zach held out his hand and she took it. The feel of his square palm against hers almost made her cry. "I love you, Husband," she said, resting her head on his shoulder as they walked down the aisle, fingers twined.

"I love you, Wife."

The words felt like vows in the gentle quiet of the church and Jolene hugged the feeling close. It was moments like this that held a marriage together for the long-term. The insight surprised her. It wasn't the hot sex of the honeymoon phase, or the children, or habit. It was the determination to stay connected, to accept these moments of grace that came even in the midst of what promised to be a hard period, to work at loving the person she'd promised to love and cherish until death. She pulled Zach to a stop and leaned up on tip-toe to kiss his cheek, inhabiting the peace of the moment and letting it work its way through her entire body before they opened the doors.

# FORTY-TWO

**IRIS**

IRIS FOUND HERSELF AT the door of Outback Cottage without conscious thought. She pounded with her fist, upset enough to consider kicking the door in and storming the bungalow. When Marian swung the door inward with a surprised and irritated expression, Iris took an automatic step forward before realization froze her. Her breath hitched and her eyes swept the area. Nothing—*nothing*—was the same. Framed photos of Colorado landscapes had replaced the mirror and cross on the walls of the small foyer. Someone had knocked out a wall to open the kitchen to the living room area. Mrs. Wellington's scratchy sofa and loveseat had been replaced with a low-end but attractive microfiber suite in a rich chestnut color. Colorful pillows and peach-colored walls made the space homey, even welcoming. Iris sucked in a thin thread of breath through her constricted throat.

White subway tiles gleamed from the kitchen's walls and the linoleum had been replaced with a wood-look laminate. Even the appliances were new. *Of course they are*, Iris thought. *It's been twenty-three years.* She let herself breathe. Her fear of the cottage didn't have anything to do with the space itself. It was about what had happened here and she was safe from that now. She was thirty-eight, not fifteen, and Pastor Matt was gone, for all intents and purposes. She could be here without hyperventilating. She took three slow, deep breaths to prove it, and looked at her mother.

Marian was wearing a gray flannel bathrobe that Iris thought had been her father's. The sight of it would have made her smile if she hadn't been so wound up.

"What are you doing—?" Marian started. "Oh, you found Angel's purse. We've been looking for it."

She held out her hand, but Iris jerked the purse away. "Where's Angel?"

"At a sleepover. I think she's far too young to be spending the night at a friend's house, but we Skyped with Keely and she said it was okay." Marian sniffed. "I was looking forward to an evening alone, so if you'll just—"

Iris fished the photo from the purse and held it up between a trembling thumb and forefinger. "Is this Noah?" she asked.

"Yes, of course. Noah and Keely. If you're not leaving, come in so I can shut the door. It's getting chilly. I wish you'd called first."

Iris walked farther into the room and faced her mother as she closed the door. She shook the picture accusingly. "There's a photo of Noah on the fridge at Jolene's house. With Zach." She paused, and thought her mother stiffened slightly.

"I'm not surprised," Marian said matter-of-factly, moving into the kitchen, her slippers flapping. "They've been best friends forever. Surely you remember that." She retrieved a glass from a cupboard near the sink. It tinked against the faucet as if the hand that held it wasn't steady. "Water?" Marian asked.

"I'm not thirsty. When I saw the photo, I thought the man with Zach must be a cousin because they look so much alike. But he's not a cousin, is he, Mother? Noah's his brother."

Marian's features squinched together. "How dare you?"

"How dare I?" Suddenly, Iris was shouting. "How dare *I*? You have lived a lie for God knows how many years and you want to act all offended with me? You slept with Pastor Matt, you had his son, and then you were cruel enough to pretend you didn't believe me when I told you, when I told you that he..." Iris turned away and stiffened every muscle, trying not to let her anger and sense of betrayal overwhelm her.

"I *didn't* believe you," her mother said. "I didn't believe he could...that he could betray me, that our time together meant so little to him!" Pain narrowed her voice to a whisper.

"Oh, that's rich, Mother. You felt betrayed? What about his poor wife? Did Daddy know?"

Marian's shoulders sagged. She slumped into a ladder-back chair at the table like a marionette whose strings had been cut. "I suppose you want to know all of it."

"Damn right." Iris sat opposite her mother and laid the photo on the table between them.

"It's funny," Marian said, her fingers with their short nails touching the photo's edge. "No one else ever guessed. They were so used to seeing the boys together, to thinking of them as friends, that they didn't notice how much they began to look alike as they grew up. People used to tell me Noah had Neil's eyes." She expelled a sharp breath. "I guess we see what we expect to see, hm? Or what we want to see. You saw the truth because you got far enough away from us all to have a new perspective."

Iris stayed quiet, waiting for her mother to work her way around to telling her story.

Marian took a long swallow of water, her throat working and then set the glass down with a decisive click. "I was sixteen when my parents heard Matthew speak at our church in Illinois and followed him here to set up the Community. We felt like pioneers, coming west in a station wagon instead of a covered wagon. The church was already here, and that strange Victorian house, so out of place in what was then an isolated corner of the county. I cried for weeks about leaving my friends, my bedroom, my softball team. Oh, yes," she said in response to Iris's surprised look. "I was a pretty good outfielder at one time and had the highest batting average on the team.

"I was so upset for so long that my parents took me to Pastor Matt for counseling. He was young then, Iris, in his early thirties. Handsome and sympathetic. Charismatic. He was so interested in me, in what I thought and felt. He asked my advice about Community matters. I was flattered. I felt—" She broke off, apparently unable to find the right words.

"I know," Iris said.

Marian nodded. "Yes, well. He was married and Glynnis was pregnant. With Esther, as it turns out. We never meant for it to happen, but one day our feelings overcame us and we made love in his office. We both felt horrible afterward. He begged my forgiveness and we agreed that it would never happen again. But we loved each other so much."

Iris fought the urge to mime retching; her mother's story was too awful for such a flippant response.

"And then I discovered I was pregnant." Marian's voice went flat and she stared into her empty water glass. "I went to him in tears, panic-stricken. He was as horrified as I. More. He told me he needed time to think what was best to do. When I came to him the next day in his office, Neil was there. I knew Neil slightly; he'd been part of the Community when we arrived and I'd spoken with him a few times—he had a little crush on me, even though he was six years older—but I barely knew him. I didn't understand what he was doing there, until Matthew told me that Neil had agreed to marry me and raise my child—he called him *my* child, not ours—as his own."

Iris reached across the table for her mother's hand, unwillingly sympathetic. Pastor Matt had victimized them both. Marian let her hand rest under Iris's for a short moment, and then withdrew it. "I agreed. What could I do? When Neil left, Matthew told me that he would always love me, but that circumstances made it impossible for us to be together the way we wanted to be. He said that Neil was a good man, that he would take care of me and the baby. He made it sound like he was the one making a huge sacrifice, Iris," Marian said, sounding disillusioned and old. "Like he was sacrificing himself so my reputation wouldn't be damaged, so he could continue to do God's work in the Community. I thought he was noble."

Iris felt ill and didn't know what to say. "Were you faithful to Daddy?"

Marian jerked back as if stung. "Of course. Matthew and I never again—"

"You were too old for him by then."

Only the briefest pause suggested Marian had heard her. "I respected Neil and I was grateful to him. In time, I came to love him. I think he loved me all along, and he always loved Noah and thought of him as his. Noah *is* his," she said fiercely, raking her fingers through her short hair, "in all the ways that count."

"Does he know? Noah?" No wonder her mother hadn't wanted him to date Esther.

Marian shook her head violently. "You can't tell him."

"He has a right—"

"You can't tell him. Neil's already lost everything—you can't take away his son."

Iris heard the plea in her mother's voice. Even if Noah had a right to know who his biological father was, it would wound Neil if the knowledge changed the way Noah related to him. Maybe Noah was happier not knowing. Most of her life, from the time she was a little girl, she'd wanted to *know* everything, because knowledge was power and power was control. Now, she hesitated. It was within her power to completely change Noah's worldview, his concept of who he was. Would that truth empower him or destroy him? It wasn't her secret to tell, Iris finally decided.

"I won't say anything."

"Thank you," Marian said with an effort.

Agitated, Iris rose and paced across the small dining area. Her footfalls made the decorative tea cups displayed on a metal étagère *tink* in their saucers. "So, when I told you that he'd molested me—"

"I couldn't believe it. I *couldn't* believe it. It wasn't until the night of the reckoning stones that I saw, in the woods, that I let myself see…" Marian's teeth snapped together. "I went to see Matthew the next night, the night you left, although I didn't know then that you were gone. I needed to know the truth, needed to hear it from him, even though I suspected I already knew, that I had heard the truth from you."

"You were there that night?" Iris arched her brows.

"Oh, yes," her mother said grimly.

# FORTY-THREE

**MARIAN**

*Twenty-Three Years Ago*

Marian strode through the woods that edged Lone Pine, counting on the noise she made trampling twigs and rustling branches to warn away any wildlife. The bears were cranky this time of year, awaking hungry from their hibernation, and Quentin Welsh had reported seeing a black sow by the motel two nights ago. She hated the necessity of skulking through the trees, but she couldn't march boldly up to Matthew's door. Not tonight. Shivering, she wrapped her arms around herself, pulling her cardigan tight at the neck. It had no business being so cold in early May. She stepped out of the woods, the smoothness under her feet signaling she was on the lawn, even though the moon was stingy and she could barely make out the turret and peaks of the Victorian house.

She saw no one as she crossed the lawn to the front porch. No surprise at past ten o'clock. Smoothing her hair, she rapped on the door. It opened almost immediately, and she fell back a step. She should have realized she might see Glynnis, but she hadn't prepared a story.

"Marian," Glynnis said in her dry, unanimated way. She had gone from being petite to fragile in the years Marian had known her, and now, with light gray hair pulled back into a low bun, and her sallow face makeup free, she looked ten years older than her rightful fifty years. "It's late."

"I know. I'm sorry. It's only—" *I need to find out if your husband cheated on me with my daughter.* She couldn't tell the truth.

"You'll be wanting to talk to Matthew about Mercy, I expect."

"Yes, I—"

"She took the stones hard; I could tell." Glynnis opened the door wider to invite Marian in. "Matthew can maybe give you some ideas for helping her through this time, bringing her to the point of desiring reconciliation with the Community."

"Yes, that's it," Marian said, stepping inside. "I'm worried about Mercy."

"He's in his study. You'll excuse me—I've got some banana bread just about ready to take out of the oven." She headed down the wall-papered hall to the kitchen.

A strange woman. Marian had always wondered what brought her and Matthew together, though she knew she couldn't see Glynnis clearly through the fog of guilt. She needed to get this over with. Knocking once on the closed study door, she opened it without waiting for an answer. She stepped inside, closed the door behind her, and stood with her back against it. The drapes were drawn and a small fire burned cozily in the hearth. Matthew sat at the desk, his broad brow propped on one hand as he read the large Bible opened on the blotter. He marked his place with a finger and looked up. A mix of emotions—surprise, consternation, fear—skittered across his face before he smoothed them away and stood, coming toward her with hands outstretched. When he got closer, she noticed the bruise, like a shadow, seeping from the corner of his mouth across his jaw.

"Marian! What are you doing here? Is Mercy okay?"

Marian brought her clasped hands up beneath her chin so he couldn't take them. This was the first time they'd been alone behind closed doors since she'd married Neil. Matthew had told her he couldn't trust himself with her, that they had to keep a distance to preserve their marriage vows, but she wondered now if he'd actually been worried that she'd enact a scene or beg him to resume their relationship if they were alone together.

"Tell me you didn't do it, Matthew." She blinked back tears. "No. Tell me the truth."

He halted, his eyes wary. "What truth is that?"

She kept her gaze on his face. Her every muscle was tight; she felt as brittle as the ice on the pond, ready to crack with the slightest pressure.

He tried a sad chuckle. "Oh, Marian, how could you think—? You, of all people."

"Exactly." She regarded him coldly. "I, of all people."

She became conscious of his body odor and realized he was perspiring beneath his maroon sweater. The smell of him brought back memories—wrong, hurtful memories—and she pushed them down. She studied him with the clear insight of a thirty-three-year-old woman, and not the bedazzled eyes of a lovesick teenager. Something gnawed at her insides ... the growing conviction that she had wronged Mercy horribly and unforgivably.

"You fornicated with my daughter."

He opened his mouth, and she could almost hear the words of denial hovering on his thick, pink tongue. But then he said, "She's so very much like you were, Marian. Your image."

She recoiled, bumping against the door. "You are a sick man. Sickening."

His eyes glinted. "God made me as I am."

Marian took two hasty steps toward him, hauled her arm back and slapped him full across the face. The blow stung her palm and rocked his head sideways. Tears wet her cheeks. She swung her arm again, but he caught her wrist and forced her backward, almost against the fireplace screen. Heat from the flames warmed her legs. "We are both guilty of horrible sins. Our relationship was wrong and sinful from the start. The only good to come from it was Noah. *My* son. Mine and Neil's. You poisoned my relationship with my daughter. You molested her, just like she said, and I refused to believe her because I thought . . . I thought—"

"I do still love you, Marian," Matthew said, trying to take her hand.

Repulsed that he could intuit her thoughts, she yanked it away and staggered back, bumping against the fireplace tools which jangled to the floor.

Another crash sounded from the hallway. Matthew shot Marian a look that warned her she had as much to lose as he did, and opened the door. Glynnis knelt on the floor, surrounded by a litter of broken china and a tray. Her hand clutched a jagged shard and she stared up at her husband, hatred burning in her eyes. "I was bringing you tea, and I heard . . . I heard . . ."

She stopped mid-sentence and her jaw hung slack, mouth ajar. Glynnis had deliberately eavesdropped, Marian suspected. What else had she overheard over the years? She began to think there was more to Glynnis Brozek, a slyness, than she had ever recognized. The heavy aroma of banana bread drifted from the kitchen and Marian knew she'd never be able to eat it again.

Matthew said soothingly, "I don't know what you thought you heard, Glynnis, but Marian was just asking my advice about poor Mercy. That misguided girl—"

"Don't touch me." Glynnis struggled to get to her feet, and breathed with effort, laying a hand on her chest. "I've known what you were for years, and turned a blind eye because I loved you, because you were the father of my children, but now—"

"Let me help you clean this up," Matthew said easily, robbing his wife's words of their power by ignoring them. He stooped to pick up slices of shattered cups and place them on the tray. "Oh, you've broken one of your mother's saucers. I know how you love that pattern. Maybe we can get it repaired."

Forcing her stiff limbs to move, Marian sidled around the pair, frantic to get out of the house. "I've got to go. Neil will be wondering where I am. Glynnis—"

The woman's now empty eyes swiveled to her and Marian found it impossible to utter the apology she knew she owed her. She banged against the newel post as she stumbled past it, and looked up at the sound of a soft footfall from the landing. A shadow moved and then Marian was out the door, leaving it ajar as she raced toward the woods and home, the stench of burning banana bread chasing her.

# FORTY-FOUR

**IRIS**

Iris sat frozen when her mother finished speaking, feeling like only stillness could keep her together. She was in the eye of a hurricane, and if she moved at all, she'd be swept into the wrecking winds and torn apart. Noah was her half-brother. Her mother and Pastor Matt had—Iris's mind refused to go there. She understood now, at least, why Marian hadn't believed her, couldn't believe her, when she said Pastor Matt had molested her. Marian had been in love with Matthew Brozek all along, even after her marriage ended their affair. Admitting that he'd slept with her daughter, that he was a pedophile who'd never really loved her the way she loved him, would have destroyed her, Iris recognized. She looked at her mother. Maybe had destroyed her.

Marian, after one brief, almost furtive look at Iris, had dropped her gaze to her lap where her fingers worried at a button on her dress.

"Do you hate him?" Iris asked.

"I did. For a while. After you left, because he's what made you go. I hated us both. I cut my hair as a sign of penitence." Her fingers pulled at one short strand. "Neil never asked why I cut it. With Jesus' help, I forgave Matthew long ago. I'm still working on forgiving myself, window by window." She made a circular motion with one hand, as if she was polishing glass. "You need to forgive him, too. Not for his sake, but for yours."

Iris stared at her mother, biting back an instinctual denial. An image of Pastor Matt as she'd last seen him, lolling in his bed as she shook it, came into her mind's eye and almost immediately faded. She looked at her mother with wonder, thinking about the years she'd spent caring for the church, trimming shrubs, steam-cleaning carpets, changing furnace filters. She'd taken the task on like a penance, Iris thought. She remembered Cade talking about going to confession and receiving Hail Marys as a punishment for something trivial. How many cleaned windows did it take to get a clean slate? Studying the way her mother's gray robe drained her face of color, how her dark eyes stood out against the pallor, troubled, beseeching, Iris realized it wasn't Pastor Matt she needed to forgive.

The knowledge thudded into her like a rockslide, making her sway in the chair. She reached for her mother's hand. It was cool, work-roughened, strong. The knuckles were slightly swollen and Iris wondered if they pained her. This hand had smoothed her hair back from her sweaty forehead when she'd had the flu, spanked her, held hers for balance when she learned to roller skate, plucked chickens for family dinners, and slapped Pastor Matt for her.

"I want to forgive, Mom," Iris whispered, and they both knew she wasn't talking about Matthew Brozek. A concept for the Green Gable sculpture rose up before her suddenly, born of what her mother had said. A window, or window panes …

Marian sniffed hard and stood to fetch a box of Kleenex. She blew her nose and returned to the table, but remained standing. "Well. It's late." Her tone suggested it was time for Iris to go.

Iris refused to budge, her mind buzzing. "So neither you nor Dad really has an alibi," she said slowly.

Giving her a sour look, Marian said, "Well, really! After all this, you're saying Neil beat Matthew after all? Or I did?"

"If you were at the Brozeks', you can't know what time Dad left the house. What if he followed you there? Cade was there before you—that's why Pastor Matt's face was bruised."

Marian looked stricken, but recovered quickly. "That's ridiculous. If you don't know by now that your father is no more capable of beating a man half to death than ... than Angel is, then you're hopeless." She stood and plucked a sponge from the sink, and began wiping down the table with short, angry swipes.

Iris remembered the look on her father's face when she told him she hadn't attacked Pastor Matt. His shock was real. Sucking in a deep breath, disturbed at the path her thoughts had taken, she asked, "Did you think I'd done it?"

Marian shot her an impatient look. "Not for one second. Not one! Why do you think I was so against Neil confessing? You didn't—don't—have it in you to beat a man to near death, any more than Neil does. A mother knows. I tried to make Neil see that, but he was convinced, with you gone, that—. He insisted on confessing. If you hadn't run off, Neil would never have gone to prison." She scrubbed viciously at an invisible spot on the table.

Iris looked at her with wonder, touched despite the acid rider by her mother's adamantine belief in her innocence. Iris changed the subject slightly. "Who do you think was on the landing?"

"What?"

"The landing. You said you heard someone. Who else was in the Brozek house?"

"Oh. I don't know. Probably Esther or Zach, wouldn't you think?"

"Yes. But they both say they were gone. Zach told me he was looking for Jolene, although he never found her, and Esther said she was at the church, working on something for Sunday school." Iris knew she'd learned something else, something about the church, but she couldn't place it. She tried sifting through everything she'd heard this week. She'd talked to Jolene and Zach about that night, to Cade … the knowledge she sought clicked like a puzzle piece locking into place. "Cade vandalized the church that night," Iris said, rising in her excitement.

"That was him?" Marian looked indignant. "Well! He ought—"

Iris spoke loudly to override her mother. "Wouldn't Esther have heard him smashing windows if she was really in the church basement like she said? Wouldn't she have come up to see what was going on, or, at least, mentioned it to the cops the next day if she was too scared to confront an intruder?"

Marian stilled and Iris locked eyes with her. "You think Esther was at the house," Marian said finally, "that she knows what happened to Matthew."

"It makes sense," Iris said with fierce exultation at having discovered the truth that would free her father. "It's the only thing that makes sense." Iris bit her lip, trying to think through what might have happened. Maybe Glynnis had finally snapped and gone after her husband with the poker. Had Esther intervened?

"If Esther was there, why wouldn't she say so? Why lie about being in the church?" Water dripped from the sponge, betraying Marian's convulsive grip.

Iris said, "I don't know. But I damn well plan to ask her."

# FORTY-FIVE

**IRIS**

BACK IN HER ROOM, having accepted her mother's advice to wait until morning to tackle Esther, Iris reached for her sketch pad with shaking hands. She wanted to still her brain, going around and around with Marian's revelations. The window idea for the award commission sang within her and she burned to get it down on paper. What if she couldn't do it, if her fingers wouldn't translate what was in her head onto the page? What if she was still blocked? She hadn't confronted Pastor Matt, after all. *Only one way to find out.* Flipping the pad open, she picked up a pencil, hesitated, and then began to draw. The lines came stiffly at first, but then more fluidly as she gave herself up to the images. Filling page after page with drawings, each one more detailed, more crisp, more exactly what she envisioned, she worked until almost dawn, afraid to stop. When the pencil finally slid from her cramped fingers, she crawled into bed fully clothed, leaving the sketch pad open on the bedside table. Happy exhaustion pressed her into the soft bed. It was back. Her gift was back. Even though she'd never had it out with Pastor

Matt like she'd planned, her gift was back. Feeling a superstitious reluctance to examine it too closely for fear that thinking about it too much might close her off again, she rolled over on her side and smiled, letting sleep steal over her.

———

Still filled with a sense of well-being, even though her talk with Esther might turn ugly, Iris approached the Victorian home at just after eight in the morning. Clouds had moved in and the day was chilly enough that Iris wore a hoodie over her T-shirt and tucked her hands into the kangaroo pocket after she knocked. Shifting from foot to foot, she waited for Esther to answer. The door stayed closed. Iris made a visor of her hand, stepped over to a window, and peered in. A sleepy dining room, empty, met her gaze. No light shone from the hall beyond.

Iris descended the veranda stairs. Damn. Where could Esther be at this hour? Maybe she was visiting her father. No, her car was under the carport; Iris had noticed it when she walked up from the church parking lot. She could be breakfasting with Zach and Jolene or a friend. Seeing the futility of going on a door-to-door hunt for Esther, Iris left her car where it was and wandered into Lone Pine in search of coffee and information.

Debby's Café hummed with activity and conversation, but Joseph Ulm spotted Iris as soon as she came in. "The usual?" he asked over the heads of two women chatting at the counter.

Feeling absurdly warmed by his greeting, Iris nodded. As he counted out her change, she asked where she might find Esther.

"Try the barn. She usually works with the alpacas on Saturdays. Stop back by for a piece of pie when you're done. That way I'll know she didn't put a pitchfork in you." He grinned again, but Iris wasn't altogether sure he was joking.

"Thanks. Say 'hi' to Gabby for me, next time you talk to her," Iris said.

"Will do. She's Gabby Von Wolfseck now, you know. She and Keith are expecting their third in July. Their oldest is coming up on fifteen. Already got college scouts watching him pitch. And the middle girl, Tracy, plays a violin that could make the angels weep."

Joseph Ulm wore a proud grandpa expression and Iris said goodbye and left before he could whip out photos.

―――

The trek to the alpaca barn on the far side of the meadow took Iris almost fifteen minutes. By the time she arrived, the sun had broken through the clouds and she was sweating lightly. Taking off the hoodie, she tied it around her waist and followed the sound of a murmuring voice into the barn. It wasn't a big structure designed to hold tractors and large livestock. Rather, it seemed to have been purpose-built for the alpacas, a rough lean-to with small pens on either side of a central aisle, most of them occupied by alpacas, and a ceiling that only cleared Iris's head by a foot and a half. Gaps where the boards didn't fit together evenly let in jewels of sunlight and air. It felt like a cross between a barn and a chicken coop, and smelled of hay and fresh water.

Iris walked softly down the aisle, an object of curiosity to the alpacas. She stopped when she came to the open door of what looked to be a storage room, filled with sacks of feed. Dust motes twirled in the sun's spotlight beaming through a small window. Esther, massive in overalls and work boots, crouched beside a brown alpaca, preparing to give it an injection. The animal didn't even seem to notice the needle go in and butted Esther's arm when she patted it.

Iris must have made some sound because Esther looked up. "She's diabetic," she said, nodding toward the alpaca. "Has to have insulin twice a day." She stood with effort and disposed of the syringe in a gallon milk jug half full of syringes. Then, she turned and met Iris's eyes, "I told the police about you, you know. About you trying to kill my father and your father taking the blame for it. You'll have to pay for what you did." Her face shone with malice.

Ignoring Esther's words, she said, "My mother and I talked last night."

"You've caused her a lot of grief."

Brushing aside Esther's comment, Iris continued, "She told me about visiting Pastor Matt at your house the night he was attacked. She went there to confront him about molesting me. She knew, you see, what he was capable of since he'd seduced her years earlier. I never knew that. Your mother overheard them talking."

Iris paused, trying to gauge Esther's reaction. The older woman's face remained deadpan, her blue stare un-nerving Iris. Iris shifted, her feet rustling wisps of hay underfoot. "You were there."

When Esther still said nothing, remained motionless, Iris plunged on. "You know what happened that night, Esther. Have you kept quiet all these years to protect your mother? Here's what I think happened. I think Glynnis lost it. She heard her husband admitting to raping not only me, but also my mother. She snapped. After my mother left, I think Glynnis picked up the poker, followed Pastor Matt to the cottage, and beat him. No one would blame her, Esther. I'm sure you don't want to see her name blackened at this late date, but think about my father's freedom. It's not right that he should die in prison. Can't you come forward and tell what really happened, clear my father?" Iris's voice and eyes pled with the other woman.

Esther blinked slowly. "My mother never lifted a hand against my father. She was a mouse. A pathetic, sniveling little mouse. Gray, blah. What he saw in her, I'll never know."

The venom in her voice startled Iris and she found herself looking around surreptitiously. There was a metal bucket, and a wheelbarrow with a small shovel in it, probably for mucking out the stalls. Nothing that looked like a weapon. Iris relaxed a bit, chiding herself for letting Ulm's joke get to her.

"My mother didn't go for the poker, she went for the phone." Anger mottled Esther's face. "She told him she was going to call the police and turn him in. He laughed at her and left, not bothering to say where he was going, but I knew. I came downstairs to stop her, and found her on the floor in the kitchen, gripping her left shoulder. She was obviously having a heart attack. All I had to do was kick the phone out of the way—she had dropped it—and wait for nature to take its course."

A chill like the cold metal tine of a pitchfork ripped up Iris's spine and she jerked. Had she misunderstood Esther? "You—?"

"I showed her the mercy God wants us to show all who suffer or are in need. I put a damp cloth on her brow and I sat on the floor with her, holding her hand and praying for her soul until her spirit left her. She couldn't talk, so I prayed for her, asking God to forgive her for thinking to betray the husband he had joined her with, asking him to make her passing painless and quick. He was merciful and just, as is his nature. It was less than twenty minutes before she died. But even that was too long."

Iris stared dumbfounded at Esther, who was eerily calm. Only her last words betrayed emotion. "Too long?" Esther hadn't admitted to murder, or even lifting a hand against her mother, but surely not summoning help for someone in distress was a crime? It was certainly a moral crime, even if the legal system couldn't prosecute.

And it made Esther one very cold, calculating eighteen-year-old. Iris edged toward the storage room door, uneasily aware that the two of them were alone and isolated.

"I went after my father, of course. I had to tell him about Mother, to assure him that he was safe. I was too late. If only Mom hadn't taken so long to die, I'd have been there. I could have saved him." Sorrow contracted Esther's face. "Your father had already attacked him when I got to the cottage, struck him down and hit him again and again. There was blood everywhere."

Iris didn't think this was the time to protest her father's innocence, so she kept her mouth shut. She touched the door jamb, the unfinished wood rough beneath her hand. A thought struck her. "You must have been very mad at him," she suggested gently. "At your father. For what he did. No wonder you struck out at him."

Esther stared at Iris for a second before catching on. She laughed. The sound rang inappropriately through the barn. An alpaca bleated. "You think I hit my father? I would never, ever have hurt him." Earnestness settled on her doughy face and she took a step toward Iris. "Never. I loved him. He was the love of my life. Even when he left me for Penelope, I didn't stop loving him. It wasn't his fault, it was hers. He didn't want to be the way he was. He fought it, you know, fought against his nature, the way God made him. He used to cry sometimes when he came into my room at night and I'd tell him, 'It's okay, Daddy.' Girls like Penelope and you tempted him, led him into sin. You were Bathshebas to his David, displaying yourselves, luring him away from God and me."

Something in Esther's voice prickled the hairs on Iris's arms. She remembered the sensations of water and terror she'd felt when holding Penelope's bracelet. "Penelope didn't die in the landslide, did she?" Iris blurted.

"It was an accident."

Iris didn't ask what Esther meant. It was too much to process at once. Esther had been Pastor Matt's first victim. Or maybe not. There was her own mother, after all. At any rate, he had molested his own daughter and when she'd grown too old for his sick tastes, he'd moved on to other girls in the Community. Esther had felt rejected and taken steps to secure her father's attentions again. Iris breathed quickly, almost hyperventilating at the implications. She sucked in a bit of hay or husk of feed and began to cough hard.

While she was bent forward, Esther grabbed her arm. Her hands were large and the pudgy fingers had a core of steel. Iris tried to wrench away, but Esther pulled her in until their faces nearly touched.

"And you," she breathed into Iris's face. "You tried to take him away, too. What none of you ever understood is that he's mine, that we share a sacred bond, a connection that is eternal. You were a wisp of fog in his life, a moment. Meaningless. I'm the one he loves." Esther's fingers tightened. She leaned into Iris and bore her back against the storage room wall, her bulk pinning her to the splintery slats, breast to breast, thigh to thigh. The intimacy of it was unnerving.

Iris fought down panic. Esther's flesh enveloped her, made her feel as if she couldn't breathe. It felt like all of Esther's three hundred fifty pounds was compressing her rib cage, making it hard to draw in air. Esther was still talking, but Iris had quit listening, intent on getting away. She didn't have enough leverage to get a knee up into the woman's crotch. Esther's hand still gripped Iris's left arm and she fought to wiggle her right hand free. The boards protested and Iris thought she felt them shift.

"... they'll all be glad you're gone," Esther was saying. "No one will look for you or wonder why you didn't come back. Not even your own mother." She maneuvered her hand up and began to wedge it toward Iris's neck. Her eyes were hard, soul-less sapphires and she pressed her lips together so tightly they disappeared into the flesh surrounding them, making her look eerily like the sock puppet dolls Iris and her mother had made together when she was a child. Esther's fingers groped for Iris's neck as her torso mashed Iris to the wall. A rank scent rose from her, adrenaline and sweat and malice oozing from her pores.

Iris knew she only had one shot. As Esther's fingers dug into her throat, she smashed her head forward into the other woman's nose and threw herself back against the wall as hard as she could, using all the power of her legs to strain backward. Blood splattered from Esther's broken nose. The woman bellowed with anger and pain, heaving herself forward to grind Iris against the wall. Esther's hand tightened around her neck, and Iris's vision began to dim at the edges, blood pounding in her head.

The wall shuddered. Just a little more ... Iris sank down as much as she could, allowing her thighs to push harder. *Crr-rack!* The boards bent, then splintered under their combined weight. Iris felt a slight gap open between herself and Esther as she fell backward. She flung herself sideways, not wanting to cushion Esther's fall or be trapped under her. A broken board gouged her thigh. She ignored the pain, wrapping her suddenly free arms around her head and ducking her chin toward her chest.

Iris hit the ground with a hard thud and lay winded for a moment. Dust and debris created a disorienting fog, but she could see the litter of torn and broken boards that had been the storage room wall and part of a pen. Hoofed feet sounded like far-off thunder as the alpacas surged inside their pens, panicked. The ones freed by the wall knocking over their enclosure trotted down the aisle and out the open door. Her left shoulder shrieked with the pain of torn muscles and blood dripped down her leg from where the board had gouged it. Her legs were trapped beneath Esther's still form.

With her left arm all but useless, Iris scrabbled backward. *An anchor. Need something to hold onto.* Her fingers brushed cold metal. With a gasp of relief, she hooked her elbow around the water trough's supports. The metal cutting into her arm, she hauled her body toward it. Bucking and pushing with her legs, she managed to drag them out from beneath Esther's heavy body. She identified a strange, ragged sound as her own labored breathing, on the cusp of sobbing. Uncoiling her arm from the trough, she pushed to a kneeling position. Grabbing the trough's edge, she began to pull herself up. A hand clamped around her ankle.

Esther yanked. Iris, still unsteady, fell forward, clipping her forehead on the metal trough. Lights sparkled behind her eyes and everything went gray. She fought for consciousness. *If I black out, I'm dead.* She kicked out with her free foot, connecting with Esther's shoulder. Esther's grip didn't loosen. Her hands climbed up Iris's calf to her knee and pulled steadily. Raising her head, Iris glimpsed the other woman's bloodied, implacable face, and her bright hair, now wild and gooped with something from the alpaca pen. Esther's breath came in little grunts and her face was frozen into a grimace.

Iris's good arm swept the ground around her and her fingers scraped a piece of wood. *Can't quite reach ... got it!* She gripped it, ignoring the slivers that bit into her palm, lifted it high, and swung hard. It glanced off Esther's head and the woman yelped. Desperate, Iris swung it again, simultaneously kicking as hard as she could. The board snagged on something and came out of Iris's hand. Esther's hold loosened and Iris crab-walked backward on her feet and one hand. She struggled up, breathing raggedly, and eyed the prone woman. Her bulk was unmoving, arms flopped forward over her head. A thin rivulet of blood crept from beneath her chin and soaked into the hay. Iris took a cautious step toward her.

"Esther?" She dropped to her knees and saw a bloody nail rising up from the board that lay beside Esther. Iris tore her hoodie from around her waist to stanch the thin trickle of blood seeping from Esther's neck and dialed 911 with trembling fingers. The small brown alpaca sidled over nervously and nosed Esther's arm.

"It's okay," Iris told the animal, more to comfort herself than to soothe the alpaca. She reached out to pat it, needing its warmth and softness, but it sidled away, leaving a trail of bloody hoof prints. Iris continued to apply pressure to Esther's wound, unsure if the woman was still breathing. Waves of relief and sadness and confusion rolled through her as she replayed events and Esther's story in her mind. She thought about treating Esther for shock but didn't think she should stop stanching the blood to do it, worried briefly about the loose alpacas and whether someone would round them up, and wondered how Jane's surgery was going. She desperately wanted to talk to Jane. Realizing dimly that her lack of ability to focus and the nausea-inducing headache probably meant she had a concussion, she touched the bump; it felt like a golf ball had embedded itself in her forehead.

A siren, thin at first but then stronger, warned of the ambulance's approach and Iris yelled, "Hurry, hurry!" before the EMTs were out of the vehicle. Relinquishing her place at Esther's side to a competent-looking woman, she let another technician help her to her feet, yelping when he tugged on her injured arm. Tears came to her eyes and she knew they were a reaction to the stress and horror of the last half hour, more than to the pain.

"I'm okay," she told the EMT. "Esther—"

"My partner's looking after your friend, ma'am. Let me take care of you."

"She's not my—" Iris broke off. She stayed silent while the efficient but taciturn EMT hooked her up to an IV that took the edge off the pain, and helped her onto a gurney that slid into the ambulance as easily as a tray of cookies into the oven. *I don't bake*, she thought, woozy from the pain medication and the concussion. All the way to the hospital she wondered what kind of cookies Greg Lansing preferred and whether she'd killed Esther Brozek.

# FORTY-SIX

### IRIS

THE DOCTORS SWABBED OUT Iris's thigh wound and stitched it, put her arm in a sling, stabbed her with antibiotics and a tetanus booster, and admitted her overnight to keep a watch on her concussion. When they let her leave Sunday afternoon, she carried with her the burden of Esther's death. A doctor who was more Marcus Welby than McDreamy sought to cushion the blow by telling Iris that Esther had died not of blood loss from the neck wound, but from a heart attack. She'd regained consciousness at the hospital and asked for her brother, the doctor said, and Zach had stayed with her until she died.

"She was a walking coronary," he said gruffly. "Bad family history. Two hundred pounds overweight. It was bound to happen sooner rather than later. Don't blame yourself." With a hearty but friendly pat that made her good shoulder ache, he signed Iris out.

———

Four days later, Iris figured she had told the story of her confrontation with Esther what felt like a hundred times. To many species of law enforcement officials from cops to investigators to ADAs, to her mother and Jolene, to Jane and Lassie and Greg via phone, to Cade, and to assorted other Community members who trickled sheepishly to her motel room door, bearing flowers and good wishes for her recovery. Her mother had offered to let her stay at the cottage to recuperate, but Iris didn't think their fragile, newly hatched détente could survive so much togetherness so she had declined and laughed to herself at Marian's relieved look. Her concussion headache and nausea had finally faded and her shoulder, though painful, was functional. She had little trouble changing the dressing on her thigh and was due to have her stitches removed on Monday. Her injuries went a long way toward convincing the police she'd acted in self-defense and the DA declined to file charges, especially after Zach Brozek filled them in on the conversation he'd had with Esther on her deathbed, where she apparently told him everything she'd told Iris, and more.

On Thursday afternoon, Cade and Iris met Marian at the cottage. Marian and Cade leaped on the story as a means of exonerating Neil. "Of course she killed him," Marian said of Esther. "She admitted to letting her mother die, practically confessed to killing poor Penelope Welsh, and to being livid about Matthew's other relationships. Victims. That poor girl," she said, pausing for a moment. "Who knows how she would have turned out if he hadn't—? Anyway, she obviously followed him here"—she gestured to the cottage where the three of them sat in the living room—"and hit out at him in fury and hurt, not meaning to put him into a coma."

"I know a reporter," Cade said leaning toward Iris with his forearms on his knees. His skin looked clearer than when Iris had last seen him and his eyes seemed less puffy. He hadn't brought the odor of cigarettes in with him and Iris wondered if he'd given them up. A chased gold band circled his left ring finger and he gave it a self-conscious twist when he noticed her noticing. Iris raised her brows slightly, earning a rueful smile in return. She hoped he and Lila would make it work, and wondered which of them had made the first overture, and how you brought a relationship back from the brink. She'd always shoved hers over the cliff before they'd lasted long enough to merit the term "relationship." Things would be different with Greg, hopefully. Definitely. She recalled her wandering thoughts as Cade continued.

"She can take this story and make Neil a cause célèbre. With Esther dead and unable to give a statement or stand trial, there's no way to persuade the courts to vacate Neil's sentence, but the parole board can consider what she told you and Zach, and take into account his record as a model prisoner and release him. Enough publicity might even get the governor to pardon him. It wouldn't be as good as having him declared innocent, but at least he'd be free."

"She said she didn't try to kill Pastor Matt," Iris said doubtfully, sipping the nasty herbal tea her mother said would help her heal quicker. She heard again the passion in Esther's voice when she declared her love for her father. "She loved him."

"People kill people they love all the time," Cade said dismissively.

"A happy outlook," Iris murmured into her mug.

"Even if the courts don't recognize Neil's innocence," Marian said, "at least the folks around here do, thanks to Zachary."

Zach Brozek, maybe as a way of dealing with his grief, had suggested that the Community celebrate a special service at the Arkansas Valley Correctional Facility Friday during visiting hours. He had—bravely and generously, in Iris' opinion—shared most of his sister's deathbed confession with the Community in a letter sent to each parishioner. He hadn't outright accused his sister of the attack on their father, but most of the Community had taken his desire to visit Neil as tacit admission. The church had chartered a bus and gotten special permission from the warden. Forty-two people were going. Iris had reluctantly agreed to attend, although she had no intention of letting herself be trapped on a bus with Community members eager to make it up to her and her father; she'd drive herself, shoulder be damned.

While Cade and Marian discussed what family photos to give the reporter to go with the story, and how to approach the governor about a pardon, Iris glanced idly around the cottage's living room. Pastor Matt had effectively died here, even though he was still breathing. What, she wondered suddenly, had brought him out here that night? The cottage back then was unoccupied, with no phone or electricity, hardly a comfy bolt-hole where he could work in peace. Maybe Glynnis had chased him with the poker and he'd run to the cottage for refuge? Ludicrous. Besides, Glynnis had gone straight for the phone, according to Esther.

Her hands went icy and she cupped them around the mug, seeking warmth from the now tepid tea. He'd used the cottage for one thing only. Was it possible that he was meeting someone? A girl. The idea trickled from Iris's brain and set her body on fire. She clicked her mug onto the table, sloshing tea onto a devotional magazine.

"Really, Iris," her mother said, rising to fetch a towel.

Iris ignored her, mind spinning. If she was right about him and Gabby Ulm, maybe he'd been planning to meet her here that night. Maybe Gabby knew the truth. Iris didn't waste time pondering what that truth might be. She only knew she had to find it. She had to know. She stood.

"I've … uh, got to go," she said to her disapproving mother and surprised Cade. "You two have this under control. I've got something I have to do."

Deliberately not telling them she was headed to Denver for fear they'd object or insist on driving because of her shoulder injury, she hurried to the door, already fishing the keys from her purse.

# FORTY-SEVEN

### IRIS

UNSURE WHAT TO DO with the information she'd gotten from Gabby Von Wolfseck, née Ulm, Iris headed for the Arkansas Valley Correctional Facility the next morning. The drive seemed longer and she wished she'd offered to let Angel ride with her as a distraction from her thoughts. She was thrilled that it looked like her father had a good chance at freedom—she was—but she knew she wouldn't be able to look at him without remembering that he hadn't believed her, had thought her capable of fabricating lies that would destroy a man's life, and many other lives. He was so oblivious to the truth of who she was that he could picture her striking a man with a weapon, lifting it high and pounding it into him again and again until flesh split, bones crunched, and his brain rattled against his skull.

Her thigh stitches pulled and her shoulder ached by the time she reached the prison, shortly ahead of the bus. Everyone was quiet, even Angel holding Marian's hand, intimidated by their surroundings, as they emptied their pockets of coins and pens. Wanting a few moments alone with her father, Iris hurried into the small visitor processing station and submitted to the vetting procedures. The process still made her uncomfortable, but didn't seem as offensive as the first time, and she marveled at how quickly one could get used to routines and rules, even distasteful ones. *Probably the secret to surviving prison*, she thought, walking past the bridge to nowhere.

Once in the visitor's area, surrounded by the humming vending machines, Iris found herself unable to sit while waiting for the guards to summon her father. She studied the offerings in all the machines, popped the door on one of the microwaves and surveyed its crusty interior, and swung around when she heard the scuff of footsteps. Her father appeared, escorted by a guard. He looked like he'd lost a few pounds and he held himself straighter. Hope could make huge changes, Iris thought.

"You look like you're doing better, Dad," she said. "Cough gone?"

He nodded, and held out his hand to her, smiling. She took his hand and sat beside him. They were quiet for several minutes before her father said, "You did it, Iris. Thank you."

She shook her head, hair swishing. "You're still in this place."

"Cade's working on that. There's the parole hearing next week —he thinks they'll free me. And the possibility of a governor's pardon. Cade's lined up a reporter to talk to me day after tomorrow. You proved me innocent to the Community," he said. "That's what matters."

"There's a lot of people here to see you."

"Because of you." He swallowed hard and allowed Iris to get him a soda from the vending machine. After taking a couple of gulps, her father said, "I spoke with Marian. She told me about Esther, how Esther must have hit Pastor Matt and gone to dispose of the weapon before returning to find me trying to help him."

Iris stayed silent.

"I'm sorry you had to kill her," her father said, rheumy eyes searching hers. "That must weigh heavily on you."

Iris nodded and squeezed his hand. She didn't mention what the doctor had said, about Esther dying of a heart attack; she knew she was responsible for Esther's death at that time and in that place.

"I've talked to enough killers over the years, some who killed intentionally, some by accident or neglect. Taking a life changes you. But it doesn't have to change you for the worse. It doesn't, Iris." He shook their linked hands.

Here was her chance, her opportunity to ask him why he hadn't believed her. The words formed in her mouth. She hesitated. What would it change? Making him explain why he hadn't believed her, whether it was out of loyalty to Marian or a refusal to accept that a man he'd revered could be responsible for such evil, was only going to make him feel badly. An apology wouldn't magically undo the past. Life didn't have a re-set button. The best you could hope for was understanding, maybe, or forgiveness. Iris thought about her mother becoming the church's custodian. Redemption might come through some big selfless act, or through a series of small sacrifices, the kind Marian had embraced. It seemed to Iris that it might also come through deliberate silence and a willingness to let go. She didn't know whether she was thinking of his redemption or her own. It didn't matter.

"I love you, Dad," she finally said.

"I love you, too, Mercy." He leaned forward and pressed his chapped lips to her cheek.

Iris closed her eyes. They sat in silence, hands still linked, until the influx of Community members began to fill the room. Marian and Angel came in and Iris moved away from her father so he could talk to his granddaughter. He was Angel's true grandfather, Iris thought, even if not by blood. His eyes filled with wonder at her approach. She hopped onto the chair Iris had vacated and, after a brief minute of shyness, was soon prattling away like she'd known him all her short life. When he chuckled at something Angel said, Iris thought her heart would burst with gladness.

"What a gift you've given them both," Jolene said quietly from beside Iris.

"They seem to enjoy each other," she said instead. "How's Zach?"

Jolene sighed and ran her fingers through the blond hair that hung loose around her face. "Coping. A bit shell-shocked, but coping. He's grieving for Esther—"

"I'm sorry."

"He doesn't blame you, Iris," Jolene said quickly. "He's grieving for his mother all over again, after what Esther told him, and he's so terribly shocked by what Esther did to her, and what she said about her relationship with their father, that he hasn't even begun to process it all. And he's grieving for his father. Not really for his father, but for his idea of him, for who he thought he was. I think he thinks he should have known what his father was doing, with Esther, if not with you and . . . and the others. He blames himself."

"He was a kid."

"That's what I told him." Jolene shrugged one shoulder. "I'm trying to get him to agree to see someone, you know, to talk it out with a professional. At the risk of sounding like a selfish bitch—"

Iris choked on a surprised laugh.

"—I will say that one silver lining is that he's agreed Matthew can continue in the nursing home, that we don't have to take him in. I feel guilty about feeling so relieved, but I just couldn't face—. He'll get better care in the nursing home anyway. A rationalization, I know," she added, biting her lower lip.

"Stop beating yourself up," Iris said, semi-impatiently. "You do more good in a week than most people do in a year. You don't want to take a comatose pedophile into your home and care for him at the expense of your marriage, your children, and your teaching. Good for you. Get over the guilt thing."

Jolene gave her a surprised look that turned thoughtful. "I will if you will," she said.

"Deal." Iris stuck out her hand, but Jolene ignored it, leaning in to hug her. After a startled moment, Iris returned the hug.

"I'm glad we're going to be friends again," Jolene said, releasing Iris. "We are, right?"

"We seem to be headed that way," Iris said, the ghost of a smile playing around her lips. "Maybe if the Community can spare you long enough, you can come see me in Portland. I'm thinking about buying a house."

She hadn't realized until that moment that she was thinking about making an offer for the house she lived in, but it felt right and she resolved to call her landlord as soon as she returned.

Zach started the service shortly after that and Iris kept to the fringe of the circle surrounding her father. For a fleeting moment, it felt like the ritual in the woods, when the Community encircled her and threw stones, but then the joy in the hymns and the warmth in the smiles erased the impression. Angel's voice piped above the others on "A Mighty Fortress Is Our God," a bright soprano that reminded Iris of Esther's. Before the song ended, she slipped out of the room without anyone noticing. She and her father had said what they needed to say for now.

She hit the road doing eighty-five. With any luck she'd have at least an hour before the bus got back to Lone Pine. She eased the accelerator closer to the floor. That should be plenty of time for a conversation best held in private.

# FORTY-EIGHT

**IRIS**

LONE PINE FELT DESERTED when Iris drove in. There had been no cars in the Sleepytime Inn's parking lot when she passed, and even though a couple of vehicles were parked along Center Street, no one strolled down the sidewalk, mowed a lawn, or rocked on a front porch. In the middle of a weekday, the residents were either at work or on the bus returning from the prison. It felt like a ghost town, Iris thought, parking in front of Debby's Café. Taking a deep breath, she pushed through the door, wanting to rip down the annoying bell, and stood by the counter with its pile of damp plastic-coated menus, apparently newly wiped.

"Coming." Joseph Ulm's voice came from the kitchen. He emerged a moment later, his welcoming smile shrinking when he spotted Iris. "Oh. Hi, Iris."

"Joe."

They faced each other silently for thirty seconds.

"Gabby called last night," Joe finally said. He scratched a spot behind his ear.

Iris nodded.

"We thought we might be seeing you."

Debby Ulm's voice came from Iris's left and she turned to see the petite woman come out of the restroom, drying her hands on her apron. Iris tensed, not liking to have to split her focus, but then Debby crossed to her husband and put her hand on his shoulder. Her face was set, defiant, the strong brows pinched in. Iris rotated her shoulders, wincing when the injured one objected, and gestured toward a booth. "Maybe we could sit?"

The Ulms moved as one to the booth she indicated and slid onto the bench, with Joe on the inside, closest to the window. Iris sat across from them and folded her hands on the table. Something about the way Debby Ulm held herself made Iris say, "I should tell you that I left a letter with Cade Zuniga after I talked to Gabby yesterday. It says I intended to come here and talk to you."

Joe looked blank, but then his eyes widened as he realized what he was saying. "Good God, Iris, we aren't the kind of people who—"

"I didn't think so," Iris said, looking not at him but at his wife who glared at her with ill-concealed fury. "If you were, you would surely have found an opportunity to finish Pastor Matt off sometime during the past twenty-three years, especially after he woke up."

"When we heard he was awake—" Debby Ulm gripped her husband's hand on the table.

"That must have scared you," Iris agreed.

"But then it seemed as if he didn't remember anything, or couldn't communicate it, if he did," Joe said. His left hand played with the sweetener packets in their small rectangular dish, lifting them half out of the dish and stuffing them back down. "We felt safe again."

"Until you came back," Debby said flatly. "I tried to persuade you to leave—"

"The phone call? My car?"

Debby nodded. "And I trashed your room."

"The rockslide?"

She hesitated, then gave a tiny nod. "I thought it would just be the one rock. I didn't anticipate that avalanche. I was at Mary Welsh's for the knitting circle when I saw you drive in and leave again. I followed you, thinking I'd convince you to go home, I guess. When you pulled over and started hiking, I ... I waited and then drove to the north rim ..."

Iris was anticipating an apology, but none came.

"Debby!" Joe gaped at his wife.

"She was going to dig it all up, Joe," she snapped. "I did what I had to do to protect you—us."

He pulled his hand away and faced Iris. "What did you tell Gabby?"

Iris found herself wanting to reassure the man who had beaten Pastor Matt and let her father go to prison for his crime. "I didn't tell her what I suspected. I told her I'd looked her up for old time's sake. She seemed glad to see me."

"She always looked up to you," Debby Ulm said, as if puzzled by her daughter's lack of judgment.

"I worked the conversation around to the reckoning stones and she fell apart, telling me that my 'bravery' in telling the truth had given her the strength to tell the truth, too. To you." Iris let her gaze rest on Joe and then on Debby. "She told you Pastor Matt was molesting her."

Debby sank her face into her work-roughened hands and Joe mangled a sweetener packet so that the white crystals spilled onto the table. He concentrated on poking them into a pile with his forefinger.

"She told you the day after the ritual, the day Pastor Matt was beaten. She hasn't connected the dots, or if she has, she's repressing the truth. But I see it." Iris put both palms flat on the table and leaned forward. "You went to the Brozek house that night, outraged and heartbroken, planning to confront him or—who knows?—planning to kill him."

"No!" Debby's voice cracked. "Joe isn't like that. He wouldn't—"

"Either Gabby told you she was supposed to meet him in the cottage, or you saw him headed that way and followed him. Did you talk to him, or just go in swinging?"

Joe cleared his throat. "He … he said Gabby was lying, that you and she were both liars. I knew my little girl wasn't lying. She was nearly hysterical, crying, when she told me what he'd done to her. She blamed herself." He fisted his hand and put the knuckles to his mouth. "My innocent little Gabby thought something she'd done or said had made that wicked pervert want her. She was only thirteen! He started to say something about the reckoning stones and Gabby, and I told him I was through with the Community, that I was going to the police. He grabbed that iron cross off the wall and took a swing at me, cut my cheek open." He rubbed his cheekbone. "I got it away from him and then … I couldn't seem to stop. I didn't mean to kill him."

Silence settled over the café as Joe finished talking. A dishwasher gurgled from the kitchen and an insect flew into the window with a tiny *thuck*.

"You let my dad go to prison for something you did," Iris said.

Joe nodded. "Yes. I made it home somehow and told Debby what I'd done—"

"I took one look at him and knew," Debby said, memories of that night darkening her eyes. "He was spattered with blood and almost catatonic, still clutching the cross in his hand. I got him cleaned up, burned his clothes, hid the cross. And then we waited."

"For the police to come," Joe said. "But they didn't. Esther found Neil standing over the body and he confessed. I didn't know"—he looked at his wife—"we didn't know how to react."

"By telling the truth," Iris said grimly. Before they could respond, she added, "But I'm not in a good position to throw stones on that front. If I'd told the truth straight off, about Pastor Matt molesting me, then maybe he would never have had the opportunity to victimize Gabby. Even if everyone called me a liar, maybe if I'd spoken up sooner, you'd have been more alert, Gabby would have been more wary. Who knows?" Weariness draped itself over her and she leaned against the booth.

"When I started this," she said, letting her head fall back so she was talking to a spot somewhere between the Ulms and the ceiling, "I wanted to discover the truth to get my father out of prison. It was some kind of quest I set myself to make up for all the years I was gone. It wasn't my fault that he confessed, thinking I had attacked Pastor Matt, but I felt responsible. I could make it up to him, redeem myself for giving in to Pastor Matt, for not telling the truth immediately, for God knows what other sins, by setting him free."

"Do you want me to tell the police the truth?" Joe asked. He looked straight at her, his expression bleak. "I'm ready to do that. I should have done it twenty-three years ago, but I didn't want anyone to know that that bastard had raped my Gabby, that she and he had—"

"Joe!" Debby put a hand on his arm as if to keep him from marching off to the sheriff's office.

"A part of me was glad to think my father had done what you did," Iris confessed, looking at Joe. "I'm not proud of that. I was actually disappointed, hurt even, to find out that he truly hadn't believed me, hadn't exacted revenge on my behalf." She paused, letting her gaze rest on a tabby cat sitting on the sidewalk. Her eyes swung back to the Ulms. "It's not my place to condone what you did or condemn you, but my father has already served twenty-three years for what you did."

Debby leaped to her feet, knocking over the salt shaker. "You can't make us—. Joe's been sorry every day for—." Her shoulders shook violently and she glared at Iris.

"Sorry isn't enough," Joe said, reaching for his wife's hand. She yanked it away.

"Don't do this, Joe. Gabby! Everyone would know she, that Pastor Matt and she—. Don't let her talk you into—"

"No one here's talking me into anything, Deb. I'm only doing what the Holy Spirit's been trying to talk me into for a quarter century." Joe slid out of the booth and took his stiff wife in his arms. She struggled, but then subsided against his shoulder. Iris watched uncomfortably as he stroked her hair and murmured to her. With his eyes shut, Joe Ulm looked resigned, even peaceful, as he comforted his wife, and Iris regretted that her father's freedom might come at the cost of his.

"You might not even have to do time," Iris said. "Esther confessed to letting her mother die, after all, so the only charges would be related to Pastor Matt's beating. Any judge or jury would sympathize with your motive, and with a good lawyer ..." She hoped his confession and his knowledge of the crime's details would be enough to outweigh her father's earlier confession. Something Debby had said niggled at her. Barely daring to hope, she asked, "Do you still have the cross? You said you 'hid it.'" She leaned forward, tensing as she waited for an answer.

Debby and Joe exchanged a look, Debby's resistant and Joe's commanding. Finally, Debby gave a tiny nod. "That night, when Joe came home with the cross that looked like it'd been dipped in blood, I knew we needed to get rid of it. But it didn't seem right to bury the symbol of our Savior in the dirt, or toss it in a Dumpster like it was just ... just trash. I couldn't make myself do it. So I wrapped it up and drove over to my parents' house in Canon City that very night. I hid it in their attic. They're in their eighties—they haven't gone up in the attic in decades. I check on it sometimes when we visit them."

It was more than Iris had dared hope for. "Thank God," she breathed.

She slid out of the booth, suddenly anxious to get away from the Ulms who were standing side by side with clasped hands, from the past, from Lone Pine. She planned to phone Cade as soon as she got outside so he could mobilize the police to search Debby's parents' house and find the cross. She trusted Joseph Ulm to do the right thing, but she sensed Debby was intent on protecting her husband, possibly even against his wishes. She didn't completely blame her, but she couldn't let her jeopardize her father's bid for freedom. Giving the pies a wistful look as she passed their glass domes, Iris pushed through the door and into the sunshine, lifting up her face to its warmth. She'd call Cade and then the airline, to book a ticket home.

# FORTY-NINE

*One month later*

IRIS CLIMBED FROM HER car outside Eclectica and carefully re-moved the boxed and tissue-swaddled award from the passenger seat. Carrying it into the store, she hugged the box to her chest and waited for Jane to get off the phone. She had recovered well from her surgery, Iris thought, and although she was still doing physical ther-apy several times a week, she'd returned to her home a week earlier, days after Iris's return. Iris had stayed in Colorado until a judge va-cated her father's conviction after Joseph Ulm turned himself in with the bloodied cross that bore Matthew Brozek's DNA, and the district attorney declined to file new charges against Neil Asher in "the interests of justice." They were still working out a plea deal for Joe Ulm. Volunteering to hang out with Angel for a weekend, Iris had given her mother and father some alone time when he was re-leased from prison. Then she'd spent an awkward day with the three of them in Lone Pine and flown to Portland, unbearably glad to be home.

Jane hung up and peered over her glasses. "Well, are you going to show me?"

With a rustle of tissue paper, Iris unwrapped the foot-tall award and placed it on the counter. "Ta-da." She stood back, waiting for Jane's reaction.

It was unlike anything Iris had ever done. For one, it wasn't a piece of jewelry, but a sculpture set on a granite base. She ran her fingers across the three-inch squares of clear glass, with lead solder to denote panes, assembled in an overlapping way so that from one direction they almost looked like birds taking off, and from another they were clearly windows. A sprinkle of tiny stones, clear quartz, made the panes shimmer, as if splashed with raindrops. A hand constructed from intertwined metal wires like an armature rose from the granite base and supported the sculpture with a cloth draped beneath the palm.

"It's windows," Iris explained, too anxious to wait for Jane's reaction. "Green Gables is a construction company, so I thought windows would work. And the hand polishing the windows—well, that's the hard-working employee who's getting the award." The piece had almost constructed itself upon Iris's return, even though she'd had to consult with a friend who did stained glass to get some tips on working with the glass panes.

"It's stunning," Jane said quietly. "Stunning." After another moment of walking around the piece, studying it, she looked up with a glint in her eye. "I foresee a lucrative new aspect to your design career, my dear."

"Spoken like an agent," Iris said, laughing. "How are you doing?"

"My physical therapist is a sadist," Jane scowled, "but I'm moving easier." To demonstrate, she took several steps across the gallery, leaning only lightly on the handsome cane her son had given her, and returned to lower herself onto a settee positioned in front of a large canvas. She patted it and Iris sat beside her. "How about you?"

"Better. I'm closing on the house in two weeks. Jolene's coming for a visit after school lets out and Greg's helping me get the yard in shape before she arrives."

"You're spending a lot of time with that young man." Jane's smile was knowing.

"We're taking it slowly. We'll see where it goes."

"Still committed to celibacy?"

"For the moment." Iris blushed, feeling a bit foolish.

Jane patted her leg. "Good for you. If you last another twenty-seven days, I win the pool. Lassie didn't think you'd go a full week."

"A pool? You started a pool?" The thought both amused and appalled Iris. She brushed Jane's hand off her leg with mock-exasperation and stood, stroking a finger along the sculpture's granite base. Lasting. Granite was made to endure, as were some relationships. Iris thought with wonder and ruefulness of her weekly Skype sessions with her parents and Angel. Angel did most of the talking. Iris was wary of opening up to her parents—it wasn't easy moving past twenty-three years of resentment and betrayal—and stuck mostly to the kind of chitchat she'd make with a stranger in a coffee shop, but at least the lines of communication were open. She hoped they wouldn't close up when Angel rejoined Noah and Keely in a few months. Six weeks ago, Iris wouldn't have risked a 2mm freshwater pearl on the chance that she and her mother would ever speak to each other again. But now...

A stray sunbeam sparked off one of the tiny window panes. It was too soon to know if she and Greg would be together long-term, but Iris felt good about him, about them. Their relationship might not—yet—be granite-strong, but they were strengthening it daily with their conversations, honesty, laughter, and kissing. World-class kissing. Maybe apatite or feldspar. She imagined the look on Greg's face if she told him she was pretty sure their relationship was as strong as feldspar, and laughed.

When Jane asked what was so funny, Iris shook her head. "Just thinking about stones," she said. She sobered. "Did I tell you they identified the remains found in the pond as Penelope's?"

Before she left Colorado, Iris had gone to see the Welshes and suggested they drag the pond in the alpaca field. They'd found the skeletonized remains of a young girl. A crack in the skeleton's skull suggested she'd been struck with something, a shovel maybe, and then dragged into the pond to drown. The girl's bracelet had apparently come off when Esther was dragging her to the pond, investigators speculated, and when the rockslide occurred that same day Esther had had the presence of mind to half-bury it among the overturned rocks. Iris shivered at the thought of Penelope lying at the bottom of the pond all these years, staring up into the blue.

"Hopefully, being able to bury their daughter properly will give her parents some peace," Jane said.

"Hopefully."

"And Pastor Matt? Is there any hope that he'll awaken again?"

Iris shrugged. "Jolene says they've moved him back to the nursing home. I guess if a miracle can happen once, it can happen again, but for now..."

"I'm sorry you never got to confront him the way you wanted to." Jane gazed at her over the tops of her purple glasses. "Cowardly man to duck back into his coma before you could give him what-for."

Iris managed a small smile. "I let him take too much over the years—my virginity, my peace of mind, my self-image, probably relationships I could have had. I'm not giving him anything more—

not 'what-for' and not even a stray thought. Whether awake or not, alive or not, Matthew Brozek belongs to the past."

The future, she thought, was a sleek curve of possibility she could shape, not without rough spots, but bright with the jewels of work and friendship and love.

# EPILOGUE

Jolene Brozek and Marian Asher sat in the chintz-decorated reception area of the nursing home, chatting in the easy yet superficial way of people who have known each other for decades but never sought intimacy. Jolene still visited her father-in-law weekly from a sense of duty and because it made Zach happy. She and Zach came together sometimes and sat, hands linked, near the bed. Zach spent most of the half-hour visits praying. Jolene wasn't sure what he prayed for and hadn't asked. For his father, she figured, and for his father's victims. For healing of all kinds and the grace to forgive. At any rate, that's what she prayed for. For Marian, sitting with the comatose Matthew Brozek was the hair shirt she had donned years ago. She had long ago given up having mental conversations with him and was now content to let her mind drift where it would when she sat with him—to her grocery list, the chores she needed to tackle at the church, the email she'd received from Noah, the funny things Angel said. Today, she'd brought Angel with her and parked her in a corner of the room with crayons and a coloring book. When she had stepped out of the room to purchase a bottled water from the vending machine and run into Jolene, she'd had no qualms about spending a few minutes chatting with her, knowing Angel was occupied with her coloring.

As Jolene was telling Marian about her trip to Portland, the patter of running feet drew their attention to the hallway. Angel burst into view, dark hair flying, eyes round. "Nana, Nana! Pastor Matt woke up! He talked to me. Come see." She grabbed Marian's hand and tugged.

"Now, Angel," Marian said, corralling the girl with an arm around her waist so they were face to face. "Pastor Matt can't talk. Remember what I told you about a coma?"

"But he *is* awake. He is. He said my name and talked to me."

The women exchanged glances and, as one, moved toward Matthew Brozek's room. It brimmed with light, the setting sun blazing through the open windows and bleaching the walls pure white. The sheer curtain billowed outward, pulled by a breeze lighter than a butterfly's wing flap. Angel's abandoned coloring book was splayed open in the corner. Matthew lay motionless under the single sheet drawn over him, as unaware as ever of their presence.

"See, he's not awake," Marian told Angel as they approached the bed. She studied the unmoving figure on the bed, her eyes drawn to the hand nearest her, blue-veined and still as marble on the sheet. Her gaze flicked to his face with the colorless lips barely parted, the chin stubbled. Something new about his stillness startled her. Holding her breath, she watched for nearly a minute but didn't see his chest rise and fall. She beckoned Jolene over. They studied Matthew's face.

"I think he's gone," Marian whispered. A breath of air stroked her bare arms and she shivered.

Jolene felt for a pulse in her father-in-law's neck and, after a long moment, nodded her head, conscious of no feeling but gratitude. "May God have mercy on his soul."

"He talked to me," Angel said crossly, folding thin arms over her chest. "Why don't you believe me?"

"What did he say?" Jolene asked, humoring the girl.

Angel approached her gratefully. "He said, 'Angel! So beautiful. Angel, Angel.' I said, 'Thank you,' like Nana told me I should when someone says I'm pretty or smart. Then I came to get you."

"He doesn't even know your name," Marion pointed out, trying not to sound testy.

Understanding seeped into Jolene. "'Angels,'" she breathed. "He said 'angels.'"

The wonder of it held her motionless. Later, she would ponder the presence of angels in Matthew Brozek's room, of all places, and question what it meant, what it might say about forgiveness and God's grace. For now, she stared at the little girl, then at the husk of the dead man, then up and around, turning in a dizzying circle so her gaze swept the corners where the walls met the ceiling, the bed, and the open window, as if one could see angels merely by looking for them.

**THE END**

# AUTHOR'S NOTE

I HAVE TAKEN SOME liberties with the topography near Colorado Springs in writing this novel. Although the city itself is largely as I've described it, there is no hamlet of Lone Pine and the ravine and rockslide do not exist in Black Forest. The landscape has more ravines and canyons 20 to 30 miles north, near Castlewood Canyon State Park, and I have simply transplanted some of that topography. The idea for the rockslide came from a visit to Slide Lake, Wyoming (near Grand Teton National Park), where 50 million cubic yards of rock and dirt sheared off and slid across the Gros Ventre River in 1925, creating a natural dam 225 feet high and a mile wide. The acres of boulders and rocks, studded with trees carried away by the slide, are much as I've described them in this book, although I've made the book's rockslide much smaller in scale.

## ACKNOWLEDGMENTS

When I set out to write this book, I knew very little about comas, jewelry-making, prisons, or how to work the legal system to get someone out of prison. I am greatly indebted to several people for enlightening my ignorance.

Ruben Manuel, award-winning jewelry designer, shared expertise, techniques, and anecdotes that helped me create Iris Dashwood, jewelry designer and maker. I hope I have been able to transfer some of his passion for his art to Iris. (I've actually gotten interested enough in jewelry-making to take a metal-working class.) I also found the books *Complete Metalsmith* by Tim McCreight and *The Encyclopedia of Jewelry-Making Techniques* by Jinks McGrath very helpful.

My brother-in-law, Robert DiSilverio, offered his legal knowledge and advice on such subjects as what kinds of charges would result in a conviction long enough to keep Neil Asher in prison for twenty-three years, and how to free him once Iris realizes he is innocent. He did a lot of research on my behalf and made it possible for me to set up a scenario in this book that won't make legal professionals groan too loudly (I hope). Any slip-ups, inconsistencies, or errors are, of course, mine. If you're in the Bay Area of California and need a great attorney, Robert DiSilverio is your man.

I am also supremely grateful to Dr. Carroll Ramseyer, M.D., Board Certified Neurologist, who helped me understand "comas" just enough to put Pastor Matt into one and awaken him briefly, and return him to a minimally conscious state. As Dr. Ramseyer continually reminded me, it's extremely rare for someone to emerge from a minimally conscious state after many years. However, it does happen. For those interested in reading about an individual who "awoke" from a coma after nineteen years, I refer you to the case of Terry Wallis of Arkansas.

A friend, William Newmiller, spent several hours telling me about the Arkansas Valley Correctional Facility and describing details of entry procedure, "offender" treatment and lifestyle, and layout. My thanks to him and good wishes for proving his son's innocence and getting him released.

As always I owe thanks to many people for reading early drafts, cheering me on, and supporting me emotionally and otherwise while I write. Thanks to my critique group, Lin Poyer, Marie Layton, and Amy Tracy, and to my mother, Joan Hankins, for comments on early drafts. A special thanks to Rev. Sally Hubbell for reading the manuscript and giving me her very helpful thoughts. This book is better than it would have been because of their input.

I am grateful every day to my husband and daughters, who fill my world with joy and make everything worthwhile.

## BOOK CLUB DISCUSSION QUESTIONS

1. Neil Asher is incarcerated, yet he is not the only character who is trapped or imprisoned in some way. What other characters are imprisoned? Are these "prisons" imposed by forces and circumstances outside the individual, or are they self-built? Are the characters freed or do they free themselves in the course of the story? If not, why not?

2. Discuss the "rock/stone" images in this novel. Obviously, the reckoning stones were used to punish and humiliate. How are other stone references/symbols positive ones? How does Iris's connection to stones influence the story?

3. How do the different characters find redemption (if they do)? Compare Jolene's path to redemption with Marian's, for instance. Is Iris redeemed in this story? Does she need redemption?

4. The ending hints that there may be forgiveness and grace even for people like pedophiles who society may consider monsters. Are there acts that are unredeemable or unforgivable? How do you interpret the ending?

5. Iris sometimes seems obsessed with finding and revealing the truth, even at great cost to herself and others. Is the truth all-important?

6. What is innocence? Are there any characters in this book who are innocent?

7. How do the flashbacks work to give the story more depth? Do they make Iris a more sympathetic character? What about Jolene?

---

I love meeting with book clubs and would be happy to join your club in person or via Skype if you discuss *The Reckoning Stones*. Contact me through my web page, www.lauradisilverio.com.

## ABOUT THE AUTHOR

Laura DiSilverio is the nationally best selling author of the Readaholics Book Club series, and more than a dozen other crime novels. Past President of Sisters in Crime, she pens articles for *Writer's Digest*, and conducts workshops and speaks at writers' conferences, universities, and literary events. A retired Air Force intelligence officer, she plots murders and parents teens in Colorado, trying to keep the two tasks separate.

*An Excerpt from* Close Call *the Next Book by Laura DiSilverio*

# ONE

## Sydney

Washington D.C., Wednesday, 1 August

When someone starts a conversation with "Are you okay?" and you have no idea what they're talking about, it's a sure sign that fate has trampled you with cleats and you just don't know it yet.

That thought zipped through my head as I slowed in the middle of a rush hour D.C. sidewalk to answer a cell phone call from my mom.

"Are you okay?" she asked, anxiety tightening her voice.

"Why wouldn't I be?" A man jostled me and I walked faster. The sidewalk was almost as jammed as the street and the pedestrians had fewer hesitations about ramming each other.

She inhaled sharply. "You haven't heard. Oh, my God. Sydney, it's George."

"George?" There had only ever been one George in my life, one George who had *been* my life, but I asked anyway, "Manley?" The name brought with it a whole lot of memories I tried to keep corralled in an "Off Limits" part of my brain. Nausea roiled my stomach and I swallowed hard. "What about him?"

"He's dead."

"How? Wha—" I was abreast of an Electronics Emporium and the display window was filled with high-def TVs. Images of me and George from long ago played on the screens. I hung up on Mom without apology and edged closer to the window. I was thirteen years younger and twenty pounds heavier on the screen; it was like looking at a badly distorted image, a fun-house mirror. My face flamed and I looked over my shoulder. No one was pointing or staring. People trotted down the Metro stairs. Jaywalkers snarled traffic. Thank God for small favors. I turned back to the window as my younger self shrouded her head with a coat to escape the reporters jabbing microphones at her.

George's image filled the screens. Oh, my God. In his sixties, his silver hair matched the gray of his suit and his hooded eyes challenged the viewer. A name and a brace of years underscored the photo: "George Manley (D/Ohio), former Speaker of the House, 1953–2016." He was really dead. Oh, my God. My knees buckled. I splayed a hand on the cool glass to keep from falling.

"Hey, lady, this yours?" A beefy stranger held my briefcase. I hadn't even felt it fall.

"What? Oh, thank you." I strangled the handle, torn between wanting to know what had happened to George and an unwillingness to hear newscasters rehash our past. The anchor, face solemn, narrated silently, and I tried to read his lips. Had he said "heart attack?" Anger prickled in my scalp and in my hands and feet. I swung away from the window. God knew I had plenty of reason to hate George, but he was dead. Why did the networks always—*always*—have to zoom in on the sordid? How sad—tragic, even—that our affair was haunting George even in death. He'd have wanted to be remembered for his education bill, for three decades of public service, not for screwing a co-ed younger than his daughter. Even if that girl had loved him more than … more than was safe.

Anger, humiliation, and something that wasn't quite sadness—more like regret—mixed up in my stomach as I pushed open the door of Sol's Deli, four storefronts away. A bell tinkled, drowned by customers shouting their orders to harried clerks, cell phones spraying Bach or the Beatles, and cash registers pinging. I inhaled a peppery hint of salami and the vinegar tang of pickles and pepperoncini. Better. My jangled nerves quieted. Leaning against a glass-fronted case, I let the cool seep through my sweat-damp dress. D.C. summers could double as one of Dante's circles of hell—one reserved for politicians, George used to say. I tore my thoughts away from George Manley. Even though I'd never live down my teenage mistake, I didn't have to relive it just because George was dead. I didn't need the painful memories spoiling my evening with Jason.

Half a pound of sharp cheddar, I forced myself to think instead, two roasted chicken dinners, and a few of those garlic olives Jason liked. Did we need more coffee? Supplies like coffee and toilet paper seemed to evaporate with Jason in the house. One more week and he'd be back in his newly-renovated condo. A pang zipped through me and I bit the inside of my lip. It'd been a little claustrophobic at first, having Jason around, but I liked bumping against him now as we cooked dinner in the small kitchen, liked hearing the details of his day and snuggling with him every night, not just on weekends. I could live with the whiskers in the sink, but his racing bicycle couldn't stay in the living room. We'd have to find somewhere else to keep it if—

"Ma'am? It's your turn." A man nudged me from behind. He bounced from one foot to the other, horn-rimmed glasses balanced on his sharp nose. "Can you hurry it up? I've gotta get my kids from daycare. They charge ten bucks for every minute you're late. Per kid."

"Sorry."

I stepped to the counter with its four cash registers and ordered, on impulse getting a piece of chocolate cheesecake for Mrs. Colwell, my neighbor with the chocolate jones and fixed income. I had to lean forward to be heard over the men on either side, both jabbering into their cell phones. The aproned clerk dumped two white bags with handles on the counter, and my phone rang.

"Sorry." I checked the number displayed on the cell phone. Mom. Calling back to check on my okay-ness. I didn't answer. I put the phone beside the deli bags and pulled out a fifty as the man on my left slapped his phone on the counter to inspect the contents of six pizza boxes and the man on my other side set his phone down to pick up coins he'd dropped.

"Sorry. I don't have anything smaller," I told the clerk, a youth with pimples and straw-colored hair. Good grief, I sounded like the battered women I'd set up Winning Ways to help: "Sorry, sorry, sorry."

"It's cool," the clerk said, making change. He peered at me in a way I'd come to dread. "You look familiar—"

I didn't need this. "Thanks." I gave him a five and a nervous smile, sidling away, desperate to be gone before he said more.

"Hey—I just saw you on TV!" He jerked his head toward the tiny television suspended above the far end of the counter. "Cool! You're that—"

Impatient, the man behind me elbowed me aside and knocked against a jar of pickles, sending a stream of briny water over the counter. The clerk sprang back. Warty green pickles rolled across the formica and plunked to the floor. I swept my phone and damp change into my purse and almost ran out the door, praying that no one had heard the clerk.

"Jesus H. Christ!" and "Oh, shit, I'm sorry!" followed me out of the deli.

Two blocks away, I paused to take a deep breath, not minding the exhaust fumes held at street level by the oppressive humidity that slicked my skin. In another half hour, this part of D.C. would quiet as the commuters fled to suburbia. Jason and I could enjoy dinner on the balcony, have a glass of wine, talk. I picked up my pace. Ten minutes brought me to the one-way quiet of G Street Southeast. Townhomes lined both sides of the street, cooled by mighty oaks old enough to remember flames shooting from the White House just three miles away, the eerie quiet of the streets during the flu pandemic, and windows darkened by blackout curtains.

A block from home, I heard the faint brrr of a cell phone, a plain ring, not my "Rhapsody in Blue" ring tone. I looked around. No one in earshot. Funny. It trilled again, from inside my purse. I knew what must have happened even as I set the deli bags down and found the phone. It was a simple pay-as-you-go model. I hadn't had a cell phone contract since my account got hacked by unscrupulous journalists when my relationship with George made the headlines. A man's voice started speaking before I could even say "hello."

"There are some new parameters to the Montoya job. It's got to look like an accident. And there's a bonus if you take care of it before the election." The voice was terse, accentless, male.

"I'm—"

"Payment as previously arranged. Make it happen." Click.

# TWO

### PAUL

PAUL JONES HAILED A taxi outside Sol's Deli. He reeked of pickle juice, a splash of tomato soup marred his white shirt, and Moira had called to tell him his father had started a small fire in the kitchen, but not to worry. Not to worry! How was he supposed to not worry when Pop's behavior grew more erratic every day? When he eluded Moira and wandered off, sometimes dressed, sometimes in bathrobe and socks, when he started to fill the tub and got caught up watching *Judge Judy* so the water overflowed and soaked the linoleum so it had to be replaced, when—

"Address?" the taxi driver asked, looking at him in the rearview mirror. His fingers tapped the steering wheel to the beat of a rap song on the radio.

Paul closed his eyes and took a deep breath through flared nostrils. Calm. He had a job to do. He couldn't afford to be distracted. Moira could handle his pop. Concentrate. After a moment he opened his eyes and gave the driver the address of his motel.

With a grunt, the driver started the meter and pulled into traffic, making the hula girl suction-cupped to the dash vibrate.

Paul eased his head back against the vinyl seat. He wasn't sure what smelled worse—the mildewy plastic of the cab or his clothes. His ability to blend in with a crowd, to rate no more detailed a description than "middle-aged white guy," was key to his success. Smelling like a pickle factory jeopardized his anonymity. As the taxi sludged along in the stop-and-go traffic, he concentrated on clearing his mind, emptying it of all thought and emotion. It was a trick he'd developed working with a Buddhist monk in Laos when he was in country for the third time in the early '70s. It kept him focused.

The opening glissando of Gershwin's "Rhapsody in Blue" trilled from his pocket, almost drowned out by the cabbie's rap crap. What the—? He pulled out the cell phone, conscious of the driver's gaze, and answered cautiously, "Yes?"

A recorded voice said, "This call is for Sydney Ellison from Dr. Field's office to remind you of your dental appointment on Monday, August 5th, at eight o'clock. If you need to reschedule, please call 555-1324."

"Go back," he told the startled cabbie.

"Huh?"

"To the deli. And turn off that fucking noise."

Paul's fingers worried at the curling end of duct tape that patched a foot-long tear in the seat beside him. Every red light and delay twanged his taut nerves. There was no relief at the deli—his phone wasn't there. No one remembered seeing it. He should never have set it on the counter, not for an instant, he berated himself. He didn't give a damn about the phone—it was pay-as-you-go and replaceable—but he needed to make sure his client didn't call and say something that could incriminate both of them if the Sid Ellison guy answered. He'd have to alert his client via email—that was safer and quicker than a face-to-face with Ellison to trade phones.

He climbed back into the cab and pulled his laptop out of its case. "Starbucks. The closest one."

# WWW.MIDNIGHTINKBOOKS.COM

From the gritty streets of New York City to sacred tombs in the Middle East, it's always midnight somewhere. Join us online at any hour for fresh new voices in mystery fiction.

At midnightinkbooks.com you'll also find our author blog, new and upcoming books, events, book club questions, excerpts, mystery resources, and more.

## MIDNIGHT INK ORDERING INFORMATION

### Order Online:
• Visit our website www.midnightinkbooks.com, select your books, and order them on our secure server.

### Order by Phone:
• Call toll-free within the U.S. and Canada at
  1-888-NITE-INK (1-888-648-3465)
• We accept VISA, MasterCard, and American Express

### Order by Mail:
Send the full price of your order (MN residents add 6.875% sales tax) in U.S. funds, plus postage & handling to:

> Midnight Ink
> 2143 Wooddale Drive
> Woodbury, MN  55125-2989

### Postage & Handling:

Standard (U.S. & Canada). If your order is:
> $25.00 and under, add $4.00
> $25.01 and over, FREE STANDARD SHIPPING

AK, HI, PR: $16.00 for one book plus $2.00 for each additional book.

International Orders (airmail only):
> $16.00 for one book plus $3.00 for each additional book

Orders are processed within 12 business days. Please allow for normal shipping time.
Postage and handling rates subject to change.